SWEET SURRENDER

She tore her lips from his. "Trey, stop it! It's wrong."

Catching her hands, he drew them both up over her head and held them captive against the wall. He brushed his lips over the curve of her cheek. "It's not wrong," he murmured into her ear.

This time there was no escaping his mouth as it captured hers with a savageness that sent waves of shock hurtling through her veins and awakened in her a hunger that had been denied for so long she failed to recognize it for what it was.

All thought of resisting him crumbled, and Samantha surrendered helplessly to the suppressed longings he aroused in her. Waves of intoxicating heat washed over her, dragging a tortured moan of desire from her throat as she returned his kiss with a fierceness that surprised them both. . . .

Diamond Books by Linda Andersen

PASSION'S PRICE
FORTUNE'S FURY

FORTUNE'S FURY

LINDA ANDERSEN

DIAMOND BOOKS, NEW YORK

FORTUNE'S FURY

A Diamond Book / published by arrangement
with the author

PRINTING HISTORY
Diamond edition / May 1992

ISBN: 1-55773-704-5

Diamond Books are published by The Berkley Publishing
Group, 200 Madison Avenue, New York, New York 10016.
The name "DIAMOND" and its logo are trademarks
belonging to Charter Communications, Inc.

PRINTED IN THE UNITED STATES OF AMERICA

10 9 8 7 6 5 4 3 2 1

FORTUNE'S FURY

Chapter
One

WHEN Joe reached the gate to the mine compound, he found Maria in tears. The only words he could comprehend of her rapid staccato Spanish were *hombres* and *restaurante*. Disregarding the pointed stare Arnie Pitts was giving them from the guard shack, Joe took Maria by the shoulders and gently shook her. "Slow down, *querida*. I can't understand you. *What* men are at the restaurant?"

Maria took a ragged breath. She rubbed the back of her hand across her wet eyes. "Señor Littleton send the men because *la señora* no pay *el alquiler*. They make everyone go away. *La señora*, she fight them, but they are too many."

Anger snapped in Joe's black eyes. So Samantha had fallen behind on the rent again. And this time, Littleton was getting nasty. "Stay here, Maria," he ordered. "I'll be back."

Joe pivoted and took off up the hill at a brisk lope. He ran easily, without tiring. As a child, he had been trained to run several miles with a rock in either hand to build his stamina. To help him learn to breathe through his nose, he would run while holding a mouthful of water. If he learned well, the elders taught him, he could be a great war chief like his uncle.

But even then things had begun changing. His people were herded like cattle onto reservations. Now, in place of the old pretend games of hunting and raiding, the young

1

boys played at getting drunk and being locked up in jail. Instead of becoming a chief, he had gone to work in the silver mines.

Joe bounded up the steps of the long, weathered wooden building that housed the mine's offices.

Miles Gilbert, the bookkeeper, sprang up from his chair when Joe entered the building. Gilbert's wire-rimmed spectacles slid down his nose, and he pushed them up into place with a forefinger. "You can't go in there!" he called out as Joe bolted across the room.

Joe ignored him and headed straight for Treyman Stern's private office.

"Mr. Tochino, please!" Gilbert implored. "Mr. Stern is in a meeting with the surveyors. He asked not to be disturbed."

Joe yanked open the office door. "Trey, Samantha is in trouble."

"I'm not leaving!" Samantha dug her heels into the floor and clung to the doorjamb, but the man was too strong for her. He wrapped one arm around her waist and jerked her against him. She kicked at him and gouged her elbow into his ribs. He merely grunted. Wedging her arm up between them, she clawed his face.

The man yelped. He abruptly released her and grabbed his cheek. When he pulled his hand away, there was blood on his fingers. "Why, you bitch!"

Samantha was already halfway across the dining room.

The man ran after her. He caught hold of the back of her skirt. They both went down. Samantha hit the floor with enough impact to knock the air from her lungs. The terracotta tiles were hard and unforgiving, and she lay, dazed, for several seconds. The sound of hammering surrounded her. Samantha realized vaguely that the man's companions were nailing boards across the restaurant's windows. She was struggling to catch her breath when the man hauled her roughly to her feet and spun her around. Before she could get her bearings, he picked her up and tossed her over his shoulder.

He carried her out the front door. A crowd had already begun gathering in front of the building. The onlookers parted to let them pass as he carried her several yards away from the building. Several men cheered as he unceremoniously dumped her into the middle of the packed-dirt street. Without a word, he turned and walked away. No one came to her aid.

Samantha scrambled to her feet. Her hair, an unforgiving shade of red that had earned her a host of uncomplimentary nicknames as a child, escaped its restraining combs and tumbled around her shoulders and down her back in a shimmering explosion of color. With an angry swipe of her hand, she brushed the fiery tresses away from her face and started back toward the building. She would be damned if she'd let them force her out of her home and her restaurant without a fight.

The man who had carried her from the building was busy boarding up the front door. Samantha marched up behind him, picked up a board from the pile near his feet, and swung it as hard as she could.

The board cracked against the man's shoulder with a sickening thud. With a cry of agony, he dropped the hammer and went down on one knee.

From behind, a hand knotted painfully in her hair, and she felt herself being jerked around. A fist crashed against her cheek, blinding her with white-hot pain and sending her reeling into the adobe wall. Her legs crumpled beneath her, and she felt herself falling. . . .

A gunshot pierced the darkness that pressed down on her. She could hear people yelling. Something gentle and warm touched her face, and she forced her eyes open to find Maria kneeling over her. Maria's tearstained face shifted in and out of focus. Samantha squeezed her eyes shut and fought back the nausea that threatened to overwhelm her.

She heard a familiar voice, low and forceful. "Unless you want me to kill you, you'd better get the hell out of here."

Relief and horror surged through her at once. She opened her eyes long enough to catch a glimpse of a tall, broad-shouldered man with dark brown hair. Trey? Why was *he* here?

"We was just doing our job," another man shot back. "Mr. Littleton paid us to shut this place down, and that's just what we aim to do."

In the split second of silence that followed, Samantha heard the soft but distinctive click of a revolver being cocked. "I told you to leave," Trey said.

"Listen here, mister, you don't got no right to—"

"*Now.*"

"C'mon, Calvin. We'd better do as he says."

"No goddamn Indian-lover's gonna tell me what to do!"

"Calvin! Let's git!"

With Maria's help, Samantha managed to sit up.

"Joe, get those boards off the door," Trey ordered. Maria scampered out of his way. Before Samantha realized what was happening, Trey bent down and lifted her in his arms.

She sucked in her breath and winced at the painful throbbing in her head. "I-I can . . . walk," she protested, unaware that she was clutching the front of his shirt. "Treyman Stern, put me down!"

Joe got the front door open, and Trey carried her into the building.

All around them were signs of the struggle that had taken place. Tables and chairs had been overturned. Dishes were smashed. Daylight filtered into the dining room between gaps in the boards that had been nailed over the windows.

Over Samantha's objections, Trey carried her through the restaurant to the small, spare apartment at the rear of the building, and laid her on the bed. He gave instructions to Maria, and the girl hastened to do his bidding.

Samantha started to rise, but Trey gently pushed her back against the pillows. "Lie still."

His closeness ignited a flame of apprehension deep within her. She hated being in the same room with him. She hated *him*. She shoved his hands away. "Leave me alone."

Trey placed a hand on the mattress on either side of her and brought his face down on a level with hers. It was a proud, arrogant face. If there had ever been any youthful softness in his lean, masculine features, it had long since disappeared. Well-defined brows arched cynically above eyes that were a dark blue-gray, like slate. Bronzed skin stretched tautly across his cheekbones, and his lips were firm and sensual. There was a small pale scar near one corner of his mouth. Tiny lines radiated outward from the corners of his eyes. "Don't do this, Sam," he said quietly.

Samantha's hazel eyes shot sparks of molten gold as she glared at him, angry with herself for feeling so helpless against the powerful emotions that churned within her. "Go to hell."

Trey's eyes darkened, but he said nothing. Maria returned to the bedroom with a towel and a bottle of Dr. Lister's Antiseptic. Trey took the items from her and spoke to her in Spanish. Casting Samantha a worried glance, Maria left the room.

Samantha pushed herself upright. "Didn't anyone ever teach you that it's rude to carry on a conversation not everyone can understand?"

Trey sat on the edge of the bed. "I'm sure someone tried," he said dryly. He dampened one corner of the towel with the antiseptic. "Look at me."

Seeing what he was about to do, Samantha grimaced and reached for the towel. "Give me that thing. I can clean my own face, thank you."

Ignoring her churlishness, Trey firmly gripped her chin in one hand and held her face still. With the wet towel, he gently dabbed at the discolored swelling beneath her left eye. "I want to talk to you about this Littleton character."

"He's none of your business."

"I'm making him my business. How far behind are you on the rent?"

Samantha winced. "Ouch! What are you trying to do? Give me a black eye?"

"You already have one. Now, sit still and answer my question."

His touch was having an unsettling effect on Samantha. The nightmarish images that had haunted her for weeks after the cave-in flickered through Samantha's memory: the night-long vigil at the shaft entrance awaiting news of those trapped in the stope; the hoisting mechanics bringing up cage after cage with men whose bodies had been crushed beyond recognition; Trey rousing her from an exhausted sleep to tell her they'd found Michael's body. . . .

The need to cry was so great that tears grated behind her eyelids and choked her throat. "Two months," she croaked.

Trey's gaze sought hers. Dark brows drew together over blue-gray eyes clouded with concern. He released her chin, and she hastily looked away. He saw her throat work spasmodically several times as she fought for control. A dull ache spread through his chest. He knew it was not the rent that was upsetting her. "There's no shame in crying, sweetheart."

Samantha snapped her head back around to impale him with her topaz-flecked glare. "I'm not crying."

Like gold dust, thousands of pale delicate freckles powdered her forehead and her chin and her nose, disappearing into a warm pink flush over her cheekbones. Her lips were soft and moist and a deep rose-apricot, and Trey felt an unbidden heat unfurl in his loins as he wondered how those lips would feel against his. "No, but you want to," he said gently. "You haven't had a good cry since Michael's death, have you?"

"What business is that of yours?"

"Sam, Michael was my friend."

Samantha dropped her feet over the side of the bed. "Some friend," she retorted. "If it hadn't been for you, my husband would still be alive."

She started to rise, but Trey caught her upper arm in a painful grip and yanked her back down onto the bed with a force that wrenched a cry of surprise from her throat. Her gaze was riveted on his face, and the cold fury she saw in his eyes sent a tremor of fear rippling through her.

"Damn it, Samantha! There is nothing I could have done to stop that explosion. Even you know enough about mining to realize that."

"If you hadn't brought in a bunch of inexperienced workers, there wouldn't have been an explosion," Samantha shot back. She tried to pull away, but his grip on her arm only tightened.

"The men were unemployed, not inexperienced."

"They were inexperienced in *this* mine."

"The miners were on strike, Sam. If I hadn't brought in replacements from the outside, we would have had to shut down completely. We couldn't afford that."

Samantha glared at him through the tears that pooled in her eyes. Her voice shook. "Of course you couldn't afford it," she said sarcastically. "You were so damned scared of losing a few dollars that you risked everyone's life just to keep that blasted mine open."

"It was a business decision. It was not a matter of risking lives. That day should have been no more dangerous than any other day down in the stope."

"No more dangerous! Trey, those men had no business being down there. Michael asked you not to hire them. He begged you. He wanted to give the strikers a few more days. You and Michael were supposed to be partners, but you wouldn't listen to him, would you? No. You had to flaunt your *sixty-five percent* ownership and send sixteen men to their death."

The hard-chiseled planes of Trey's face were taut with barely suppressed anger. He had to exercise supreme control to bite his tongue and not fling her accusations back in her face. What Samantha had never been told about that day was that the explosion was not an accident. Someone planted dynamite in one of the tunnels that had been closed off. Michael Drury was supposed to have been at the mill overseeing the assembly of the new furnaces. What he'd been doing in the mine that day was a question no one had been able to answer.

There was a peculiar tightness in Trey's chest. It had been a year since Michael's death. There was nothing to be gained by telling Samantha the truth now; she had already suffered enough. Trey released her arm and stood up. "After we get this place back in order, you and I are going to sit down with the books and work out—"

"You and I aren't doing anything. I told you several months ago I never wanted to see you again. I meant it, Trey. I want you to leave."

The sudden leaping of the muscle in Trey's jaw was the only outward sign of his annoyance. "We are going to sit down with the books," he repeated firmly. "We are going to work out a budget. And *you* are going to learn to follow it." He started to leave.

Samantha's expression immediately became mutinous. "You might have owned controlling shares in the Concha Mine, Treyman Stern, but the Drake House is mine. You have no right butting in and telling me how to run it."

Trey stopped just inside the doorway. Bracing one hand on the doorjamb, he turned back to face her. His expression was a mask of stone. "I once promised your husband that I would take care of you should anything ever happen to him," he said in a low, portentous voice. "Knowing how you felt about me, I've kept my distance. Well, no more, Samantha. I intend to keep that promise to Michael, whether you like it or not. When you've shown that you can manage this place without running yourself into debt and provoking your creditors, I'll back off and give you free rein. Until then I want you to promise me that you won't make any decisions without consulting me first."

Hurt, then disbelief, then outrage flickered across Samantha's face in rapid succession. The man's gall was unbearable. It was not enough that his greed had driven her husband to an untimely death. Now he was trying to redeem himself by alluding to a promise Samantha doubted he ever had any intention of keeping. She exploded. "When are you going to get it through your thick skull that I don't want your blasted help?"

One dark brow arched meaningfully. Trey's gaze never wavered from hers. "When you get it through yours that I didn't kill your husband."

Samantha's nostrils flared in righteous anger. She turned her face away and refused to look at him. "What I should do," she bit out between clenched teeth, "is get the sheriff over here and have you arrested for trespassing."

"Then, why don't you?"

Samantha snapped her head around to glower at him. Why indeed? she thought angrily. She didn't have the slightest idea what was stopping her, and that infuriated her above all else.

Trey accepted her silence as the closest he was going to get to a concession. Samantha was nothing if not stubborn. Without another word, he turned and walked away.

Joe and Maria had cleaned up much of the mess in the dining room. Maria came to Trey, her young face pinched with concern. She worried that Samantha would be angry with her. She knew how Samantha felt about Mr. Stern, but she did not know of anyone else to turn to for help. "*La señora?*" she asked hesitantly.

Trey forced a smile. "She'll be fine. I think right now she's more upset with me for being here than she is with the ruffians who trashed the place." He looked at Joe. "Take Maria home; then head back up to the mine. I want you there for shift change. The incident here at the restaurant may have been intended as a diversion."

Joe nodded. "Will Samantha be safe?"

"I'll stay here tonight, just in case Littleton's men decide to come back."

After they left, Trey hung out the Closed sign and locked the door. He turned to find Samantha standing at the cash register. She pushed the drawer shut and crossed her arms defensively. She didn't look at him. "They took all the money," she said.

Trey righted a chair. "Did you recognize any of the men?"

She shook her head.

"What about Littleton? Has he been here?"

"I've never seen Mr. Littleton. He lives in Phoenix."

"If you've never seen him, how do you pay your rent?"

Samantha knew Trey wouldn't stop badgering her until she told him everything. Perhaps if he realized all this was beyond his control, he would forget his ridiculous promise to Michael and leave her alone. "I deposit the money into an account at the bank. Richard handles the lease."

A muscle in Trey's jaw knotted. It was all he could do to keep his dislike from showing on his face. A handsome, distinguished fair-haired young man who was a perennial favorite among Myterra's female population, Richard Winters was president of the First Territorial Bank. As far as Trey was concerned, any man who had a hard time looking you straight in the eyes when he was shaking your hand was a weasel. That he had been openly courting Samantha for the past four months did nothing to improve his standing in Trey's eyes. "First thing in the morning we are going to the bank to pay your rent."

He just wasn't going to give up, was he? "I don't have the money. I already told you those men took everything."

"We are going to the bank," Trey said firmly. "I'll help you with the money. I also want to take a look at your lease. I have a bone to pick with your Mr. Littleton."

"Are you sure you weren't hurt?" Joe asked. Maria was so tiny, he often worried about her. Physically, she was no match for most women, much less for a pack of undisciplined men bent on destruction.

"I am fine. I am glad you and Señor Stern come. La Señora Drury, she is a proud lady. She do everything herself, but sometimes she try to do too much."

Once they passed the intersection at Fifth, few women, and no ladies, were to be seen on Main Street. Maria shuddered and slipped her hand into Joe's. She kept her gaze averted and tried to ignore the stares that followed them as they walked briskly down the dirt thoroughfare. Joe could feel her trembling, and he squeezed her hand in reassurance.

Indians and Mexicans were not welcome on Main Street.

Main Street was home to no fewer than fifty saloons, nearly one for every hundred Myterra men. Most were concentrated along a strip of Main Street from Fifth Street southward to the barrio on the edge of town. Each saloon boasted its own peculiar attraction, from imported delicacies to wrestling matches and target shooting. McAlpin's claim to fame was an oyster bar, with oysters from San Francisco Bay and fresh spring trout. The Shamrock Parlor featured a chop stand where a man could wash down his fried chops, steaks, or ribs with a mug of ale. Fifteen of the establishments claimed to have private gambling rooms. Some of the saloons that fronted on Main Street opened in the rear onto Union Street, also known as Virgin Alley. Brothels and dance halls lined both sides of Union Street. There were nearly as many houses of prostitution in Myterra as there were saloons.

Joe did not like the idea of Maria walking alone through this part of town every day to get to work. He accompanied her whenever possible, but his duties at the Concha Mine often denied him the opportunity. Trey was an accommodating employer, who would permit him to leave the mine whenever he asked, but Joe was careful not to abuse a valued privilege. Trey had already risked much for him.

It was Joe's promotion to crew foreman that had set off the chain of events leading to Myterra's worst mine disaster. Men who had previously objected to working alongside the Apaches assigned to their crews blatantly refused to work *for* one. Marty Dennison, the night shift supervisor, had called for a general strike.

Never one to commit himself to an unpopular decision, Michael Drury had wanted to try to appease the miners. Trey held firm. Any man not willing to work would be replaced.

Strikers barricaded the road leading to the Concha Mine, preventing the miners who had been hired as replacements from entering the compound. Sheriff's deputies were engaged to escort the replacement workers across the picket lines. One man was shot. Negotiations with the miners' union came to a virtual standstill.

At midmorning on the eighth day of the strike, a violent explosion rocked the entire valley. At first no one was even certain what had happened. Then the news came that the Kingman stope had collapsed. Sixteen men were killed and scores of others injured. Some said the explosion had been caused by a failed powder charge. Others said the miners had hit a gas pocket. Four months passed before anyone discovered the dynamite casings in a tunnel that had been sealed off before the explosion because it was considered unsafe.

Rumors and accusations proliferated. No one escaped suspicion. Michael Drury's presence in the mine that day was questioned. Trey's absence from the mine was questioned, and his judgment in sending the men below was still being criticized.

Joe sometimes wondered if it was all worth it. It might be better, he reasoned, if he resigned from his position as crew foreman. Many of his cousins had already quit working in the mines and returned to the reservation at San Carlos.

That solution irritated Joe. He was not a quitter. And there were no other jobs available in Myterra. He wanted to marry Maria, but he refused to take her to San Carlos where she would be no more welcome among his people than he was among hers.

Maria's footsteps slowed as they neared the end of the street. "*La señora*, I think she is afraid," Maria said softly.

Joe cast her a sharp glance. "Of Littleton's men?"

Maria shook her head. A small laugh burst from her lips. "Señora Drury does not fear men. She say they are like little boys. She say they turn their backs on God for a good piece of pie."

Joe laughed. He could hear Samantha saying something like that. She was the most outspoken woman he knew.

Maria's expression became pensive. "I think she is afraid of herself. She is afraid to love again. There is much pain in her heart."

"Her husband died, Maria. Some people grieve for a long time."

"I think Señor Stern likes *la señora*. I think he be better *marido* for her than Señor Winters. I do not like Señor Winters. When he look at *la señora*—"

Joe caught Maria's elbow and turned her to face him. His expression was serious. "What about me, Maria?" he asked. "Would I be a good husband?"

Dismay flickered behind Maria's brown velvet eyes. She shook her head. "Please, do not ask of me—"

"I love you, Maria. I want to marry you."

"It is wrong."

"Why? Because I'm Apache? Or because I don't believe in your Christ?"

Maria averted her gaze. "It is wrong," she repeated.

Joe released her elbow. He knew Maria wanted to get married as much as he did. He also knew that both her family and the church would frown on a marriage between them. Maria was a devoted daughter and a devout Catholic.

It would not be easy for her to go against the dictates of either her family or her religion. He pulled her to him and kissed the top of her head. "I'm sorry, *querida*. I won't pressure you."

Maria tried to smile. "Someday my father will know you are a good man. He will give us his blessing. Then we will have a wedding."

The false hope that shone in Maria's eyes tore at Joe's heart. They both knew Señor Velásquez would never consent to the marriage. Mexicans and Apaches had always been enemies. And the three years he had spent at the Indian school at Carlisle Barracks, where he had learned to talk, dress, and even think like an Anglo, had not altered the fact that he was an Apache.

Placing two fingers beneath her chin, Joe tilted Maria's face up toward his and gently, tenderly kissed her. He wanted her so badly that he had even considered resorting to his ancestors' tactics and abducting her from her father's house. The only reason he did not was that he knew the shame would destroy her, and he did not want to take away her dignity. For now the feel of her lips on his would have to be enough.

Maria sighed when he finally pulled away. "I must go," she said.

"Be careful, *querida*."

An impish smile suddenly lit Maria's heart-shaped face. "I think you will be a handsome *marido*," she teased. Rising up on tiptoe, she planted a kiss on his chin. "I love you."

Anger gnawed at Joe's gut as he watched Maria disappear between the thick-walled adobe buildings that distinguished the barrio from the rest of Myterra. The rules Maria's culture imposed upon her would not even permit him to walk her to her own door.

Someday, he vowed, he would make Maria his wife. And he would do it in a way that would make her proud. Someday he would find a way.

Trey snapped the cashbook shut and rubbed one hand wearily over his eyes. He looked up at Samantha, who was sitting across the table from him. In the soft golden glow of the lamp, the bruise beneath her left eye was not as garish as it had been in the daylight. She had not repinned her hair, and it cascaded over her shoulders in a glorious riot of untamed curls. Her expression was rebellious. "I've gone over the accounts three times," he said in the stern tone of an adult chastising a child. "Even taking into consideration the rise in the cost of food, your overhead is still relatively low. With the amount of business you take in daily, by all rights, you should be the richest woman in town. What are you doing with the money?"

"That's none of your business."

"Sam, don't start," Trey cautioned.

"Then stop hounding me about the money."

"I'm trying to help you."

Her eyes smoldered. "I've already told you, I don't want your help. I can manage just fine by myself."

"As you did this afternoon? If Joe and I hadn't arrived when we did, Samantha, there's no telling what those men would have done."

"All they did was board up the place."

"Not to mention knocking you around."

"Next time I'll be ready for them. All right?"

"No, it's not all right. You might not give two cents for your own hide, damn it, but think of Maria. Do you want her to get hurt?"

"Of course not."

"Then use some common sense, woman! Next time they're not going to stop at giving you a black eye and nailing a few boards across the windows. Your only defense is in not *giving* them a next time."

Samantha had an overwhelming urge to claw Trey's handsome, arrogant face to ribbons. Being forced to endure his company was bad enough; that he was making sense was insufferable. No matter how much she hated accepting his help, she couldn't risk Maria's safety. Maria and Joe were her friends. If anything happened to either of them, she would never forgive herself.

She held up her hands in defeat. "You're right," she said tartly. "I am apparently lacking in any measure of common sense at all. Therefore, I'll concede to your better judgment. Please excuse me, Mr. Stern, but I am tired. It has been a trying day, and I would like to go to bed. Since you have already made it perfectly clear that you have no intention of leaving tonight, you may use the spare blankets in the hall closet. If you can find a soft spot out here on the floor, please be kind enough to inform me of its location. I'll make every attempt to land on it next time I'm pounced on by a man attempting to evict me." To her chagrin, her voice quavered.

She pushed back her chair and stood up. "We open the doors at five o'clock. If you're not up by then, you're going to get trampled." She started to reach for the lamp.

Trey caught her wrist. Concern creased his brow. "Are you sure you're all right?"

Samantha stared numbly at his darkly tanned fingers closed around her pale, freckled wrist. Her throat tightened. No, she wasn't all right. In spite of her insistence to the contrary, she was scared. Very scared. And confused. She didn't understand what was happening to her or why the feel of Trey's hand on her wrist was having such an unnerving effect on her. She was dangerously close to crying. If she didn't leave the room immediately, she was liable to do the unforgivable and burst into tears.

She took a deep, steadying breath. "I'm taking the lamp with me," she said, ignoring his question. "If you wish to continue perusing my account books, you'll have to get the lamp from the kitchen."

Trey had never felt so helpless in his life. Samantha was hurting; that much was obvious. Yet he was aware that she would flatly refuse any comfort he tried to offer her. He wondered if she was still capable of accepting tenderness from anyone. Or had her desire to love and be loved perished along with her husband?

He released her wrist. "Good night, Sam," he said quietly.

Samantha hesitated. She felt she should say something. At the very least, she should thank him for chasing off Littleton's men earlier. "There is some cold fried chicken in the icebox, if you get hungry," she heard herself say instead. "The bread is wrapped in a towel in the pantry. Maria makes good bread." Her voice faltered. She reached for the lamp.

Without warning, a gunshot shattered the window nearest them, pelting them both with shards of flying glass.

Chapter
Two

SAMANTHA screamed.

Trey seized her arm and yanked her down under the table. "Are you hit?"

She shook her head. Her eyes were wide and dark in her ashen face. She did not appear to have been cut by flying glass.

"Don't move," Trey ordered. Keeping his head below the level of the tabletop, he reached up and placed Samantha's cash journal over the lamp's glass chimney, snuffing out the flame.

Darkness engulfed the room. No sound came from the alley. In the distance they could hear the tinkling of a player piano coming from one of the saloons. At the broken window, a breeze caused the muslin curtain to flutter.

Samantha wrapped her arms around herself. She could not stop shaking. Who would want to kill her? Surely Mr. Littleton would not have sent his men on such a mission? After all, if she were dead, he wouldn't be able to get his money. In the ten months that she had been operating the restaurant, nothing like this had ever happened before now. She shuddered.

Trey placed a reassuring hand on her shoulder. "Stay here," he said in a low voice. "I'm going to take a look around."

He had removed his gun belt earlier and draped it across

the back of his chair. He eased the revolver from its holster. Crouching low, he darted to the window. Broken glass crunched beneath his boots. He straightened up. Keeping his back pressed close to the wall, he carefully pushed the curtain aside and peered out into the darkness.

He moved his head slightly, and the moonlight glanced off his profile, illuminating his strongly sculpted features. He quickly pulled back into the shadows.

Samantha nervously moistened her lips. "Can you see anything?" she whispered.

Trey didn't answer. He let go of the curtain and moved silently to the next window.

Huddled beneath the table, Samantha fidgeted. She wanted to know what was happening. Her heartbeat sounded unnaturally loud in the stillness.

After a minute Trey returned to the table and buckled on his gun belt.

Samantha crawled out from under the table. "What's wrong?"

"I want you to stay here. No matter what happens, you're not to leave this room."

"Trey, where are you going?"

"Stay here."

"Would you please tell me what's going on?" Impatience sharpened Samantha's voice.

In the next instant he was gone. The front door closed behind him with a soft click.

Samantha knotted her hands in frustration. "Bastard," she muttered angrily. The least he could have done was tell her what he was going to do, instead of leaving her standing here in the dark feeling like an ignorant fool.

She went to the window and peeked through the curtain. Outside the restaurant, all was still. Several blocks away a gunshot sounded in the vicinity of Main Street, its sharp retort muffled by the closely packed buildings and the din from the saloons. It was the same night after night. The miners poured into the saloons, eager to ease the monotony of their lives with overpriced benzine whiskey, rigged gambling tables, or the attentions of one of Myterra's numerous pox-ridden prostitutes. Before long a fight would ensue, and someone would be wounded or killed. The weeks when the army payroll arrived were even worse. The saloons would fill up not only with excitement-starved miners but also with soldiers from nearby Fort McCrae. It was not unusual for a barroom brawl to escalate into a full-fledged riot.

Samantha could not see Trey anywhere. She wondered where he had gone.

When several minutes passed and he still did not return, she began to worry. Suppose something had happened to him? Suppose the gunshot had been a lure to draw him away from the building?

A muted scraping noise from the rear of the building caused Samantha to start. A window being opened? Her pulse raced. Had she locked the kitchen door? She couldn't remember.

Then she heard the sound again, followed by a dull thud. Her breath caught in her throat. Someone else was in the house with her.

Don't panic, she admonished herself. She fought to get her erratically beating heart under control. Surely Trey should have returned by now.

Samantha reminded herself that she had an advantage over whoever was in the kitchen. She knew her way around the restaurant, even in the dark, whereas an intruder would be unfamiliar with his surroundings. He might have the advantage of greater physical strength; she could rely upon the element of surprise.

Careful not to make a sound, Samantha made her way

across the dining room. If she only had a weapon, she thought. Unfortunately, any implement she might possibly have used, such as a knife or a rolling pin, was in the kitchen.

Her hand rested on the back of a chair. It wasn't her first choice for a weapon, but it might buy her a few needed seconds, she reasoned.

She picked up the chair.

Damn it, Trey, where are you?

She paused in the doorway to the kitchen and looked around. Because it faced the alley, the kitchen was darker than the dining room. She could see no one. The pantry door stood ajar, as it usually did; the latch had been broken when she rented the place, and she'd never gotten around to replacing it. Gripping the chair by its seat, she moved stealthily along the perimeter of the room.

Her heart pounded in her ears. Even her breathing sounded unnaturally loud in the smothering silence.

She stopped.

Although she could hear nothing, she could *feel* the presence of someone else in the room. That she could see no one terrified her. Gooseflesh erupted on her skin.

She had to get out of there.

Whirling around, Samantha collided with a tall, shadowy figure in the darkness. Fear exploded in her chest. With a cry of sheer terror, she raised the chair up over her head and brought it down hard.

Trey threw up his arm, deflecting the blow. He seized the chair and wrested it from her hands.

Driven by panic, Samantha lunged at him. He caught her by the shoulders and forced her back against the wall. "Samantha!" he said sharply.

At the sound of his voice, relief surged through her, nearly driving her to her knees. She struggled to catch her breath and get her rapidly beating heart under control. "You scared me," she blurted out.

"I scared you? Damn it, woman, I could have shot you!"

"I-I'm sorry. I didn't know it was you."

"What in the hell are you doing back here anyway? I told you to stay put."

"I heard a noise. And when you didn't come back, I was . . . afraid." Her voice faltered as she became acutely aware that he was standing so close to her that their thighs touched. Warm and moist, his breath caressed her forehead. Even in the darkness, she could see the intensity of the expression in his eyes as he studied her face.

Awareness crackled like heat lightning in the silence that stretched between them. Samantha's heart beat so fast it hurt. Trey relaxed his grip on her shoulders and began gently rubbing one thumb back and forth along the ridge of her collarbone. His touch ignited a dull, throbbing ache deep down inside her. Samantha frantically clamped her thighs together against the disconcerting sensation, but even that failed to quench the searing heat that spread like wildfire through her veins. Trey slid one hand up the side of her neck and into her hair, and Samantha sucked in her breath as an uncontrollable shudder rocked her entire body.

His head descended.

Reality returned with brutal swiftness. Realizing what he was about to do, Samantha quickly turned her head away. "Trey, don't."

He turned her face back toward his. "Yes," he whispered huskily.

He covered her mouth with his. Samantha stiffened. She wedged her hands between them and pushed as hard as she could against his chest. She tore her lips from his. "Trey, stop it! It's wrong."

Catching her hands, he drew them both up over her head

and held them captive against the wall. He brushed his lips over the curve of her cheek. "It's not wrong," he murmured into her ear.

She squirmed and twisted, trying to escape the persistent pursuit of his lips. "Trey, *please!*"

Easily holding both her hands with one of his, Trey cupped her face firmly with his free hand and held it immobile. This time there was no escaping his mouth as it captured hers with a savageness that sent waves of shock hurtling through her veins and awakened in her a hunger that had been denied for so long she failed to recognize it for what it was.

All thought of resisting him crumbled, and Samantha surrendered helplessly to the suppressed longings he aroused in her. Waves of intoxicating heat washed over her, dragging a tortured moan of desire from her throat as she returned his kiss with a fierceness that surprised them both. It had been a long time since she had experienced a man's touch, and now her body demanded full measure of what it had been denied.

Trey released her wrists and encircled her waist, pulling her hard against him. He could not get enough of her. His strong hands explored the hollows of her back and the soft curves of her body with a fevered urgency. He parted her lips with his and boldly delved his tongue into the honeyed recesses of her sweet, warm mouth, ruthlessly searching out her very soul.

Samantha threaded her fingers in his thick wavy hair and leaned drunkenly into his embrace, crushing her breasts against his rock-hard chest. Her tongue fenced with his, sometimes thrusting, sometimes retreating, but always returning for more.

Finally she tore her mouth away from his with a strangled sob and buried her face against his chest. This is wrong, her tormented mind screamed. Terribly wrong. How could she have forgotten that Trey had betrayed her husband, costing him his life? How could she allow her body's weaknesses to defile her husband's memory? Was her love for Michael so insignificant that she would forsake it all for a moment of lust with his rightful adversary?

Trey folded his arms around her trembling form and held her close. He rested his chin against the top of her head. "It's all right, Sam," he whispered. "I won't let anything hurt you."

Drawing a ragged breath, she pushed him away. "Let go of me."

"Samantha, don't."

"I said, *let go.*" Samantha wriggled out of his embrace. Shaking violently, she crossed her arms in front of her and moved out of his reach. Her legs felt too weak to support her. She was having difficulty catching her breath. Trey's ardor had left her mouth feeling bruised and her integrity violated.

She thought of Michael and how she had shamed him.

Guilt and remorse filled her with acute, unforgiving pain. Tears flooded her eyes. The grief that she did not permit herself to feel, that she associated with weakness, suddenly threatened to overwhelm her.

Trey touched her shoulder and she flinched. "Sam?"

She shrugged off his hand. "Please, leave me alone," she said in a thick, tear-choked voice. She wiped her eyes with her fingertips. "We'll need to sweep up the broken glass," she said shakily, struggling to get her fragile emotions back under control. "There's a broom in the pantry. If you'll start on that, I'll find something to cover the broken window . . ."

She broke off, unable to continue. She fled to her bedroom and slammed the door behind her.

Trey dragged a shaky hand over his jaw. Christ! The woman was a veritable powder keg. He'd never seen so much pent-up fire in a woman. How long had Samantha been suppressing her own needs? Since her husband's death, or before? Trey tried to picture Samantha and Michael kissing with such a lack of restraint, but the image eluded him. In fact, he was having a difficult time visualizing Michael Drury at all. Sandy hair came to mind, and a ready laugh. Beyond that, it was almost as if the man had never existed.

Trey glanced at the closed door that separated them like an impenetrable wall. He was torn between wanting to go to Samantha and take her in his arms and hold her until her grief abated, and respecting her need for privacy.

Tonight two truths had been revealed to him. The first was that behind Samantha's tough, independent facade was an untapped reservoir of deep, intense passions.

The second was that he wanted her.

When the first customers came through the door of the restaurant at ten minutes after five o'clock in the morning, there was little to suggest that anything unusual had taken place there the day before. The shards of glass had been swept up and brown paper tacked over the broken window until the pane could be replaced.

To Samantha's relief, Trey had left shortly before dawn. She had slept fitfully, knowing he was sleeping in the next room. At least she assumed he had slept. None of the blankets in the hall closet had been touched.

Her hands shook as she pinned up her hair, pulling it away from her face so tightly it made her scalp ache. She wanted no reminders of the way it had looked last night, wild and provocatively touchable. That done, she let her arms drop to her sides and stared in dismay at her reflection in the mirror. What she saw disturbed her.

In spite of the severity of her hair and the high, primly buttoned collar of her shirtwaist, in spite of the faint shadows beneath her eyes that attested to her lack of sleep, in spite of a whopping purple bruise beneath her left eye, there was a new softness in her face. Her lips seemed fuller, her cheeks pinker, and her pupils larger and darker than she remembered, giving her the dewy-eyed appearance of a woman who had just spent a blissful night in the arms of the man she loved. She narrowed her eyes and glowered at the image in the mirror, but the instant she relaxed, the dreamy expression abruptly returned, more pronounced than before.

Chastising herself for her foolishness, she went to her bed and sat down on the edge to put on her shoes. She tried to tell herself that she had behaved so shamefully last night only because she had grown unaccustomed to being in the company of men since Michael's death, but the lie did not sit well with her. She was well accustomed to being around men; most of the customers who patronized the restaurant were men. Men in general did not even faze her, and she seldom granted them a second thought.

Treyman Stern flustered her, however, and she didn't know why. She had spent so much time in the past year just trying to avoid him that he had almost become a fixation with her. The restaurant had been her salvation. Because it forced her to concentrate on day-to-day survival rather than allowing her to dwell on Michael's death, she had thrown herself wholeheartedly into its operation. Yet even hard work, she soon discovered, failed to exorcise the restlessness that gnawed relentlessly at her insides. It was as if she were forever searching for something and not finding it. Trey's presence, on the other hand, haunted her with all too much of something she did not want: memories of the past.

Maria was kneading bread dough in the kitchen when Samantha finally emerged from the bedroom. *"Buenos días,* señora," she said cheerfully when Samantha entered the room. She pursed her lips and winced when she saw Samantha's black eye. "That man, he hit you hard, no?"

Samantha's hand flew to her cheek. She thought of what Trey had said about Maria getting hurt, and her expression became serious. "Maria, if you're afraid to work here after what happened yesterday, I'll understand."

Maria smiled secretively. Wiping the flour off her hands with a towel, she went to the pantry and returned with a sawed-off double-barreled twelve-gauge scattergun. "Next time, señora, we will be ready for them."

Samantha's eyes widened. "My God, Maria! Where did you get that thing?"

"It belong to my brother Guillermo when he ride with the Wells Fargo. He no need it now. He marry Elena, and she make him stay home and work on her papa's hacienda."

Samantha shuddered. "Just looking at it makes me ill. Please, Maria, put it away. I hope we'll have no need to use it."

At midmorning Trey returned. He had washed and shaved, and looked none the worse for having spent the night sleeping on the dining room floor. His black coat hugged his broad shoulders without a wrinkle, and the crisp lines of his trousers emphasized his long, well-proportioned legs. The whiteness of his starched collar above his black waistcoat contrasted sharply with his tan. "Are you ready to go to the bank?" he asked from the kitchen doorway.

Samantha's face was flushed from the heat in the kitchen. Wispy curls had escaped her hairpins and softly framed her face, defying her earlier attempts at austerity. She avoided Trey's gaze. "I'll be ready in a moment," she snapped.

Maria was rolling out flour tortillas for dinner. At Samantha's sharp tone, Maria lifted her brows slightly and she cast a startled glance in Trey's direction.

Trey winked at her. His blue-gray eyes twinkled mischievously.

Suppressing a smile, Maria went back to work.

The silent exchange did not go unnoticed. Samantha pressed her lips together in annoyance and dried her hands on her apron. "Maria, will you be all right here while I'm gone?"

"Si, señora. Sarah and me, we will be fine."

Sarah Morrissey, the woman who came three times a day to wash dishes, had arrived and was busy cleaning up after the breakfast rush. She had already agreed to stay with Maria until Samantha returned from the bank.

Samantha reached behind her and untied her apron. "Let me get my shawl and I'll meet you out front," she said testily.

Trey was waiting for her beside the buggy. "I thought you might want to ride," he said when she finally joined him.

"Do I have a choice?"

"No."

A conspicuous silence hung between them as Trey drove across town. Samantha sat stiffly beside him, her back rigid and her chin held unnaturally high as she tried unsuccessfully to keep her skirts from brushing against his legs. Trey shot her an occasional amused glance. Finally he could no longer suppress a chuckle. "You might as well stop pretending that nothing happened between us last night," he chided gently.

Samantha bristled. "I think you're attaching too much significance to a mere kiss."

"I would hardly call that a mere kiss, Sam."

"Trey, drop it. As far as I'm concerned, nothing happened. And it certainly won't happen again. You may rest assured of that."

Neither of them spoke again until they reached the bank. Without waiting for Trey's help, Samantha started to climb down from the buggy, but he placed one hand firmly over hers, detaining her. His expression was solemn as his gaze met and held hers captive. "For a figment of my imagination, Sam, you're one hell of a passionate woman."

Hot color crept up Samantha's neck, all the way to the roots of her hair. Angry sparks danced in her hazel eyes. She jerked her hand free, but the heat of his touch lingered disconcertingly on her skin.

When they entered the bank, Richard Winters emerged immediately from his private office. He was dressed in an expensively tailored suit of pale gray silk, and not a strand of his silver-blond hair was out of place. He looked just as polished, just as dashing, as he had last Sunday when he'd asked Samantha to marry him.

Concern clouded Richard's light blue eyes as he hurried forward to greet them. He clasped Samantha's hand with both of his. "Samantha dearest, what happened? Are you all right?"

Normally Richard Winters's solicitude would have made Samantha feel pampered. This morning, however, it merely annoyed her. She pulled her hand free of his grasp. "I'm fine, Richard. Honestly."

"But your eye! Who did that to you?" He glanced suspiciously at Trey.

Samantha was acutely aware of Trey's hand closing possessively around her arm. "I'd rather not discuss it right now," she told Richard. She swore silently. Just what was Trey trying to prove? she wondered. Still, she made no effort to shrug off his hand. For the first time since entering the bank, she became aware that her heart was beating unnaturally fast, and she felt almost relieved to have Trey here beside her.

"I understand you are custodian of Samantha's lease for the Drake House," Trey said. There was no mistaking either the impatience in his voice or his dislike of Richard Winters.

Richard drew back as if offended. "I am sorry, Mr. Stern, but my business dealings with Mrs. Drury are confidential."

"It's all right, Richard," Samantha put in quickly. "Trey is helping me."

Surprise flashed across Richard's face and was quickly suppressed. "But of course," he said smoothly. He extended a well-manicured hand toward an open door bearing a brass plate engraved with his name. "If you will kindly step in here, we can discuss this in private."

Still holding Samantha's arm, Trey led her through the doorway. "Insolent pup," he muttered under his breath, just loud enough for Samantha to hear.

Samantha jabbed him in the ribs with her elbow. "Hush!" she whispered sharply.

A massive desk of polished dark mahogany anchored a red Oriental carpet in the center of the office. The tall, narrow windows were covered with wooden blinds, which were adjusted to deflect the morning sun. Behind Richard's desk was a leather-upholstered armchair with a high back. Two intricately carved straight-backed chairs stood at precise angles in front of Richard's desk. Trey thought wryly that the angles, if measured, would prove to be equal.

Richard closed the door. "Please sit down."

Trey escorted Samantha to a chair. Once she was seated, he pulled the other chair away from the desk, slightly altering the angle, and lowered his tall frame to the seat in a single fluid motion. He leaned back and casually stretched out his long, well-muscled legs.

A barely perceptible frown marred the banker's forehead as he circled his desk and sat down. He folded his hands in front of him. "Is there a problem with the lease?" he asked.

Samantha cast Trey an uncertain glance. Trey was eyeballing Richard with an intensity that bordered on rudeness. "I want to see it."

Richard looked at Samantha and arched one brow questioningly.

Samantha inclined her head.

His expression revealing nothing, Richard opened a deep bottom drawer of his desk. He fingered through several files before withdrawing one. He passed the heavy brown paper folder to Trey. "You will find that everything is in order," he said. "The lease is straightforward. As Samantha can tell you, I went over it thoroughly myself before permitting her to sign it. Knowing how inexperienced women are in these matters, I did not want her duped into committing herself to unfavorable terms."

Samantha bit her tongue. She did not appreciate being treated like a gullible child without any sense. Still, considering the mess she'd managed to get herself into, she decided it was best to keep a civil tongue in her head, at least for now.

Samantha watched Trey from the corner of her eye. His face was ruggedly handsome and his profile strong, she thought. Somehow he seemed more at home in this imposing office with its heavy masculine furnishings than did Richard. Trey's brows drew together and down as he perused the documents in the file. Finally he snapped the folder shut and handed it back to Richard. "I want a draft drawn on my account sufficient to cover Mrs. Drury's rent payments for the next four months in addition to what she currently owes. It's to be sent to Littleton immediately," he said.

Samantha stared at Trey in disbelief. She opened her mouth to protest, but the words stuck in her throat.

Richard Winters leaned forward, his expression one of overwhelming concern. "Samantha dearest, why didn't you tell me you were having trouble meeting the rent? We could have renegotiated the lease."

"Stay out of this, Winters. This is between Samantha and me."

"On the contrary, Mr. Stern. As Samantha's financial adviser, I am very much concerned with her welfare."

Samantha scowled at him. "Richard, you keep my lease in your desk drawer. That does not make you my financial adviser."

"But, Samantha, I am only trying to help."

"Richard, *please!*" She rounded on Trey. "I can't let you do this."

"Consider it done," Trey said curtly. He turned his attention to Richard. "I'll sign whatever documents you need to initiate the transaction."

"Trey, that's too much money!" Samantha insisted. "I can't accept it."

"I also want to arrange a meeting with this Morris Littleton who owns the property," Trey said.

Richard frowned. "May I ask why?"

"No, you may not. It's a private matter."

Richard's gaze fell to the middle of Trey's chest and remained there as he spoke. He moistened his lips. "I am afraid a meeting is impossible at the moment. Mr. Littleton travels extensively. He is not in the territory."

"When will he return?"

"Not for several weeks."

"I see," Trey said slowly, fixing his gaze on the other man with a single-minded intensity that made the banker's avoidance of it all the more obvious.

Samantha felt the color rise in her cheeks. In spite of her annoyance with Richard, she felt embarrassed for him. She wished Trey would stop glowering at him.

A knock sounded at the door.

Richard consulted his watch, then abruptly rose to his feet, signaling the end of their meeting. "I apologize for the interruption," he said, "but I am scheduled for another appointment at this time. If you will step out into the lobby with me, I will inform the teller of your wishes, and he will prepare the bank draft for you."

Feeling vaguely dissatisfied with the outcome of the meeting, Samantha stood up. She could not look at either Richard or Trey without feeling irritated with both of them. Trey reached for her elbow, and she jerked her arm out of his reach.

The movement did not go unnoticed. Richard started to open his office door for her, then stopped, nearly causing Samantha to collide with him. Startled, she jerked her gaze up to his.

Richard gave her his warmest smile. "Are we still having dinner tonight?" he asked her.

Samantha started to shake her head. "Oh, Richard, I can't leave the restaurant again so soon after—"

"Samantha dearest, you promised. Besides, I have a very special surprise for you tonight."

Uncomfortably aware that Trey was listening to every word, Samantha reluctantly relented. "It'll have to be late . . . after the dinner rush."

"I'll call for you at nine o'clock."

Although Samantha couldn't see Trey's face, she could have sworn he was glaring at her. She was relieved when

Richard opened the door and she escaped into the bank lobby.

Twenty minutes later, when she and Trey were on their way back to the restaurant, Samantha finally spoke her mind. "You didn't have to be so rude to him," she said curtly.

Trey held the reins loosely. He cast Samantha a sideways glance. "To whom?"

"You know good and well to whom, Treyman Stern, and don't try to deny it."

"This makes the second time this week you'll have had dinner with him," Trey interjected.

Surprised that he seemed so well informed of her actions, Samantha felt her face grow warm. "That, Mr. Stern, is no concern of yours. Besides, we're not talking about me. We're talking about you, so quit trying to change the subject. Why were you so uncivil back there?"

"Are you sweet on him?"

"Trey!"

"All right, Sam, I'll tell you why. Truth is, I can't stand the man."

"What has he ever done to you?"

"Not a damned thing."

"Then, why do you dislike him?"

"I don't like the way he combs his hair."

Samantha's mouth dropped open. "That's the most ridiculous thing I've ever heard!"

The muscle in Trey's jaw knotted. He hadn't meant for Samantha to take him literally. "Did you read that contract before you signed it?" he asked.

"I scanned it. Why? Is there something wrong with it?"

"Not with the contract. Just with your landlord. I'd be willing to bet you a month's wages the man doesn't even exist."

"What makes you say that?"

Trey's expression became guarded, giving Samantha the impression he felt he'd already said too much. He shrugged. "Just a hunch."

Annoyed that he would arouse her curiosity only to cut her off just when the conversation was getting interesting, Samantha pressed her lips together and jerked her gaze back to the front. "If *I'd* said that, you would have made some sarcastic comment about woman's intuition," she said testily.

Trey chuckled. "Probably," he agreed.

Samantha shot him a disparaging glance. "Trey, the Drake House is my restaurant. If there is something fishy about the lease, I have a right to know."

"I agree."

"Then tell me!"

Trey mulled over that one a moment. "Can you make a trip to Phoenix?" he finally asked.

"That would take several days. I can't afford to close the restaurant for that long."

"You can't afford not to," Trey said quietly.

They made the rest of the trip back across town in silence.

"I need to go up to the mine for a while," Trey said when he dropped Samantha off in front of the restaurant. "I'll stop at Mason's on the way and have him send someone out to measure the window for a new pane of glass."

"Trey, wait." It galled Samantha immensely to know she was indebted to Trey, but what might have happened if he hadn't helped her? She knew Trey was not exaggerating when he questioned her landlord's character; she had seen evidence of that deficiency yesterday when he'd sent that bunch of ruffians to evict her from the Drake House. "I don't want you to think I don't appreciate what you've done for me," she said. "I'll pay you back as soon as possible. I promise."

Trey's expression grew serious. "I'm not trying to humiliate you by helping you out. I hope you understand that."

Samantha shifted uncomfortably and turned her gaze down the street. "I've never owed anyone money before," she said in a low voice.

The stubbornness in her proud, unyielding profile brought a reluctant smile to Trey's lips. "It makes you feel helpless," he commented softly. "As if you'd given away control of your own life."

He had discerned her thoughts so precisely that Samantha was momentarily caught off guard. She turned to look at him and was surprised to see the understanding in his warm blue-gray eyes. But whatever satisfaction she might have gotten from his sympathy was tempered by her awareness of how easily he could manipulate her. "The only thing it gives you control over is my money," she said sharply. "And don't you ever forget it."

Trey could not help laughing. "With you to remind me, sweetheart, that'll be about as easy as forgetting the way you kiss." He touched the brim of his hat. "I hope Winters chokes on his steak."

Fuming, Samantha watched as he drove away. She didn't know who angered her more—Richard Winters, who patronized her, or Trey, who was being a pain in the neck.

She pivoted and strode into the restaurant. Even more than with the other two, she was angry with herself. If she hadn't gotten herself into such a pickle, she wouldn't have to contend with either of them.

When Trey returned to his office, two men were waiting to see him. One of the men, Ian Hunter, was an agent for the Consolidated Silver Corporation and had worked with him and Michael Drury two years ago on plans for the new stamp mill.

Ian stood up and extended his hand. " 'Tis good to see you again, Stern," he said. A tall, clear-eyed young man with a faint Scottish burr, Ian Hunter had a firm handshake that Trey liked. "This is Gaylord Whittaker. He's a geologist from Consolidated's home office."

Trey sized the man up as he shook his hand. Whittaker was much older than most of the men Consolidated sent to Arizona Territory. His thick, bushy sideburns were completely gray. "Are you a native of Chicago, Mr. Whittaker?" Trey asked.

"Pittsburgh," Gaylord Whittaker said. "Relocated to Chicago ten years ago."

Trey motioned to the men to be seated, then took his own chair. "What brings you gentlemen to Myterra?"

Ian removed a bound bundle of papers from his inside coat pocket and placed it on Trey's desk. He came straight to the point. "Consolidated wants to make you an offer."

Trey's expression was closed and unreadable. He made no move to pick up the papers. "Ian, you were informed last time you were here that the Concha Mine is not for sale."

"I haven't forgotten. I'm also aware that your circumstances have changed in the past year. You're sole owner of the mine now, Stern. And with the price of silver down to under sixty cents an ounce, you're operating at a loss. It would be to your benefit to consider our terms."

"If I'm operating at a loss," Trey said slowly, "what makes you think Consolidated can do better?"

Gaylord Whittaker leaned forward. "Mr. Stern, ore samples taken from the Concha contain measurable amounts of gold. It's my belief you are sitting on top a major lode. Consolidated has the financial resources to go down there and locate that lode."

"It's something to consider, Stern," Ian put in. "If the President is successful in his push to have Congress repeal the Sherman silver law, the Concha's only hope for survival is with gold."

Ian Hunter was not telling Trey anything he didn't already know. Trey knew that rolling back the Silver Purchase Act would spell doom not only for him but for every silver miner in the country. Cleveland had been hell bent on putting the country on a gold standard ever since he resumed office in March. Without the government's promise that the Treasury would purchase a minimum of four and a half million ounces of silver every month, nearly all that was currently being mined in the United States and its territories, Trey had no guaranteed buyer for his ore.

Bracing his elbows on the arms of his chair, he steepled his hands and studied the two men over the tips of his fingers. He drew his brows together pensively. "Hypothetical situation," he proposed. "Consolidated buys the Concha, sinks a large sum of money into exploration and development, and comes up with nothing. No gold, no new lode, not even a worthwhile deposit of copper. What then?"

Ian shrugged. "Consolidated swallows its losses and continues to mine silver."

"At a loss?"

Ian hesitated. "Not necessarily."

"That's what I thought. I'm sorry, gentlemen, but my dealings with Consolidated Silver will continue to be limited to operation of the stamp mill. The mine is not for sale."

Gaylord Whittaker shook his head. "You're a fool, Treyman Stern."

A slow, deliberate smile spread across Trey's features. "Look at it this way: if my men strike gold, then I'll be a very wealthy fool."

Just then the emergency whistle sounded, its piercing high-low, high-low warble calculated to send a shiver of dread through anyone who heard it.

Trey surged from his chair. On his way out of the office, he grabbed a safety lantern and a coiled rope from a hook behind the door.

Ian Hunter and Gaylord Whittaker exchanged glances. Each knew what the other was thinking: the whistle had last been used when the Kingman stope collapsed.

Chapter
Three

DOWN in the town, church bells took up the alarm and passed it on, filling the air with their urgent clanging. People poured out of shops and houses. Some hurried up the hill. Most stood in the streets, their anxious gazes turned toward the mine compound.

Wiping her hands on her apron, Samantha followed her customers out the front door. Her heart pounded. The memories of what had happened the last time the warning whistle sounded were suddenly painfully fresh in her mind. Like everyone else, she stared up the street at the stamp mill that loomed over the town, its two giant stacks belching thick black smoke into the air.

Beside her, Maria was wringing her hands, her hysterical Spanish punctuated by broken sobs. She started up the street, but Samantha caught her arm and held her back. "Stay here, Maria. You'll only be in the way."

Maria pressed a fist against her mouth. Tears streamed down her face. Samantha understood Maria's fears. Maria's father and two of her brothers worked day shift at the mine.

So did Joe.

Samantha released Maria's arm. She knew she had no right to hold her back. No one had been able to hold Samantha back the day she'd found out Michael was trapped.

Maria's long braids flew out behind her as she tore up the hill. She cut between the buildings and disappeared from sight.

Samantha turned and went back inside the restaurant. The place was empty. Some of the customers had tossed money on their tables on their way out the door; others had left their meals uneaten. Sighing, she began to stack the dirty dishes. She knew she had to keep busy. She could not allow herself to speculate about what might have happened up at the Concha. To do so would only cause her to fret and worry.

She would check the larder, she told herself, fighting to keep a clear head. If whatever happened at the mine led to an all-night vigil, as it had when the Kingman tunnel collapsed, the rescue workers would need to eat. She would make sure she had enough provisions to serve them a cold dinner.

During the day, news trickled from the mine compound down into the town. One of the hoisting cables had snapped, dropping the cage that carried the miners below. The cage had not fallen all the way to the bottom, but had become wedged at an angle in the shaft. Six men were trapped inside.

Samantha fried some chicken, prepared jugs of lemonade, and spread thick slabs of freshly baked bread with sweet butter. The kitchen was hot and airless, and perspiration trickled down her temples. Several times she had to go into her bedroom and splash cold water on her face. Even though it was nearly October, the days were still uncomfortably warm.

Late in the afternoon Maria returned to the restaurant. Her face was pale, and she looked as if she wanted to cry.

Samantha made her sit down with a glass of cool lemonade. Between sips, Maria spilled out what she knew.

"I don't understand," Samantha said. "Why don't they just go down and attach a new cable to the cage?"

"If the cage fall, all will die."

Maria explained that men were going to go down into the mine through the old entrance and place lagging timbers through the crosscuts below the cage, forming a safety net across the shaft. If the cage fell before a new cable could be attached, it would land on the timbers a few yards below instead of falling all the way to the bottom of the shaft.

It was the craziest thing Samantha had ever heard. She could not believe Trey was going to attempt something so dangerous. The slightest movement could dislodge the cage. If the men installing the timbers could not get out of the way fast enough, they risked being crushed if the cage fell.

Joe and Trey were among the men who had gone below to block the shaft.

Samantha gave Maria some food to take back up to the mine. "See if Mr. Connelly will let us borrow his wagon to carry the rest of it," she instructed the girl.

Although Samantha's regular customers usually came into the restaurant at some time during most days, today nearly all of them remained at the mine. Business was slow. Samantha sent Sarah Morrissey home. She counted the day's receipts, and her heart sank. How was she ever going to repay Trey what she owed him if she could not turn a profit?

During what was normally the peak dinner hour the restaurant attracted only one customer, a grisly little man who looked as if neither he nor his clothes had seen a washtub in weeks. Concealing her distaste, Samantha served the man. Usually a man's unkempt appearance did not bother her; she'd seen more honest dirt than that on most of the miners who came in after a twelve-hour shift in the tunnels.

The man wolfed down his food, causing Samantha to wonder when he'd last eaten. There was something vaguely familiar about him that she could not place. When he had finished the last of the fried chicken, the man wiped his hands on his pants and sat looking around the empty dining room.

Samantha refilled his coffee cup. "Would you like to order dessert?" she asked.

The man's eyes narrowed as he looked at her. "You run this place alone?"

Something in his tone caused the fine hair at the back of Samantha's neck to bristle. "I have help," she said warily.

The man looked away. He might have been handsome once, Samantha thought, observing his profile. She surmised that hard liquor had done more to age him than hard work. His complexion was ruddy, and fine broken veins stretched across his prominent cheekbones.

He nodded toward the broken window. "That could use fixin'."

"The glass is on order. May I get you anything else? A slice of pie?"

"Actually, ma'am, I thought I might be able to help out. Do some odd jobs to pay for my meal. I'm pretty good with my hands."

Samantha sighed. I should have guessed, she thought. She wished the man had told her he couldn't pay before she fed him. Not that it would have made any difference; she had yet to turn away anyone who was hungry. She just didn't like feeling she had been taken advantage of. "I don't need any help around here right now," she told the man. "You might check down at the hardware store. Mr. Stickley sometimes needs an extra hand."

"About my food," the man hedged. "I don't have any money."

"It's on the house. With the accident up at the mine today, business wasn't any good anyway."

He gave her an odd look. "There was trouble at the mine?"

She started clearing away his dishes. "A cable snapped. The cage was wedged in the shaft. Last I heard, no one was hurt. Would you like a slice of pie? It's apple."

"I'd better get going. You say I might be able to get a job at the hardware store?"

"You can ask. I can't promise anything, though."

"You've already done plenty. I'm much obliged for the meal. That was the best home cookin' I've had in years, since my wife passed on." He shook his head. "Things've been tough, with the mines closing down right and left. I got laid off two months ago. Haven't been able to find another job since."

Samantha felt a twinge of guilt at turning the man away. Even though there was something about him that made her uncomfortable, she could not help feeling sorry for him. "If you can't find work, come back in a few days," she heard herself say. "By then I should know when I'll be getting the new glass for the window. I'll need help installing it." *Please bathe first*, she added silently.

"Thank you, ma'am. I'll keep that in mind."

After he left, Samantha screwed up her face in disgust. What a stench! Even the flies were keeping a respectable distance, she thought dryly. While her heart went out to the old man, she wanted to kick herself for encouraging him to return.

The evening dragged. When it became evident that no more customers were going to come into the restaurant, Samantha closed the doors.

It was still early. Richard wasn't due to call for her for another hour and a half. If she hurried with the cleaning, she would have time to bathe and pin up her hair before going out to dinner.

She sighed wearily. She wished she hadn't agreed to have dinner with Richard tonight. It didn't seem right, going out and enjoying herself while men were still trapped in the mine.

When she finished sweeping the dining room floor, she went outside to sweep the front steps.

The temperature had dropped considerably once darkness had fallen, and the night air was pleasantly cool. Down on Main Street lively strains of music mixed with ribald laughter filled the air.

Maria had not returned to the restaurant after delivering the last of the food, and Samantha worried about her. She didn't know if Maria had gone home or stayed up at the mine waiting for Joe.

Up the hill, at the entrance to the compound, she could see lanterns bobbing. Just as they had the night she waited for news of Michael.

Trey's voice rang in her ears: *Samantha, they found him. I'm sorry.*

She swallowed hard.

I'm sorry, Samantha.

"Damn you, Michael, why did you have to leave me?" she whispered thickly. Her throat hurt.

Michael has been dead for a year, Samantha.

Tears stung Samantha's eyes. "There were so many debts, Michael. I lost our house . . ."

You haven't had a good cry since Michael's death, have you?

"I lost your half of the Concha, too. Trey owns the entire mine now. He bought . . . he bought your notes."

I promised your husband I would take care of you.

Samantha took a deep, shuddering breath. There was a terrible, burning ache in the middle of her chest. She stared up the hill at the lanterns and at the dark shadows of the smokestacks silhouetted against the night sky. The lanterns blurred and swam before her eyes. "I miss you, Michael. I miss you so much . . . it hurts—" Her voice cracked.

In the distance, a shout went up, then another, bringing Samantha abruptly back to the present. She could hear cheering coming from the mine compound.

They had gotten the men out! This time there would be no funerals to attend. No wakes that somehow had to be endured. No women left without husbands or sons; no children deprived of fathers.

They had brought the men out safely, but instead of being relieved, Samantha felt angry. She felt jealous. Why couldn't they have saved Michael, too? Why were other women permitted to keep their husbands while hers was taken from her?

Ashamed of herself for harboring such uncharitable thoughts, Samantha turned and went back inside. Trey had been right about one thing: Michael was dead. No amount of wishful thinking was going to bring him back. It was time to put the past behind her and get on with her life. It was time, she reasoned, to give some serious consideration to Richard's offer of marriage.

Richard called for her at precisely nine o'clock. "You look especially beautiful tonight," he said as he helped her into the open carriage. "I've never seen that dress before. Is it new?"

Samantha felt the color rise in her face. Even though the white cotton dress with its row of tiny French tucks across the bodice was outdated by a good three years, it was the nicest of all her gowns. It had also been her wedding dress. She self-consciously touched the high lace-trimmed collar. "I-I don't wear it often," she stammered. "Only on special occasions."

Richard settled beside her on the seat and picked up the reins. "I'm honored that you consider dinner with me a special occasion," he said somberly.

Neither of them spoke much on the way to the hotel. Several times Samantha opened her mouth to apologize to Richard for Trey's rudeness to him that morning, but she could not make the words come.

At the Silver Queen Hotel, the headwaiter led them through the elegant pink and gray marble dining room to a secluded alcove near a pair of French doors leading to the terrace. Even though Richard had brought her here regularly over the past four months, the richness of the place still made Samantha uneasy. She always felt hopelessly gauche and underdressed, even when she was wearing her best. Richard, as always, was impeccably turned out, this time in black silk.

After Richard had ordered wine, he turned to Samantha. His brow furrowed. "How is your eye?"

Samantha fidgeted. She'd tried covering the bruise with rice powder, but it had only made her complexion look pallid and artificial, so she had washed it off. "It's healing. It doesn't hurt so much."

Richard reached across the table and took her hand. "I found out what happened yesterday," he said. "I've spoken with Sheriff Calder. A reward has been posted for any information leading to the arrest of the men who attacked you."

"You didn't have to do that."

"What else was I supposed to do? Those men are dangerous!"

Samantha curbed the impulse to tell Richard she had already figured that out on her own. He was only trying to be helpful. "I shouldn't have any more trouble with them. Please don't worry about it."

"But I do worry about it. I worry about you. Darling, you know I don't like the idea of you living down in that part of town. There are too many unsavory characters down there. I never know what manner of harm is going to come to you."

Samantha smothered a laugh. "Richard, I've spent most of my life in that part of town. I grew up there. My customers are miners and their families. A little dirt on a man's clothes doesn't make him an unsavory character."

"What about the men who attacked you? They weren't exactly upstanding, law-abiding citizens."

"No, but—"

"Samantha dearest, I have it from reliable sources that not one person, with the possible exception of Treyman Stern, even attempted to help you yesterday. For all that I dislike the man, I do owe him that."

Samantha extricated her hand. "It's over and done, Richard. I wasn't seriously hurt, and I don't want to talk about it." She did not add that it disturbed her, too, that no one else had come to her assistance. Myterra had changed. A few years ago no one would have dared to treat a woman so shabbily. Now that there were more of them in the territory, women seemed expendable somehow.

Richard was pensive. "I thought you had severed your ties with Treyman Stern," he finally said. "Why are you letting him help you now? You could have come to me."

Samantha made a pretense of arranging her napkin across her lap. Just why *was* she letting Trey help her? If she knew the answer to that . . . She shrugged. "It's strictly a business arrangement. I'm going to pay him back as soon as I can.

You know I don't like to be indebted to anyone."

"Samantha dearest, have you forgotten what Stern did to your husband?"

"Richard, please—"

"The man is a scoundrel. He's not helping you out of the goodness of his heart. He's doing it to manipulate you."

"I don't believe that."

"Treyman Stern is not happy unless he has control over everyone and everything. Why else do you think he hurried to buy out your husband's share of the mine when he was killed? Greed, darling. Pure, unadulterated greed."

Samantha paled.

Richard refilled their wineglasses. "Just this morning Stern turned down another offer from Consolidated Silver. They offered him a partnership, with excellent terms, I might add. But Stern wouldn't hear of it. He refuses to give up an ounce of control over that mine."

"Richard, please, couldn't we talk about something else?"

Richard Winters immediately looked contrite. "Darling, I'm sorry. It was terribly vulgar of me to bring up such a delicate subject. Please forgive me."

The waiter brought their dinner, and Samantha was thankful for the diversion. Still, she found her usual appetite lacking. Even though her veal was exquisitely prepared in a delicate wine sauce, it seemed to want to stick in her throat.

Her thoughts kept returning to what Trey had told her earlier of his suspicions regarding her landlord. If Morris Littleton didn't exist, then just where was her rent money going each month? She thought of asking Richard about it, but held back. Richard was likely see such an inquiry as a slight to both his intelligence and his integrity. No, she decided. She would wait until she had proof before she broached the subject. After all, Trey could be wrong.

"You're not eating," Richard remarked after a few minutes. He had been enjoying a rare steak. He put down his fork. "Is everything all right? Your veal is done the way you like it, is it not?"

"It's fine. I'm just not very hungry."

Worry clouded Richard's eyes. "Are you ill?"

"No. Just tired."

"You work too hard."

"Richard, don't start."

"I promise, Samantha, I won't say anything about giving up the restaurant. I know how much it means to you. But that doesn't stop me from being concerned."

Samantha met Richard's solemn gaze across the table. He seemed sincere. Yet she could not help feeling wary. Until a few weeks ago he'd been adamant about her quitting the restaurant. He didn't want his wife working, he had told her. It was the one thing that had kept her from accepting his marriage proposal. She dabbed her mouth with her napkin. "Are you saying you won't mind if I keep the restaurant?"

An indulgent smile touched the corners of his mouth. "No, darling, I can't lie to you. I do mind. But I also want you to be happy. If you really enjoy it that much . . ." He left the statement unfinished.

"It's not a matter of enjoyment but of security. I don't want to wind up as I did when Michael died, with no money, nothing to fall back upon."

"Samantha! How many times do I have to tell you? I'll never let that happen to you. I'll take care of you. You'll never have to worry about money again."

Every nerve in Samantha's body felt ready to snap. "I've heard that before," she said curtly.

"From whom?"

"From Michael."

A sharp laugh escaped Richard's lips. "Samantha, that's different. Michael was only a—" He broke off at the sudden fury that streaked across Samantha's face.

Fire blazed in her hazel eyes. "Only a what?" she demanded. "Only a miner?"

"That is not what I meant."

The legs of Samantha's chair scraped the floor as she pushed away from the table and stood up. She snatched her shawl off the back of her chair.

She was halfway across the hotel lobby when Richard caught up with her.

"Samantha, wait!"

Richard caught her arm and spun her around. "Samantha, I'm sorry. I didn't mean to imply—"

"Let go of me."

"Please listen to me. I'm trying to explain."

"I said let go!"

Samantha's voice reverberated across the sumptuous lobby. Both she and Richard glanced around to find the hotel clerk staring at them.

Richard frowned his displeasure. Still grasping Samantha's arm, he propelled her across the lobby and into a small sitting room. He firmly closed the door.

The instant he released her arm, Samantha turned away and wrapped her arms around herself, something she unconsciously did whenever she was upset.

"Samantha," Richard said softly.

Her head snapped up, but she refused to turn and look at him.

Richard rubbed one hand along his jaw. "Love does strange things to a man," he said quietly. "It makes him crazy. It makes him say things he doesn't mean."

Samantha struggled to get her anger under control. If she lost her temper now, Richard might withdraw his offer of marriage—although, at this point, she was not certain she even wanted to marry him. If Richard Winters thought of Michael as *only a miner*, how did he see her? After all, she was a miner's daughter. And she had been a miner's wife.

Richard took her gently by the shoulders and pulled her back against him. He brushed his lips against the top of her head. "I'm sorry, Samantha. Truly I am. I know you must think me a callous brute, and it would be no more than I deserve if you were to walk out of here and refuse to ever speak to me again. It's just that I get so insanely jealous whenever I even think of you with anyone else. The thought of another man . . . touching you . . ." His voice trailed off.

Samantha leaned the back of her head against his shoulder and closed her eyes. He was gently kneading her shoulders, and the sensation was relaxing. She sighed. "Richard, you have nothing to be jealous of. If anything, the other men in this town envy you. You're wealthy, you're successful, you're handsome. The women, heaven knows, practically swoon at your feet. What more could you possibly want?"

"You."

She shook her head. "Oh, Richard, I—"

He turned Samantha around to face him. "Say you'll marry me, Samantha."

I'll marry you, Samantha thought, but she couldn't make her mouth form the words. Even though she knew, from a practical standpoint, that marrying Richard was probably the smartest thing she could possibly do, she could not shake the unpleasant feeling that she would be giving up far more than she would be getting in return. "I don't love you, Richard," she said. "I like you, but . . . I'm not in love with you."

"I know that. I also know that I can make you very happy. In time you may even grow to love me. All I ask is that you give it a chance."

Samantha moistened her lips. "I want to keep the restaurant."

Annoyance flashed in Richard's eyes, then was gone. "Samantha, you know how I feel about my wife working. But as I said before, if it means that much to you, then I'm willing to bend. However, you must promise me that you won't work so hard. I want you to engage more employees so that you're not waiting on tables yourself."

"Richard, I can't afford to hire more—"

He placed a forefinger against her lips, silencing her. "We'll work it out, darling. Trust me. Right now, however, I have a surprise for you."

Richard took Samantha's hand. "I've been wanting to give this to you for a long time," he said. "I can't wait any longer. You need not give me your answer now, but I do want you to promise me you will think about it. And I want you to wear this while you decide."

Samantha stared in astonishment at the huge diamond solitaire ring he slipped onto her finger. She had never seen a gem so large. Indeed, it looked almost lethal. She gave Richard a look of dismay. "Oh, Richard, it's lovely. But I can't possibly—"

"You can, and you will."

"What if I lose it? I can't wear this in the restaurant." A picture flickered through her mind of one of her customers biting into a biscuit only to crack a tooth on the massive diamond. "What if the stone falls out while I'm working?"

Richard laughed. "Samantha dearest, you worry about the most inconsequential things. Nothing will happen to the ring. And if it does, I'll buy you another. There's plenty more where that came from, believe me. Now come here and give me a kiss. I've been aching to kiss you all evening."

As Richard lowered his head to hers, Samantha could not help wondering what Trey's reaction would be when he saw the ring.

The two shift supervisors and fourteen of the Concha's sixteen crew chiefs had assembled outside Trey's office. The men from the day shift were tired and dirty. All were subdued.

A lock of dark brown hair fell haphazardly over Trey's forehead. Blood had crusted along a gash over his right eyebrow. He had removed his coat and vest, and his white shirt was soiled and torn and smeared with blood where he had wiped his brow with his sleeve. Exhaustion deepened the lines on his face. He held up the section of cable that he had detached from the cage's headframe. "Can anyone explain this?"

An ominous hush fell over the room. A few of the men shuffled their feet and stared sullenly at the floor.

Finally, Marty Dennison spoke up. "Looks like a worn cable to me."

Trey's eyes narrowed as he studied the other man. The night shift supervisor, Marty Dennison was a short, barrel-chested man with a thick neck and an unusually prominent brow-bone ridge that protruded over his eyes, making them appear sunken. Trey had never particularly liked Marty. The man possessed a quick fist and a short fuse. He seldom thought before he reacted, but he knew the mechanics of mining, and he knew how to get the men to work. Trey handed the cable to him. "Take a closer look."

Marty frowned as he examined the cable. "I guess it wasn't worn," he said, returning the cable to Trey.

It was all Trey could do to keep his temper in check. Anger hardened his face and lent an edge to his voice. "I'd hoped we had seen the end of this nonsense," he said, observing each man in turn. "Obviously I was mistaken."

No one said a word.

A tic beneath Trey's left eye twitched. "I'm going to say this only once, so I want you to listen very carefully. Another frayed cable." He paused. "Another missed powder charge. Another incorrectly positioned rock bolt. Any more *accidents* at all, and every last one of you will be given your wages and escorted off the premises."

A murmur of protest rippled through the room.

"Aw, c'mon, Trey," Carl Lemner blurted out. "You're not being fair."

"With nearly four hundred unemployed miners in this town, I don't need to be fair," Trey returned icily. "You are all responsible for the men assigned to you. If you can't keep abreast of what your men are doing while they are below, I'll hire supervisors who will. You're dismissed."

The men silently trooped out of the building. Several of them cast resentful glances in Trey's direction as they passed him.

Joe Tochino hung back. After the others had gone, he followed Trey into his office. "That cable was meant for me," he said.

Trey placed the papers Ian Hunter had left with him in his desk drawer and locked it. "You don't know that," he said sharply.

Joe felt his hackles rise. "Who else could it have been for?"

"There were six crews below this morning. Any one of them could have been in the cage when the cable snapped."

"It's starting all over again, Trey. The miners don't want to work with an Apache."

"If they don't like it, they're free to leave."

Joe shifted uneasily. He knew Trey did not mean to snap at him; he was exhausted. They all were. Yet while all the men on the rescue team had worked hard to free the miners trapped in the cage, it was Trey who ultimately bore the responsibility for the miners' safety. If the cage had fallen, Trey would have shouldered the blame. Still, Joe could not help feeling a sense of betrayal at his friend's sudden remoteness. He took a deep, steadying breath. "Maybe I should be the one to leave," he said quietly.

Trey's eyes were icy and unresponsive. "Joe, if you're going to resign, then resign. But you'd better have a damned good reason for doing so. I don't consider your men not wanting to work with you a good reason. Half of the men in this town wouldn't work for me if they could get jobs elsewhere." He retrieved his coat from the back of his chair and draped it across his arm. "You've been here since six-thirty this morning. If you're going to be of any use to either of us tomorrow, you'd better go home and get some sleep."

By the time Trey left the building, his temper was dangerously close to snapping. More than once today he had feared the cage would slip before they could move sufficient lagging timbers into place. He had hoped someone would come forward and identify the guilty party, but if the men knew who had cut that cable, they weren't talking.

The mill workers for the night shift were arriving at the compound when Trey drove through the gate. Unlike the miners, the men at the stamp mill, who were employed by Consolidated Silver, worked an eight-hour shift. It had been a bone of contention between him and the miners ever since the mill opened. The miners failed to acknowledge what the mill workers sacrificed for the shorter workday.

After reminding Paddy Sweeny, the night gate guard, to make sure everyone signed the log upon entering and leaving the compound, Trey snapped the reins and urged the horse down the hill toward the town. He had one more stop to make before turning in for the night.

All day the thought of Samantha having dinner with Richard Winters had grated on him. Why couldn't Samantha see that the man was an unprincipled lout? Trey could not believe she was smitten with the banker; he'd always given her credit for having more intelligence than that.

He was also aware that Samantha's dislike of him had increased proportionately with her association with Winters.

The first months following Michael Drury's death had been filled with pain and uncertainty for both of them. Samantha, left penniless, had sold nearly everything she owned in order to come up with the security deposit on the rent for the Drake House restaurant. Trey had scrambled to buy out Michael's notes of indebtedness before Consolidated Silver could get its hands on them—notes for which Michael had put up his share of Concha Mine as collateral. If he and Samantha saw little of each other then, it was less because of the painful memories the chance meetings evoked than because they were both too immersed in trying to survive.

Then Samantha had begun seeing Richard.

Trey did not begrudge Samantha male companionship. In all honesty, he had expected her to remarry long before now. She was a beautiful, vibrant woman in a town where men still outnumbered the fairer sex ten to one.

But Richard Winters? Trey could not suppress his annoyance. Anyone but Richard Winters, he thought derisively.

Winters had begun to visit Samantha on the pretense of having her sign some papers extending her lease on the restaurant. Then he began to make a habit of dropping in whenever he "happened to be passing through."

If the distance between Samantha and Trey had once been born of necessity, it continued now by design. Samantha went out of her way to avoid him. When he tried to find out what was wrong, she angrily confronted him with the often rocky business relationship he'd had with her husband. His explanations, he soon found, fell on deaf ears. Samantha firmly believed he had betrayed Michael.

Finally, four months ago, Samantha had told him she didn't want to have anything more to do with him. During those four months, until yesterday, he had relied on Joe to keep him informed of her welfare.

No more, he told himself. Last night he had come to the realization that he wanted Samantha for himself. If Samantha was sufficiently over her grief to let herself be courted again, then she could add another suitor to her list.

He intended to give Richard Winters some competition.

The dining room was dark when Trey reached the Drake House, but a lamp still burned in the kitchen. Trey drove around to the alley. He jumped down from the seat and lifted the crate containing Samantha's lemonade jugs off the floor of the buggy. On his way to the door, he stopped to peek in the window to see if Samantha was in the kitchen.

She was standing at the sink. She was in her nightclothes, and her feet were bare. Her hair hung down her back in a mass of coppery curls. Glass sugar dispensers were lined up on the drainboard next to the sink. Samantha placed a funnel in the top of one. When she raised the canister to pour sugar into the funnel, the lamplight shone through her gown and wrapper, erotically silhouetting her figure against the fabric.

Trey swore inwardly at his body's immediate response to Samantha's vivid beauty. His gaze followed the seductive curve of her breasts down to the indentation at her waist, and over her gently rounded abdomen. He fought back the wave of longing that gripped him. Damned fool woman, he cursed silently. Samantha was no naive schoolgirl. She knew better than to stand half dressed in front of an uncovered window.

Bracing the crate against his thigh, he went around to the kitchen door and knocked.

He heard a movement on the other side of the door. "Who is it?" Samantha called out.

"Trey."

Samantha quickly slid back the bolt and opened the door. "Oh, Trey, I was so worried about you. Did everyone get out all right? My God, look at your eye! What happened?"

Trey didn't answer. He entered the kitchen and placed the crate on the floor.

Samantha pushed the door shut and hurried to the sink. "I'll get you something for your eye."

Trey straightened up. As Samantha worked the pump at the kitchen sink, his gaze fell on the glittering diamond on her finger. He swore silently. "How was your evening?"

Samantha held a clean dishcloth under the running water. "It was very nice, thank you. Go sit over there."

Nice? Trey thought irritably. Just what did she mean by "nice"? It had to have been one hell of an evening for Sam to come away from it with a stone that big on her finger.

Trey pulled the chair away from the kitchen table and sat down. Samantha stood with her back toward him. Her hair hung below her waist, its undisciplined ends licking at her hips like flames as she lifted her arms to wring out the cloth. The room suddenly felt unbearably warm.

"That was a very generous thing you did, sending the food up to the men." In spite of his kind words, his voice was unduly harsh.

A slight frown creased Samantha's brow as she carried the wet cloth to him. "There wasn't much else I could do. I wanted to help."

"It was also very shortsighted of you."

Samantha stopped short. Her mouth dropped open. Dumbstruck, she stared at him.

"You're running a restaurant, Samantha. Not a charity. You can't afford to give away food. In the future I suggest you use your head and show a little more restraint. Pay your bills first. Then you can be as extravagant as you want."

Samantha had pressed her lips together so tightly a circle of white ringed her mouth. Her gold-flecked eyes smoldered. "You ungrateful skinflint!" she managed to choke out. "I spend all day worrying about you, wondering if you are all right, scared to death something would happen to you, and all *you're* concerned with is how much it cost to feed you and your men."

She snorted inelegantly. "That's all you worry about, isn't it? It all boils down to money. Money, money, money! It wouldn't surprise me in the least if that cable got frayed because you were too damned miserly to replace it!" Without warning she lifted her arm and hurled the dishcloth at him. It struck Trey full in the face with a loud, wet plop.

Trey surged up off his chair and snatched the dishcloth away from his face. His hand shot out and snapped around her wrist, wrenching a startled cry from her throat as he yanked her hard against him.

His fingers bit into her wrist as he held her hand up to allow the light from the kitchen lamp to reflect off the diamond on her finger. Cold fury burned in his blue-gray eyes. "When it comes to greed, sweetheart," he ground out, "you haven't done too badly yourself." He flung her hand away from him.

Before Samantha had time to gather her wits about her and come up with an appropriate response, he pivoted and stalked out of the building, slamming the kitchen door behind him and leaving Samantha to stare after him in open-mouthed shock.

By the time Trey reached Chandler's Livery, his temper had begun to cool. He didn't know what was wrong with him. First he'd barked at Joe, then at Samantha. He regretted taking his frustrations out on Samantha; she had no way of knowing that the cable was not frayed, but had been cut.

Still, her taunt rang in his ears, haunting him with echoes of the past. Before the other man's death, he and Michael Drury had argued incessantly about money. Michael's tendency to want what was best for the mine at any given moment had often clashed with his own long-term goals. Perhaps, if he had been more flexible and more receptive to Michael's ideas, they would not have been at loggerheads so often.

And he and Samantha would not be quarreling now.

Jimmy Chandler spit out a seed stalk he'd been chewing on when Trey arrived. "I heard about what happened up at the Concha," he commented as Trey unhitched the horse. "That was a mighty fine piece of work you did up there, Mr. Stern, gettin' those men out."

Trey paid him for the week's stabling. "I didn't do it by myself, Jimmy. I had plenty of help."

The old man shrugged. "All the same, them miners should be grateful to you for saving their lives. By the way, there was a man here looking for you earlier. Not a local. He kept glancing over his shoulder like he was being followed. Wouldn't leave his name."

"Did he say what he wanted?"

"Nope. Just asked me if I knew a man named Tyler Stern. I told him I knew a Treyman Stern, and he said, 'That's the one.' I figured he'd find you sooner or later, so I told him you were most likely over at the Drake House if you couldn't be found at the mine."

There was a peculiar tightness in Trey's chest. Only one person still called him by his middle name, Tyler.

A tense gnawing in his stomach, Trey finished up at the livery and walked the last block home. What, he wondered uneasily, was Liam doing in town?

The house was dark. Trey almost expected his uncle to be waiting inside for him, then decided that wasn't possible; Liam didn't have a key. No, Trey thought, the old man was probably down on Main Street getting drunk.

Trey fumbled with the key in the dark. His fingers felt numb. He got the same nerve-deadening feeling every time he was forced to deal with Liam.

Behind him Trey heard the crunch of gravel. He turned. Two doors down, a man hovered in the shadow of a thick adobe doorway. His hat was pulled down low, hiding his face. Trey called out, "Who's there?"

The man edged away from the building.

Trey frowned, remembering what Jimmy Chandler had said about Liam being followed. "Liam, is that you?"

The man moved his hand, and before Trey could react, there was a brilliant flash of red light in the darkness and the sharp retort of a gunshot.

A stabbing pain seared Trey's right hand. He swore aloud and reflexively grabbed his hand, but before he could move out of the way, a second shot slammed into his shoulder, sending him reeling backward. He grabbed for the door, but his fingers closed around air and he lost his balance, cracking the back of his skull on the wall as he fell.

Chapter
Four

JOE leaned against the bar, his hands curled around a glass of whiskey. He watched while the bartender tried to dissuade Charlie Cousins from buying another drink.

"Sorry, old man, they're beautiful, but I can't take them. I still haven't sold the last ones you gave me." The bartender pushed the ornate silver and turquoise earbobs back across the counter toward the gray-haired Apache. "Put these where you won't lose them, Charlie. Then go home and sleep it off. You've had enough for one day."

Taza Parks joined Joe at the bar. "Charlie's been drinking it up since early this morning. His old lady was in here twice today, looking for him."

Joe cast Taza a sidelong glance. They had gone to the Indian School together, but upon returning to the reservation, Taza had let his hair grow back. He now wore it down to his shoulders with a red bandanna tied around his head. "You get another job since leaving the mine?" he asked.

Taza shook his head. "No point in looking. No one wants to hire a *shkit-ne* anyway."

Taza's use of the derogatory term for their people grated on Joe's nerves. He looked away so Taza wouldn't see his aggravation. The other man's attitude of self-defeat annoyed him. Too many of the Apache had already given up on bettering themselves and trying to adapt to the white man's world. Not that he could blame them. He just wanted more out of life. He raised his glass to his mouth.

"You still working for Stern?" Taza asked.

Not for long, Joe thought, and his reaction surprised him. He couldn't imagine working for anyone else. Trey had been good to him. "For the time. Eli's quitting at the end of the month. That just leaves Eskelta and me."

Taza snickered. "It's not worth it, with Dennison and his men always out to stab you in the back. I'm glad I got out of there."

Joe swirled the whiskey around in the bottom of his glass. Maybe Taza was right. Maybe it wasn't worth it. Maybe there was something more out there for him than going down into the stopes day after day.

Taza signaled to the bartender. "You still seeing that *na-k-aya* girl?" he asked Joe. "What's her name, Maria?"

"I'm still seeing her."

"Pretty little thing. Too bad her old man won't let you marry her." Taza shoved his empty beer bottle toward the bartender and lifted a finger to motion that he wanted another.

Joe fished a coin out of his pocket and placed it on the bar. "Here, it's on me."

The bartender's face lit up. It wasn't often that the customers paid for their drinks with real money. Since the tavern, located half a mile from town, was the only saloon within miles that admitted Apaches, payment was more likely to be made in jewelry or baskets or hides, whatever the Indians brought in to barter.

"Aren't you having anything?" Taza asked.

Joe set his half-finished whiskey away from him. "I need to get going. I have to work tomorrow."

Outside the tavern, Joe nearly tripped over a body huddled on the ground in front of the door.

A grayed head lifted. The man mumbled a few barely intelligible words in Apache.

Torn between pity and disgust, Joe bent down and grasped the old man's arm. "Come on, Charlie. I'll take you home."

Charlie Cousins clutched the front of Joe's shirt as he staggered to his feet. Joe grimaced at the sour whiskey smell that emanated from the old man. Slipping one arm beneath Charlie's arms, Joe supported most of Charlie's weight on his slight, wiry frame.

There had to be more to life, Joe thought as he led Charlie Cousins away from the tavern, than working the mines, getting drunk, and growing old.

"You're damned lucky I came along when I did," Liam Stern said testily. "You always were an ornery cuss. If you'd had it your way, you woulda laid there and bled to death."

A muscle worked in Trey's jaw, but he said nothing. He did not like being indebted to his uncle.

"Got any idea who shot you?" Sheriff Calder asked Trey.

Dr. Goss tied off the bandage he had wrapped around Trey's chest, and Trey carefully pulled on his shirt. A similar bandage bound his right hand. "None, Sheriff. It was too dark to get a good look at him. He wasn't very tall, though. Maybe five-eight, five-ten at the most. And he was thin."

Unfortunately the description fit most of the men in Myterra. "What about his voice?" the sheriff asked. "Was there anything distinctive about it? Did he speak to you at all?"

"I called out to him, but he didn't answer."

Sheriff Calder asked Trey a few more questions that failed to elicit any significant answers; then he and Dr.

Goss took their leave. "Send someone out to get me if you remember anything else that might be of help," the sheriff said. "In the meantime, I'll have my men scout the area. I'll let you know if something turns up."

After Goss and Calder left, Liam carried the blue enamel coffee pot to the table and filled their mugs. "How're you feeling?"

Trey's shoulder ached. His hand throbbed. And there was a pulsing knot on the back of his head. How in the hell was he supposed to feel? Better than you smell, he thought. He wondered when was the last time Liam had bathed. "You haven't told me what you're doing in town," he said.

"Do I need a reason to visit my brother's boy?"

"That depends. Who's tailing you?"

"Always were the suspicious one, weren't you? The least you could do is thank me for hauling your carcass off the street and sending for the doc." Liam knew how to dodge a question.

Behind him, Trey heard his uncle rummaging in the cupboard. "I don't keep whiskey in the house," he said tersely. "If you're looking for a drink, you'll have to go elsewhere."

Liam returned to the table with a cold biscuit. "I've been dry for nigh on a year now," he said, sitting down. "If you'd bother to come home now and then, you'd know that."

Trey said nothing.

"Your cousin Jolene got married to that Martinez fellow down in Ajo," Liam continued. "Raymond blistered her rear end when he found out she was taking up with a Mexican, but by then it was too late to do any good. Jolene was already three months gone and starting to show. Raymond finally figured it was better to have a greaser for a son-in-law than a bastard for a grandson."

Trey knew what was coming next. It was the old "spare the rod and spoil the child" sermon. God knew he'd heard it often enough as a kid, usually when Liam was beating the hell out of him.

"I told Raymond he shoulda taken that girl in hand years ago, but you know how he is with them kids. He's too soft on them, just like your ma was with you. 'Better to reason with them,' he says. Ha! Lot of good reasoning did, with Billy now in jail and Jolene dropping dark-skinned brats all over the place." Liam shook the half-eaten biscuit at Trey. " 'Look at my Tyler,' I told Ray. 'Fine upstanding boy. Never a lick of trouble with the law. And do you know why? Because I took a belt to his backside twice a week and put the fear of the Almighty in him. You gotta let them kids know who's boss or else, first chance they get, they'll walk all over you.' "

If Trey hadn't been so weak from exhaustion and loss of blood, he would have been tempted to give Liam a taste of what the old man had been dishing out all these years. As it was, he barely had enough strength to get up and leave the room so he wouldn't have to listen to Liam's preaching. He pushed back his chair and stood up. "I'll get you a blanket," he said wearily. "You may bed down here in the kitchen."

"And just where do you think you're going?" Liam called out to his departing back.

"To hell, probably," Trey muttered under his breath. "I need to get cleaned up and head on over to the mine," he said audibly. "It'll be daylight soon."

"You just spent half the night trying to meet your Maker. You should be in bed, you stupid fool."

Trey ignored him. "There's bacon in the *alacena* if you want to cook yourself some breakfast," he tossed over his shoulder.

*   *   *

Trey struggled with the key to his office. With his right hand in bandages and his arm in a sling, he felt clumsy. Dust motes danced in the early morning sunlight that streamed in through the windows. No one else was about. It was still too early for Miles Gilbert, his bookkeeper, to arrive.

When he finally managed to unlock the door, Trey went into his office and sat down. He closed his eyes. Perspiration had beaded across his upper lip, and beneath his tan, his face was ashen. Liam was right: he should be in bed. But the thought of remaining in the same house with his uncle had filled him with such revulsion that he had to get away.

He did not believe that Liam had come to Myterra just to visit him. It was more likely that he needed money or was on the run.

His emotions had been mixed last night when he'd first seen Liam. He was thankful Liam had found him and sent for Dr. Goss, but that was where his gratitude ended. There was no love lost between him and his uncle; he had considered the score between them settled that day fourteen years before when he had left San Manuel with nothing more than the clothes on his back and an unwavering determination never again to allow himself to be at Liam's mercy.

Trey had been only eight years old when his father, Caleb Stern, was thrown and trampled to death by a horse he was trying to break to the saddle. Determined that the two thousand acres Caleb had left to his wife and son would stay in the family, Liam had wasted no time stepping into his older brother's shoes. Trey's mother, a young widow with a child to feed, had gratefully accepted Liam's help and then his offer of marriage.

Their first months together were good ones. Liam adopted Trey. He made improvements on the ranch. He drew up plans for a new house surrounded by wide shady verandas.

Then one Saturday Liam went into Tucson and didn't return for two days. He'd been drinking.

Overnight everything changed. When Liam drank, he became abusive. When he was dry, he was self-righteous. When Trey was eleven, Liam lost the ranch in a game of five-card stud and moved his family into a rented shack in Mammoth. He took a job stacking gold ingots at the stamp mill, but was soon fired for drinking. Mammoth was a small town, and Liam's propensity for showing up at work smelling like a distillery hampered his efforts to find another job. The rent came due and went unpaid. Liam was in the Mammoth jail nursing a hangover when the landlord and the sheriff came to the house and moved the family's meager belongings out into the street.

The next five years had found them in one mining town or another—McMillenville, Nugget, Silver King, Patagonia, Greaterville, San Manuel—wherever there was work and Liam's reputation had not preceded them.

When Trey was sixteen, his mother died. He left. Liam begged and threatened and cajoled, but Trey refused to return home. As far as he was concerned, Liam was out of his life.

So what did the old man want from him now?

"Can I trouble you for a moment of your time, sir?" came a voice from the doorway.

Trey's eyes snapped open. It took him several seconds to remember where he was. His thinking was clouded. "Come in, Amos," he said unevenly. "Have a seat."

Amos Flaherty, the day shift supervisor, pulled the door shut behind him. "You hurt yourself down in the shaft yesterday?"

"It's nothing serious," Trey said. He had decided to keep quiet about being shot, and Amos had just handed him the perfect pretext. It would be best for the time being, he thought, to let everyone think he'd been injured while he was below. "What's on your mind?"

Amos sat down. He looked troubled. "If I knew who cut that cable, I'd tell you," he said.

Bracing an elbow on the arm of his chair, Trey pensively rubbed a forefinger back and forth across his upper lip as he studied the other man. "Tell me something. Do you think the miners still object to working with Joe Tochino and his cousins?"

"Well, sir . . ." Amos hesitated, as though searching for the right words. "Them boys is hard workers, every last one of 'em—"

"That's not what I asked you, Amos."

"Marty Dennison don't like 'em, if that's what you're getting at," Amos said. "But I don't think he'd do nothing like cut the cables. The man's got a wife and four young 'uns to feed. He's not one to risk losin' his job."

Trey said nothing. He knew Amos wouldn't implicate anyone without proof.

"There is something I thought you ought to know, Mr. Stern," Amos continued. "There's going to be a union meeting tonight."

"Miners or mechanics?"

"Miners. I heard Silas Jenkins might be there."

One dark brow shot upward. Although it had never been proven, it was rumored that Silas Jenkins had cold-bloodedly killed the superintendent of the Oro Belle gold mine near Patagonia. Trey hadn't known Jenkins was in Myterra. "Did Dennison call this meeting?"

Amos shook his head. "That's the odd thing, Mr. Stern. No one knows who called it. The fliers just suddenly appeared out of the blue this morning at the union hall."

*   *   *

When Maria arrived for work, her eyes were red-rimmed and swollen. Samantha's anger mounted as she listened to Maria's account of what had happened when she returned home last night.

Maria blew her nose into her handkerchief. "My father say he will send me to Sonora to stay with *las monjas* if I do not stop seeing Joe."

It took Samantha a moment to realize what Maria was saying, and when she finally did, indignation flashed across her face. "With the nuns! Maria, you can't be serious. Would your father really send you to a convent?"

"*Sí,* Señora Drury, if I disobey him, it is what he will do."

Samantha plunked her hands on her hips. Determination shone in her gold-flecked eyes. "Well, we'll just have to see about that, won't we?"

All morning Samantha's mind churned. There had to be some way to get Maria and Joe together that would meet with her father's approval.

Samantha lined up four plates along the length of her arm, each plate piled high with the restaurant's most popular breakfast—steak, eggs, fried potatoes, and biscuits—and retrieved the coffee pot from the back of the stove. "There's no two ways about it. You're just going to have to elope," she called out to Maria before disappearing into the dining room.

The restaurant was packed. It seemed that those men who had gone without eating yesterday were making up for it today. She set the coffee pot on the edge of a table and distributed the plates. "May I get you gentlemen anything else?" she asked as she refilled the miners' coffee cups.

John Ruskin grinned at his companions and winked at her. "A million dollars?"

Samantha laughed. "I'll talk to my supplier and see if he'll special-order it for you. You want jam or honey with those biscuits?"

"How about a kiss?"

"Behave yourself, John, or I'll tell Maddie you were down at the Caledonian last Wednesday gambling away her egg money."

The big burly miner drew back and stared at her in surprise. "Now, how'd you find out about that?"

Samantha smiled sweetly. "I have my methods."

On her way back to the kitchen, Samantha stopped at another table. "More coffee over here?"

"Naw, I've had enough," a miner said. He leaned back in his chair and rubbed his stomach. His shirt buttons looked about ready to pop. "That fried chicken you sent up to the Concha yesterday was real good, Sam. That was a right neighborly thing for you to do."

Samantha's smile became strained. That's not what your employer thinks, she thought sourly. "I'm glad you liked it. Are you paying together or separately?"

"I'm picking up Cal's."

Samantha began stacking the plates. "Yours will be a dollar fifty. Jimmy, yours is a dollar. And your pancakes, Roger, will be fifty cents. I'll meet you at the register."

She returned to the kitchen with the coffee pot in one hand and a pile of dirty dishes in the other. Sarah Morrissey took the plates from her.

Maria handed her two more orders. "We cannot elope. It is wrong."

"Why would it be wrong? A civil ceremony is legal in the Territory of Arizona. That's all that matters."

"Not in the eyes of God and the church, señora."

"What if you got married first, then got the priest's blessing afterward?"

Maria stared at her as if she'd lost her mind.

Samantha shook her head. "Forget I said that. It was a bad idea anyway. Sarah, would you take that batch of biscuits out of the oven before it burns?"

At midmorning, after the breakfast rush had waned, Sheriff Calder came into the restaurant and sat down.

Samantha went to take his order. "What can I get for you, Sheriff?"

"You still running that steak special?"

Samantha nodded. "Steak, three eggs any style, fried potatoes, buttermilk biscuits, and all the coffee you can drink for a dollar."

Sheriff Calder chuckled. "Do you know, Mrs. Drury, you're the only one in town who charges me for my meals? Everywhere else, I eat for free."

Samantha filled his coffee cup. "Look at it this way, Sheriff. When I break the law and you have to arrest me, you won't owe me any favors."

The sheriff's expression turned serious. "Mrs. Drury, when you get a few minutes, I'd like to ask you some questions."

Remembering what Richard had told her about putting up reward money to help capture the men who had tried to evict her from the restaurant, Samantha suddenly felt embarrassed. After all, *she* had been at fault for not paying her rent. "Really, Sheriff, none of this is necessary."

"I think it is, Mrs. Drury." He inclined his head toward the chair opposite him. "Why don't you have breakfast with me?"

Samantha hesitated a moment before accepting. "That would be very nice, Sheriff. Thank you. How do you want your eggs?"

"Over easy. And could you substitute some of Maria's tortillas for the biscuits?"

A few minutes later, with her hair tidied up and wearing a clean shirtwaist, Samantha joined Sheriff Calder at his table.

"That all you're having?" he asked, quirking a brow at her cup of black coffee.

"It's all I have time for. As soon as I finish here, I need to start getting ready for the noon crowd."

The sheriff smeared butter and honey on a soft, warm flour tortilla. "You seem to be doing a booming business here. How's everything going?"

Samantha tried to sound nonchalant. "As long as I pay my rent on time, I don't have any problems," she said lightly. "Sheriff, about the reward money, I know Richard meant well, but there's really no need for—"

"I'm not here to discuss Richard Winters, Mrs. Drury. I want to know more about your involvement with Treyman Stern."

The question caught Samantha completely off guard. She made no attempt to hide the pique in her voice. "My *what?*"

"Why so touchy?"

Samantha's lips thinned into a line of irritation. "Sheriff, Treyman Stern and my husband were business partners. I've seen very little of him since Michael's death, and I'm certainly not *involved* with him."

"Am I to understand that he bailed you out of a sticky financial situation recently?"

"What does that have to do with anything?" Samantha did not like what the sheriff was insinuating.

"Just answer the question, Mrs. Drury."

"Yes," she said curtly. "He paid my rent on this place."

Sheriff Calder cut off a bite of steak and popped it into his mouth. He chewed slowly, his expression thoughtful. "Stern was here late last night," he commented after he'd swallowed.

Was nothing sacred in this town? Was her every move subject to public scrutiny? "Yes," she bit out.

"Why?"

"If you must know, Sheriff Calder, I had sent some food up to the mine for the rescue workers. Mr. Stern was merely returning the containers."

"At midnight?"

Heat flooded Samantha's face with angry color. She abruptly pushed back her chair and stood up. "I am finding your questions vulgar and impertinent, Sheriff. If you are trying to find out whether or not Mr. Stern spent the night with me, the answer is no. He did not. Now, if you will excuse me, I have a restaurant to run."

"Just one more question, Mrs. Drury."

Samantha turned to face the sheriff. She crossed her arms defiantly and peered down her nose at him. Her toe beat an impatient tattoo on the tile floor.

Sheriff Calder eyed her steadily over the rim of his coffee cup as he took a long, unhurried drink. Finally he set the cup down and leaned back in his chair. "Mrs. Drury, do you have any idea who would want to kill Treyman Stern?"

"Stern, you haven't heard a word I've said."

Trey turned away from the window. It took every ounce of determination he could muster to ignore the ache in his shoulder and concentrate on what Ian Hunter was saying. "I heard you, Ian. I'm just not buying it."

Ian ran his fingers through his hair in a gesture of frustration. "What is it about Consolidated's offer that you don't like? 'Tis as good an offer as you're going to get, with the country in a recession. The unions have been fighting for eight-hour shifts. Here's your chance to give the miners what they want."

"At a reduction in pay," Trey countered.

"The miners will receive the same pay they receive now. The only difference is, they'll be working eight hours a day instead of twelve. You can't ask for more generous terms than that."

Trey studied the other man through narrowed eyes. Finally he returned to his desk and lowered his tall frame into his chair. Aside from the sudden evacuation of color from his face, his expression gave no indication of his discomfort. "All right, I'll consider Consolidated's offer to buy out the Concha. On one condition."

"And that is?"

"I want a guarantee, in writing, that the men will continue to be paid in cash, the same as they are now."

A look of dismay flitted across Ian Hunter's face. "Stern, what you're asking is highly irregular—"

"In cash," Trey repeated firmly. "Not in scrip."

The two men eyed each other evenly across Trey's desk. "And if I can't get you that guarantee?" Ian asked slowly.

Trey's smile did not extend to his eyes. "Then we have nothing to discuss."

By the time the entrance to the mine compound came into sight, Samantha was out of breath and had a stitch in her side from running. There had been no answer when she knocked on the door of Trey's house, and when she'd gone to Chandler's Livery, she'd found that his horse and buggy were gone. He had to be at the mine. Where else could he have possibly gone?

She could not believe someone would try to kill Trey, especially after he'd spent all day yesterday risking his life to save the men trapped in the cage. For all his other faults, no one could accuse Trey of shirking his duties or of avoiding danger.

The angry words she had flung at him last night weighed heavily on her conscience. If she'd only thought before she'd spoken, he would not have left the restaurant in a blind rage. One of these days, Samantha scolded herself, your hot temper is going to buy you a great deal of unhappiness.

As Samantha neared the gate, she encountered Miles Gilbert, also heading toward the mine compound. "Miles!" she called out.

The bookkeeper stopped and turned, his expression one of disbelief. He pushed his spectacles up on his nose. "Why, Mrs. Drury, what a pleasant surprise," he said. "You're looking lovelier than ever, if I might be so bold. What brings you up to the Concha today?"

"I need to see Mr. Stern," Samantha said breathlessly. "Is he in?"

Miles nodded. "He was in a meeting with Ian Hunter when I left to take the deposit to the bank."

Samantha let out her breath in a long whoosh of relief. At least Trey was all right. "Do you mind if I walk with you?"

"By all means, please do. We'll need to sign in at the guard shack."

Samantha saw Arnie Pitts lounging against the doorjamb of the guard shack, watching them through half-closed eyes as they approached. She had never liked Arnie, although she didn't know why. There was just something about him that made icy prickles erupt on her skin whenever she saw him. She struggled to keep her dislike of him from showing on her face. "Good morning, Arnie."

Arnie wiped his hand on his pant leg. There was a red mark on one cheek where he had been digging at his skin. "Morning, Mrs. Drury," he said. "I haven't seen you up here since the explosion last year. Too bad about your husband. Things just haven't been the same around here since he was killed."

"Mrs. Drury needs to sign in," Miles said curtly.

Arnie glowered at the bookkeeper. "Why didn't you say so?" He stepped back and let Samantha into the guard shack.

Samantha hastily entered her name in the logbook, then hurried back outside to wait while Miles signed in.

"That's the new assay office," Miles pointed out a few minutes later as they walked up the hill. "Consolidated Silver built it as part of the new mill. Consolidated has big plans for this area. They want to expand and put in a smelter down along Aravaipa Creek. That's what Mr. Hunter is discussing with him now. That, and the possibility of purchasing the Concha."

Samantha cast him a sharp glance. "Trey's going to sell out?" Disbelief echoed in her voice.

"He doesn't want to," Miles replied. He adjusted his spectacles. "But between the pressure Consolidated Silver is exerting on him, and the union's demands for reforms, he might not have a choice."

Samantha stopped and placed a restraining hand on the bookkeeper's arm. "Why are you telling me these things, Miles?"

Miles's expression was solemn as he regarded her. "I've heard some of the rumors about how Mr. Stern cheated your husband out of his share of the earnings and how he only looks out for his own interests. The rumors aren't true, Mrs. Drury. Not a single one of them. I've been keeping the books for the Concha since it incorporated three years ago, and I'd swear on the Bible that every penny the mine has ever brought in can be accounted for.

"And I'll tell you something else," Miles went on. "Since the price of silver started dropping, the men's wages have come directly out of Mr. Stern's pockets more often than not. The mine is producing; it's just not making any money. If it weren't for Mr. Stern, the Concha would have gone under months ago."

Troubled thoughts churned in Samantha's mind as she and Miles Gilbert walked the rest of the way to the weathered wood-frame administration building that housed the mine's offices. If the Concha was doing so poorly, she wondered, why had Trey paid her rent on the Drake House for four months in advance? And he accused *her* of being shortsighted!

The door to Trey's private office was closed. "Mr. Stern must still be in conference with Ian Hunter," Miles said. "You're welcome to wait for him if you'd like."

After thanking him, Samantha wandered absently around the outer office. A long counter, like the one at the bank, now separated the bookkeeper's desk from the entrance. Aside from that, little had changed over the past year. The third floorboard in from the front door still creaked when one stepped on it. The wooden telephone box on the north wall still hung at a slightly crooked angle, as it had when it was first installed. Samantha was even willing to bet the window behind the bookcase was still stuck shut.

Suddenly she found herself face to face with the door to Michael's old office. Hesitantly she reached out and touched the nameplate on the door: Michael B. Drury. It had never been removed.

The blood pounding in her ears, she opened the door and went inside.

The office was dark. Shades had been mounted over the windows. Cases of dynamite were stacked along one wall. The room was now being used for storage.

Samantha closed her eyes as a wave of misery so acute it felt like physical pain swept over her, heightening her sense of loss and desolation. "Oh, Michael," she whispered into the stillness. Her throat closed up. "Please tell me how I'm supposed to go on without you. . . ."

After a while the silence seemed to take on a significance of its own, calling out to her, touching her with an urgent awareness that something was amiss. Puzzled, Samantha looked around her, trying to discern just what it was about Michael's office that she found so troubling.

Slowly the realization dawned that it was too quiet. Michael's office was adjacent to Trey's. If Trey were still meeting with Ian Hunter, their voices would have penetrated the common wall.

Samantha went to the wall and pressed her ear to it. Nothing. Nothing at all. Samantha swore silently. Damn it all, she thought. She'd been waiting for nothing. Trey wasn't even in there. Or if he was, he was alone.

Going back out into the main office, Samantha went to Trey's office and knocked on the door. "Trey, are you in there?"

Miles glanced up from the ledgers he'd been footing and eyed her oddly. "Is something wrong?" he asked.

"I don't know." Samantha opened the door. Her breath caught in her throat.

Trey lay sprawled on the floor behind his desk. The front of his shirt was saturated with blood.

Samantha flew to Trey's side and knelt beside him. His face was a deathly shade of gray. He was barely breathing. "Oh, my God! Miles! Call the doctor!"

Chapter
Five

DR. GOSS knotted a clean bandage around Trey's chest. "What were you trying to do, young man?" he asked. "Dig your own grave? You should be in bed, resting."

It was so unusual to hear someone take the upper hand with Trey that Samantha had to suppress a smile. "I'll see that he gets home, Dr. Goss," she volunteered.

Trey shot her a venomous glance. His jaw was clenched so tightly, Samantha thought he would crack a tooth.

The elderly physician glanced from one to the other. "You're lucky Mrs. Drury found you when she did. If she hadn't, you wouldn't be here right now," he told Trey. He closed his medical bag and stood up. "That's the last time I'm going to bandage you up, boy. If you make that wound start bleeding again, you're on your own. I don't have time to waste on patients who can't follow orders."

Samantha saw Dr. Goss to the door. When she returned to Trey's office, he was trying to work his arm into a clean shirt. Thank goodness he kept a change of clothes on the site, Samantha thought, remembering the times Michael had been forced to borrow a clean shirt from Trey. "Here, let me help you."

"Who appointed you my keeper?" Trey demanded impatiently as she eased the shirt up over his shoulders.

Dr. Goss had warned Samantha that the pain medication he had given Trey would make him either sleepy or irritable. She smiled brightly. "I did. Now, sit down before you faint again, and face me so I can button you up."

Too drained to put up much of a protest, Trey did as she commanded. "Sam, I appreciate what you've done, but you need to get back to the restaurant. I'll go home when I finish up here."

Bending over him, Samantha frowned in concentration as she buttoned his shirt. "Too late. I've already sent Miles after your buggy."

"I didn't tell you to do that."

"I know. You were out cold."

Trey shook his head in exasperation. "Samantha, what are you doing up here, anyway? Why aren't you down at the restaurant?"

"I closed it down for the rest of the day."

"You can't afford to do that. What in the hell was going through your mind?"

"I was worried about you, you hardheaded fool. And if I hadn't come here, you'd probably be dead now, so quit your bellyaching."

"Sam." Trey's hand closed over hers. He held it against his chest.

She glanced up.

Gratitude darkened Trey's eyes. "Thank you," he whispered hoarsely.

Sudden tears blinded her and choked her throat. What if she'd been too late? What if he'd died? Just thinking it brought a sharp stab of pain to her heart. She took a deep breath. "Come on. I'll take you home."

As they left the mine compound, Samantha was acutely aware of Arnie Pitts's curious gaze following them. She drove through the gate without stopping to sign out.

Trey leaned back against the seat. His face was pale.

Samantha cast him a sidelong glance. "You aren't going to swoon on me, are you?"

He gritted his teeth against the pain in his shoulder. "Not if I can help it."

They had just turned down Sherman Street when Trey suddenly ordered Samantha to stop the buggy. By this time his face was as white as his shirt.

"Trey, what's wrong?"

"Turn . . . the buggy around."

She stared at him in disbelief. "Trey, we're almost home."

"No," he bit out. "Not there."

He wasn't making any sense. Samantha wondered if he was becoming feverish. "I'm taking you home," she said firmly.

"No!"

The vehemence of his protest made Samantha flinch. She stared at him, not knowing what to do. The glazed look in Trey's eyes worried her.

Trey ran his tongue over his lips. "Anywhere . . . else." He struggled to get the words out. "Not . . . there."

Samantha's brow furrowed. What reason would he have for not wanting to go home? "Would you rather go back to the restaurant?" she asked.

Trey's eyelids closed and his shoulders sagged. He nodded feebly. "Yes."

After what seemed an eternity, Samantha managed to get Trey to her own small apartment and onto her bed. Before his head even hit the pillow, he was sound asleep.

Samantha felt his forehead. He wasn't feverish. Perhaps it was just the medicine Dr. Goss had given him that was making him so lethargic. That and exhaustion. Fatigue seemed to have been permanently etched into the lines of his face, making him seem far older than his thirty years.

A sympathetic smile touched her mouth as she surveyed the tall, broad-shouldered man sprawled unconscious on her bed. "And just think," she said aloud. "I wanted to punch Sheriff Calder in the nose this morning just for hinting that you had spent last night here. You're determined to make an amoral woman of me, aren't you, Treyman Stern?"

Samantha removed Trey's boots. The fact that he did not even stir when she accidentally dropped his foot over the side of the bed when the second boot came off attested to the extent of his fatigue. She placed his foot back on the mattress. "If anyone asks, you slept *on top* of the covers."

That evening, after the seven o'clock shift change at the mine, Joe made his daily stop at the restaurant to see Maria. Samantha explained that she had sent Maria and Sarah home early and told him why, then asked him if he would stay and have dinner with her.

Joe grinned, showing even white teeth in his bronzed face. "You know I never turn down a free meal," he said.

After they had eaten and Samantha had refilled their coffee cups, she asked Joe if he knew who would want to kill Trey.

"Could be anyone," he answered. "The men were pretty shaken up last night when Trey said he'd fire all of us if there were any more accidents."

"But that's ridiculous! Accidents happen no matter how careful you are. Trey wouldn't fire everyone because a cable became frayed."

Joe eyed her steadily. "It wasn't frayed, Samantha. Someone cut it."

Samantha felt as if someone had punched her in the midsection and knocked the air from her lungs. She leaned back in her chair, shock written on her face. That anyone would deliberately do something to endanger the lives of the other miners was unthinkable. But the worst part was not knowing if the man working next to you day in and day out was the one responsible for the sabotage. "Who would do such a despicable thing?" she asked.

"You tell me and we'll both know." Joe pushed back his chair. "Listen, I'm going to take care of Trey's horse, then head on over to the union hall. Maybe I'll overhear something. Thanks for the supper."

"Please be careful. You don't know what those men will do if they catch you snooping around." Samantha followed him to the door. "Joe, may I ask you something?"

Joe donned his hat. "What do you want to know?"

"The explosion that killed Michael . . . That wasn't an accident either, was it?"

Joe had not missed the slight tremor in her voice. Very few people in Myterra knew for certain what had happened that day. He'd always felt that Trey owed it to Samantha to tell her the truth, but Trey had been adamant about protecting her.

Until now Joe had respected Trey's wishes and had kept silent. Now that Samantha had asked him straight out, however, he couldn't lie to her. "No, Samantha," he said quietly. "The explosion wasn't an accident."

At the lectern, Dieter Vogel raised his fist, drawing cheers from the men crowding the union hall. "We've had enough of Stern keeping from us what we have worked hard for," he said in his slightly accented English. "We are the ones who risk our lives day after day in that mine, not Stern. We should be the ones to decide who we want to work for."

Vogel waited for the yelling and applauding to wane before continuing. "I have been informed by a reliable source that Consolidated Silver Corporation has extended a legitimate offer to Treyman Stern to buy the Concha Mine." The German went on to list the advantages of ownership by Consolidated: authorization to use company housing and company stores, benefits which, for now, were limited to employees of the stamp mill; medical care by company physicians; Consolidated would even build a secondary school so the miners' children could advance beyond the sixth grade, which was all Myterra currently offered. But the real gem among Consolidated's offerings was the proposed eight-hour workday, something no union member could lightly dismiss.

"Some of us are barely scraping by as it is," Roger McKenna called out. "If our wages are cut by four hours a day, we'll starve."

"That's right," another miner shouted. "My youngest has the lung sickness from breathing the tailings that blow down from the mill. Half of what I make goes to pay the doc. Is Consolidated going to pick up the tab for that?"

Dieter Vogel held his hands up, palms outward, to calm the now restless group. "Men, you misunderstand me. The only cut Consolidated Silver Corporation will make is to your hours, to put you on the same three-shift schedule as the mill workers. Your wages will remain the same: twelve hours' pay for eight hours' work."

In the back of the room a small, hard-eyed man listened to the proceedings with more than a passing interest. He wasn't a local, but then, union meetings often attracted those who had no more at stake in the issue at hand than a mild curiosity. No one paid much attention to him when he slipped out the door.

When he reached the elegant two-story frame house on Elden Street, he found Richard Winters pacing in his study. "Well?" Richard asked impatiently. "How did everything go?"

Silas Jenkins grinned. "Like clockwork. Vogel's got 'em convinced Consolidated's the answer to their prayers."

Winters went to his desk and unlocked a drawer. He withdrew a small leather pouch from the drawer and placed it on the desk top.

"Is that what we agreed on?" Jenkins asked.

"No, it's a third of that. You will get the rest when the assignment is completed to my satisfaction. And no more mistakes. Sheriff Calder has been asking too many questions."

Jenkins picked up the pouch and tucked it into his shirt pocket. "Quit gettin' so jumpy and the sheriff won't suspect a thing. If anyone's gonna blow this job, Winters, it'll most likely be you." He patted the bulge in his shirt pocket. "Only reason I'm lettin' you get away with not paying me everything up front like you promised is because I know where to find you. Start holding out on me and you might not live to regret it."

The light in Richard's eyes turned cold. "Are you threatening me?"

Jenkins rammed his hat down on his head. "Keep up your end of the bargain and you won't have to worry about it."

Richard had a sudden desire to wrap his hands around Silas Jenkins's neck and squeeze the life out of him, but his anger was tempered by a gnawing sense of urgency. As soon as he'd gotten rid of Treyman Stern, he decided, he would have to do something about Silas Jenkins.

The bedroom walls glowed a deep silver-rose in the early morning light. Trey could not remember at first where he was. How long had he slept? He felt groggy.

The bedroom door was closed. Trey glanced at the pillow beside him. It had been slept on, but when he touched it, the white cotton pillowcase with its delicate pink embroidered hemstitching was cool to the touch. He wondered how long Samantha had been up.

Sitting up required more of an effort than Trey had expected. With his good hand, he rubbed the stiffness out of the back of his neck. Damn, I need a shave, he thought as he rubbed his hand across his jaw.

He looked around the bedroom. Aside from Samantha's hairbrush, which sat neatly on a white doily on top of her bureau beside the porcelain pitcher and washbasin, there was little adornment to soften the room's austerity. It was not an unfriendly room, merely a simple one. Samantha had never gone in for the frills and gewgaws other women seemed to like, Trey thought. He remembered asking her what she wanted for a wedding present when she and Michael were married. She had laughed and told him candidly that she didn't want anything that required dusting.

He couldn't remember what he'd ended up buying for her.

Had it been only three years ago? It seemed more like three lifetimes.

Suddenly the bedroom door opened.

Clean folded towels in her arms, Samantha stopped short, surprise stamped on her face. "I didn't know you were awake. How do you feel?"

Like hell, Trey thought, but before he could reply, another realization crowded into his mind. He was disappointed—disappointed that he had not awakened early enough to see Samantha before she pinned up her hair. He wanted to see it again tumbling like wildfire over her shoulders. He wanted to touch it. He thought of the indentation in her pillow, and truth pierced the wall of denial he had erected around himself. Just how long had he been in love with Samantha? Two days or two years? Or had it happened long before that? Even before the wedding? He didn't trust himself to speak. "Much better, thank you," he managed to say.

Samantha hesitated a moment before stepping farther into the room. She placed the towels on the bureau next to the washbasin. "I thought you might want to clean up a bit when you awakened," she said over her shoulder. There was a raw edge to her voice. "I brought you some clean towels. Maria just put the kettle on, so you should have hot water in a few minutes." She opened the top drawer of the bureau and pulled out an elongated wooden case. "You may use these, if you like. Michael . . . would have wanted—" Her voice broke.

Trey saw her head drop and her shoulders suddenly hunch as if someone had struck her a blow in the stomach. Fighting the spinning in his head, he pushed himself up off the bed. He went to her and placed his good hand on her shoulder. "Samantha?"

She lifted her head and met his gaze in the mirror over the dresser. Her eyes brimmed with unshed tears. "I think . . . Michael would have wanted you to have these."

She placed the open case on the dresser. Inside, on a bed of dark green velvet that was a little threadbare in spots, lay a pearl-handled straight razor, a shallow-bowled shaving mug, and a small mirror with a folding stand.

A long-forgotten memory flashed before Trey's eyes with the blinding intensity of a bolt of lightning.

On the morning of the wedding Michael had been up at the mine office getting ready. He'd brought the shaving kit with him. "It belonged to my father," Michael had told him when he opened up the straight razor. "Pa used to wonder if I'd ever have enough whiskers to warrant using the thing." Michael had then rubbed one hand over the healthy growth of stubble on his jaw and laughed. "Wouldn't Pa be surprised to see me now?"

Trey felt his throat swell. He didn't trust himself to speak. His hand tightened on Samantha's shoulder.

Without thinking, Samantha reached up and placed her hand over his. Trey withdrew his hand and engulfed hers in a tight clasp. In the mirror a silent understanding passed between them.

Through the tears that glittered in her eyes, Samantha attempted an uncertain smile. "Joe will be by around six-thirty with your buggy to drive you home," she said. "When you finish getting cleaned up, come out to the dining room and eat some breakfast before you go. I'll send Maria in with your hot water."

Liam was sitting at the kitchen table warming his hands around a mug of coffee when Trey returned to the house. He had shaved and washed and eaten a hearty breakfast down at the Drake House, but he still felt a bit unsteady on his feet.

Liam, however, had not shaved, and Trey noticed that his beard was mostly white. "You didn't come home last night," Liam said, his tone accusing. "Where were you?"

Trey ignored the question. He went to the stove and poured himself a cup of coffee. He held the pot unsteadily. He wasn't accustomed to using his left hand. "You still haven't told me why you are here."

"Let up, Tyler. A man's got a right to visit kin."

"How long are you staying?"

Liam rubbed his jaw. "Well, I don't know. I kinda thought—"

"Did you get fired again?"

Liam bristled. "It's not what you're thinking, boy. I told you the other night I quit the bottle. A whole bunch of us was laid off. The mill burned down, and the owners are talking about pulling out. They said it was too expensive to rebuild."

Trey carried his coffee mug to the table and sat down. He eyed his uncle evenly. "Get to the point."

"Blast you, Tyler. I'm tryin' to ask you for a job! What do you want from me? You want me to get down on my knees and beg?"

Trey took a deliberately long draft of coffee. Instinct told him to walk away from Liam and not let the old man goad him into a fight, but he stayed put. This was his house, and he was not going to let his uncle run him out. He set his mug on the table. "I don't have a job to offer you."

"Aw, c'mon, Tyler. You own a mine! If anyone can give me a job, you can."

"You don't belong here, Liam. Go back to Tucson and see if Raymond can use you on the ranch."

"Hell, Tyler, I'm not a cowhand! I'm a miner!"

"So are the other four hundred unemployed men in this town."

The two men glared at each other across the table. "What's that got to do with it? I'm family."

Trey realized that Liam was not going to take a hint. He was going to have to be blunt. "The truth, Liam, is that I'd give any one of them a job before I'd even consider hiring you."

"Why? Are they better than me?"

"No, just more reliable."

Liam came up swinging. He smashed his fist into Trey's face, toppling both him and the chair and sending him crashing into the wall. "You rotten bastard! All I've done for you and this is the thanks I get! I brung you up like you were my own. You and your ma woulda starved to death if I hadn't come along and married her when I did." Liam rubbed his knuckles. "If you didn't have that arm in a sling, I'd take you out behind the house and teach you some manners."

Trey righted the chair and hauled himself unsteadily to his feet. Blood trickled from the corner of his mouth. "I doubt it. The trouble with you, Liam, is that you take on only those you know you can beat—women, children, and injured men. You don't have the guts to fight fair." He jerked his head toward the door. "I want you out of here today. You've overstayed your welcome."

The restaurant was closed on Sundays. The streets of Myterra were quiet. In the morning most of the town's law-abiding citizens were to be found in church. The rest were sleeping off the effects of the previous night's revelry.

It was hot and dusty. Dark clouds pressed down over the valley, promising some relief from the withering heat.

Samantha stood near the edge of the small cemetery adjacent to the church, staring down at the three simple headstones. Her mother's was the oldest of the three, and the plain lettering had been worn by the elements. She'd only been thirty-two when she died of yellow fever. Samantha had just turned sixteen. Four years after that, two weeks after her marriage to Michael, her father was swept away in a flash flood. After the waters receded, his body was found several miles outside town.

Michael's grave was a little apart from the others. The wildflowers she had placed by the headstone last Sunday had long since dried up, and most of them had blown away.

She usually talked to Michael when she came here, telling him about the little details that filled her days. Today, however, words eluded her. Before, she had always felt Michael's comforting presence when she came here, but today the cemetery seemed strangely empty, as if Michael were no longer there to listen to her.

She swallowed hard and fought back the sudden rush of tears. She was alone now. Her family was gone. Michael was gone. She was alone in a mining town where silver had ceased to be king, and the community's prosperous existence was threatened by the daily influx of unemployed miners. If the Concha closed, she might as well shut down the Drake House. There would be no one left with any money to pay for meals. Then what would become of her? She could go somewhere else and start over, but where? She had no living relatives that she knew of. And what would she do? Opening another restaurant would require money, something she did not have.

Or she could marry Richard Winters.

She still had not given him an answer. She didn't know what was holding her back. She liked Richard. He was everything a woman could desire in a husband. He was young. He was attractive. He was successful. Even the least impressionable woman could not fail to be affected by his charm.

Yet no matter how desirable a husband he might be, Samantha could not ignore the fact that, of late, every time she considered marrying Richard, thoughts of Treyman Stern crept into her mind. When Richard took her in his arms and kissed her, she had begun to imagine it was Trey kissing her. When Richard took her dancing at the Silver Queen Hotel, she imagined it was Trey twirling her around the ballroom. It was extremely difficult to think of marrying one man when her thoughts were becoming increasingly obsessed with another.

It troubled her that she felt so drawn to Trey. He'd been Michael's best friend and, in the end, his adversary. She felt she was being disloyal to Michael by renewing her ties to Trey. Still, knowing Trey was there for her gave her a sense of security that she had sorely missed since Michael's death. And no matter how annoyed she became with him for interfering in the operation of the restaurant, she could not pretend she wasn't grateful for his help.

Perhaps Richard was right, she thought uneasily. Perhaps she should give up the restaurant. It wasn't as if she truly enjoyed running it. It was, however, the one thing that was hers and hers alone. If she gave it up, she would have nothing left to call her own. She would be completely dependent upon Richard, the way she had been upon Michael.

From inside the church, the organist struck up the beginning strains of a hymn. Samantha hastily dried her eyes on her sleeve and turned to leave the cemetery. She did not want to be present when the church service ended. She had stopped attending services shortly after Michael's death, when the Reverend Mr. Crowley began devoting more and more sermons to the doctrine that it was a woman's duty to marry and bear children. The final straw had come when he looked directly at her and declared that an unmarried woman was an abomination against God and against nature. She had not returned to the church after that except to visit the cemetery.

At least Richard would be pleased, she thought as she walked home, to know that she had taken his advice and hired a new employee to help out at the Drake House.

Back at the restaurant, Liam had just finished installing the new glass in the window when Samantha returned. His hair was slicked back with pomade, and there was a cut on his chin where he'd nicked himself shaving. "It fit like a charm," he told her. "I'll need to touch up some scratches I made on the frame, though. If you got some extra paint, I can take care of those right now."

"I really appreciate your fixing the window today," Samantha said. "I hated asking you to come in on a Sunday, but I thought it best to do this when the restaurant was closed."

"I'm just thankful to have a job, ma'am," Liam said. "If it wasn't for you, I'd still be sleepin' in the streets. At least now I can pay for a bed down at the rooming house, and I'm eating better'n I have in years."

When the old man had come back to the restaurant to ask if Samantha still needed someone to install her new window, he'd looked worse than he had the first time she saw him. As he told her how his nephew had thrown him out, she'd been seized with indignation. She had almost asked him who his nephew was so she could refuse to serve him if he ever came into the Drake House, but stopped just short of doing so. She would be likely to lose not only the nephew's patronage but that of his friends as well. And until she got out of debt, she couldn't afford to do that. Besides, she had enough to worry about without interfering in something that was none of her business.

What she could do, however, was give the old man a job. With every one of Sarah Morrissey's children down with the chicken pox, she needed a dishwasher. She could also use someone to clear tables and help clean the restaurant after it had closed for the day. She couldn't afford to pay him much, she explained to him, but he could eat free, and he could have most Sundays off.

And if she ever found out who the man's nephew was, she thought, she just might overrule her better judgment and give the selfish scoundrel a piece of her mind.

"I'll get you the paint," she told Liam. "When you're finished there, you may go. I'll need you back here at five o'clock tomorrow morning."

It was past noon when Liam finally left. Samantha was just getting cleaned up to go to the mine to meet with Trey when she heard someone knock on the kitchen door. She rebuttoned her dress and went to answer the door.

Samantha's insides clenched when she saw who it was. She knew without asking why Eulalie Carter had come. "I would like to help you," she said in response to the woman's tearful plea, "but this is the second time this month that you've asked me for money, and I really don't have—"

"I wouldn't ask you for help if I wasn't desperate," Eulalie hastily put in. "There hasn't been any milk in the house for little Darryl for the past week, and we've been getting by on bread and dried beans for so long that the rest of the kids have been looking downright peaked."

Samantha could not help feeling resentful. Eulalie had never paid back any money she'd lent her in the past. She knew that if she gave Eulalie money again, she would feel like a sucker. If she refused, she'd feel guilty. "Eulalie, your husband got paid on Friday. What happened to the money?"

Eulalie's chin began to quiver. "Jerry lost it . . . in a game of craps. . . . Oh, Samantha, if anyone ever finds out, we'll be the laughingstock of Myterra."

Maybe that was what Jerry needed to straighten him out, Samantha thought peevishly. Even though she felt sorry for Eulalie, she was beginning to feel that she was being used. She sighed. "All right," she said wearily. "I'll see what I can spare. But you and Jerry are going to have to come to terms about his wages, Eulalie. I can't keep bailing you out every time you need money."

Relief passed across the other woman's face. "God bless you, Samantha. You are an angel come down to earth. You won't regret this; I promise you."

Samantha forced a smile. She was already beginning to regret it.

Trey's house had been a part of the old trading post that used to serve Fort McCrae until the army post moved to a flatter site downstream. It was built right up close to the street, with few windows on the street side to admit either the late afternoon sun or the stares of curious passersby. It was a small, simple dwelling, with four-foot-thick adobe walls that kept out the summer heat, and floors made of old bricks set in sand. All three of the main rooms—the kitchen, the bedroom, and a sitting room that Trey had turned into a study—opened onto an interior courtyard that was a pleasant place to sit, even on summer evenings. The kitchen was the most primitive of the rooms. It did not even have an icebox. Instead, Trey used the old *alacena*—a cupboard ventilated to the outside—that had been built into the kitchen's north wall when the house was erected. When the Concha had been prospering, before the recent dramatic drops in the price of silver, Trey had thought of moving into a larger, more elegant home, then decided against it. The small, unpretentious house suited him well.

Until now.

What the house lacked, Trey realized as he looked up from his desk in the study, was a woman's touch. Not ruffles and knickknacks and all those other dust catchers, as he called them, but a certain softness. A certain warmth. The elusive fragrance of a woman's perfume.

It was not hard to imagine Samantha's presence in the house. He could see her moving gracefully from room to room, and hear her throaty laughter. He could see her magnificent hair spread out across the pillows of their bed, and feel her long legs wrap around him, drawing him into her. He could visualize the subtle yet powerful changes in her body as their child grew to term in her womb, and feel its miraculous quickening.

Trey closed his eyes and groaned inwardly. Even if he could exorcise Michael Drury's ghost from their lives long enough to persuade Samantha to marry him, what in the world made him think he might be a good father? His memories of his own father were too faint to be of any use, and he refused to follow the example his uncle had laid down for him. Could he be firm without being dogmatic? Could he discipline without resorting to brutality? Or would his temper snap at the slightest provocation, the way Liam's had?

He thought of his mother and of the abuse she had suffered at Liam's hands during the last eight years of her life. Trey had always sworn he would never treat a woman the way Liam Stern had treated his mother, but how could he be certain? He had planned never to marry, partly because he believed that children learned by example. Once the newness of marriage wore off, once his guard was down, would he behave any better than his uncle?

After a while, he closed the ledgers. The picture did not look good. If the Concha's finances didn't improve soon, he reasoned, he might be forced to seriously consider Consolidated's offer. Barring any unforeseen events, he had enough capital left to keep the mine operating at full production for another six months. If, in the meantime, Congress repealed the Sherman Silver Purchase Act, he couldn't guarantee staying open even that long.

He looked at his watch. He had a two o'clock appointment with Samantha at the mine office to go over her books for the Drake House. Perhaps when they were finished he could take her out to dinner.

Unlike the rest the Myterra, the mine did not slow down on Sundays. Since the company incorporated three years ago, production had expanded to twenty-four hours a day, seven days a week. Some of the miners had objected to working on the Sabbath, not so much for religious reasons but because it interfered with their Saturday night drinking. The furor had died down when the men discovered that Sunday shifts yielded a pay differential.

When Trey arrived at the compound, he went first to the hoisting station. Unlike many mine owners who seldom set foot in their mines or came into contact with the men who labored for them, Trey liked to assure himself firsthand that everything was running smoothly. After the cable incident, the frequency of his visits had increased. He wasn't taking any chances.

Excitement charged the air at the hoisting station. Amos Flaherty, Carl Lemner, and several miners were talking among themselves in animated voices. Trey wondered why they weren't below with the rest of the men. "What's going on here? Is something wrong?"

Grinning, Amos broke away from the others and came to him. He handed Trey a fist-sized chunk of ore. "Sir, we've struck *gold!*"

Trey turned the ore over and studied it. Unlike the chunks of quartz laced with gold that they had previously unearthed, this one was almost solid metal, so pure he could dent it with his thumbnail. "Where did you find this?"

"Lemner's crew located it. We don't know yet if it's a pocket or a vein, but it looks to be about three feet across."

Trey glanced at Carl. The other man's expression was one of barely contained glee. Trey cautiously suppressed his own excitement. It was too soon to get his hopes up. "I want to see this discovery of yours," he said. He removed his identification tag from the board on the wall and slipped the chain over his head. "I'm going below."

It took ten minutes for the cage to make the three-thousand-foot descent into the bowels of the mountain. At the transfer station, Trey and the other men boarded the rail cars that would then carry them down another thousand feet along a narrow-gauge track through a tunnel.

The interior of the mine was cool and damp. Winter and summer, the temperature below stayed an unwavering fifty-eight degrees. Water trickled down the tunnel walls and out through the drains installed in the floor.

The rail tunnels were the only areas of the mine completely illuminated by electricity. In the areas where the ore was actively being mined, Trey had insisted on using safety lanterns in addition to the electric battery lamps. The men did not like the old oil safety lanterns because they required frequent inspections and cleanings, but they had one advantage over the newer electric lamps. Whereas the flame of the safety lamp would elongate in the presence of poisonous methane gases, or go out completely when there was insufficient oxygen, the electric lamps gave off no warning at all.

Finally they reached the drift that Carl's crew had been digging when they made the discovery.

The passageway was so low the men had to bend over to keep from striking their heads on the support timbers. Trey hunkered down to examine the dark, malleable streak in the quartz that Joe pointed out to him.

It was gold, all right, in as undiluted a form as Trey had ever seen it. He'd heard of mines in South Africa producing solid masses of pure gold, but none here. Usually the gold mined in this region was found embedded in quartz in nearly invisible flakes or was mixed with silver or copper.

Trey turned to Carl. "Keep digging. We'll start another drift parallel to this one. If this deposit proves worth pursuing, we'll proceed with a cave-in. It'll be safer than dynamiting."

The sky was dark and threatening as Samantha mounted the hill toward the Concha, the cash journal from the restaurant tucked beneath her arm. Trey was going to show her how the mine's books were kept, so they had decided that it would be more convenient for her to bring her single journal up to the mine than for him to cart the Concha's numerous journals and ledgers down to the restaurant. He had promised to show her how to set up separate inventory and payroll accounts as well as how to plan for unexpected expenses—such as broken windows.

She had not seen Trey since he'd spent the night at the Drake House. At first she had felt self-conscious, sharing her bed with him. Yet lying next to him had felt strangely right, and the soothing sound of his deep, even breathing had soon lulled her into a peaceful, dreamless sleep.

Although she could not say exactly what had caused it, something had definitely changed between them the next morning—a truce of sorts. She knew he had been touched to receive Michael's shaving gear. Even those who had known Trey the longest seldom saw beyond the tough, hard-bitten image he chose to show the rest of the world. He wore that image like a suit of armor, she mused. But armor shielding him from what? Closeness? Vulnerability? How little she really knew about him, she thought sadly, even after all these years.

When she reached the gate, to her dismay, she saw that Arnie Pitts was again on duty. Didn't he ever have a day off? Steeling herself against the revulsion she felt whenever she saw him, she stepped inside the guard shack to sign in.

He leaned close to her and peered over her shoulder as she entered her name in the logbook. His hand cupped her backside and lingered. "Too bad about them fellas roughin' you up down at your place last week," he said. He smelled of stale whiskey. "The sheriff ever find out who they were?"

Samantha rammed the pen back into its holder and rounded on him. "Don't you ever touch me again!"

"You might try being a little nicer to me," Arnie said. He raked her with his narrowed gaze. "A pretty widow woman like you . . . all alone. Hell, I might even be able to do you a favor or two."

Color consumed Samantha's face. "Get out of my way."

Arnie grinned at her. He moved away from the door to let her pass. "Don't say I didn't offer," he called out to her departing back.

Samantha was shaking so badly she had to fight to regain her composure. What angered her most was that there was an element of truth in Arnie's implication. She was a widow, and she was alone, which made her an easy target for men like Morris Littleton's ruffians—and men like Arnie Pitts who could not keep their hands to themselves. Even the playful flirting and bantering that went on down at the restaurant was fraught with insinuation.

By the time she reached the mine office, the first huge drops of rain had begun to fall.

The door was locked. Samantha pounded on it, but to no avail. A dust devil swirled across the compound, kicking up her skirt and blowing grit into her eyes. Shielding her eyes with one hand, she looked around for some sign of Trey, but he was nowhere to be seen. Thunder rumbled in the distance. "Damn you, Trey, where are you?"

Sheriff Calder was waiting for Trey when he returned to the mine office. The sheriff was wearing a yellow slicker to protect himself from the downpour. "Your man on guard duty told me I'd find you here," he called out through the torrent.

Trey, his clothes drenched, unlocked the door and let the sheriff into the office. It was nearly three o'clock. He hoped

Samantha had not ventured out in the storm.

Sheriff Calder removed his hat. Water poured from the brim of the Stetson. "That cloudburst sure came up in a hurry. Turned Fremont Street into a river in no time at all."

"I can believe it," Trey said. "What brings you out in this weather, Sheriff?"

"Just thought you might be interested in knowing that I've arrested the man who tried to kill you."

Chapter
Six

"JOE?"

Joe jumped up from the cot. He grabbed the iron bars of his jail cell. "Don't believe him, Trey. It's not true. I wasn't anywhere near your place the night you were shot."

Trey looked at the sheriff. "What is the meaning of this?"

Sheriff Calder hung his dripping hat on a hook just inside the door. "I got a witness who claims Tochino here was pretty upset over the dressing-down you gave the boys up at the mine the day that cable broke. Says he was down at Mike's Tavern, drinking and bragging that he was going to teach you a lesson."

"That's a lie!"

The sheriff threw the Apache a look of impatience. "After he left Mike's, Tochino went to your place to wait for you."

"Damn it, Sheriff! I told you I took Charlie Cousins home. If you don't believe me, go ask him."

"I did. Charlie says he doesn't remember seeing you."

"Damn!" Joe punched at an invisible target in frustration. "Sheriff, you have to believe me. I took Charlie home. He was so drunk he could barely stand."

"You know of anyone who can verify that?"

"The bartender. He refused to serve Charlie another drink.

And Taza Parks was there. I bought him a beer."

"Can anyone verify that you *took Charlie home*?"

Despair flickered in Joe's eyes as he met Trey's gaze through the confining bars. He said nothing.

Trey shook his head. "Sheriff, I don't know what's going on here, but you have the wrong man."

"Sorry, Trey, but I have a witness who says he followed this man to your house after he left Mike's. Unless Tochino comes up with someone who can prove otherwise, I have no choice but to keep him locked up."

"I'll put up the bail money."

"Won't do any good, Stern. Arraignment isn't until tomorrow morning. Until then Tochino stays here."

Trey felt his own frustration rising. "What time is the hearing?"

"Ten o'clock."

Trey didn't know what else to do. He felt helpless, and that annoyed him. "Listen, Joe. We'll get you out of here. Don't worry about your job; you'll draw full wages."

Sheriff Calder followed Trey out the door. The rain had stopped. "I wouldn't hold my breath on the bail," he told Trey. "Judge Gates is a tough one. He's not likely to release Tochino on any kind of bond."

"Listen, Sheriff, I believe you when you say Charlie Cousins doesn't remember Joe taking him home. But I don't believe Joe was the one who shot at me. What about the others who were at Mike's Tavern that night? Have you questioned any of them? Have you talked to Taza Parks?"

A look of annoyance passed behind the sheriff's eyes. "Who do you think turned Tochino in?"

Samantha knew the instant she saw Trey's face that something was wrong, but she had been nursing her anger for a good two hours and she didn't feel particularly forgiving.

She had changed into dry clothes but had left her hair down so it would dry, and it curled around her face in soft coppery tendrils that belied the smoldering fury in her gold-flecked eyes. Without a word, she slammed the kitchen door in his face, but before she could bolt it, it came flying open again.

Samantha gasped and jumped back from the door as it crashed against the wall.

Trey closed the door with a resounding bang. His expression was tense. "We need to talk."

Samantha's chin shot up in rebellion. "Our appointment was for two o'clock," she said tersely. "*I* was on time."

"Samantha, I'm sorry, but something—"

"Sorry? I waited for you for over half an hour! I got drenched. The ink ran in my journal, and now that's ruined. And as if that wasn't enough, I had to endure Arnie Pitts putting his filthy hands where they don't belong and making suggestive remarks to me." She leveled a finger at him. "And I'll tell you something else, Treyman Stern. If that . . . that *slag heap* who calls himself a gate guard ever touches me again, I'll see to it that he walks bent over for the rest of his life!"

Trey's eyes abruptly narrowed. "Pitts touched you?"

Samantha defensively folded her arms across her chest. Her gaze dropped, and she stared sullenly at the floor as she struggled to get control of her tangled emotions. Tears grated behind her eyelids, and she had to bite down on her bottom lip to keep it from trembling. She wasn't certain whether she was more furious with Trey or Arnie or herself. For several days she had been on the verge of crying, and she hated herself for being such a ninny.

"Sam, answer me. Did Arnie Pitts touch you?"

"It's not important." Her voice shook. "Look, you're going to get sick if you don't get out of those wet clothes.

I'll see if I have anything of Michael's that you might be able to wear. *Then* we can discuss why you stood me up."

With a puzzled frown, Trey watched her exit from the room. Sometimes there was no reasoning with the woman, he thought irritably. And yet as she was blasting him with her anger he had begun to realize it was directed not so much at him as at Arnie Pitts. Damn that Pitts, he swore to himself. He intended to have a word with that young man. If Pitts ever so much as looked at a woman again in an unseemly manner, he would find himself out of a job before he had time to draw his next breath.

Trey stripped down to his trousers and draped his wet clothes across the drainboard to dry. It felt good to take off the sling. He flexed his arm, easing the stiffness out of the unused muscles. That morning, when he rewrapped the bandages around his chest and hand, he'd noticed that the wounds were healing quickly. A few more days and he would be able to remove the bandages as well.

When several minutes passed and Samantha did not return to the kitchen, Trey grew concerned. He could hear no sounds of movement from the next room.

He found her on the floor of her tiny bedroom, kneeling before an open trunk. Her head was bowed, and she was clutching a faded blue plaid shirt. Her shoulders shook with silent sobs.

Trey went to her. He hunkered down beside her and placed a hand on her shoulder. "Sam, are you all right?"

A strangled sound exploded in her throat. She buried her face in the blue shirt. Her entire body shook with uncontrollable sobs.

Trey lowered himself to the floor. Taking care not to strain his right shoulder, he hoisted Samantha onto his lap. She tried to pull away, but his arms closed around her. He placed a hand behind her head and drew it down onto his shoulder. "It's all right, sweetheart," he said gently. "Go ahead and cry. Get it out."

She sagged against him and buried her face against his neck as the grief she had held inside for so long finally erupted in wave after wave of unstoppable, agonizing pain. Scalding tears poured from her eyes to drench Trey's neck as well as the shirt she still clutched in a fierce grip. The harder she tried to stop crying, the faster the tears came until finally she gave up fighting altogether and succumbed to violent, unrestrained weeping that felt as if it would tear her very soul apart.

For nearly an hour she wept.

She wept for Michael, whose life had been cut short by a tragedy that should never have happened. She wept for the lost dreams, for a marriage that had promised so much, and for the children of that marriage who would never be.

But most of all she wept for herself. For the first time since Michael's death, she grieved for herself and for all she had lost. She allowed herself to weep for the terrible, over-whelming loneliness that had become so much a part of her life that she hardly recognized it for what it was anymore.

Gradually her tears began to wane, and she became aware that Trey was holding her in his strong arms and rocking her, as one would a child. His big hand gently stroked her hair. As she quieted, he bent his head and lightly brushed his lips against the top of her head. "Welcome back," he said softly.

Samantha opened her mouth to speak, but the only thing that came out was a convulsive breath. She was weak and exhausted, and her head throbbed. She let her eyelids droop.

She was not aware she had fallen asleep until Trey shifted his position. A small, startled cry tore from her throat as she awoke with a start.

Trey smoothed her hair back from her face and kissed her forehead. "I need to stand up, sweetheart," he urged gently.

He helped her get into bed. "Stay here," he said as she sank back against the pillow. "I'll make you some tea."

Feeling utterly drained, she closed her eyes and nodded. She wished the spinning in her head would go away. "Trey?"

He stopped in the doorway.

Samantha forced her eyes open and tried to focus her gaze on him. "Thank you," she whispered feebly.

Trey knew she wasn't referring to the tea. His expression softened. "Get some rest. I'll be back shortly."

After he had gone, Samantha closed her eyes as weariness engulfed her. She didn't know what had become of Michael's shirt. She supposed she must have dropped it. It had begun to pour again, and the sound of the rain lulled her into a peaceful stupor. In the kitchen, she could hear Trey move the heavy cast-iron kettle into place on the stove. Just knowing he was in the next room brought her a measure of comfort.

By the time Trey returned with the tea, she had managed to sleep a little. He set the tray on her dresser. "How do you feel?"

She struggled to sit up. "Shaky," she replied candidly.

He came to the bed and adjusted the pillow behind her back. "Feeling any better?"

Oddly, she did feel better. She felt incredibly tired, more tired than she had ever been in her life, and yet she also felt lighter, as though a tremendous weight had been lifted off her shoulders. She nodded.

Trey lit the lamp on her dresser. It cast a golden glow over the room. Outside, the rain was still coming down.

Samantha raised one hand to her eyes, shielding them

from his view. "I hate to have you see me," she said with a self-conscious laugh. "I know how I look when I've been crying."

He carried the tray to the bed and placed it beside her on the mattress. He took her hand and pulled it away from her face. Samantha grimaced.

Trey had been about to offer her words of comfort, but judging from the open challenge he saw in her tear-ravaged eyes, he doubted she would believe him. One corner of his mouth began to twitch in suppressed mirth. "You're right," he said solemnly. "It's pretty frightening."

She uttered a choked laugh. "You weren't supposed to agree with me," she scolded. She pulled her hand free and wiped her eyes with her fingertips.

He handed her a handkerchief and she blew her nose while he drew a chair up beside the bed. "Mind if I join you?"

"Only if you pour. My hands are shaking so badly, I might spill it."

As he added sugar and milk to their tea, Samantha's gaze was drawn to the play of lamplight across the bunched muscles of his shoulders, and she felt an odd tingling in the pit of her stomach. She swallowed hard and tore her gaze away. "Did you find a place to put your clothes?"

"I hung them in front of the stove. They're almost dry." He handed her a cup. "Careful. It's full."

She took a sip of the tea, then leaned her head back against the wall and closed her eyes as the hot liquid worked its soothing magic. "That feels good going down," she murmured.

Trey studied her face in the soft glow of the lamp. The crying spell had left her face blotched and swollen. In the years he had known her, Samantha had never been more vulnerable than she was now. He knew he would have to tread carefully to keep from alienating her again.

She opened her eyes to find him watching her. She gave him an uncertain smile. "Thank you for staying with me," she said unevenly.

Understanding warmed his deep blue-gray gaze. "That's what friends are for."

His face blurred and swam before her eyes. She swallowed hard against the lump that swelled in her throat. "Do you know what I've missed most since Michael died?" Her voice was little more than a pained whisper. "I miss having someone to talk to."

"I miss him, too, Sam. Michael was more than just a business partner to me. He was my closest friend."

"Then why were you two always fighting?"

The accusation in her voice tore at Trey's heart. "We didn't fight," he said. "We disagreed many times, yes, but we never fought."

Samantha's eyes glistened with unshed tears. "Trey, every time Michael wanted to do something at the mine, you said no. Every innovation he came up with, you vetoed. It hurt him so much that you had so little regard for his ideas." Her voice cracked.

Regret passed behind Trey's eyes. He took her cup from her. He set the tray on the floor beside the bed and stood up. "Scoot over."

She made room for him on the bed, and he sat down beside her. She felt self-conscious sitting on her bed with him, especially since he was not wearing a shirt, but since he had already spent one night in her bed, it seemed hypocritical to put up a fuss now. She stiffened a little, but otherwise did not protest when he placed his arm around her shoulders and drew her against him.

"Sam, Michael was a brilliant man. I had a great deal of respect for his ideas. Unfortunately, it would have been impractical to institute many of them until the mine began showing a profit."

"Trey, Michael put everything we had into that mine. You had no right to deny him a voice in how it was run."

Trey did not respond. His face was set in a taut mask. He absently stroked Samantha's shoulder as he stared unseeing at some undetermined point across the room.

A tear ran down Samantha's face and hung from her chin. She wiped it away with the back of her hand. "If it's just a matter of money, why won't you consider Consolidated's partnership offer?" she asked in a choked voice. "You keep emphasizing costs, and yet you won't accept any help. You seem to want . . . to need to have complete control. Consolidated tried to make you an offer again last week, and you refused to listen to them."

Trey cast her a sharp glance. "Where did you hear that?"

"Richard told me," Samantha replied without thinking. She dabbed at her eyes with the sodden handkerchief. "Trey, the point is, if Consolidated is willing to provide the financial backing to expand the mine and build a smelter, why *not* accept their offer? Yes, it would mean relinquishing some control, but in the long run it would be worth it. You'll be able to afford to put the men on eight-hour shifts. You'll be able to provide company housing and all the other benefits the unions have been demanding."

"Sam, it's not that simple."

"Why *not*? What is holding you back?"

Trey glanced down to find Samantha looking up at him, her hazel eyes silently pleading. He smoothed a wayward curl away from her face. His thumb brushed lightly against her forehead. A furrow creased his brow. "If I sell to Consolidated, the men will no longer be paid in cash. They'll be paid in scrip, the same as the mill workers."

"But, Trey, look how well off the mill workers are! Their

housing costs them almost nothing. They have company doctors. And the company stores have the lowest prices in town."

"Yes, that's true. But you have to remember, Sam, scrip can be spent only in company stores, whereas cash is welcome anywhere. If the miners start drawing their wages in scrip, the company stores will no longer have to compete with the other merchants for the miners' patronage. It will be guaranteed. Prices will shoot up. Any merchant unwilling to accept payment in scrip—which is redeemable only at a steep discount—will be forced out of business. Including you."

"I don't believe that." In spite of her denial, Samantha knew inwardly that Trey spoke the truth.

"Sam, it's happened in every company-owned town across the country. We'd be naive to think it can't happen here."

A look of despair crossed Samantha's face. "I've never seen so many greedy people in my life."

Trey battled a smile. "I'm not the only one?"

Samantha sniffled and threw him a disparaging glance. "You're ruining my perception of you," she said peevishly. "It was easier when I believed you were corrupt and mercenary."

Trey's expression became solemn. "What was easier?" he prompted gently.

Fresh tears burned Samantha's eyes. She turned her head away. Her throat constricted. "Hating you."

Trey cupped her chin and turned her face back toward his. "Sam, look at me."

She tried, but the lean, handsome face before her was a tanned blur. A tear streaked down her cheek, and Trey brushed it away with the pad of his thumb. "I'm sorry you ever felt that way," he said quietly. "I would never intentionally do anything to hurt you. I hope you know that."

There was a terrible pain in the middle of Samantha's chest. "I think I've always known that," she whispered thickly.

For a moment neither of them moved. The sound of the rain drumming steadily on the tin roof acted like a natural fortress, cutting them off from the rest of the world and heightening their almost painful awareness of each other.

Trey's eyes darkened. He slid his fingers into her hair, and Samantha knew even before he lowered his head that he was going to kiss her. This time, instead of fighting him, she tilted her head back and leaned into his embrace, her eyes closed and her lips slightly parted as he kissed her eyelids, tasting the salty tears that clung to her lashes. He brushed his lips down the curve of her cheek. His breath was like warm velvet against her skin. He kissed the corner of her mouth and gently teased her lips, drawing moist circles along her soft, full bottom lip with the tip of his tongue before finally claiming her mouth in a deep, satisfying kiss.

She returned his kiss with reckless abandon, sliding one hand behind his neck to pull his head down to hers. The blood rushed into her head, filling her ears with a dull roar that blocked out all awareness of anything except the feel of Trey's lips on hers and his strong arms as they closed securely around her.

His kiss deepened. He moved his mouth over hers, savoring its sweet warmth and devouring its softness with a savage tenderness that left them both trembling and aching for more. Samantha was only half aware of him moving her pillow out of the way and easing her down onto the bed.

His mouth left hers to explore the hollows of her neck while his hand sought her breasts and he gently caressed the soft swells through the thin cotton of her dress. His fingers found the row of dainty whalebone buttons, and he began unfastening them.

He lifted his head, and Samantha opened her eyes to find him watching her with an intensity that fanned a steadily growing fire of longing deep inside her.

Trey tugged on the ribbon threaded through the eyelets embroidered along the bodice of her chemise, freeing her breasts from their fragile restraint. He brushed the confining fabric aside, and Samantha sucked in her breath as his fingers grazed her bare skin.

He lowered his head to her breast.

A low moan sounded deep in Samantha's throat as his mouth closed around a sensitive nipple. She threw her head back and closed her eyes, helpless against the raging passions that swept over her like a prairie fire. It had been so long since she had experienced a man's touch that she had almost forgotten how good it could feel. Yet nothing she had ever experienced had felt as wonderful as this. She felt as if she were floating. Trey stroked and caressed her breasts with skilled hands and teased her burning flesh with his tongue, drawing her higher and higher into a delirious, wonderful, swirling mist of untapped desires. She was so caught up in the dizzying sensations that she was not aware of him gathering her into his arms and holding her close.

Trey stroked the back of her head and combed his tanned fingers through her tangled tresses. "Are you all right?" he asked gently.

Lying beside him with their legs intertwined and her head cradled in the hollow of his shoulder seemed more natural than anything she had ever before experienced, and that both puzzled and surprised her. She drew her head back to look at him, a dreamy, dazed look in her golden-hued eyes that caused the blood to pound through his veins. "If I were a lady, I would never have let you do that," she said, almost ruefully.

Trey thought that if she kept looking at him with that irresistible mixture of innocence and seductiveness, he was going to lose all control over his actions. He tenderly brushed his knuckles along her jawline. "Sweetheart, I wouldn't trade you for all the ladies in the world."

Samantha caught her lower lip between her teeth and averted her gaze. Although her long copper-tipped lashes partially hid the bewilderment that clouded her eyes, the deepening furrow between her brows left no doubt as to the roiling uncertainties that churned within her as her fingertips glided down the broad slope of his shoulder and along the edge of the bandage wrapped securely about his chest. The unexpected shattering of long-held convictions had left her feeling as though the ground had been jerked from beneath her feet. She swallowed hard several times before she was able to speak again. "A part of me feels I'm being disloyal to Michael, lying here with you and letting you touch me," she said in a low, stricken voice. "Yet another part of me wishes . . ." Her voice trailed off. She nervously moistened her lips.

"Go on," Trey urged quietly. "Another part of you wishes what?"

Samantha lifted her eyes to his, and the undisguised long-ing she saw in his smoldering smoky blue gaze stripped away the last of her defenses. "That you hadn't stopped," she whispered.

Trey groaned. He rolled onto his back, carrying her with him. Her fiery hair tumbled down around them as he settled her on top of his hard-muscled length, cloaking them both in a shimmering veil of flames.

"Trey, your shoulder," Samantha cautioned, but the warn-ing was lost as Trey buried his hands in her hair and pulled her down to him, silencing her protest with a fierce, almost rough, kiss. His lips were hard and searching, leaving her mouth burning with fire and igniting in her body a clamoring need that demanded to be satisfied. Her breasts tingled as they brushed against the dark hair on his chest. She began returning his kisses with a fevered urgency, parting his lips with hers and engaging his tongue in an erotic duel.

Trey moved his hands down over her back to cup her buttocks and pull her even tighter against the part of him that felt as if it would burst with longing for her. He found the hem of her dress and inched it up over her hips, exposing her rounded cotton-encased bottom to his caresses.

Suddenly Samantha stopped kissing him and drew back her head. She could have sworn she had heard someone knocking on the front door. "Trey . . ."

He wrapped his arms around her and crushed her to him. "Hush," he ordered huskily before recapturing her mouth with his own.

Samantha's senses reeled out of control. Every place their bodies met felt as though it were ablaze. She wished they could stay as they were forever, touching and kissing and holding each other. She wanted him to make love to her, she realized dimly. Yet when his hand slipped inside the waistband of her underdrawers to stroke her bare skin, she somehow managed to regain possession of her sanity. She tore her mouth away from his. Her breath came in short insistent gasps. "Trey, there's someone at the door."

Trey scowled at the impatient pounding on the front door of the restaurant. "Ignore it. Whoever it is will go away."

He started to pull Samantha back down to him, but she firmly resisted his efforts. "Trey!"

He reluctantly relaxed his hold on her. Displeasure knitted his brows and crackled like heat lightning in his beautiful eyes. "All right, I'll go see who it is."

"No!" Horror surged through Samantha at the thought of the rumors that would fly if anyone discovered him here half dressed. "Stay here. *I'll* go see who it is." She scrambled off the bed and buttoned her dress with trembling hands.

Trey's gaze dropped to the seductive sway of her hips as she left the room, and he muttered a curse under his breath. Whoever was at the door had better have a damned good reason for coming here.

Samantha hastily smoothed out the wrinkles in her skirt and raked her fingers through her hair, giving it a hard shake before unlocking the door.

Even before the door was open, Maria, a rebozo draped over her head, burst into a stream of unintelligible Spanish.

Samantha grabbed the girl's arm and led her into the restaurant. "Maria, what's wrong? Come inside. You're getting drenched."

Maria's chest heaved as she tried to catch her breath. "It is Joe, señora. My brother Roberto, he say Joe is in jail. Roberto say Joe shoot Señor Stern."

"Maria, that's ridiculous!" Samantha turned at a sound behind her. Trey had put his shirt on and was just coming from the kitchen. His expression was grave.

Maria skirted Samantha and went to Trey. "Señor Stern, it is not true." Her voice trembled. "Joe, he say you are like his brother. He never try to kill you."

Trey placed a consoling hand on her shoulder. "I know Joe didn't do it, Maria. There's been a misunderstanding. Don't worry. Joe will be freed tomorrow."

"You *knew* about this?" Samantha's tone was incredulous.

Trey met her searching gaze over the top of Maria's head. "Taza Parks told Sheriff Calder that he followed Joe to my place the night I was shot. He claims he saw Joe shoot me."

"But that's preposterous!"

"Sam, you know that, and I know that. The problem is convincing Calder. And Judge Gates."

Judge Gates! The color drained from Samantha's face. Judge Gates would never release Joe on bond. An Indian attack had taken the lives of several members of his family, and Gates harbored a deeply rooted hatred of the Apaches. Nearly twenty years had passed since then and times had changed, but Gates had not. Just last month he had sentenced a sixteen-year-old Apache youth to be hanged for stealing a couple of chickens. Fortunately the boy had managed to escape the night before his scheduled execution, but the incident had stirred old hostilities between the Indians and the townspeople. She nervously moistened her lips. "Trey, this is insane. Why would Taza Parks make such an outrageous allegation?"

"I wish I knew. I went to Mike's Tavern right before I came here. The bartender remembered seeing Joe and Parks together that night, but he doesn't know where they went after they left the saloon. I haven't been able to locate Parks."

Samantha began pacing. "Trey, we have to do something. We can't just let an innocent man be locked up."

"Sam, short of helping him escape, there's nothing we can do right now. Joe's hearing is tomorrow morning. I intend to be there with him."

"I want to go to Joe," Maria said. "My father, he does not know I am here."

Trey's hand tightened on Maria's shoulder. "I'll take you up to the jail so you can see him."

"I'm coming, too." Samantha started toward the bedroom to get a shawl.

"You're staying here," Trey said firmly. "After Maria has seen Joe, I'm going to take her home. Then I'm going to go up to the mine and ask some questions about Taza Parks."

Samantha fidgeted. She didn't know if she was upset because she was being left behind, because Trey had neglected to tell her Joe had been arrested, or because she was just beginning to realize how close she had come to giving herself to Trey. She defensively crossed her arms in front of her. "Will you tell me what you find out?"

Understanding softened the hard lines of Trey's face. He longed to take her in his arms and kiss her senseless, but his shoulder was giving him fits. As much as he wanted to carry Samantha to bed and make love to her, he doubted that he could have sustained the effort for a respectable length of time even if Maria had not been present. "As soon as I learn anything, I'll let you know. All right?"

She gave him an almost resentful look from beneath her lashes. "And be careful," she scolded sternly. "I don't want to have to break *both* of you out of jail."

Across the street from the restaurant a man stood in the alley between the buildings, his hat pulled down low and the collar of his coat turned up against the rain. He watched as Trey drove away with Maria, then noted the time. Mr. Winters would be interested in learning that Treyman Stern had just spent over two hours alone with Samantha Drury. It was the kind of information Winters was paying him good money to report.

Chapter
Seven

THE atmosphere in the restaurant was unusually subdued during the breakfast rush. Maria spoke little as she prepared the meals. Since Sarah Morrissey still had not returned, Liam helped with the cleaning up and the dishes. As Samantha waited on the customers, she strained her ears for bits of conversation that might give her a hint at what was happening down at the courthouse.

Samantha's eyes were a little puffy from crying the night before, but otherwise she felt much better than she had in months. She felt as if a great weight had been lifted from her shoulders. All this time she had never realized that she was still carrying around her grief for Michael and letting it control her life.

Last night, after Trey and Maria left, she had sat down and done some serious thinking. She had come to the conclusion that she was not ready to marry again. In spite of her worries over having enough money to survive, she realized that she rather liked living alone and not having to answer to anyone but herself.

She also realized that she would be doing a great disservice both to Richard and to herself if she married him. Richard needed a woman he could cosset and spoil and lavish with extravagant gifts. She had removed the diamond from her finger and placed it in her dresser drawer for safekeeping until she could return it to him. She doubted she would ever fully appreciate Richard's efforts to woo her, because he always tried to buy her affection with material things on which she placed little value.

The breakfast rush was long over when Trey finally arrived at the restaurant. Samantha had sent Liam down to Mason's Mercantile for supplies, so only she and Maria were present when Trey arrived. He had come straight from the courthouse. She poured coffee for the three of them, and they sat down in the empty dining room.

"Judge Gates refused to set bail," Trey told them. "He's holding Joe in custody until his case goes to trial."

"When is that?" Samantha asked.

"November twentieth."

"November twentieth! Trey, that's a month away!"

Maria's lower lip began to quiver as she stared down into her coffee cup. She said nothing.

Beneath the table, Samantha reached for Maria's hand and gave it a squeeze. She turned a challenging gaze on Trey. "Didn't you tell Judge Gates that you and Joe are friends and that you don't believe Joe was the one who shot you?"

"I did."

"Then why won't he let Joe go? How in the hell is Judge Gates going to hold a trial when the victim isn't willing to press charges?" Samantha was so angry she didn't realize she'd sworn.

"Sam, the case against Joe isn't that clear-cut. My word has very little bearing in the matter."

"And Taza Parks's does?"

"Unfortunately, yes."

Samantha shoved back her chair. "This has gotten out of hand," she said hotly. "I'm going down to that courthouse and talk to Judge Gates myself."

"Samantha, sit down!"

He had spoken so sharply that Samantha was momentarily taken aback, and she unthinkingly slid back onto her chair. She stared at Trey with a mixture of hurt and bewilderment.

Trey's expression was unreadable. "If the charges against Joe involved only me, it would be a different story," he said. "Joe is also being charged with cutting the hoisting cable at the mine."

Samantha's mouth fell open.

Maria lifted a tearful gaze to Trey's face. "It is a lie, Señor Stern. Taza Parks, he tell terrible lies about my Joe."

"Is Taza responsible for this prevarication, too?" Samantha demanded.

"Unfortunately, yes."

"Well, then, somebody had better find that young man and get to the bottom of this before he ruins Joe's life completely."

The light in Trey's eyes turned cold. "Taza Parks's body was found by the reservation police in San Carlos last night. They believe he was shot some time within the past two days."

Samantha suddenly felt sick to her stomach. "Surely they don't think Joe did that, too?"

Trey said nothing, but Samantha saw the answer in his eyes. She groaned inwardly.

Suddenly Maria burst into tears.

Samantha reached for her hand, but Maria pulled away. In a flurry of emotionally charged Spanish, she jumped up from her chair, upsetting her coffee cup.

"Maria, wait!" Samantha called out, but the girl bolted through the dining room and into the kitchen. The kitchen door slammed loudly after her.

Samantha started to go after her, but Trey caught her hand. "Leave her alone," he said quietly.

"Trey, someone should be with her."

"Right now, Sam, she just wants to be alone."

A terrible aching lump pressed against Samantha's throat. She had never felt so helpless in her life. Her two dearest friends were having their lives torn apart by malicious lies, and there was not a damn thing she could do to help them. She propped her elbow on the table and dropped her forehead into her palm. A choking silence filled the room, pressing down on them. "Trey, what's happening to this town?" she asked wearily.

Trey slowly released his breath in a long sigh and tilted his head back to stare aimlessly at the rough plaster ceiling. "I don't know, Sam," he finally said. "I honestly don't know."

Samantha tried to keep from staring at the jail as she rode past in Richard's carriage. Both the jail and the sheriff's office were dark. She wondered if Joe was in there alone. Trey was planning to go to Phoenix in the morning to hire a good lawyer to handle Joe's defense. He had promised to stop by the restaurant before leaving town.

Richard cast her a sideways glance. "You're awfully quiet tonight."

I'm exhausted, Samantha thought. Maria had not returned to the restaurant after running out, and she and Liam had managed both the lunch crowd and the dinner rush alone. "I'm just worried about Joe," she said instead. She was not willing to endure another lecture from Richard on how hard she worked.

"It is an odd case," Richard agreed. News of Joe's arrest had spread rapidly through the town. "It would seem to be more than mere coincidence that the man who betrayed your friend should die before he could testify in a court of law."

Samantha tensed. "Are you saying you think Joe is guilty?"

Richard gave her an indulgent smile. "Of course not, darling. A man is always innocent until proven guilty."

Somehow his words did little to reassure her. She changed the subject. "I hired a new employee at the restaurant."

"I'm glad to hear it. You need all the help you can get down there. I don't like to see you driving yourself to exhaustion day after day. Who is it?"

"His name's Liam Smith. He's been out of work for several months, so he was willing to accept what I'm able to pay. He'll be doing a little bit of everything—washing dishes, waiting on tables. He replaced the broken window yesterday."

Richard was grim. Liam Smith. He'd never heard of the man. But he had ways of finding out what he wanted to know. "Did you check his references?" he asked off-handedly.

"I didn't ask for references." Samantha had a hard time keeping the irritation from her voice. "He was hungry and willing to work. That's all the recommendation I needed. If he doesn't work out, I'll fire him and hire someone else. It's that simple."

"Nothing is ever that simple where you are concerned, my dear. You have a soft heart, and people are inclined to take advantage of you."

Like Eulalie Carter, Samantha thought. It was no wonder she was having trouble keeping ahead of her obligations.

They finally reached the big white house on Elden Street. Instead of taking her to the hotel for dinner, Richard had insisted on a private, informal meal at his home. He escorted Samantha into the elegant glass-walled conservatory at the rear of the house. Gaslight peeked through the profusion of exotic plants that gave the room the feeling of a tropical rain forest. Giant ferns arched across the stone path leading to a small elevated pavilion. In the center of the pavilion a table had been set for two with the most elegant silver and crystal and bone china Samantha had ever seen. A bottle of white wine with a name she dared not try to pronounce was chilling in a silver bucket filled with ice chips.

Samantha unconsciously folded her arms. "When you said an informal dinner, I thought you were referring to ham sandwiches and a jug of lemonade. I never expected anything like this."

Richard wrapped his arms around her from behind and eased her back against him. He trailed his lips against the top of her head and down along her temple. "You had best accustom yourself to it, my dear," he whispered huskily in her ear. He nipped at her earlobe with his teeth. "I plan to indulge you like this every day until you agree to marry me."

"Richard . . ." There was a note of dismay in Samantha's voice. She squirmed out of his embrace and turned to face him. "Richard, we need to talk—" Her words were cut short as he caught her by the shoulders and lowered his head to hers.

Although she tried, Samantha could not lose herself in his kiss. As he moved his lips over hers, she was both horrified and ashamed to find herself gauging him against Trey. In comparison, Richard's kisses seemed mundane, almost mechanical. Silent words of rebuke echoed in her head. Why did it even matter how he kissed? She had already decided to turn down his offer of marriage, for completely unrelated reasons. At least she hoped her reasons were unrelated. She would be a fool to reject Richard's proposal simply because his touch did not set her body ablaze with passion and longing.

Richard pulled away and straightened his back. Bewilderment deepened the vertical crease etched between his fair brows as he regarded her. "Do I dare ask what you were thinking just now? You were miles away."

"Richard, we *must* talk."

He tenderly kissed her forehead. "Later. Right now I want to show you what delicacies I had prepared for you."

Samantha barely heard him as he recited what was beneath each dome-shaped silver cover. Richard wasn't making this any easier for her, and the longer she delayed, the harder it was becoming to break the truth to him.

No sooner were they seated and the wine poured than Hodges, the butler, came into the conservatory and whispered an urgent message to his employer.

Giving her an apologetic smile, Richard placed his napkin on the table and pushed back his chair. "Do not make the foolish mistake of getting a telephone," he told her. "It can be a terrible intrusion at times."

While she waited, Samantha sipped her wine and nibbled on a piece of crusty bread spread with pâté. She pensively observed her surroundings. Even Richard's greenhouse was more opulent than anything she was accustomed to, she thought as she noticed the vast variety of exotic plants that filled the conservatory. When she was a child, she had often wondered what it would be like to live surrounded by such luxury. Yet now, when all she had to do to make it hers was say yes, she found she didn't want it.

With a tired sigh, she took the diamond ring from her reticule and placed it on the table. There was no point in dragging this out any longer than necessary. She would tell Richard the minute he came back.

As she sat there waiting for him to return, she began to get the distinct feeling that she was being watched. She looked around her, but could see nothing. Aside from the steady rippling of water from the triple-tiered stone fountain, all was quiet. Here and there, through the jungle of tropical plants, patches of night-blackened glass from the conservatory's windows stared back at her like dark, furtive eyes.

Samantha shuddered. She was letting her imagination get the best of her, she told herself. Still, the feeling of being watched did not go away, and she was glad when Richard returned.

He gave her a tight-lipped smile. "I think I am going to take my own advice and have that idiotic contraption disconnected," he said as he sat down. "A telephone is fine for the bank, but at home it becomes a nuisance." He noticed the ring. "So *this* is what you wanted to talk about." He fixed his cold blue gaze on her. "May I ask why?"

Samantha nervously moistened her lips. "Richard, please don't take this the wrong way. I'm simply not ready to get married again."

He eyed her steadily over the rim of his glass as he took a sip of wine. Finally he set the glass down. "To me, you mean."

"To anyone."

"Not even to Treyman Stern?"

Samantha began to feel defensive. "This has nothing to do with Trey."

Richard leaned back in his chair. He slowly traced a fingertip around the rim of his glass as he regarded her. "You were with him last night."

The color drained from Samantha's face. It took every ounce of willpower she could summon to remain unflustered. "He came to tell me about Joe's arrest," she said with a calm she was far from feeling. "Then he took Maria up to the jail so she could visit Joe."

"He was there for two hours before Maria arrived, Samantha."

Samantha could not believe what she was hearing. Realizing that she was gripping her wineglass so hard her knuckles had turned white, she released the glass before it could shatter and placed her hands in her lap. Anger glittered in her eyes. "What were you doing? Spying on me?"

"Don't be absurd."

"Well, pardon me," she returned snidely. "I wasn't aware that I shouldn't take offense at having my actions policed."

"Samantha, you are blowing this way out of proportion. No one is policing your actions. But this is a small town, and an attractive widow is an easy target for the local gossips."

His condescending tone irked her. She placed her napkin on the table and stood up. "I think it's time for me to leave."

"Sit down, darling, and let's discuss this logically."

"There's nothing to discuss. Good-bye, Richard."

He followed her out the door. "I'm not going to let you leave like this."

He reached for her arm, but she recoiled from his outstretched hand. "Don't touch me."

"Samantha! For God's sake, what is wrong with you?"

She tried to get her escalating temper under control. Until now she had tolerated Richard's advances, and she had nearly convinced herself she wanted them. Now, for no reason that she could fathom, she suddenly hated Richard Winters, and she didn't know why. She had to force herself to look him in the eye. "There's nothing wrong with me that a good night's sleep won't cure. I'm tired, and I want to go home."

"I'll have the carriage brought around."

"No. I'll walk."

"I won't hear of it. It's too dangerous."

"Richard, I've been walking at night in this town since

long before you moved here. I'm capable of taking care of myself, thank you."

"Darling, do you realize the risks you'll be taking? You were already attacked once. Surely you don't want to tempt fate again so soon?"

His reminder of the incident at the restaurant annoyed rather than frightened her. "Mr. Littleton has received his rent," she said testily. "I doubt that I need to worry about his men coming after me again. At least not for the next four months."

Richard held up his hands in mock defeat. "All right. Safety aside, I'll feel better knowing you made it home without incident. Will you at least humor me in this?"

Although as she didn't want him to drive her home, she was shrewd enough to realize that it was probably the only way he was going to let her leave. She did not relish the thought of sitting beside him in the carriage all the way home, but she was thankful that this would be the last time. "All right, Richard. I am very tired, and a ride home would be nice."

Samantha didn't know how she was able to endure the drive home. She did not understand why she suddenly had such an extreme aversion to Richard. Perhaps the revulsion had been there all along and she had simply chosen to ignore it.

When they reached the restaurant, Richard helped her out of the carriage and unlocked the front door for her. Cupping her chin, he tilted her face up and tenderly brushed his lips against her forehead. "I'll call on you tomorrow evening," he said, his tone solicitous. "Try not to work so hard, darling. You worry me."

Samantha merely nodded. She decided it was best not to tell Richard that she had no intention of seeing him tomorrow. He would find out soon enough.

When she was finally inside, Samantha slumped against the locked door. Her heart was beating unnaturally hard, and icy prickles stung her skin. She briskly rubbed the sides of her face with her palms to make the unpleasant tingling sensation go away. A shudder rippled through her. The thought of spending the rest of her life sharing Richard's bed and letting him touch her made her feel physically ill. She sensed that her body was trying to tell her something that her mind had long denied. She had expected to feel some sadness at putting an end to her association with Richard; instead, she simply felt relieved.

It was not quite four-thirty the next morning when Trey arrived at the restaurant. Samantha had already been up for half an hour. She had lighted the stove, made coffee, and begun setting out the ingredients for breakfast. She was dressed but had not yet pinned up her hair, and it tumbled about her shoulders and down her back in soft, tantalizing waves.

"Do you want breakfast before you go?" she asked after she locked the kitchen door behind Trey.

"Just coffee, thanks."

She carried two mugs and the coffee pot into the dining room.

"Are you going to be all right here while I'm gone?" Trey asked while she filled the mugs.

She placed the pot on an iron trivet and sat down opposite him. "I'll be fine. If Maria and Sarah don't come in today, Liam and I can handle the work by ourselves."

Trey felt the fine hairs rise along the nape of his neck. He arched a questioning brow at her. "Liam?"

"Liam Smith. He's the handyman I hired. Now, before you complain that I didn't consult you first, I want you to know that he has been a big help to me, and I don't know how I would have gotten through the past few days without him. He does everything from fix windows to wash dishes and wait on tables. Besides, he's cheap."

Unease clouded Trey's eyes as he took a drink of the hot coffee. Liam Smith. Liam Stern. It was too much of a coincidence. "Is he reliable?" he asked.

"Very."

That didn't sound like Liam, Trey thought. His uncle didn't know the meaning of the word "reliable." Besides, he couldn't imagine Samantha hiring anyone as unkempt as his uncle. His expression lightened somewhat. "Just be careful," he cautioned. "If anything happens while I'm away, get Sheriff Calder."

Samantha avoided making any promises. She still had not forgiven Sheriff Calder for arresting Joe on what she considered false charges. "How long do you think you'll be gone?" she asked instead.

"No more than three or four days, I hope. I want to make sure Joe gets the best lawyer in the territory. If necessary, I'll go to Tucson."

Samantha's hair fell forward, partially covering her face as she stared down at her hands. "It's so strange," she began in a low voice, "the things that are suddenly happening around here. First the restaurant is ransacked. Then someone cuts a cable at the mine. You get shot. Joe is arrested. Taza Parks is killed. And all within a matter of days. I can't help but feel there's a connection, although for the life of me I can't figure out where or why." She lifted a contemplative gaze to his face. "It seems almost as if someone is out to destroy this town."

"I've been thinking the same thing. Unfortunately, I don't have any answers."

Samantha took a deep breath and squared her shoulders. "While you're in Phoenix," she said, "do you think you'll have time to look up Mr. Littleton?"

"I'd already planned on it."

"Thanks. This is a bad time for me to try to get away from the restaurant."

Trey had not missed the note of uncertainty in her voice. He reached across the table and took Samantha's hand. "If it's any consolation to you, I hope I'm wrong about Morris Littleton. Little good ever comes of suspecting the worst about someone."

Samantha pulled her hand free of his and folded her arms in front of her. She seemed to be doing that a lot lately. "There is something I think you should know, and I want you to hear it from me before the rumormongers in this town get hold of it." She paused and tugged on her bottom lip with her teeth for a moment before continuing. "Richard and I aren't going to get married. I returned his ring last night."

Trey looked momentarily stunned. "I'm sorry."

He sounded so sincere, it was Samantha's turn to look surprised. "I thought you'd be glad."

Trey chose his words carefully. "It never makes me glad to see your dreams dashed, Sam. No matter how I feel about Winters, the only thing that really matters is your happiness."

"I don't want you to think this has anything to do with what happened between us the other night. It doesn't. I've simply decided that I don't want to get married again. For the time being I'm content living by myself and making my own decisions."

Trey eyed her steadily. "I want to court you."

In spite of her efforts to be calm and sophisticated, Samantha felt the color rise in her cheeks. "I can't promise anything."

Trey realized that, while it had been more than a year

since Michael's death, her emotional separation from him was still painfully raw, so her answer was neither more nor less than he'd expected. Suddenly the pale scar at one corner of his mouth disappeared into a boyish dimple. A mischievous twinkle danced in his eyes. "I might as well warn you now, Sam: when I see something I want, I don't give up until I get it."

There was no mistaking the implication behind his words, and in spite of her insistence that she was unswayed by the intimacy they had recently shared, Samantha felt an unexpected surge of excitement at the prospect of being pursued by Trey. A smile, faint and fleeting, flickered across her features. "Perhaps I'd best warn you, Mr. Stern, I'm not easily caught."

The first gray light of morning was beginning to fill the valley as Trey packed his saddlebags with the sandwiches and apple turnovers Samantha had made for him. That done, he turned back to tell her good-bye, and he thought she had never looked more beautiful or more tempting than she did at this moment.

She was standing in the kitchen doorway, her slender figure silhouetted in the light of the oil lamp. The lamplight glanced off her hair, making it shimmer with the precious red-gold of a desert sunset. He went to her and braced one hand on the doorjamb behind her head. With his other hand, he lifted a sweetly scented tendril away from her face. "Are you sure you'll be all right here while I'm away?"

Samantha gave him a reproachful look. "You've already asked me that three times this morning."

Trey was silent a moment. "Sam, I know this is none of my business, but may I ask why you broke off your engagement to Winters?"

For the first time in all the years she'd known him, Samantha saw a reflection of her own uncertainty and vulnerability in Trey's eyes, and she sensed his loneliness. She knew without asking what he wanted to hear, but she could not bring herself to say it. Not yet. Not until she'd had a chance to sort out her own feelings. She reached out and placed her palm flat against his chest and felt the steady, reassuring rhythm of his heart. "Let's just say I don't like the way he combs his hair," she said softly.

It was not the answer he'd wanted to hear, but Trey knew it would have to be enough for now. He also knew that, even though no commitment had been spoken between them, she would be here when he returned.

Trey slid his fingers into her hair and lowered his head. His lips were firm and warm against hers. Samantha wrapped her arms around his waist and leaned against him as they indulged in a long, tender, unhurried kiss. All too soon Trey reluctantly pulled away. "Be careful," Samantha said as he swung up into the saddle.

He grinned at her and touched the brim of his hat. "Don't worry. I intend to claim the other half of that kiss the minute I return."

As she watched him ride away, Samantha's throat tightened. She unconsciously folded her arms. "God help me, Treyman Stern," she whispered at his departing back, "but I think I'm falling in love with you."

Maria did not return to the restaurant that day or the next. By the second night, exhausted from running the restaurant with no one but Liam to help her, Samantha locked up the building and headed down Main Street toward the barrio. She had to find out if Maria was all right.

She walked quickly, keeping her head down to discourage passersby from trying to talk to her. She could have taken a more circuitous route, but Main Street was the best-lighted street in town and, in spite of its reputation for rowdiness, probably the safest road to travel after dark.

Horses were crowded into the hitching space in front of the saloons. Through the swinging doors, Samantha caught glimpses of blue uniforms among the miners' traditional corduroy and flannel. It must be payday at Fort McCrae, she thought.

From one of the saloons very close to her came loud squeals of feminine laughter. Suddenly the squeals escalated into shrieks. The swinging doors of the Caledonian flew open. Two men, locked in a death grip, rolled over and over and out into the street amid a flurry of gunshots. Dozens of men, their spirits heightened by liquor, shoved their way out of the saloon, goading the two on with shouted obscenities.

Samantha drew her shawl tighter about her shoulders and broke into a run.

By the time she reached the barrio, she was gasping for air, and she had to stop to catch her breath before venturing any farther. Still breathing heavily, she made her way down a narrow dirt path, careful to count her steps as she went along. Even though she had been to Maria's house several times, she still had to concentrate on the directions to keep from getting lost in the maze of dark, thick-walled alleys. Finally she reached the house. She lifted the heavy iron knocker and let it drop.

Maria's father opened the rough-hewn plank door.

Señor Velásquez was a short, thickset man with thinning hair and a warm smile. Tonight, however, there was no laughter in his brown eyes. Samantha shook his hand. "Señor Velásquez, I have come to see Maria." She spoke slowly so that he would understand her.

Maria's father nodded his comprehension and waved to her to enter. His voice reverberated against the walls. "Maria! *Ven acá!* Señora Drury *quiere hablar contigo.*"

The heavy door creaked shut behind her on iron hinges.

Señor Velásquez left Samantha standing in the sparsely furnished entryway. On one white plastered wall, candles in tin sconces flanked a Cristo carved of pine. Below the pine crucifix, on a small table draped with an embroidered linen cloth, an elaborate silver niche held a painted figurine of Our Lady of Guadalupe. Another, more primitive niche fashioned from saguaro ribs contained a nativity scene. Samantha shifted uneasily. It was the first time Maria's father had not invited her into the *sala*.

Maria's bare feet made no sound on the packed-dirt floor. Only the sudden flickering of the candles alerted Samantha to her presence. She turned.

Maria smiled weakly through tear-reddened eyes. "I am glad you come to see me," she said in a shaky voice. "I was afraid I would not get to say good-bye to you."

Samantha reached for Maria's hand. "Maria, what do you mean, good-bye? What's wrong? I've been worried sick about you."

Maria placed a forefinger against her lips, signaling to Samantha to keep her voice down. "I do not want my father to hear," she whispered. She pulled a silver chain with a delicate silver crucifix from her pocket and pressed it in Samantha's hand. "Please, señora, give this to Joe."

Samantha stared, dumbstruck, at the necklace.

"My father is afraid Joe will try to see me when he is away from jail," Maria continued in a hurried whisper. "He say it is best for me to go away. My brother Roberto, tomorrow he take me to Sonora to the nuns."

"Maria, that's terrible! Joe will be heartbroken. He loves you!"

"It is best."

"And what about me? Maria, I can't run the restaurant without you. It's your cooking that everyone loves."

Fresh tears welled in Maria's eyes, and her chin began to quiver. "Señora, please . . ." Her voice broke.

Samantha immediately felt contrite. "Oh, Maria, I know I'm being selfish, but I don't want you to go!" She was on the verge of tears herself. "Would it help if I spoke with your father?"

Maria shook her head. "It is decided."

"Maria!" Señor Velásquez called out.

"I must go," Maria blurted out. "I will miss you, señora." She rose up on tiptoe to kiss Samantha's cheek. "*Vaya con Dios*. Tell Joe I love him." She turned and fled down the hall.

Maria's brother Roberto escorted Samantha back to the restaurant. He refused to discuss his father's decision to send Maria to a convent, and after several failed attempts to start a conversation with him, Samantha fell silent. She clutched Maria's crucifix in her fist as she walked along beside him. She felt as if someone had dealt her a blow to the stomach. It hurt to breathe. She could not believe she might never see Maria again.

Once inside the restaurant, Samantha had not taken more than a few steps into the dining room when she banged her shin on something in the dark and nearly fell. She felt around her. Her fingers closed around the leg of an overturned chair.

Cold tendrils of apprehension wrapped themselves around her spine. When she left the restaurant earlier, everything was in its proper place.

She stood without moving and listened.

Nothing.

Not a sound came from anywhere in the building.

Gradually her vision adjusted to the darkness.

All around her, tables and chairs had been overturned.

She took another step and sugar crunched beneath her shoe. Carefully she made her way to the kitchen. Her hands shook as she lighted a lamp.

The kitchen door was standing ajar. The lock had been broken. The floor was littered with broken dishes. Bins of sugar and flour and cornmeal had been overturned, and their contents scattered.

A week's worth of staples had been ruined.

The cash register, miraculously, had not been touched. Samantha hastily counted out the money in the cash drawer and was somewhat unnerved by the fact that it all seemed to be there. Had robbery been the motive, the money would have been the first thing taken.

The sound of a horse whinnying outside the restaurant drew Samantha's attention, and she looked up to find Richard standing just inside the front door, shock written on his face as he looked around him. "Good heavens," he murmured. "What happened here?"

Chapter Eight

WHAT does it look like? Samantha nearly blurted the question out, but she caught herself and bit back the retort. She folded her arms in front of her. "It would seem, Richard, that my restaurant has been vandalized."

Richard came to her. "Are you all right, darling? Were you hurt?"

"No, I wasn't hurt. I wasn't even here." Samantha stiffened as he pulled her into his arms.

"Samantha, this is twice now that something like this has happened to you. I can't allow you to stay here any longer."

She shrugged out of his embrace. She did not want him touching her. "That's not your decision to make, Richard," she said, piqued. "I'll clean up here and have the locks changed. Everything will be fine."

"Everything will *not* be fine. You won't be safe until you are out of this building. I want you to pack some things and come home with me."

"No."

"Now, no arguments, darling. I insist. You will have a suite of rooms at your disposal—"

"Richard, I said no."

"I will not allow you to place yourself in jeopardy. Now, be a good girl and do as you are told. Go pack some things and—"

"Damn you, Richard! *I said no!*"

He stared at her in surprise.

Samantha raked her fingers through her hair in frustration. "Richard, it's not necessary for you to be so overprotective. I can manage just fine on my own."

"Of course you can. I just don't like the idea of you staying in this building alone at night."

"Well, I am not going home with you, and that's final. Now, if you will please get out of here, I would like to start cleaning up some of this mess before I have an army of ants and God knows what else in here."

He looked hurt. Samantha knew she could have phrased the request a little more civilly, but she was in no mood to put up with Richard's possessiveness.

Instead of leaving, Richard extended his hands toward her. "I wish you would talk to me, darling. I came here last night, but your lights were out and—"

"I was in bed," she said tersely. She had lain in bed with the covers pulled up to her chin, listening to his persistent knocking on the front door and hoping it would sink in that she did not want to see him.

"Samantha, I told you I was coming. Why didn't you wait for me?"

"Because, quite frankly, Richard, I didn't want to see you. I didn't want to talk to you. I don't want to talk to you now. So please leave."

"All right, I'll leave. But I'll be back. With Sheriff Calder."

"Richard, no! I don't want Sheriff Calder here. I can handle this myself."

Richard's eyes narrowed, and his mouth took on an unpleasant twist. "I am sure, Samantha, that even your friend Treyman Stern would want you to send for the sheriff," he said icily.

By the time Richard returned with Sheriff Calder, Samantha had righted all the chairs and tables and pushed them up against one wall so she could clean the floor.

"Looks to me like someone's trying to send you a message," the sheriff said after walking through the restaurant and surveying the damage. "You got any idea who?"

"Joe Tochino has an alibi, so you can forget about pinning the blame on him," Samantha bit out.

Richard threw her a sharp glance. "Darling, Sheriff Calder is only trying to help—"

"I don't want his help. Or yours. I wish you would both leave."

"Samantha dearest, you're being irrational. Please try to cooperate."

"Winters, I think it would be best if you left now," Calder said. "I can take over here."

"Sheriff, I planned to take Mrs. Drury to a safe place to spend the night."

Samantha shot him a withering glance. "I wish you'd clean out your ears, Richard. You seem to be suffering a hearing loss. I've already told you I have no intention of going anywhere with you."

"Samantha, what on earth is the matter with you?"

Her patience rapidly waning, Samantha marched to the front door and yanked it open. "Richard, if you don't leave right this minute, Sheriff Calder is going to have to arrest *me* for attempted murder."

Richard's expression became hard and resentful. Somehow managing to maintain his dignity, he strode to the door. He stopped and looked down at Samantha. "Please let me know if there is anything I can do," he said with strained politeness.

Samantha avoided his gaze. "Good night, Richard."

After he had gone, Sheriff Calder chuckled softly.

"According to rumor, the two of you were about to tie the knot."

Samantha bristled. "Sheriff, my personal life is not open to discussion. May we please get on with business?"

Calder rubbed the back of his neck. "Your personal life, Mrs. Drury, may very well be the reason for all the trouble you keep having here."

"What is that supposed to mean?"

"Mrs. Drury, Richard Winters and Treyman Stern are the two most powerful men in this town, and you have been seeing a great deal of both of them. It would not surprise me in the least if one of them is trying to oust the other from competition." He paused. "Do you have any idea where Stern is tonight?"

Samantha saw red. "Yes, I do," she said angrily. "He is in Phoenix, hiring a lawyer to defend Joe Tochino. Furthermore, since he's the one who paid the rent on this place, I seriously doubt he would try to destroy it. I suggest, Sheriff Calder, that you spend a little more time enforcing the law and a little less time listening to local gossip."

Her outburst did not even seem to faze him. In fact, Samantha had the distinct feeling that he had deliberately provoked it. A small smile touched his mouth. "Interesting thing, gossip," he said. "It's amazing what you can learn if you keep your ears open." He nodded toward the kitchen. "You might want to wedge a chair beneath that doorknob until you can get the lock repaired. Good night, Mrs. Drury." He put his hat back on and left the building.

It was all Samantha could do not to slam the door after him. Arrogant ass, she thought peevishly. She was beginning to dislike Calder nearly as much as she disliked Richard. That he would even suggest that Trey might have something to do with vandalizing the restaurant made her furious.

She picked up the broom and began attacking the floor. "I won't stand for it," she said hotly as she swept up the debris. "I won't just sit back and let my friends be falsely accused. If I have to, I'll go after the real culprits myself."

In the meantime, however, she knew she had to find a way to keep the restaurant running. She would have to hire another cook. She had to order more supplies. And she needed to have a new lock installed on the kitchen door.

She gave the floor a particularly vicious swipe with the broom. "Every time I start to make progress," she blurted out resentfully, "something like this happens to set me back. I'm tired of working my damned tail off for *nothing*." Her voice quavered, and she stopped to take a deep breath and get her careening emotions back under control. Threatening tears stung her eyes and choked her throat, but she fought those back, too. Feeling sorry for herself was a luxury she could not afford. She didn't have the time.

After she finished sweeping the dining room, she started on the kitchen. It galled her to see the wasted flour and sugar that had been dumped. It was a shame, she thought as the broom sliced a path through the spilled flour, that she couldn't simply sift the flour and reuse it.

She suddenly stopped with the broom suspended in midair as inspiration knifed through her. She glanced at the door, then down at the flour. Her pulse quickened as she remembered an incident from her school days. Maybe, she thought, just maybe the flour wouldn't be wasted after all.

She wasn't quite sure how she was going to do it, but if Matthew Collins could douse their fourth grade teacher with a bucket of water suspended over the schoolroom door, then she could figure out how to rig a similar snare using a container of flour.

She also intended to start sleeping with Maria's sawed-off shotgun beside her bed.

"If Stern will not willingly sell to Consolidated Silver," Dieter Vogel said, "then we must force him to sell."

Marty Dennison eyed him sharply. "You suggesting another strike?"

Vogel inclined his head. "We must be prepared to fight for what we want, no matter how long it takes."

"Are you forgetting what happened the last time?" Carl Lemner asked. The three men were standing at the chop bar at the Shamrock Parlor, discussing the mine over a platter of fried pork chops and tankards of beer. "If Stern orders us back to work and we don't comply, there are enough unemployed miners in this town to replace every last one of us."

Marty Dennison snorted. "You goin' yellow on us, Lemner? Stern can hire all the replacements he wants. Won't do him any good if the men can't even get to the mine, now, will it?"

Carl picked a sliver of meat from between his front teeth. "I just don't have a good feeling about it. Tempers have been running pretty hot ever since Joe got himself arrested. Calder's liable to think *we're* the ones who are out to get Stern."

"What about Amos?" Vogel asked. "Can we count on him?"

"Don't hold your breath," Marty retorted. "Flaherty's been talkin' it up on the day shift how Tochino's bein' falsely accused."

"He's got a point," Carl said. "Joe's crew was going up and down that shaft right along with the rest of us."

"Since when are you standin' up for Apache Joe?" Marty demanded.

"I'm not. I'm just saying I don't think he had anything to do with cutting that cable."

Vogel changed the subject. "The biggest problem we are going to have is money. There is only enough left in the union treasury to support the strike for three weeks. If it goes longer than that, the men are going to want to return to work."

"Then maybe we should wait," Carl suggested. "If we don't have enough money to see this thing through to the end, it's all liable to be for nothing."

"Aw, c'mon, Lemner," Dennison said. "You're always looking for some excuse to back out. I'm beginning to think you're turnin' tail on us."

"Gentlemen, please," Vogel implored. "Whatever we decide to do, we must all work together. Dissent within the ranks will only guarantee our failure."

A few feet down the bar, Silas Jenkins downed the last of his beer. He wiped the back of his hand across his mouth and rammed his hat down on his head. It was time to pay Richard Winters a visit. Of course, if Winters wanted to know what he'd overheard tonight, he was going to have to come up with the rest of the cash he owed him. Jenkins was getting awfully tired of working without pay.

Joe wiped his mouth on the napkin and placed his dinner tray on the floor next to his cot. "Thanks. That's the best meal I've had since I've been in here."

From the other side of the bars, Samantha gave him a rueful smile. "Sorry about the meat pie being broken apart. Sheriff Calder wanted to make certain I wasn't trying to smuggle a weapon into your cell."

"Do you blame him?"

Samantha shrugged. "I'm not feeling very magnanimous toward him right now."

Joe was thoughtful for a moment. "You know, Samantha, the sheriff could be right about whoever broke into the Drake House."

"Surely you don't think Trey had anything to do with it?"

"No, but someone could be trying to make it appear that Trey is guilty."

Samantha expelled her breath in a sigh of frustration. "I don't like what's been happening, Joe. It's just like last year all over again. Everyone is suspicious of everyone else. You don't know whom you can trust anymore."

Joe stared down at the tiny silver crucifix that hung around his neck, and Samantha wondered if he was thinking of Maria. "No," he said quietly. "You never know."

Immediately Samantha felt ashamed of thinking only of herself when Joe was hurting so much. She closed her hands around the iron bars and rested her forehead against them. "I'm sorry about Maria, Joe. It all happened so . . . suddenly . . ." Her voice trailed off.

Joe glanced up. An intense light burned in his dark eyes. "When I get out of here, I'm going after her."

A frown puckered Samantha's forehead. "It wasn't Maria's fault; I hope you know that. She loves you."

"I'm going to find her, Samantha. And when I do, I'm going to marry her. If I have to, I'll go to the padres and become a Catholic."

Samantha lifted her head and stared at him. "I thought you weren't a believer."

"I believe in the Great Spirit. I think the Great Spirit and Maria's God are the same. It is men who make them different."

Samantha wasn't sure Maria would see it that way, but she said nothing. The last thing Joe needed was her pessimism.

* * *

There had been no more trouble at the restaurant since the night it was vandalized. Still, not wanting to take any chances, Samantha carefully suspended a flour-filled apron over both the front and back doors every night before she went to bed. If her intruder decided to return, he was going to be in for a big surprise.

Richard, to Samantha's relief, had stayed away. She overheard one of her customers say that Winters had escorted Mathilda Marston to Emma Hayden's coming-out party. At first she had felt a twinge of jealousy. Even though she had been the one to break off their association, she could not help feeling that Richard had wasted little time finding someone to replace her.

It was past eleven on Saturday night when Samantha finally blew out the lamp and turned in. Her body ached with fatigue. Unless she could hire dependable employees who learned quickly and could work under a minimum of supervision, she might as well close down the restaurant completely. She could not keep going like this day after day, doing most of the work herself. Sooner or later she was going to collapse from sheer exhaustion.

She had no sooner dozed off than a sound from the alley caused her to jerk awake. She lay without moving. Her heart pounded in her ears. She heard a rattling noise at the kitchen door. Someone was testing the doorknob.

Very quietly she pushed back the covers and dropped her feet over the side of the bed. She reached for the shotgun.

Without making a sound, she tiptoed toward the kitchen, clutching the shotgun. Her white nightgown was the only thing visible in the darkness.

Someone knocked loudly on the kitchen door. "Samantha, are you awake?"

Trey!

"Just a minute!" Samantha called out. She hid the shotgun in the pantry, then ran to the door and threw back the bolt. Trey was back! He must have just gotten into town. She opened the kitchen door.

Suddenly a cloud of white engulfed her, filling her lungs, suffocating her.

Trey swore aloud. "What the—"

Samantha coughed and gasped for air. She took an angry swipe at her face with her sleeve. How could she have been so stupid? Flour tickled her nose, and she sneezed.

Behind her, she heard Trey moving around the kitchen. "Where do you keep the matches?" he asked.

"Beneath . . . the lamp," Samantha choked. She screwed up her eyes and tried to brush the flour off her face.

The flame in the lamp flickered and dipped as Trey slipped the glass chimney into place, then swelled to a warm, mellow glow.

For a minute Trey just stared at Samantha, unable even to react, much less speak. She was standing in the open doorway. Flour covered every inch of her, from her hair to her bare feet. It settled into the hollows beneath her eyes, giving her the appearance of a raccoon, and masked her lips. Above her an apron dangled from a nail that had been driven into the ceiling. Samantha reached up to wipe her cheek, shaking more flour loose from the folds of her nightgown.

The chuckle started somewhere deep down inside Trey. A small, barely perceptible tremor at first, it welled up inside him until his broad shoulders were shaking uncontrollably with silent laughter.

Samantha slammed the kitchen door shut. "That's right. Go ahead and laugh. You think it's funny, don't you?"

Still laughing, Trey shook his head. Mirth sparkled in his blue-gray eyes as he started toward her. "Sweetheart, if you had any idea how you look right now—"

His words were cut short as Samantha scooped up a handful of flour from the floor and hurled it at him.

The flour dispersed into a powdery cloud before it ever reached him. Annoyed that she had not even struck her target, Samantha started to bend down for another handful, but Trey caught her arm, stopping her. He pulled her against him, and his mouth hungrily covered hers.

The anger left Samantha in a rush. She leaned into his embrace as he folded his strong arms around her. Starved for his touch, she wrapped her arms around his waist and clung fiercely to him, her fragile emotions spinning out of control as she surrendered to the forceful domination of his lips.

After a seemingly endless, wonderful, drugging kiss, Trey gently withdrew. "I told you I was going to claim the other half of that kiss the minute I returned," he said huskily.

Samantha started to lift her eyes to his, but her gaze stopped just below the end of his nose. A reluctant smile tugged at the corners of her mouth. The front of Trey's shirt was covered with flour and her kiss had left a pasty white ring around his mouth. She pressed her lips together to keep from laughing, but not before Trey had seen her smirk.

"Now look who's laughing," Trey chided her. He started to lick the flour from his lips, and Samantha lost control. Her shoulders hunched forward in helpless laughter.

"I think . . . I should . . . warn you," she managed to get out, "that flour has seen . . . better days."

She reached up to brush the ring from his mouth, but Trey caught her hand and held it to his lips. He kissed her knuckles, then folded his fingers around hers and held her hand tightly. A puckered red ridge ran along the base of his thumb where the bullet had grazed his hand. He lifted his gaze to the apron dangling precariously from the ceiling. "Do I dare ask?"

Beneath the coating of flour that obscured her face, Samantha felt her cheeks grow warm. "I don't think that would be a good idea," she said sheepishly.

Trey looked down at her. The fine lines at the outer corners of his eyes deepened. His eyes twinkled. "At least now you know your snare works."

She shrugged. "For all the good it did. The only thing I caught was a man who smells as bad as his horse."

Trey feigned a wounded look. "I'll have you know I rode most of the day to get back here. That's good honest sweat you're smelling."

"Horse sweat, you mean," she said, still laughing. "The water in the kettle should still be hot. I'll fill the tub while you get out of those clothes. Do you need to put up your horse for the night?"

Trey could have sworn that sounded like an invitation. "I left him at Chandler's. He needed a rubdown by the time we got into town."

Samantha started for the door. "I'll get you some clean towels. Are you hungry?"

Trey's gaze dropped to her hips, and he felt the heat stir in his veins. Only for you, he thought. He was beginning to think it had been a mistake to come here. All the way back from Phoenix he had been thinking about Samantha, and the provocative images that had kept his mind occupied for the hundred-thirty-mile journey had raised his desire for her to a dangerous level. He did not entirely trust himself around her. "I stopped in Globe to eat," he said.

"Oh," Samantha said. Then, as if remembering what she had originally set out to do, she hastily added, "I'll get the towels."

When she returned to the kitchen a few minutes later, she had brushed the flour out of her hair and had also donned a clean nightgown and her wrapper. Her freshly scrubbed face shone. She smelled faintly of lavender. She handed him a towel and a washcloth. "You can spread the towel on the floor to stand on. I'll set the other one on top of the stove so it will be warm when you finish bathing."

Even though he was accustomed to taking care of himself, Trey had to admit that he rather liked having Samantha do little things for him, like preparing his bath and bringing him a towel. For the first time in years, he felt as awkward as an untried youth. "I could go down to the bathhouse," he suggested.

"And pay two dollars just to get wet? That's crazy!" The wide-eyed look she gave him was deceptively innocent. Trey knew Samantha had to be aware of what his bathing here might lead to. She was no naive schoolgirl.

"Besides," Samantha continued a little too quickly, "I have a lot to tell you, and this may be the last chance we'll get to be alone for a while, because I'm going to be very busy for the next few weeks." Suddenly unsure of herself, she faltered. "Unless, of course, you'd *rather* go down to the bathhouse."

"Not particularly." Trey's voice sounded oddly raw. A gleam of interest smoldered in his blue-gray eyes.

Samantha shifted self-consciously. "I'll get the tub."

Trey felt an unexpected tingle travel down his spine. The only other woman who had ever let him bathe in her house had also extended an invitation to spend the night. Samantha was being more circumspect but hardly any more subtle. "Tell me where it is," he said thickly. "I'll get it."

As Trey hauled the copper hip bath out of the pantry, Samantha swept up the flour. Then she went to the sink and began filling a bucket with cold water. "Go ahead and empty the kettle into the tub," she said as she worked the pump. "I'll put some more water on the stove to heat."

Samantha talked nonstop as they filled the tub, telling him everything that had happened while he was away. She knew it was just a nervous reaction to having Trey here, but she chatted on anyway, desperately needing to fill the silence with something, no matter how inane. She told him about Maria's leaving, about her intruder, and about Sheriff Calder implying that Trey might have had something to do with the break-in. "That man made me so angry I wanted to spit in his eye. I'm beginning to wish someone would run against him in the next election. He's getting too complacent. He thinks no one's going to challenge him."

"Calder's done as good a job as any sheriff Myterra's had in the past," Trey reminded her.

Samantha rolled her eyes. "I wouldn't call arresting Joe 'doing a good job.' "

Trey told her about the lawyer he'd hired. "His name's Kendall. He'll be in town next week to meet with Joe."

Samantha turned to gape at him. "Perry Kendall?" she asked. She'd heard of him. Everyone in the territory had. He had defended Carlos Rodriguez, an immigrant farm laborer, on charges of setting fire to his wealthy employer's house, and he had won. "He's supposed to be *good*."

"The best, from what I was told." Trey started to unbutton his shirt. "If anyone can clear Joe's name, he can."

Samantha dried her hands on a dish towel. "I'll get you some soap," she said, searching frantically for an excuse to leave the kitchen while he undressed. Everything was happening too quickly.

In her bedroom she stopped with one hand on the dresser for support. Her heart was pounding so hard it hurt. This was insane, letting Trey bathe here, in her kitchen. She knew what was likely to happen between them. Not only that but she was beginning to realize that she actually *wanted* it to happen.

She caught her reflection in the mirror. Her eyes seemed unusually large and dark, and her lips looked temptingly full. Her hair tumbled like wildfire over her shoulders. She drew her wrapper tighter around her and defensively crossed her arms. She wasn't afraid, exactly. But it had been a long time. A very long time.

By the time she returned with the soap, Trey was already in the tub. His back was toward her. The tub was too small for him, and his bare knees stuck out at an awkward angle, making him seem especially vulnerable. Although not as tanned as the rest of him, his legs were nonetheless long and strongly muscled. Dark hair clung wetly to the pale skin of his legs.

The muscles rippled through his broad tanned shoulders as he lifted the washcloth and squeezed it over his head. Water ran down over his head, causing the hair at the nape of his neck to separate into glossy dark brown curls.

An awakening hunger spread through Samantha at the sight of Trey's unclad body. It was a purely physical sensation, primitive and instinctual, unlike anything she had ever before experienced. She hastily stifled the unfamiliar feeling, telling herself that it was all in her imagination and that she simply wasn't accustomed to having men bathe in her kitchen, but no matter how she tried to talk herself out of it, the peculiar sensation would not go away.

She uttered a small cough, alerting Trey to her presence. "I brought the soap," she said with an outward calmness that successfully masked her nervousness. She went to the tub. Careful not to let her gaze drop below his chin, she handed him the soap. "Call me if you need anything," she said. "I'll find something for you to wear." Her voice faltered. Not waiting for Trey's response, she turned and fled the room.

She retrieved a pair of pants and an old shirt of Michael's. This time the faded, familiar items did not unleash a flood of tears. She felt a little sad, but the sharp edge of her grief had blurred, and it no longer overwhelmed her. Michael was part of an irretrievable past, and she was learning to live with her memories instead of letting them control her.

She took the clothes into the kitchen. "I hope these fit," she said. She draped them across a chair. "I think you're broader through the shoulders than Michael was."

Trey cast her a sharp glance, his eyes searching her face. He wasn't sure just where he stood with Samantha. While he sincerely hoped she was finally overcoming her grief for Michael, he could not be certain. Her behavior tonight puzzled him.

Samantha went to the tub. "Hand me the soap. I'll wash your back."

Trey suddenly felt as if every nerve in his body had awakened, alerting him to danger. "You don't have to do that."

Samantha was so close to him she could see where the stubble on his jaw was beginning to turn silver. She pushed up her sleeves and knelt behind the tub. "I want to."

Taking a deep breath, he handed her the soap and washcloth. "Thanks," he said warily.

She soaped up the washcloth. "I used to do this for Michael sometimes," she said. "I cut his hair, too. I never could get it quite even around his ears."

It was on the tip of Trey's tongue to tell Samantha he didn't want to talk about Michael, but he kept silent. If the slight wavering in her voice was any indication of her agitation, then she was like a coiled spring, ready to snap.

He tucked his chin under and leaned forward as she rubbed the soapy washcloth over his back in broad, sure strokes, careful to avoid the still-tender area near his shoulder. Then she changed to small, hard circles that made him feel as though he were being deprived of several layers of skin as she worked up a thick lather. Once he grew accustomed to her brisk touch, however, he had to admit that it felt good. Damned good, in fact. A shudder of pure pleasure worked its way up his spine and radiated out through his limbs. His shoulders jerked spasmodically, then relaxed.

He nodded toward the apron still hanging over the kitchen door. "That wouldn't have stopped an intruder."

Samantha followed his gaze. "I know. But doing it made me feel a little less helpless."

Trey didn't like the idea of her staying in the house alone, and he said as much.

"Now, don't you start on me, too," Samantha said sternly. "I've already been through this with Richard. He wanted me to come and stay with him." She didn't need to see his face to know what he was thinking. He was jealous! She could feel it in the abrupt tightening of his muscles beneath her fingers. "Don't worry," she said lightly. "I told him no."

For no particular reason Trey suddenly felt angry. He didn't know if it was hearing Richard Winters's name that had set him off, or the unpleasant nagging feeling deep in his gut that Samantha was baiting him. He glared at the apron. "Good," he said. His tone was surly.

Samantha had to suppress a smile. Not only was he jealous, she thought, but he was making no attempt to hide the fact. She tossed the washcloth over his shoulder. It hit the water with a splat. She stood up. "You rinse off, and I'll get you the towel."

"Sam!"

She turned back, puzzled by his unusually sharp tone. "Yes?"

Before she knew what was happening, Trey seized a fistful of her nightgown and gave it a hearty jerk, causing her to lose her balance and tumble backward. She gasped and threw her arms out to stop herself from falling, but to no avail. Water surged up over the sides of the tub as she landed unceremoniously on Trey's lap.

Chapter
Nine

SAMANTHA squealed as the water saturated her night-gown and wrapper all the way to her waist. Wedging her elbow against Trey's chest for leverage, she fought to push herself up out of the tub. "Let me up!"

His arms closed around her, trapping her. He yanked her hard against him. "Stop it!"

The brittleness of his voice caught Samantha off guard. "Stop what?" she demanded hotly. "*You're* the one who pulled *me* into the water."

"*Stop playing games.*"

Samantha immediately ceased struggling and turned her head to stare at him in bewilderment. The anger she saw burning in his eyes told her she had not imagined his sharp tone. "I-I don't know what you're talking about."

"You know damned well what I'm talking about. From the minute I walked through that door tonight, you have been dallying with me."

Her eyes widened. "I have not!"

"*You have*. And don't try to deny it. If you have some-thing on your mind, speak up. Coyness doesn't suit you, Sam."

Humiliation crept up Samantha's neck like a brilliant red veil. She pressed her lips together and turned her face away, not certain whether she was more angered with him or with herself. She knew she had been leading him on, but to what purpose? Was she falling in love with him, as she had begun to suspect? Or was she merely seeking to fill the void that had been left in her life by Michael's death?

She wanted Trey; she couldn't deny that. What she was having trouble accepting, however, was how *badly* she wanted him. She wanted to feel him inside her, to lose herself in his touch. She could already feel the aroused hardness of him pressing against her bottom through her sodden nightclothes, and that flustered her even more, because it turned a fanciful desire into an all-too-imminent probability. "What do you want me to say?" she bit out between clenched teeth. "That I hate myself for feeling so confused when I'm with you?"

"If that's what you're feeling, yes."

The dusting of freckles on her face was barely visible through the scarlet stain on her cheeks. Trey's gaze fell to the rapidly jumping pulse in the side of her neck. He had a pretty good idea what was troubling Samantha. In fact, he was willing to gamble everything he owned on it. "There's no shame in wanting someone to hold you and love you," he said gently.

If it had been possible for Samantha's face to turn any redder, it would have. That Trey could so easily discern her most private thoughts made her feel exposed and vulnerable. To her disgust, sudden tears filled her eyes. Her throat ached. "Damn you," she croaked.

Trey's expression became solemn. He reached up and brushed a gleaming copper lock away from her face. "Sam, look at me."

Drawn almost against her will by the gentle firmness of his command, Samantha turned her head. Warm blue-gray eyes that brimmed with tenderness and passion gazed steadily into hers. A warm, pulsing ache that had been steadily growing deep down inside her suddenly became more acute, tormenting her with agonizing demands that she could no longer ignore. Trey's smoldering gaze dropped to her lips, and the fragile threads that remained of Samantha's prison of self-denial snapped.

Trey slid his fingers into Samantha's hair, and drew her head down to his. Her eyes closed and her lips parted as she sought his kisses with a feverish desperation that welled up inside her like a volcanic eruption, consuming her with its soul-devouring fire.

Heedless of the constraints of the small tub, Samantha turned slightly in his arms and wrapped her own arms around his neck as she returned his kisses without restraint. Trey drove his tongue into her mouth again and again until she was delirious with longing. Their closeness was a powerful aphrodisiac, luring them both into a drugged, unthinking state of arousal. Samantha pressed closer to him, unable to get enough of the addicting sensations he was unleashing in her with his masterful touch. Her head reeled and she was powerless to think as his hands roved down over her back to cup her bottom and lift her higher and closer against him. Through the wet, clinging gown, he alternately stroked and kneaded her tender flesh. When his knowing fingers began to trace a path along the intimate hollow between her buttocks, Samantha cried out, and a convulsive shudder racked her body.

Samantha buried her face in the side of his neck and shuddered again and again. Shaken, she clung to him. She did not know what had overcome her. He had not even touched her most sensitive areas, and yet she had lost all control over her reaction to his caresses.

Trey wrapped his arms around her and cradled her close against his pounding heart as she drifted back down to earth.

Finally Samantha lifted her head and fixed a dazed, glassy-eyed look on him. The lean, hard lines of his face were taut with barely restrained passion. She touched a trembling hand to the lips that had so recently ·claimed hers. "I-I want . . . you," she whispered achingly.

Trey's heart swelled inside his chest. The words he had never expected to hear from her lips pierced the wall he had spent a lifetime building around his emotions. His eyes darkened with longing. Planting his hands on Samantha's waist, he lifted her out of the water. "Get up."

No sooner had her feet touched the floor than he was standing behind her. Water pooled at their feet, turning the tiles a dark burnt brown-red. "I'll get the towel," Samantha said, but before she could move, Trey had slid one arm behind her knees and swung her up into his arms.

With a small cry of surprise, Samantha threw one arm around his neck. She held on tightly as he carried her into the bedroom. The mattress dipped beneath their combined weight as Trey braced one knee on the mattress and lowered her dripping form to the bed.

In the darkened bedroom, Trey's broad shoulders were silhouetted against the lamplight that poured into the doorway from the kitchen as he knelt over her. His wet skin glistened as if illuminated by thousands of tiny points of light. He slid one hand beneath her nightgown and hooked his fingers in the waistband of her drawers. "Take them off," he ordered huskily. The pebbly roughness of his voice sent shivers of anticipation surging through Samantha's veins. Without hesitation, she did his bidding. Seconds later her nightgown and wrapper joined her drawers on the floor.

Trey silently cautioned himself to slow down and not rush, but the sight of Samantha's naked body nearly robbed him of all resolve. God, how he wanted her. Samantha lay back on the pillows, and it was all Trey could do not to surrender to the urge to lower his body to hers and drive himself into her.

Instead, he grasped a slender ankle and lifted her foot to his mouth. With torturous deliberation, he began kissing her foot, tickling her instep with the tip of his tongue. Samantha gasped and tried to pull her foot away, but he held it firmly. He kissed her ankle, her calf, the throbbing pulse in the delicate hollow behind her knee.

Every passion, every wild longing Samantha had ever felt in her entire life, welled up inside her now, filling her with a flood of desire that burned in her veins like liquid fire. She wanted to touch him, too, and return his caresses, but when she tried to reach for him, her arms would not respond; she was too caught up in the storm of pleasurable sensations that he was evoking in her. By the time his lips reached the sensitive flesh of her inner thigh and began moving slowly upward, every nerve in her body felt as though it were charged with electricity.

Trey kissed and caressed and fondled every soft, tender inch of her, arousing her first with gentle, skillful hands, then continuing the agonizing torment with his lips and tongue. He caressed her breasts, gently cupping them in his big hand and teasing the sensitive crests with his thumb until they stood erect against his palm. Then he lowered his head to her breast.

Samantha's back arched. She dug her fingers into his hair and held his head tightly to her breast as he tantalized the swollen nipple with his tongue. She felt certain she would die from the erotic torture, and yet she wanted it to go on forever. Her breath came in rapid, shallow gulps.

If Samantha's ravenous response to his touch stunned him, his own powers of self-discipline amazed Trey even more. He wanted her so badly he felt he would explode from the sheer agony of holding back. Yet each twisting, turning, writhing movement he elicited from her served only to fuel his determination to prolong her pleasure as long as was humanly possible. Somewhere along the way, his own gratification had become secondary to his desire to meet her needs.

As his hand traced a fiery trail over her abdomen and along the insides of her thighs, her body strained toward him, but he maddeningly avoided the very centers that clamored loudest for his touch, leaving her feeling frustrated and vaguely unsatisfied. Then he slid his hand down into the soft, damp triangle between her legs, and Samantha thought she would die of pure pleasure as his skillful fingers wrought their delicious torment, taking her from one trembling peak to another.

Then, just when she thought she could endure no more, Trey gently but firmly parted her thighs and shifted his weight over her. She felt his probing hardness and instinctively raised her hips to receive him, but he did not enter her. "Samantha, look at me," he whispered harshly.

Bewildered that he should suddenly stop short of giving them both the release their bodies demanded, she opened her eyes, not comprehending what he wanted from her. He was poised over her, his face hard with barely leashed passion, the bunched muscles of his shoulders and upper arms straining beneath his weight.

His intense gaze burned into her. "If you want me to stop," he managed to get out, his voice strained, "please tell me now."

Samantha's throat tightened with emotion at the realization that he was putting his own needs aside to give her one final chance to deny him ingress to a part of her that had once belonged to another. That Trey cared enough about her to give her such a choice touched her deeply.

Rising slightly, she took his face between her hands and kissed him tenderly on the lips. "If you stop now," she murmured against his mouth, "I'll never forgive you."

Time seemed to stand still as he slid slowly into her, filling her with a warmth so sweet and so intense that Samantha felt as though she had lived her entire life for this one moment. He withdrew slightly, then shifted forward again and again, taking each measured thrust a fraction deeper than the one before, until Samantha thought she would go insane if she could not have all of him.

Pleasure welled up inside her, making her feel wonderful and miserable at the same time. With each plunging stroke, broken, disjointed images of the past flashed through her mind, then disappeared before she could grasp their meaning. Moaning incoherently and tossing her head on the pillows, she drove her hips hard against Trey's, frantically seeking to assuage the terrible burning ache that throbbed inside her. Tears pooled in her eyes and slid down her cheeks, although she didn't know why she was crying. "Please," she whispered. Her voice broke.

Fiercely restraining his own rampaging desires, Trey quickened the momentum of his deep, driving thrusts, determined to give Samantha the release she so desperately sought before succumbing to his own body's demands.

Samantha felt her control rapidly slipping away. She was vaguely aware that a part of her had been resisting surrender, but now that choice seemed to have been taken from her. She felt as if she were floating, spinning higher and higher through a cloud of delicious, intoxicating heat, her body stretched taut, straining for something just beyond her reach.

Then the clouds parted, and Samantha's entire world exploded.

Her back arched and a low scream tore from her throat. Trey caught her to him and smothered her cry with his mouth, taking her lips in a long, passionate kiss before driving himself into her one last time.

Samantha's body shuddered convulsively, and she unthinkingly sobbed out his name as one tremor after another rippled through her body like the aftershocks of an earthquake.

Gathering her in his arms, Trey rolled onto his side and held her close against his pounding heart, unwilling to release her just yet. He wanted this moment to last forever.

He threaded his fingers through her hair and massaged the back of her neck.

Finally her tears subsided, and a peaceful calm unlike anything she had ever known seeped through her veins. It felt like the most natural thing in the world to be lying here with Trey, their arms wrapped tightly around each other and their legs entangled. Taking a deep, shuddering breath, she tilted her head back to look at him. "Thank you," she whispered.

A low chuckle rumbled in Trey's throat. It was the first time in his life a woman had ever thanked him for making love to her, and he wasn't certain what to make of it. He smoothed a rebellious curl away from her face. "No thanks required. I enjoyed it, too."

An easy silence settled between them. Samantha's eyelids drifted shut, but she soon realized that she was not at all sleepy. Her body felt as if it had been charged with new life. She turned slightly in his arms and rested her head in the hollow of his shoulder. Her fingertips played idly across his chest, unaware of the arousing effect her innocent touch was having on him. She touched the puckered scar just below his collarbone. "Does it still bother you?" she asked.

"Not much."

Samantha's hand stilled on his chest. After a few minutes Trey looked down at her, thinking she might have fallen asleep, but her eyes were open, and she was staring at the soft light that filled the doorway from the kitchen. "Do you want me to put out the lamp?" he asked.

Samantha did not need to ask what he meant by that. The implication was clear. A warm flush crept up her neck. "Yes, please," she whispered.

Trey extricated his arm from beneath her. "Stay here."

While he went into the kitchen, Samantha picked her wet clothes up off the floor and draped them across the back of a chair to dry, then retrieved a clean nightgown from her dresser drawer. Her hands shook as she filled the washbasin on top of her dresser. She could hear Trey in the next room, testing the window and door locks. Not counting the time he had collapsed on her bed from loss of blood, this would be the first night since Michael's death that she had not slept alone.

A small voice in the back of her head whispered that she was inviting scandal by letting Trey stay the night, but she forcibly pushed the criticism aside. She was not a smitten adolescent, recklessly endangering her chances for marriage; she'd already experienced a satisfying marriage and had no intention of marrying again. She was sure the Reverend Mr. Crowley would have something sufficiently condemning to say about that, but she didn't care. For now she was content to feel loved and wanted. That, she rationalized, was more than many people ever had.

By the time Trey returned to the bedroom, Samantha had washed and put on a dry nightgown and was brushing out her hair. For several minutes he stood in the doorway, entranced by the tiny yellow-white sparks of electricity that popped in the darkness as she tugged the brush through the thick, luxuriant tresses.

Pride and protectiveness swelled inside him as he watched her. It made him feel good to be here with her. A shiver of longing sped through his veins, and a knot rose in his throat at the thought of how empty his life would be without her. If he had ever doubted that he loved her, he had no doubts now. He loved her more than he'd ever thought it possible to love anyone, and that frightened him. If anything happened to Samantha, he would lose his will to live.

I love you, he thought. "Have I ever told you how beautiful you are?" he asked in a low, gravelly voice like rough velvet that struck a vibrant chord deep inside her.

She turned to see him coming toward her, and her heart turned over.

Gently but firmly, Trey took the brush from her hand and placed it on top of the dresser. Then he reached for Samantha. "Come here, woman," he commanded, and she leaned into his arms as his head descended.

For a moment Samantha did not know where she was or why it was light outside. Then she remembered that it was Sunday and the restaurant was closed. She had arisen before dawn every day for so long that she had forgotten what it was like to sleep late.

Clutching the covers to her, she struggled to sit up. She turned her head to stare at the rumpled pillow beside her, and a brilliant crimson flush engulfed her face. Where was her nightgown? She remembered Trey taking it off her, but not where he had tossed it.

He had made love to her several times during the night, at times taking her with a vigor that made her head reel and at other times lingering over her with a selfless tenderness that made her heart swell with love for him. Once, she could have sworn she had actually cried out, "I love you," but she couldn't be certain. If she had, Trey had made no mention of it. She vowed to exercise more caution in the future. She no longer questioned her love for Trey, but she didn't want to lead him to expect more from her than she was willing to give.

She heard the heavy clang of an iron pot being placed on the stove. Was Trey in the kitchen? She swung her feet over the side of the bed and winced at the sharp ache in her thighs and lower back. She had used muscles last night that she'd long since forgotten she had.

Completely dressed, his dark brown hair freshly combed, Trey appeared in the doorway carrying a tray. Samantha gasped and snatched the covers higher up over her breasts.

He grinned at her obvious embarrassment. "Hope you're hungry."

Her curiosity piqued, Samantha stretched her neck to see what was on the tray. "You made breakfast?" she asked skeptically.

Trey frowned and feigned affront. "Are you questioning my culinary abilities?"

"No, of course not. I'm just—" She faltered. He had made bacon and scrambled eggs and corn bread and coffee. Her mouth began to water. "I'm just not accustomed to being waited on," she finished. She hadn't realized until now how hungry she was. She began searching around in earnest for her nightgown.

Trey set the tray on the foot of the bed. Bending down, he retrieved her nightgown from the floor. A mischievous twinkle danced in his eyes. "Looking for this?"

The blood rushed to Samantha's face so quickly it made her ears roar. She extended her hand. "Yes, thank you." She started to rise, then hesitated. "Could you . . . uh . . . turn around? Please?"

A smile tugged at the corners of Trey's mouth. After last night Samantha's sudden modesty seemed misplaced. There wasn't an inch of her body that he hadn't touched and kissed and explored. Still, he good-naturedly went along with her request to turn his back.

Once his back was toward her, he folded his arms across his chest and tapped his foot with mock impatience.

Not trusting him to stay turned around long enough for her to get dressed, Samantha scrambled to put on the nightgown. She was just working her right arm into the sleeve when Trey casually tossed over his shoulder, "Are you aware that you even have freckles on your—"

"Trey!"

He chuckled softly. "There, too," he added.

Samantha threw him a withering glance. "You may turn around now," she said as the hem of the gown settled around her ankles. She extracted her long hair from beneath the neckline and gave her head a shake that caused the unruly red locks to tumble around her shoulders.

Trey's gaze traveled appreciatively down the length of her. "Damn, you're beautiful," he murmured.

Not certain whether she was more embarrassed by the compliment or by his indelicate reference to her freckles, she pretended indifference to both. "You couldn't see all my freckles," she said offhandedly. "It was dark."

"Who said I saw them? I *tasted* them. Freckles have a taste all their own."

Sternly suppressing the urge to laugh, Samantha rolled her eyes. "Let's hope your cooking is better than your jokes," she said. She smoothed out the covers and propped up a pillow to lean against. "Where's your plate? Aren't you eating, too?"

"I already ate. Once I smelled the food, I couldn't wait." He hesitated, then added in a suggestive drawl that caused her to blush profusely, "I worked up a monstrous appetite last night."

While Samantha enjoyed the breakfast he had made, Trey sat on a chair beside the bed and told her about his trip to Phoenix.

After listening to him tell about finding Morris Littleton's house and speaking with several people who informed him that this wasn't the first time the man had used violent tactics on tenants who fell behind on their rent, Samantha shook her head and sighed. "I guess we're right back where we started. I was just starting to believe that he didn't even exist."

Trey cradled his coffee cup between his hands. "If he didn't exist," he said slowly, "you would have to decide who has the most to gain by running you out of here."

"Richard," Samantha said without hesitation.

Trey nodded. "He'd be the logical choice, since he controls the lease."

"And collects the money," Samantha added. "That still doesn't explain the second attack on the restaurant, though. By then Mr. Littleton had received the rent money. What would he gain by having the place vandalized?"

"Your guess is as good as mine. Of course it's quite possible that Littleton wasn't behind what happened while I was gone. Maybe someone just wants it to look as if he was."

Samantha chewed on a piece of corn bread while she mulled that one over. Suddenly her brow furrowed and she stared down at the corn bread in her hand. "What did you put in this?"

"Like it?"

"It's good. It's a little sweeter than the recipe I use. And it doesn't crumble. Since Maria won't be coming back, I'll have to find a substitute for her tortillas. Mine aren't as good as hers are."

When Trey didn't respond, Samantha arched a questioning brow. "Well, are you going to divulge your secret or not?"

He drained his coffee cup and stood up. "Try bribery," he suggested, his blue-gray eyes twinkling. "It works every time."

Samantha glowered at him. "I'm sure it does," she shot back sarcastically.

"Are you finished?"

She nodded.

Trey bent down and placed a hand on either side of her on the mattress. "When I come back from seeing Joe, how would you like to go on a picnic? Just you and me."

He was so close that Samantha could smell the soap he had used to shave with. She was glad she was sitting down, because his nearness made her knees weaken. She battled back the urge to reach up and touch his tanned face. "I-I think I'd like that," she stammered, suddenly feeling as awkward and uncertain as a young girl.

"Good. Don't pack a lunch; I'll pick up something for us."

"From where?" It had never occurred to Samantha that he might prefer someone else's cooking to hers. A twinge of jealousy streaked through her.

Trey kissed her on the lips and winked at her. "You'll see." He took her tray and stood up.

Samantha scrambled out of bed as quickly as her sore muscles would allow and followed him to the kitchen. "Don't you want me to bring anything?" she asked. She was beginning to feel put out.

"Just some more of those delicious freckles," Trey said lightly. "For dessert."

Not about to be outdone, Samantha dashed in front of him, blocking his way to the sink. "I'll make a deal with you. I'll bring the freckles and you give me your corn bread recipe."

She was so innocently charming, standing there in her nightgown and bare feet, trying to bargain with him, that Trey swore she could have lured a saint into sin. He threw his head back and laughed. "*That*, sweetheart, isn't bribery. That's extortion!"

Ian Hunter lowered the binoculars and handed them back to Gaylord Whittaker. "If you want the truth," Ian said, "I think we're going to have a difficult time going in there without Stern finding out."

From where they stood on top of the hill, the two men had an unobstructed view of the original entrance to the Concha Mine. Abandoned in favor of a more accessible entrance downhill, the old hand-dug opening had been boarded shut.

"We'll get in," the older man said confidently. "If need be, we'll create a diversion."

Ian shifted uneasily. He was uncomfortable with the latest orders he and Whittaker had received from Consolidated's home office. They had been instructed to enter the mine, illegally if necessary, and determine whether the Concha contained enough high-grade ore to make it worth forcing Treyman Stern to sell. He did not like the strong-arm tactics his employer was adopting.

Still, as long as Consolidated was paying his salary, Ian felt he owed the company his loyalty. "The miners' union is planning another strike," he told Whittaker. "A big one. If Stern brings in replacements, as he did during the last strike, anyone who sees us will think we are just substitute miners."

Whittaker nodded. "I want to take a look at that drift where Lemner's crew discovered the gold. When do you think the miners will act?"

"There's another union meeting tomorrow night. Perhaps something will be decided then."

In the back of the top drawer of her dresser Samantha found the vial of perfume. She could not remember when she had last used it, since she seldom wore perfume. She removed the stopper and raised the vial to her nose, half expecting the expensive fragrance to have long since gone rancid.

To her surprise the perfume was still good. She dabbed some on the insides of her wrists and between her breasts and took a deep breath as the scent of exotic Oriental spices filled the room. She replaced the stopper and smiled to herself. Trey wasn't going to know what hit him.

She slid her chemise over her head, and her smile faded as she saw her reflection in the mirror.

Trey's earlier playful teasing about her freckles had dredged up some painful memories. As a child, she had suffered the taunts of other children because of her red hair and her freckles. When she was nine, a classmate's superstitious parents, sincerely believing Samantha had been marked by the devil, had refused to allow her to attend their daughter's birthday party.

Clutching the gift she had carefully wrapped in white tissue paper, she had run all the way home from the girl's house and burst into tears in her mother's arms. Her mother had tried to console her by telling her that freckles were angel kisses and that God must surely love her for giving her so many. It had taken every ounce of restraint she could muster not to blurt out that she didn't want angel kisses; she wanted to go to Becky Weed's birthday party.

She had finished dressing and was pinning up her hair when she heard the back door open. With her chin tucked under and several hairpins held between her lips, she went out to the kitchen, her hands deftly inserting pins into the heavy coil at the nape of her neck as she walked. She could not wait to see Trey again.

Suddenly, she stopped and snatched the hairpins from her mouth. "Richard! Don't you believe in knocking?"

Richard Winters stopped in the middle of the kitchen and drew back, a hurt expression on his face. "Darling, I was worried about you. When I found the front door locked, I went around—"

"The front door is always locked on Sundays. The restaurant is *closed*."

Richard's usual composure seemed strained. His complexion was pallid, and there were dark shadows beneath his eyes. "I need to talk to you."

Samantha steeled herself against the beseeching note in his voice. "We have nothing to discuss."

"Samantha, please. This is important. My carriage is out front. Why don't we go somewhere—"

"Richard, I'm sorry. I have other plans. Now I must ask you to leave."

Frustration flashed across Richard's face. He was nervously twisting his hat, something Samantha had never seen him do. "Just five minutes. Please?"

There was something oddly pathetic about Richard's behavior, Samantha thought uneasily. He was not his normal confident self; he seemed unusually downtrodden today. Her resistance weakened. "All right," she agreed. "Five minutes. But you must promise me you will then leave."

Richard took a deep breath. "A man with whom I do business told me something that troubled me greatly. You might not have any cause to worry, but I thought it important that you know. It's about the man you recently hired. His name isn't Smith. It's Stern. Liam Stern. He's Treyman Stern's uncle."

Chapter
Ten

TREY made three stops on Main Street to find everything he wanted. Samantha, he mused, was going to be surprised to find out that her lunch was being provided by the best gaming halls in town. Tucking the tin of smoked oysters into the basket he had borrowed from the Caledonian Saloon, he climbed up onto the buggy seat and picked up the reins. He hoped Samantha liked the items he'd selected. He wanted to make this day extra special for her.

His visit with Joe had gone well. Joe had reacted to Trey's choice of an attorney with mixed emotions. "Kendall's good, but he's not cheap," Joe had said. "And he doesn't take on charity cases. As soon as he discovers I can't afford to pay him, he'll drop me faster than a stick of dynamite with a lit fuse."

"Kendall stated his terms up front, Joe. If he loses the case, you owe him nothing. If he wins, you can pay him in installments."

Still, Joe was skeptical. "What's to stop me from skipping town and reneging on my obligations?"

"You won't."

"Kendall doesn't know that."

"No, he doesn't. What he does know, however, is that I'll cover your debt. If you skip town, you'll have to answer to me."

They talked for a few more minutes, then Joe broached a subject that was a matter of concern for both of them. "Trey, I'm worried about Samantha. That restaurant is too easy to break into. With all that has happened recently, I don't think she is safe there by herself."

A frown deepened the furrows between Trey's brows. "Do you have any idea who tore her place apart while I was away?"

Joe shook his head. "No money was taken. Whoever it was intended to give her a scare. Why, I don't know."

That could be anyone, Trey thought uneasily. He wished he had more to go on. He made a mental note to hire someone to guard the place at night. Samantha wouldn't like it, but she would have to accept it. He would sleep better knowing she was out of danger.

After leaving the jail, Trey ran a few more errands before returning to the restaurant.

He sidestepped the mud puddle he had made that morning when he emptied the bathtub into the alley and rapped on the kitchen door and went in.

Samantha was sitting at the kitchen table going over her cash journal. She looked up when he entered.

Trey set the picnic basket on the floor just inside the back door and went to the kitchen sink. "Sorry it took me so long," he said over his shoulder as he unscrewed the top of his canteen. "I had to make several stops to find everything I wanted. Are you about ready to go?" The pump creaked as he began working the handle.

Samantha closed the cash journal and slowly stood up. Her mouth was set in a thin line. "I have something to ask you," she said icily.

Trey straightened and turned to face her. A chill coursed through his veins at her taut expression. Something had happened. "Sam, what's wrong?"

She met Trey's wary gaze without wavering. "Is it true that Liam Stern came to you, looking for a job and a place to stay, and you refused him both?"

Trey felt as though the ground had just been jerked out from beneath him. How in the hell had she learned about that? He thought he'd seen and heard the last of Liam when he ordered him out of his home. But then, he sourly reminded himself, he had thought the very same thing when he left San Manuel as a sixteen-year-old kid with nothing but the clothes on his back. That itinerant uncle of his was turning out to be a recurring nightmare he could not shake.

"Is it true?" Samantha repeated curtly.

He slowly released his breath. "Yes."

The undisguised hurt that flashed across Samantha's face told Trey she had been hoping desperately that he would deny it. Her voice shook. "Why is it that every time I start to think I might have been wrong about you, that you just might be a decent human being after all, you turn around and do something to prove me wrong?"

Irritated that Samantha appeared to have already judged and condemned him, he was torn between wanting to explain the situation to her and turning around and walking out. He decided on the former. "Sam, listen to me. There is no love lost between Liam and—"

"I'm not talking about love, Trey; I'm talking about compassion for a harmless old man. When he came to me, he had been out of work for months, and he hadn't eaten since God knows when. And *you* just coldly turned him out into the streets, with no place to go."

Trey's anger escalated dangerously. His eyes smoldered. "He *had* a place, Sam. And he lost it. Do you hear me? He lost it in a poker game!"

"He is still your uncle, for God's sake!"

"He is also the same lying, conniving drunk who drove my mother to a pauper's grave!"

Surprise flashed across Samantha's face, but before she could respond, Trey circled the table and came toward her. "That's right, Sam," he said in a cold, bitter voice. "That *harmless old man* drove my mother to her grave. But not until he'd gambled away everything she had ever owned, and not until he had beaten every shred of dignity out of her."

Samantha instinctively took a step backward, fear surging through her at the blazing fury in his eyes. "Trey, I'm sorry. I didn't know."

He caught her by the shoulders, and Samantha swallowed the scream that swelled in her throat. He gave her a hard shake that caused her head to snap back. "He killed her, Sam. He killed my mother as surely as if he'd taken a gun and shot her. *He killed her!*"

Suddenly aware of the pressure he was exerting on Samantha's arms, Trey released her. He ran his fingers through his hair in a gesture of frustration, and fought to get a grip on his temper. It frightened him to realize how close he had come to snapping. The look of terror he had seen in Samantha's eyes cut deep into his heart. It was the same look he had seen in his mother's eyes time and time again when Liam had gone after her in a drunken rage. Only this time *he* had caused it. This time he was the one responsible for betraying a woman's trust. Not Liam. "Sam, I'm sorry," he said thickly. His voice shook and all color drained from his face. "I don't know what came over . . ."

Without finishing, he pivoted and strode from the building, slamming the door behind him.

Samantha rubbed her arms. She could still feel the places where his fingers had dug into her flesh. She could not stop trembling. Never in her life would she forget the sick horror she had felt when Trey seized her. She shuddered to think what might have happened had he not regained control of his temper.

Her gaze fell on the picnic basket sitting by the back door, and her throat constricted. Less than twenty-four hours ago, she had been a woman basking in the priceless warmth of feeling loved and wanted. Now . . . She didn't know what she was feeling now. She only knew that it hurt more than anything she had ever felt.

Richard's hands shook as he worked the combination to the bank's safe. The thought of that mangy bastard sitting in his office right now, waiting for him, made his blood churn. Jenkins had nearly outlived his usefulness. He was going to have to give some serious thought to planning the man's demise. Something that would not leave a trail.

He gave the lock a final turn and swung the door open. He removed a small sack of gold coins from the safe and walked calmly back to his office. He bristled.

Silas Jenkins was lounging in *his* chair, with his booted feet propped up on *his* desk, hands folded across his stomach. "This is a pretty fancy place you got here," Jenkins said, his assessing gaze traversing the room. "I could get used to this."

Richard crossed the room and tossed the sack on top of the desk. "Here's your final payment," he said stiffly. "If you think you're going to get more out of me, you are mistaken."

Jenkins lowered his feet to the floor and straightened. "I ain't asking for more than what you owe me." He pocketed the money.

"Aren't you going to count it?"

"Any reason I should?"

"No. Of course not." Richard forced a smile and changed the subject. "I still expect you to be at that union meeting tomorrow night. It was part of our agreement."

"So was killing Stern," Jenkins reminded him.

"I want you to stay away from Stern," Richard said sharply. "I have other plans for him."

Jenkins snickered. "What you really mean is that you don't want to take any chances Stern might die and leave the mine to someone you can't buy off."

"My plans for Stern are no concern of yours," Richard said quickly. Too quickly. It troubled him how often Jenkins managed to discern his motives. For a petty criminal, the man could be disturbingly astute. He abruptly changed the subject. "Do you remember what you're supposed to say at the meeting?"

With a sigh of impatience, Jenkins rose to his feet. "Suppose I go back to the hotel and rehearse my lines."

Richard's mouth tightened. One of these days Jenkins was going to push him too far. "There is no need for sarcasm. I am merely being cautious."

After Jenkins left, Richard wiped off his desk top, realigned his chair, and straightened the blotter. He was loath to touch anything that low-class vermin had contaminated. He would be relieved when he no longer required Jenkins's services.

By the time Samantha reached the mine compound, her arms ached from carrying the heavy basket. She set it on the ground and went up to the guard shack. Arnie Pitts was on duty again. Samantha swallowed her dislike of the man. "Is Mr. Stern here?" she asked.

Arnie Pitts did not look up from the newspaper he was reading. "No, ma'am. He didn't come in today."

Bewilderment furrowed Samantha's brow. Not only was

Arnie not ogling her but his manner almost passed for politeness. She wondered if Trey had spoken to him about harassing her. "Thank you, Arnie," she said warily. She turned around and went back to her basket.

This time Arnie did look up. His nostrils flared, and his eyes narrowed as he watched Samantha bend down to retrieve the basket. Bitch, he thought. She'd damned near gotten him fired, runnin' to Stern and complainin' that he'd diddled with her. One more time, Stern had warned him, and he would join the ranks of the unemployed. If he hadn't needed the money so blasted much, he would have told Stern just what he could do with his lousy job.

Samantha hoisted the basket onto her hip. If Trey wasn't at home, she decided, she would leave the basket on his doorstep. She simply didn't have the strength to carry it back into town.

All afternoon her thoughts had dwelt on the discord that had erupted between her and Trey. Until today she had never realized how much pent-up emotion Trey was holding inside him. Somehow she had always thought him immune to common vulnerability; he always seemed so strong, so invincible. Until today she had never given any thought to the type of childhood he must have endured or to the influences that had forged him into the man he was today: a little too aloof, a little too cynical, a little too—she struggled for the right word—*responsible*.

She suspected that, before today, she had only seen the side of Trey that he permitted the world to see. That there was so much more of him hidden from view both intrigued and saddened her. She did not know why he would choose to hide behind a facade that was almost cold in its impartiality. All she knew was that she felt more miserable than she had in a long time. She could not bear this new rift that had sprung up between them.

The sun was just dipping over the mountains when she reached the block of low-slung adobe buildings where Trey lived. She set the basket on the ground and knocked on his door.

There was no answer. She knocked again. A sick feeling churned in her stomach. Suddenly it became imperative that she see him, to assure herself that he was all right.

She had nearly given up hope that he was home when the door swung open.

Surprise, then wariness, registered in Trey's eyes when he saw her. The lines on his face seemed to have deepened perceptibly since this morning, and he appeared years older.

Samantha gave him a hesitant smile. "Someone promised me a picnic," she said softly. "I've come to collect."

Dismay and regret flashed across Trey's face. "Sam, don't do this," he cautioned. "It's no good."

She lifted her chin in stubborn resistance. "I won't let you shut me out, Trey," she said firmly. "You stood by me while I was working out my grief for Michael. I wouldn't be much of a friend if I abandoned you when you needed someone, now, would I?"

Trey started to shake his head. "I don't need anyone."

"Like hell you don't," Samantha shot back. "We all need someone. Even you."

The tone of fierce protectiveness in Samantha's voice made Trey's throat hurt. It didn't take much effort to visualize her jumping into a fray like a lioness to defend her cubs. Suddenly he ached to hold her. "Sam . . ." His voice broke, and he had to take a deep breath to regain control. "Would you like to sit out in the courtyard?" he finished hastily. He felt unaccountably awkward.

Understanding softened Samantha's eyes. "I'd love to."

Carrying the basket, Trey led the way through his study.

"You haven't seen this place since I shored up the walls and replaced the roof, have you?" It was easier to talk about tangible things. Things that didn't hurt.

"No, I haven't. You've done a lot of work. I'm pleasantly surprised at the outcome." She *was* surprised. When Trey had first moved into the building, it had been more of a derelict than a dwelling. Now a feeling of calmness emanated from the thick whitewashed adobe walls. The furnishings were few and uncluttered. There were no frills here, nothing to distract the mind from the enjoyment of a private refuge. That Trey's tastes so exactly mirrored her own gave her an odd feeling.

The doors to the courtyard stood open, admitting a gentle breeze and the last of the fading light. On the tile-paved terrace, huge clay pots overflowing with geraniums and marguerite daisies crowded around the door. Against the west wall an ancient bougainvillea spread its crimson-clad branches across the sand-colored adobe. Samantha wasn't certain what to make of it all. She had never thought of Trey as a man who liked tending flowers. But then, how much did she really know about him?

Trey set the basket down on an old table that had weathered to a pleasing silver-gray. "This is my favorite part of the house," he said, indicating the courtyard. "In the summer it's almost too hot out here, but in the winter it becomes a very enjoyable place to sit." He turned and nodded at the shuttered windows across the courtyard. "That place has been vacant for nearly a year. I've been trying to negotiate with the owner to sell it to me, but he keeps holding out in the hope that his daughter and son-in-law will move back to Myterra from Tucson. Someday I'd like to own this entire building."

Trey's voice had quavered slightly as he spoke, and Samantha realized with a pang that this was probably the first time he had ever spoken to anyone about his hopes and plans for the future. Trey simply wasn't accustomed to talking about himself or his dreams.

Going to him, Samantha wrapped her arms around him from behind and rested her cheek against his back. "What would you do with this place if you owned it all?"

Trey clasped her hands and held them against his torso. He absently rubbed a thumb along her wrist. "The main room across the courtyard faces east," he reflected aloud. "It's big, and the ceilings are high. I think it would make a nice kitchen. You could open the doors to the courtyard and let in the morning breeze. I'd build a ramada across the south wall, though, to break up the summer sun. And this courtyard, being protected from the street, would be a safe place for children to play."

His words conjured up such a vivid picture of domestic tranquillity that Samantha's eyes closed and a sigh escaped her. She tilted her head back and braced her chin against the muscled hollow between his shoulder blades. "Planning on a large brood?" she teased unthinkingly.

Trey stiffened. "I don't know about you," he said, abruptly changing the subject, "but I'm hungry. Pull up that chair and make yourself comfortable, and I'll get the other one from the kitchen."

Acutely aware of what she had done to break the spell of intimacy between them, Samantha asked shakily, "Shall I unpack the picnic basket?"

"If you want to. I'll be right back."

As she watched him return to the house, Samantha felt like kicking herself. Too late, she'd realized that her remark about children had touched a nerve.

But why? She racked her brain, but answers eluded her. All she knew was that something terrible must have happened for him to be so defensive about having a family.

And that something terrible was linked to Liam Stern.

Trey put on a pot of coffee while Samantha unpacked the basket and laid out the foods he had purchased earlier. There were crusty rolls stuffed with a spicy shredded-beef filling, pickled beets and tiny sweet gherkins, fancy smoked oysters, sardines in mustard sauce, dried apple turnovers, dates, soft ripe figs, and a dozen other delicacies that Samantha doubted she would have ever thought of packing for a picnic. That Trey had gone to such effort touched her deeply.

As they ate, night gradually fell, and under the anonymity of darkness, Trey gradually opened up. "Sam, I want to apologize for my outburst earlier today. Liam has always been a sore subject with me. It was unfair of me to take my anger out on you."

Trey told her what it had been like for his mother and him after his father died, and bit by bit, the unpleasant story of a household terrorized by an unpredictable drunkard unfolded. He spoke at length of his mother's suffering at his uncle's hands, of being evicted from one house after another as the rent came due and went unpaid, and of leaving a number of towns under a cloak of shame because of Liam's inability to hold down a job for long. While he barely touched on the times his uncle had beaten him, Samantha suspected that there was far more to the story than Trey was telling her. A man who would so cruelly mistreat his wife was unlikely to show any great fondness for her child.

Suddenly she understood why Trey had never married.

"It scares the hell out of me, Sam," Trey said quietly, "to think I might become like him. Earlier today, before I could regain control of my temper, I saw the fear in your eyes, and it made me sick to think what I might have done . . ." His voice trailed off.

Samantha reached across the table and placed her hand on his. "You're not like your uncle. If you were, you wouldn't have been able to stop yourself today. You would have flown into a rage, then made excuses for yourself afterward."

"You don't know that."

"Yes, I do." She didn't know how she knew; the words seemed to come from somewhere deep down inside her. "Trey, you're a warm, caring man. And I think you'd make a wonderful father. Don't let what your uncle did to you and your mother stop you from marrying and having a family of your own, if that's what you want."

Trey closed his hand around hers. For several long moments, they sat in silence, occupied with their own thoughts. When Trey finally spoke, his voice was so low that Samantha had to strain to hear him. "I've never told anyone else about Liam," he said in a thick, emotion-laced voice. "I always thought it was something I could put out of my mind and forget. But I can't. Day and night, it's always there. The pain never completely goes away. Sometimes I wonder what my mother and I ever did to deserve what Liam dished out. I've tried to forgive him, Sam, but I can't. Some things you just never forgive."

Trey tilted his head back, and a small, choked sound came from his throat as he swallowed hard. "When I was a kid, I used to lie awake at night, thinking of ways to kill him; I hated him that much. The problem was, I never had the guts. I could never get beyond wishing him dead."

Samantha had a difficult time comprehending the depth of Trey's hatred for his uncle. Her own parents had been kind, loving people. But what if they had been cruel? Could she have escaped their clutches emotionally unscathed? How many children followed in the footsteps of their elders instead of blazing their own paths? What surprised her the most was that Trey, instead of being beaten down by his uncle's cruelty, had emerged a stronger, more compassionate person because of it.

"Thank you for telling me," she said softly.

Trey turned his head to look at her. "I didn't want anyone to know. I don't know why. In ways, it just hurt too much to talk about it."

Samantha could not see his face clearly, but the anguish in his voice broke her heart. "And now that you have talked about it," she prompted gently, "does it still hurt?"

She could feel his gaze boring into her. "Yes," he said after a moment. "It still hurts. But I'm not afraid of it as I was before."

They talked awhile longer. Then the two of them cleared the table and carried the dishes into the house. "I'll dry if you'll wash," Samantha suggested.

"That's very kind of you, but it's not necessary," Trey said unevenly. He was still feeling a little shaky after baring his soul.

A laugh bubbled up in Samantha's throat. "Actually, I wasn't being kind at all. I hate to wash dishes."

When the last dish was dried and put away, Trey took Samantha home. It was a clear, pleasant night, and instead of going to the livery and hitching up the buggy, they walked at a leisurely pace. Samantha's attention was drawn to the mill's furnace stacks on the hill. "Trey, what's going to happen if Cleveland rescinds the Sherman Silver Purchase Act?"

He followed her gaze. It was on the tip of his tongue to tell her that the legislation was nothing to worry about, but he knew it would be unfair to keep the truth from her. The success of Samantha's restaurant hung on the future of silver as much as the rest of Myterra did. "I don't know," he said instead. "Most likely we'll have to cut back production. At worst, I may end up shutting down the mine completely."

And Myterra, Samantha thought, would become a ghost town.

Her brows drew together as she pondered a question that had been troubling her these past few weeks. She cast Trey a sidelong glance. "May I ask you something?"

"Certainly."

Samantha chose her words carefully. She did not want to get Miles Gilbert into hot water for revealing the mine's financial problems. "With the economy so uncertain right now, why did you pay my rent so far in advance?"

"I wanted to make certain that you were taken care of," Trey replied without hesitating.

"But for four months? Trey, if the mine shuts down, so will the restaurant. I doubt Mr. Littleton will return any of the rent money, and I'll certainly be in no position to repay you."

"No, but you'll have a roof over your head, and that's more important to me than the money."

Tears stung Samantha's eyes, and she had to blink hard to fight them back. She slipped her hand into his as they walked. "What did I ever do to deserve you?"

Trey squeezed her hand. "I keep asking myself the same thing about you."

The night sounds from Main and Union streets grew louder the closer they came to the restaurant. Samantha tried to imagine what the town would be like if all the saloons and dance halls and brothels closed down, but she could not. They had been a part of Myterra for as long as she could remember. Still, she could not honestly say she'd be sorry to see them go.

And what about her? she wondered. She had no place to go. If Myterra died, she would be left alone. And penniless.

The thought of being alone did not unduly trouble her, but it did make her wonder if her disinclination to remarry might jeopardize her chances of survival. She was realistic enough to know that what one wanted to do and what one needed to do to survive were not always compatible. Perhaps she would be wise to give some serious consideration to her future.

When they reached the restaurant, Samantha handed Trey the key and he unlocked the door. He did not open it immediately, however, but stood with his hand on the knob. "Sam, about what I told you earlier . . ." He paused to search for the right words. "The discord between Liam and me should have no bearing on how you run this place. If my uncle is doing a good job for you and you're satisfied with him, then I'll trust your judgment. I won't interfere. I promise."

Samantha knew how much it had cost Trey to make that concession, and she respected him even more because of it. "I haven't yet decided what I'm going to do about Liam," she said honestly. "With Maria gone, it's difficult to say what will happen. I can't run the place alone, and I can't pay the help much." Sensing Trey's concern, she forced a smile. He had enough on his mind without worrying about her. "I'll think of something," she said lightly. "I always do."

Trey went inside with her. While Samantha lighted a lamp, he checked out the empty building. "Everything seems to be in order," he said, returning to the kitchen. "Will you be all right here?"

She nodded. "I'll be fine."

He hesitated. "Well . . . good night."

He started toward the door, and Samantha suddenly felt as if she were on uneven footing. "Trey?"

He stopped and turned.

She nervously moistened her lips. "Would you . . . would you like to . . . stay?"

His expression was taut. "I don't think that would be a good idea, Sam. Maybe another time."

His words, no matter how kindly spoken, sent a flame of humiliation surging into her face. Her chin shot up defensively. "Of course," she said stiffly. "Another time."

For a minute Trey stared at her, wondering at her abrupt change in tone. Then, when the realization struck him, he could not suppress the rumble of laughter that welled up inside him. "Sam, if I keep baring my soul to you, my pride is likely to suffer, but the truth is, I think I overdid it last night. Much as it galls me to admit it, I'm not as young as I used to be." When he saw her expression soften, he reached for her and drew her into his arms. He had no intention of leaving until he'd had his fill of kissing her. "And you, you redheaded minx, are more woman than even I know what to do with."

Samantha hung a Temporarily Closed sign on the front door of the Drake House and went back into the kitchen. She had lain awake most of the night, grappling with her conscience: about Liam, about the restaurant, about hiring a replacement for Maria. It had been nearly morning when she finally drifted off to sleep, exhausted, but satisfied with her decisions.

Her cash journal lay open on the kitchen table. If she planned carefully, she could pay Trey back for the first month's rent and still have enough left over to buy the supplies she would need. It was a good plan, she thought, but she did not want to get her hopes up until she had made a few visits and corralled some support for the venture. She made a mental note to consult Trey before committing herself. While she would have the final say in the matter, she wanted to be certain she was not overlooking anything. If anyone could locate the weaknesses in her plan, he could.

At ten minutes before five o'clock, just as he had every working morning since she'd hired him, Liam arrived. Samantha felt a pang of guilt over what she was about to do, but she firmly forced her misgivings aside. Now that she had reached a decision, she knew she would be disappointed in herself if she did not implement it.

"Morning, Mrs. Drury," Liam said as he hung his hat just inside the kitchen door. "There's a touch of frost in the air. I don't think winter's long off."

Samantha closed her eyes and took a deep breath. Don't remind me about winter, she thought guiltily.

"You all right, Mrs. Drury?"

Samantha's eyes flew open. A sick feeling churned in her stomach. Now that she knew of Liam's relationship to Trey, the familial resemblance seemed to jump out at her. She had always thought there was something familiar about Liam; now that she knew why, she could not understand why she hadn't figured it out before. "Yes, I'm fine," she said shakily.

Liam shifted nervously from one foot to the other. "I saw the sign out front. I take it you're closing down until you can get more help?"

Samantha was torn between staring at the once-handsome face that was both familiar and strange to her, and looking away in revulsion. Images flashed through her mind of a vulnerable woman and a defenseless little boy whose lives had been cruelly shattered, and any sympathy she might have felt for Liam Stern withered and died.

She sucked in her breath and squared her shoulders. "My plans for the restaurant don't concern you, Mr. Stern," she said stiffly. "I'm giving you two weeks' advance wages. As of today you no longer work here."

Chapter
Eleven

IT took Liam a moment to realize that she'd used his real name instead of his assumed one, and when the truth finally registered, the surprise on his face hardened into a grimace of antagonism. "So the ungrateful bastard's been turnin' your ear," he spat. "He always was a troublemaker, that kid. I tried like hell to make him follow the straight and narrow, but he was so damned thickheaded—"

"Mr. Stern, what happened between you and your nephew is no concern of mine. What does trouble me, however, is the fact that you lied to me. If you can't even be truthful about your name, how can you expect me to trust you?"

"If I'd told you my name, you wouldn't have hired me!" Liam protested.

"Possibly not. But that, Mr. Stern, was my decision to make, not yours to tamper with. I've written you a letter of reference, attesting to the fact that you were hardworking and dependable during the time you were in my employ. It does, however, refer to you by your legal name. I wouldn't recommend trying to deceive anyone else."

The cold, hard look in Liam's eyes sent a chill through Samantha's veins. He took the money and the letter she held out to him and, without another word, turned and stalked from the building.

Completely drained, Samantha slumped down on a chair. She braced her elbows on the table and lowered her head into her hands. Her heart was beating so fast it hurt.

The decision to fire Liam had not been an easy one to make. He had been a good employee, even if she had never felt completely comfortable with him. But no matter how hard she tried, she could not ignore the years of misery he had caused Trey and his mother. Her decision had been based strictly on principle, and those were often the hardest decisions to make because they were seldom rooted in practicality. She had an uneasy feeling that this decision was going to come back to haunt her.

All morning long she planned and made lists. Sarah Morrissey returned, and Samantha put her to work taking inventory of everything in the pantry. The two women talked little as they worked, but every now and then their gazes met and held while they waited out the persistent pounding on the front door. "This is the first time in all the years I've lived here that I can remember the Drake House being closed on a weekday," Sarah commented. "I guess no one knows quite what to make of it."

Samantha gave her a wan smile and tried to ignore the knocking. She had instructed Sarah not to answer the door; once they started doing that, they would not be able to get any work done.

At midmorning, Sarah went home to check on her children, and Samantha headed into town. By the time she finished her business and started up the hill toward the mine, excitement shone in her eyes and had heightened her color. This would work. She *knew* it would.

Arnie Pitts was not on guard duty. Paddy Sweeny gave her a heartfelt welcome. "Haven't seen you in a month of Sundays," he said, grinning. "You're lookin' mighty fine, lass, if I might say so."

Samantha thanked him and entered her name in the log. "Why are you on duty now, Paddy? Did you ask to be taken off the night shift?"

"Nah. Pitts didn't show up this morning, so I stayed on for an extra shift."

"Surely you're not going to work your regular shift tonight?" Samantha asked. "You must be exhausted."

He winked at her and said conspiratorially, "Time and a half makes anything sweeter, lass. Davy Collins is fillin' in for me tonight."

After she finished signing in, Samantha hurried up to the mine's administrative building.

Miles Gilbert jumped to his feet when she entered the office. He pushed his spectacles up on his nose and stared at her in surprise. "Good morning—I mean, good afternoon, Mrs. Drury. Is there something I can do for you?"

"I'd like to see Mr. Stern, if he's here."

No sooner had she spoken than Trey emerged from his office, his brows drawn together in concern. "I thought I heard your voice. Is everything all right?"

"Everything is fine. May I talk with you a moment?"

Trey stepped aside and motioned her into his office. Suppressing a smile of amusement at the curious stare that Miles Gilbert gave her as she crossed the room, she went into Trey's office.

He shut the door behind them. "Why aren't you at the restaurant? What happened?"

Samantha laughed. "Nothing happened. I just wanted to see you. Actually, I need to see your accounting books. I want to make some changes at the restaurant, and I need to be certain I'm going about everything the right—"

She broke off as Trey's hand clamped on her shoulder. He turned her around and drew her toward him. "Come here, woman," he said huskily.

Samantha slid her arms around his waist and raised her lips to his. "I missed you last night," she whispered against his mouth.

He folded his arms around her, securing her in his protective embrace, and his lips were firm and coaxing as they caressed hers with slow, shivery kisses that melted through Samantha's limbs like warm, sweet honey. When he finally pulled away, he kissed the tip of her nose, her eyelids, her forehead, before drawing her closer against him and holding her as tightly as he could without hurting her. He buried his face in her hair. "Damn, you feel good," he murmured thickly.

Samantha sighed and closed her eyes. Beneath her cheek she could feel the steady, comforting beat of his heart, and she thought nothing would make her happier than to stay here in his arms forever.

Trey chuckled softly. "Do you know how hard it is to get any work done with you on my mind?" he asked. "I've been damned near useless all morning."

Samantha tilted her head back to look at him with glowing eyes. "*I've* had a very productive morning," she boasted.

Releasing her, Trey listened attentively while she told him her idea. "I've been promised the use of a wagon and a team for two dollars a day. Jack Petrie has agreed to supply all the ice I need, and Mr. Mason will keep us stocked with all the bottled mineral water and Hire's herb tea we can sell. With a little bit of planning, I can turn as good a profit as I do now, but with less work. I'll continue serving breakfast at the Drake House, since it's my big money-maker, but after that, I'll lock the doors for the rest of the day and start preparing for the midday dinner deliveries. The supper rush barely pays for itself, so I will discontinue it entirely."

The more Trey heard of Samantha's plan to take the midday meals to her customers rather than have them flock to the restaurant, the more he liked it, but for purely selfish reasons. While he had never been completely comfortable with the idea of Samantha waiting on tables and catering to the rowdy miners who frequented the restaurant, he now felt a new protectiveness toward her. The suggestive remarks and ribald jokes, about women in general and often about Samantha in particular, that had punctuated the miners' conversations for as long as he could remember now aroused a dangerous fury in him. He would feel better knowing she was not trapped in that building with no one to turn to for help, should anything happen. "Who will drive the wagon?" he asked.

"I will, until I can hire someone to do it for me." Samantha sighed and added wearily, "I don't know what's wrong with me. I suppose I'm getting tired of dealing with customers all day long."

As she spoke, a disquieting feeling nagged at the back of Trey's mind. The logical person to drive the wagon would be Liam, and Samantha had not said one word about him. His eyes narrowed. "Where's Liam?"

"He no longer works for me," she said, not quite meeting his gaze. She opened her reticule and removed several bank notes. "Before I forget, I have something for you," she continued hastily. "It's the first installment on what I owe you. If I plan carefully, I should be able to pay you—"

"Sam, look at me."

Her heart missed a beat. She knew there was no avoiding this conversation, no matter how much she longed to do so. She nervously moistened her lips. "I did what I thought was best," she said in a low voice. She shifted uneasily and looked away.

"Sam . . ." Trey placed two fingers beneath her chin and tilted her face up.

Not quite certain how Trey was going to react to the news that she had fired his uncle, no matter how much he professed to hate him, Samantha felt a sick churning in the pit of her stomach as she met Trey's searching gaze.

There was a touch of sadness behind the gentle understanding in Trey's eyes. "Sam, if I'd known how this was going to affect you, I would have never—"

Samantha placed her fingertips on his lips, silencing him. "Trey, don't. I made the decision; I'll take responsibility for it."

He clasped her hand and pressed a kiss into her palm. "I'd feel better if you hadn't acted so hastily," he said. "Maybe I was wrong and you were right about Liam. Maybe he has changed over the years and I've just been too closed-minded to see it."

He's changed so much there wasn't even a spark of remorse in his eyes when I confronted him, Samantha thought cynically. She lifted her chin stubbornly. "Trey, it wasn't an easy decision for me to make, and I assure you I didn't reach it in haste. I did what I felt in my heart was right. I did it . . ." I did it because I love you, she thought. She took a deep breath. "It's done, and I'd rather not discuss it any further," she finished.

Trey inclined his head in acceptance, but the troubled look that clouded his eyes did not go away.

They talked for a while longer about Samantha's plans for changing the restaurant to a meal-delivery service. Trey voiced his support, made suggestions, and even offered to spread the word among the miners. He also recommended several former miners whose injuries had cost them their jobs, but who still might be able to drive the wagon for her, and Samantha promised to contact them.

"Take this back until you get the business going." Trey tried to give her the rent money she had just paid him. "Once you're on your feet and running, then you can pay me."

Samantha firmly shook her head and refused to accept the money. "I'm going to do it right this time," she said. "That means no unnecessary debts and no careless record-keeping."

And no more handouts, she added silently. She was tired of being taken advantage of by people who knew her to be easily swayed by a woeful tale. She lifted her chin and arched a brow at him. "Speaking of record-keeping, I seem to recall *someone* insinuating that I didn't know what I was doing and needed help setting up my accounts properly," she teased.

A twinkle crept into Trey's eyes. "Oh, really?"

Samantha nodded. "In fact," she continued in a playful tone, "that *someone* said he was going to help me get my books in order whether I wanted his assistance or not."

"Overbearing brute, isn't he?"

"Extremely." A choked giggle belied Samantha's poker-faced solemnity. "But he kisses very well." She hesitated, then added mischievously, "Among other things."

Several minutes later, with Samantha's lips throbbing and her color high from being kissed senseless, they went back out into the main office.

Trey hunkered down before a bookcase and removed several books. "This one is for cash receipts," he said, handing Samantha a tall, thin leather-bound volume. "Your general disbursements and payroll disbursements are recorded in separate journals. And this one," he continued, removing yet another volume, "is the ledger in which you enter the totals from your journals and calculate your profit or loss. Gilbert, may I borrow a pencil and tablet?"

"Certainly, Mr. Stern."

Before Miles could give Trey the items he had asked for, the front door opened and Ian Hunter entered the building with Richard Winters on his heels. "We're here to see Stern," Ian said. "Is he in?"

Trey rose to his feet. "I'm here."

Ian's gaze remained riveted on Samantha for a moment before returning to Trey. "I'm sorry," he said hastily. "I didn't realize you were with someone." His gaze drifted back to Samantha. "Mrs. Drury, I believe? You may not remember me, but your husband and I—"

"I remember you, Mr. Hunter. It's nice to see you again." Samantha inclined her head toward Richard, and her stomach turned over at his pained expression. "You, too, Mr. Winters." She lowered her gaze and pretended to study the journal in her hands. She could feel rather than see Richard staring at her. Her hands shook as she turned the pages.

The tension between Samantha and Richard did not go unnoticed. Trey and Ian exchanged glances. Miles Gilbert ducked his head and suddenly appeared to be concentrating very hard on the figures before him. Trey touched Samantha's elbow. "Sam, do you object? This shouldn't take long."

Samantha's bright smile failed to disguise the distress in her eyes. "I don't object. I'll just look through these books, if it's all right with you."

Trey's expression softened in understanding. "Of course it's all right. If you have any questions, Gilbert should be able to help you."

The two men followed Trey into his office. The door closed after them, and Samantha released her breath in a whoosh. She had not realized she was holding it.

Miles glanced up at her from his desk. "Are you all right, Mrs. Drury?"

Seeing Richard had upset Samantha more than she had realized it would. She hadn't quite overcome her suspicion that Richard had told her about Liam Stern, not out of concern for her welfare, but in an attempt to drive a wedge between her and Trey. She was beginning to wonder why she had ever even contemplated marrying the man.

She took a deep breath. "I'm fine, Miles," she replied shakily. "Really I am."

She wondered just whom she was trying to convince.

Armed with a pencil and tablet, Samantha sat on a stool at the counter that separated Miles Gilbert's desk from the entrance door and looked through the books Trey had lent her, occasionally pausing to take notes or to ask Miles a question when an entry wasn't clear. It was difficult to concentrate on what she was reading. The voices coming from Trey's office were just loud enough to make her aware of the men's presence but not loud enough for her to comprehend what they were saying. They did not distract her so much as they aroused her curiosity.

Suddenly the door to Trey's office opened. Richard came out and closed it quietly behind him. He went to the counter where Samantha was sitting. "Darling?"

Samantha bristled. She had hoped Richard would not make a point of speaking with her. That he would address her with an endearment annoyed her, especially since Miles Gilbert was within earshot. Trying to be nonchalant about the matter, she marked her place on the page with a forefinger and looked up.

Richard looked as if he had not been sleeping well. His expression was taut. The skin beneath his eyes was creased and shadowed, and his complexion was sallow. Even his fair hair seemed to have lost its usual luster. Samantha felt a twinge of pity for him.

Richard gave her a wan smile. "You look beautiful," he said in a low voice. "I've missed you."

"Richard, please. This is neither the time nor the place—"

"We need to talk."

Samantha shook her head. "Richard, I can't. I'm busy."

"Have luncheon with me."

"No."

"Darling, please. This is terribly important to me. I will not trouble you again after this, I promise."

Samantha rubbed one hand across her brow in frustration. "You're making this extremely difficult," she said, attempting unsuccessfully to keep the pique from her voice. "Why can't you just take no for an answer?"

"For God's sake, Samantha!" Richard blurted out, his voice rising. "We were going to be married! Have you no regard at all for the love we once shared?"

Miles Gilbert lifted his head to stare at them.

It was all Samantha could do not to blurt out to Richard that she had never loved him, but she bit back the remark. Perhaps she should have lunch with him and settle this between them once and for all.

She snapped the journal shut. Annoyance hardened the light in her eyes. "All right, Richard, I'll have lunch with you. But I want you to promise you'll leave me alone after that."

"Of course, darling. Whatever you wish."

Samantha returned the account books to Miles. "I think I have everything I need," she said. "Please tell Mr. Stern I said thanks for letting me see them."

Miles stood up. "I will, Mrs. Drury. Will that be all?" He glanced from Samantha to Richard and back again, then shifted uncomfortably.

Tell Trey I love him, Samantha thought. "Yes, that will

be all. May I call on you again if I have any questions?"

"It will be my pleasure, Mrs. Drury."

The minute Richard left the office, Trey rounded on Ian Hunter and leveled an accusing finger at him. "If I didn't like you personally, Ian," he ground out between clenched teeth, "I would have you escorted from the premises and barred from reentering."

Ian's jaw tightened. "I can't say that I blame you. But the terms are Consolidated's, not mine. All I'm doing is relaying the message. Don't take your venom out on me."

"Who brought Winters in on this?" Trey demanded.

Ian leaned forward in his chair and rested his forearms along his thighs. "Whittaker," he answered honestly. "The two had dinner the other night and took an instant liking to each other."

Trey muttered an oath under his breath. He left the window and sat down at his desk. He was well aware that having the railroad come through Myterra would be the best thing ever to happen to the town. Unlike those who resisted progress and the resulting changes, he *wanted* the railroad to come into Myterra. Instead of hauling the silver by mule-drawn wagons through the mountains to San Manuel, they would be able to ship it directly to the smelters in San Francisco.

Still, he didn't have access to the kind of money Southern Pacific was demanding, and he absolutely refused to accept a loan from Richard Winters, no matter how tempting the offer was. He leaned back in his chair and eyeballed the man sitting across from him. His brows were drawn together, and there was a hard glint in his eyes. "When do you need my decision?"

"Southern Pacific has given us until the middle of November to respond. I'd rather not wait that long, though. There is too great a chance they may withdraw their offer."

Trey swore inwardly. "What will happen if I refuse your terms?"

Surprise flickered across Ian's face. "You'd do that?"

"I might."

Ian studied his hands. He had hoped it wouldn't come to this. He did not like being the go-between in what had already become an unfairly weighted game. "Consolidated wants the Concha," Ian said in a low voice.

"What will happen?" Trey repeated slowly, deliberately.

"If forced, Consolidated is prepared to put up the entire cost of bringing the railroad into Myterra."

"But . . . ?"

Ian took a long, unsteady breath. "Ore from the Concha will cease to be accepted into the mill for processing. Nor will you be permitted to use the railroad to ship it elsewhere."

Trey stared at the other man long and hard. "In that case, I might as well just terminate everyone and shut the mine down," he said bitterly.

Ian glanced up at him. "Or sell out."

"You're not eating," Richard prodded gently. "Perhaps you'd rather have something besides the capon?"

Samantha put down her knife and fork and dabbed her napkin on her lips. "Richard, why did you insist on bringing me here? I told you I don't like this place."

He studied her with hurt bewilderment. "The Silver Queen Hotel has the best restaurant in town," he protested.

"The most elegant, you mean."

"Is there something wrong with that?"

Samantha leaned forward and whispered angrily, "Yes, there is something wrong with it. I don't belong here. Look around you, Richard. Everyone is dressed up, and

I'm wearing a faded cotton shirtwaist."

"But you look lovely, darling."

"I look out of place."

Richard sighed and pushed back his chair. "Shall we go somewhere else?" he asked.

There was a definite challenge in his eyes that told Samantha he expected her to back down. She knew she was being belligerent, but she no longer cared. He'd monopolized her time for the past hour, yet had not bothered to explain why it was so imperative that he speak with her. She placed her napkin on the table. "Yes."

Displeasure flickered in Richard's eyes and was gone. Forging his expression into an agreeable mask, he stood up and circled the table to pull out her chair. He remained conspicuously silent, however, and Samantha suspected he was having a difficult time controlling his temper.

It was not until they were safely within the confines of Richard's carriage that he finally spoke his mind. "May I ask why you are indulging in this childish behavior?" he asked. He snapped the reins, causing the horses to surge forward with a start.

Regaining her balance, Samantha folded her hands on her lap and stared straight ahead. "For the same reason you indulged in it back at the mine," she said tersely. "It's highly effective, isn't it?"

She felt rather than saw Richard stiffen beside her. "I suppose I owe you an apology," he conceded.

Samantha said nothing.

Richard turned his attention to the street, and neither of them spoke again until they reached the restaurant.

Richard reined in the team. "I spoke with Mr. Littleton."

Samantha had been about to climb down from the carriage. She stopped and turned an apprehensive gaze on Richard as foreboding touched an icy finger to her spine.

"Knowing how much the restaurant means to you," Richard continued in a low, emotionless voice, "I had previously made arrangements to purchase the Drake House from him. It was to have been my wedding gift to you."

Samantha felt as if Richard had just landed his fist between her eyes. All color drained from her face. She stared at him in disbelief, anger and uncertainty knotting inside her. Just when had Richard purchased the building? According to what he had told both her and Trey, Morris Littleton should still be out of town. She felt as if she had just been manipulated into a corner. "When did you do all this?" she asked unevenly.

Richard evaded the question. "I know this must be awkward for you, darling," he put in hastily. "At the time it never occurred to me that you might turn down my proposal. I still love you, Samantha; I always will. And I certainly don't want you to feel obligated to me in any way. But I still want you to have the restaurant. It is my way of thanking you for the months of enjoyment your company gave me."

As he spoke, Samantha felt her temper rapidly building. She knew exactly why Richard had bought the restaurant; as always, he was trying to buy her loyalty and affection. "Trey paid my rent for several months in advance," she said shakily. "What became of that money?"

"There is no need to trouble your pretty head with that, darling; it's already been taken care—"

"I asked you a question, Richard. Where is the money?"

"The money has already been returned to Mr. Stern," Richard said, a note of weary indulgence in his voice. "I had the funds deposited in his bank account this morning."

Samantha gripped the edge of the carriage seat. She wasn't certain if she was more relieved that she no longer owed Trey such a vast sum, or angered at Richard's meddling in her life.

"I don't want to hurt you, Richard, but I don't know how to make my feelings any clearer to you without being blunt. I do not love you. I do not want to marry you. I do not want—"

"Samantha dearest, I am not trying to coerce you into marrying me, if that's what you—"

"Damn it, let me finish," Samantha blurted out, trying to corral her seesawing emotions. "I do not want any more gifts from you. Not even the restaurant. Do you understand me?"

"Samantha, it was merely a token of my—"

"Clean out your ears, Richard, and listen to me. *No more gifts!*"

He drew back slightly, pain and rejection frozen on his face. "I—I don't know what to say," he stammered.

Samantha gathered up her skirts and started to rise. "Unless it's 'good-bye' I don't want to hear it." No sooner were the words out of her mouth than she wished she could take them back. She reached out to touch his hand, and he started as if she'd stabbed him. The raw hurt in his eyes made her feel guilty. "Richard, I'm sorry. I didn't mean to be cruel. I just . . . I just want to put some distance between us for the time being." She took a deep breath. "I'll move my belongings out of the Drake House as soon as I find another place. You've made it impossible for me to stay here any longer."

He turned his head away and swallowed several times. He said nothing.

Knowing that anything else she said would only worsen matters, Samantha climbed down from the carriage. Richard drove off without speaking, leaving her standing in the middle of the street.

Samantha rubbed one hand across her brow and sighed wearily. There was a terrible ache in the middle of her chest, and she felt like crying. She felt terrible about hurting

Richard, but she also felt resentful that Richard was able to manipulate her so easily through guilt.

She also had a new problem on her hands. What was she going to do about the restaurant?

By the time Trey left the mine compound, he was as light-headed and weak-kneed as he had been in the first days after he was shot. He felt as if the ground had suddenly opened up, creating a chasm beneath him, into which he was in danger of falling. He felt as if he no longer had control over his own life.

If the Consolidated Silver Corporation's previous attempts to insinuate its way into the Concha had annoyed him, this most recent ploy made him outright furious, because its ultimate intent was to drive him out of business. Working with the Southern Pacific Railroad, Consolidated had agreed to put up half the capital needed to bring the railroad through Myterra if the Concha Mine would put up the other half. If he refused, he would be barred from doing business with any of Consolidated's holdings, the railroad and the mill included. His only alternatives were to agree to merge with Consolidated Silver or to accept a loan from the First Territorial Bank, a loan that would effectively put him under Richard Winters's control. The first option he found ethically compromising. The second, repugnant.

When he reached the restaurant, he drove around to the alley and climbed down from the buggy. The back door was propped open with a brick. At least Samantha had made it home all right, he thought. He'd been worried when he'd heard that Winters had pressured her into leaving the Concha with him.

The kitchen was in utter chaos. Packing crates, loaded with dishes and pans and cooking utensils, stood in the middle of the floor. The few clothes that Samantha owned were draped across the kitchen table. The place looked as if someone were just moving in. Or out.

Samantha backed out of the pantry. Her face was flushed and her hair was askew, and she muttered an oath under her breath as she swept spilled rice onto a sheet of newspaper that she had plastered to the floor by dampening one edge. All afternoon, she had fumed over Richard's purchase of the Drake House. At times she had been so angry she'd wanted to throw something; at other times she had been on the verge of tears. Richard Winters's "love" for her was becoming an obsession she did not know how to deal with.

"What's going on here?" Trey demanded.

Samantha whirled around. She had not realized Trey was there. His patronizing tone did nothing to calm her frazzled nerves. "What does it look like?" she shot back. "I'm moving out."

"You're *what?*"

Realizing that she was unfairly punishing Trey for something that was not of his doing, Samantha immediately felt contrite. She propped the broom against the wall and dragged her sleeve across her forehead. "I'm sorry. I didn't mean to bark at you. I'm just so furious right now, I can't think clearly."

She was so distraught that she failed to see the strain in the fatigued lines of Trey's face. Bending down to fold the paper around the debris, she continued angrily, "Richard bought this place from Morris Littleton. He said he was going to give it to me for a wedding present, although I'm finding that awfully difficult to believe. He hates this place. It was the one thing that kept me from accepting his offer of marriage. He didn't want me to work here, and I did. We fought about it continually."

She bunched up the newspaper and placed it on the drainboard by the sink. "Whatever his reasons, I'm having none of it. I told him in no uncertain terms that he has made it impossible for me to stay here."

As she talked, Trey felt as if steel bands were closing around his chest. Perspiration beaded across his forehead. "Where will you go?" he asked. His voice sounded unnaturally hollow.

Samantha dusted her hands off on her apron. "I don't know, and I don't care," she said hotly. "If I have to, I'll sleep on the street. Richard Winters is going to have to get it through that hard head of his that he can't control my life. I told him I was moving out, and that's precisely what I intend to do."

Something in Trey snapped. "Damn it, Samantha! I have enough on my mind without having to worry about you, too! Don't you ever think before you act?"

Samantha froze at the biting fury in his voice. She stared at him, unable to move, her mind reeling from his outburst. His harsh words had struck her like a blow, delivering criticism when she wanted sympathy. She felt betrayed.

An uneasy silence hung over the room like a thick, choking cloud.

Trey raked his long fingers through his hair and pressed his fingertips against his closed eyes. He shook his head. "Forgive me," he said slowly. "I had no right to shout at you."

Samantha defensively folded her arms across her chest. Her throat ached, and she felt dangerously close to bursting into tears. She stared at the floor.

Trey started toward her, and Samantha's head shot up. Hurt and anger glittered in the tears that pooled in her eyes. "Stay away from me," she said hoarsely.

Heedless of her command, Trey went to her anyway. Taking her by the shoulders, he drew her stiff-backed, unyielding form against him, then folded his arms around her. "Forgive me," he whispered into her hair.

Samantha could feel his large body trembling, and she had to fight even harder against the tears that threatened. Her throat tightened. "I hate it when we argue," she said in a raw, emotion-filled voice.

Trey's arms tightened around her. "Forgive me?" he asked again, and there was so much aching uncertainty in his voice that Samantha nearly lost control. Unable to speak, she unfolded her arms and wrapped them around Trey's waist. They held on to each other with a gentle fierceness, letting their touch heal the wounds their words had caused.

Later, after they had eaten a light supper, they sat at the kitchen table and talked. Trey told her what had happened at the mine earlier, and Samantha felt his anguish. "I don't know what to do, Sam," he said. "If I sell out, I'll feel as if I'm letting the miners down. On the other hand, if I accept that loan from Winters . . ."

He left the sentence unfinished.

A heavy weariness settled over Samantha. She felt guilty for thinking only of herself when Trey was faced with a decision that could affect the life of nearly everyone in Myterra. She reached across the table and touched his hand, and his strong fingers closed around hers. "Tomorrow morning I'll go to the bank and tell Richard I'll stay in the restaurant." She shook her head when Trey started to object. "You were right; I did act impulsively," she said. "I'll have Richard draw up a new lease on the restaurant, only this time it will be on a month-to-month basis. In the meantime, I'll look for another place to rent. I don't want you worrying about me. I'll be fine."

There was a touch of sadness in the gratitude that filled Trey's eyes. "You don't mind staying here for a while longer?"

I'd do damn near anything for you, Samantha thought. She smiled sheepishly. "I'd be lying if I said I didn't mind."

Trey lifted her hand to his mouth and brushed his lips across the backs of her knuckles. "You know, Sam, after days like this, all I want is to go somewhere where no one knows me and start over. I often wonder what's stopping me."

Their gazes met and held. Samantha saw the torment in Trey's eyes and she wished she could say something to comfort him. "We can't run away from our problems," she said softly. "Somehow they always manage to catch up with us."

Trey thought of Liam, and bitter bile filled his mouth. His mouth tightened.

Sensing the sudden change in his mood, Samantha placed her napkin beside her plate and stood up. "What we can do, however," she said, circling to his side of the table, "is try to escape them for a while."

Trey did not miss her suggestive tone. He pushed his chair away from the table and drew her down onto his lap. "Are you trying to seduce me?" he teased.

Samantha slid her fingers into the dark waves at the nape of his neck and lowered her head to his. "Yes."

Even as he surrendered to the sweet warmth of her kiss, a part of Trey's mind remained warily detached. He could not help wondering what else could go wrong.

Dieter Vogel raised his hands, signaling for silence in the noisy union hall. "These disruptions must cease," he said sternly, eyeing with derision the miner who had sparked the last wave of dissension. "We will accomplish nothing unless we present a united front."

"Who's going to feed our families?" another miner demanded to know. "Your fancy words don't mean a thing when the young'uns bellies are empty."

John Ruskin nodded in agreement. "He's right, Vogel. Guarantee food on our tables, and we'll back the strike. Otherwise you're going to have to count me out."

"Quit bein' such a sissy-pants, Ruskin," Marty Dennison bit out. "If you want something bad enough, you gotta be willing to pay for it. No one's gonna hand it to you on a china plate."

"I won't starve my family for the sake of a strike," another man shouted.

"Gentlemen, gentlemen, please!" Vogel glared at the men. "This squabbling is getting us nowhere. The fact is, we are all going to have to endure temporary discomfort. But isn't what we are fighting for worth the sacrifice?"

"Is money the only thing standin' in the way of a strike?"

In the sudden hush that fell over the room, everyone turned to see who had spoken. "Who the hell are you?" Marty Dennison demanded.

Silas Jenkins ignored Dennison. His penetrating gaze was fixed on Vogel.

Dieter Vogel studied the other man as if sizing him up. "I do not believe we have met," he said cautiously. "Who are you?"

"I asked you a question, mister. 'Is money your problem?'"

"Lack of it would be more accurate," Carl Lemner supplied.

In the strained silence that followed, Jenkins frowned and idly pretended to be studying his nails. The miners shifted uneasily as the tension in the room quickly mounted. Everyone stared at Jenkins, waiting to see what he would do next. Finally Jenkins dropped his hand. "Suppose I tell you I know someone who is willing to fund the strike?"

A stir rippled throughout the crowd.

Recognition flickered in Marty Dennison's eyes, and his ruddy complexion paled as he stared at Jenkins. What was *he* doing here?

Dieter Vogel's eyes narrowed. He was shrewd enough to know that Jenkins was not likely to reveal his source. "For how long?" he asked instead.

Jenkins folded his arms across his chest and looked Vogel straight in the eyes. "For as long as it takes."

Chapter
Twelve

AS sleep gradually left her, Samantha became aware of a delicious heat spreading through her limbs, making her feel as if she were floating on a warm, liquid cloud. A callused hand—part of the dream, yet infinitely more real than the dream—caressed her breast with a rough tenderness that made every nerve in her body ache with desire. She sighed contentedly and stretched, her fogged mind clinging to the dream in a desperate attempt to keep it from slipping away.

Something warm and wet fastened around her nipple, wringing a gasp from her as the erotic sensations condensed into sharp stabs of pleasure. Her eyes flew open, and the dream evaporated.

Trey pressed a kiss to the hardened bud and lay back down beside her, his head propped in his hand. His other hand stilled on her breast. "Good morning, sleepyhead," he teased huskily.

"What time is it?"

"Five-thirty."

Samantha grimaced. "You awoke me in the middle of a dream."

Trey chuckled. "It must have been some dream. You were purring like a kitten."

Samantha curled up against Trey. "Just a few more minutes," she mumbled against his chest.

He drew up the blankets and tucked them around her. "I enjoyed last night."

The corners of Samantha's mouth curved into a sleepy smile. "Mmmm . . ."

His hand slid beneath the covers to stroke her hip. "You're purring again."

Samantha tilted her head back and rested her chin against Trey's chest. Her eyes were closed. "You don't sound groggy. You sound as if you've been awake for a while."

"I've been thinking about the restaurant."

"What about it?"

"You know the empty house that adjoins mine, the one that's been boarded up?"

"Mmmm?"

"If the owner won't sell right now, he might consider renting to me. It would be a good place for the restaurant; it's close to the mine, and there's enough room for a small dining area."

Samantha's sleep-drugged mind grappled with the suggestion. "Where would I stay?" she asked.

"There are sufficient rooms in the place for you to set up living quarters for yourself. Or you could stay with me."

A laugh rumbled in Samantha's throat. "The gossips would have a field day."

"They wouldn't if we were married."

Samantha stiffened. Suddenly awake, she pushed away from Trey and sat up. "If this is your idea of a joke, it's not funny."

Trey rose up on one elbow. "Do you think I'm joking?"

It hurt to breathe. Samantha felt as if she were suffocating. "I-I'll go put on a pot of coffee," she stammered. She rolled to her feet and snatched her wrapper off the foot of the bed in a single unbroken movement.

"Sam, wait."

Samantha fled the room.

By the time she reached the kitchen, she was shaking. She pulled on her wrapper and tied the belt with trembling hands. She did not know what had come over her. Trey's mention of marriage had caused something inside her to snap, and she didn't know why. Even Richard's proposal had not affected her like that. But then, she had not loved Richard. She loved Trey, and for no fathomable reason, that made the prospect of marrying him even more frightening. She wrapped her arms around her middle, squeezed her eyes shut, and tried to stop shaking. She didn't understand what was happening to her. She felt as if she were being forced to confront something she had long been avoiding, although she could not explain exactly what.

Trey came into the kitchen. He had donned his pants, but his feet were bare and he was shirtless. After going to Samantha, he took her by the shoulders and turned her around. He cupped her chin firmly in one hand and tilted her face up toward his. He strained to see her face in the darkness. "Sam, what's wrong? What are you afraid of?"

Her throat tightened. Of loving you too much, she thought. She swallowed hard. "I-I don't know."

Trey let his fingers slide into her hair. "It scares me, too, Sam," he said gently. "It's not easy for me, knowing I can't even guarantee that I'll be a good husband and father. All I can promise is that I'll do my damnedest not to repeat the mistakes my uncle made."

Samantha shook her head. "This is all so . . . sudden."

"Is it?"

While the forefront of Samantha's mind screamed *yes*, a tiny, nagging voice deep down inside her told her she had known all along that the threads of her life were inseparably woven among those of Trey's. Married or not, it was impossible to imagine living without him. Still, she needed more time to think. "Trey, I only recently stopped seeing Richard, and I'm not ready to—"

"Sam, I'm not Richard Winters. I don't want to control your life. I won't make you give up the restaurant and I won't interfere in how you run it—" Trey broke off suddenly as he felt, rather than saw, Samantha's disbelief. A rueful smile touched his lips. "Yes," he admitted, "I did try to interfere, and I'm sorry. I don't know why I did it; I think I was reacting out of fear that you would slip through my fingers again."

Samantha became very still. "Again?" she whispered.

Trey took a deep breath. "I love you, Sam. I've loved you for a long time. It just took me a while to realize it."

Poignantly aware of how her own perception of love had changed over the years, Samantha turned her head slightly and pressed her cheek against Trey's hand. "There are no fireworks, are there?" she asked in sympathetic understanding.

"No fireworks," he agreed. "And no stars."

Standing in the darkened kitchen, exchanging feelings instead of caresses, Samantha felt even closer to Trey than she had when they were making love. Her heart was beating so loudly she wondered if Trey could hear it. "What did you find instead?" she prompted softly.

Trey thought a moment before answering. "That few things in life bring greater pleasure than waking up next to your best friend."

That he considered her his best friend touched something deep inside her. "I love you, too. I think I always have."

"Will you marry me?"

"Suppose I promise to think about it?"

"I can live with that." Even though he knew it was unrealistic to expect an immediate answer, Trey had to fight to keep the disappointment from his voice. After untying the belt at Samantha's waist, he slid the wrapper off her shoulders and lowered his head.

"What are you doing?" Samantha asked, although she already knew the answer. She closed her eyes and allowed her head to fall back as Trey's lips moved down her throat. While she had a hundred chores to do before daybreak, she did not want this moment to end.

Trey cupped her breasts in his large hands and gently stroked the sensitive peaks with his thumbs as his lips moved down her throat. "Influencing your decision," he murmured.

If Joe had met Perry Kendall on the street, he would not have given the attorney a second glance. As it was, he was having a difficult time believing that this wizened little man with his squinting blue eyes and his sun-weathered face was the one who was supposed to get him acquitted of the charges against him. Perry Kendall looked more like a down-on-his-luck prospector than the high-powered criminal attorney he was reputed to be.

Kendall tilted his chair back against the wall and stared unseeing at the iron bars that imprisoned both him and his client. "Tell me again where you went after you left Mike's Tavern."

Suppressing his resentment at what he felt was an uncharacteristic lack of good judgment on Trey's part, Joe recounted again the events of that fateful evening when he had helped a drunk old Indian find his way home.

When he had finished, Kendall chuckled softly. "You sure as hell pissed someone off."

"Tell me something I don't already know," Joe retorted.

Kendall brought the front legs of his chair back down to the floor and leaned forward to eye Joe sternly. "Listen here, young man. I don't give a damn what you think of me, but you'd better start giving some consideration to that hide of yours. You're a marked man, Tochino. Someone wants you to swing from the end of a rope, and if we can't find out who it is in the next few weeks, that's precisely what you're going to do. So you can quit looking at me as if you think I'm a rat that crawled out of the sewer, and start trying to figure out who wants you out of the way." He stood up. "Sheriff, I'm ready to leave now," he called out.

Joe surged up off his bunk. "Where are you going?"

"To Mike's Tavern, then out to San Carlos to do some looking around. While I'm gone, I want you to do some good hard thinking. Make a list. Put down the name of everyone you've looked at the wrong way in the past ten years, be it man, woman, or child."

Out in the sheriff's office, Trey waited impatiently. "Well?" he asked when Kendall, escorted by Sheriff Calder, entered the room.

"Tell me about this Taza Parks," Kendall said. "What was he like?"

Trey rubbed one hand along his jaw. "I didn't know him very well. He was a hard worker, when he wanted to be."

One shaggy brow arched questioningly. "Wanted to be?" Kendall echoed.

Trey's brows knitted together as he tried to remember the handsome, sometimes rebellious young man who had once worked for him. "I suppose Taza was like many young people," he said. "He was impatient, he gave up easily, and he seemed to have a chip on his shoulder. Other than that, I honestly don't remember."

"When did he quit working for you?"

"During the last strike, when the miners were protesting Joe's promotion to crew foreman. Taza was one of the first Apaches to resign and return to the reservation at San Carlos."

Kendall's blue eyes narrowed until they were mere slits in his tanned face. "Do you think he would be a likely target for easy money?"

Trey eyed the other man evenly. "Are you suggesting someone might have paid Taza to shoot me, then blame Joe?"

"Not necessarily. But it's a possibility worth investigating."

Samantha chewed on the end of her pencil as she studied the figures before her. "According to my calculations," she said, "we'll break even just with the sandwiches. Anything over that will be profit."

Sarah Morrissey refilled their coffee cups and joined Samantha at the kitchen table. "I can't honestly say I'll miss the lunch rush. The smell of frying bacon first thing in the morning is about all my stomach can handle."

Samantha cast the other woman a sharp glance.

Sarah smiled, almost guiltily. "Two months," she replied to Samantha's unvoiced question.

Samantha wasn't certain if she was happy or dismayed by the news that Sarah was pregnant. She tried to smile, but the result was more of a grimace. "Oh, Sarah, I know I'm being selfish, but I can't afford to lose you. Without you, I might as well give up."

"Don't worry about that. I can't afford to quit. Every time we start to get a little bit put away, it seems something happens to drain us dry. If it's not one of the kids getting sick, it's Connor's back spasms acting up again. Really,

Samantha, I sometimes think I would have been better off staying an old maid."

Sarah's disillusionment with marriage did nothing to help Samantha with her own dilemma. She did not know why she was having such a difficult time deciding whether to accept Trey's marriage proposal. She had no doubt that she loved him; if anything, she loved him too much. Within a painfully short time, she had lost all those she loved either to death or to misfortune. Both her parents and her husband were dead. Maria was now gone, and Joe was in jail. If she lost Trey, too . . .

"Samantha?"

Samantha forced her attention back to the present to find the other woman looking at her oddly. "Did you say something?"

"I asked if you wanted me to start baking the pies for tomorrow's run after I put the rest of the dishes away."

"That would be a big help. When I finish at the bank, I'll stop by Mason's Mercantile to make certain everything is ready to go. Do we need any supplies?"

"Some more vanilla beans maybe, to flavor the sugar."

"Do we have enough wrapping paper?"

"Enough to last the week. Mr. Mason said the new shipment should be in any day now."

After she had freshened up and changed her clothes and made Sarah promise to do no heavy lifting, Samantha took one final glance around the kitchen before leaving. She was not looking forward to seeing Richard. Every encounter she had with him of late seemed to disintegrate into an argument. She hoped she could get through this meeting with him without losing her temper.

Richard was with a client when she reached the bank, and she wound up waiting for the better part of an hour until he was free. Before long, the chair on which she sat in the main lobby, waiting for him, grew uncomfortably hard, and it was all she could do to sit still and not squirm in an unladylike manner. Her legs grew numb, and there was no feeling in her toes when she tried to wiggle them.

After what seemed an eternity, Richard emerged from his office. Ian Hunter was with him. Samantha quickly stood up, but feeling was slow to return to her legs, and the abrupt movement nearly landed her on the floor.

The two men turned to look at her.

Ian smiled a greeting, but Richard's expression grew taut. His face looked haggard, as though he had spent a fitful night. The details over which he had control—his impeccably tailored suit, his highly polished shoes, his unruffled, neatly combed hair—contrasted sharply with the dark shadows beneath his eyes and his almost sickly pallor. The Richard who stood before her now was a far cry from the handsome, self-confident man she had nearly married. Samantha felt a stab of guilt.

Richard and Ian spoke in low tones for a few minutes more, and then Ian took his leave, inclining his head toward Samantha on his way out the door.

Richard stepped aside to allow Samantha to enter his office, then held a chair for her while she sat down. "It's a beautiful morning," he commented offhandedly as he circled his desk to his own chair.

"Yes, it is." Samantha placed her folded hands on her lap and tried not to fidget.

Richard managed a tight smile. "That color is very becoming on you."

Samantha stared down at her hands. Ecru lace peeked out from beneath the wrists of her forest-green jacket. "Thank you," she said uncomfortably. She didn't know how to begin, but the pleasantries they were attempting to exchange were doing more to increase the tension than to lessen it.

Finally she lifted her head and met Richard's gaze directly. "Richard, I've come to discuss the restaurant."

He sucked in his breath. "I saw the Closed sign on the front door."

"It's only temporary. I'll be resuming business tomorrow." She hesitated. "I would like to continue my lease, but on a month-to-month basis. I have the first month's rent here." She started to open her reticule.

Richard leaned forward. "Samantha, the restaurant is yours. You need not—"

"No, Richard, the restaurant is not mine. It's yours. You bought it."

"But I bought it for you, darling."

Anger flashed in Samantha's eyes. "Richard, please don't start."

Richard stood up and went to the window. He crossed his arms over his chest and buried his face in one hand. His back was toward Samantha.

Samantha shifted uneasily. He was not making this any easier for her.

Richard lifted his head and took a deep breath. "Tell me what went wrong," he pleaded in an uneven voice. He was still staring out the window. "I don't understand this rift between us, darling. Tell me where I failed you."

Samantha's stomach knotted. She hated these feelings of pity he aroused in her, because they made her feel as if she was wrong to be angered by his manipulating. "You didn't *fail* me, Richard. I just don't think we're right for each other."

He rounded on her, desperation hardening his pale blue eyes. "We were right for each other until you started seeing Stern behind my back," he accused.

Samantha's mouth dropped open in astonishment. Remembering herself, she snapped it shut, then said, "Richard, when are you going to get it through your head that you have no hold on me? We were never officially engaged. I never consented to marry you. I accepted your invitations to dinner because I enjoyed your company. That is all. You do not own me."

Richard ran his fingers through his hair, upsetting its neatness. "I thought that buying the restaurant for you would make you happy, but obviously it did not. I am at a loss, darling. What do I need to do to prove my love for you?"

Icy prickles of unease touched the base of Samantha's spine as she fought to curb her rising frustration at Richard's refusal to hear what she was saying. It was becoming apparent that another approach was needed, if only to get her through the business negotiations necessary to extend her lease for another month or two. It also seemed ironic that she had no trouble telling Trey to go to hell when he provoked her, while with Richard she found herself treading on eggshells out of fear of his reaction. Her reservations went beyond mere politeness; she was beginning to feel that she was dealing with someone who was mentally unbalanced.

She took a deep breath and forced a superficial smile. "Perhaps we can start over, Richard, and take things a little slower this time."

Confusion clouded his eyes. "I thought you hated me."

"I don't hate you, Richard. I-I'm very fond of you." The lie left a bitter taste in Samantha's mouth. She nervously moistened her lips. "It's just that I'm so busy with the restaurant right now that I really have no time for a social life. Perhaps when I've been able hire someone to replace Liam and Maria, and get back on my feet again, I'll have more time."

"Did you let Liam Stern go?"

"Did you think I would keep him on after what you told me?"

Richard looked contrite. "I didn't make it any easier for you by revealing his identity, did I?"

"No, Richard, you didn't. But what's done is done, and there's no point in dwelling on the past. Now, please, sit down so that we can discuss the lease. I'm making some changes in the restaurant, and I need your cooperation."

Samantha lost track of the time as she told Richard of her plans for carrying the meals to the customers rather than having them come to her. Excitement shone in her eyes, and her voice conveyed a gaiety she hoped was more convincing than she felt, for she found herself carefully weighing each word before uttering it; she did not want to say anything that might arouse Richard's fury or his suspicions.

Richard, however, was quick to voice his reservations. "I'm glad you will not be waiting on tables any longer," he said, "although I fail to see how driving a lunch wagon is any less demeaning."

Although it annoyed Samantha that Richard found manual labor demeaning, she was careful to keep her feelings from showing on her face. "I'll only be driving it temporarily, until I can establish the route and train someone to take over." Smiling coquettishly, Samantha reached across the desk and placed her hand over his. "Please say you'll help me, Richard. I don't think I can do this on my own."

"I would do anything for you, darling. I thought you already knew that. Tell me what you need, and I'll do everything within my power to get it for you."

By the time Samantha left the bank, her head was pounding and she felt sick to her stomach. She hated women who used their charms to get what they wanted, and she hated herself for resorting to the ploy. Even knowing that she had gotten exactly what she wanted—a new month-to-month lease on the Drake House—was little consolation for the guilt she felt over deceiving Richard. In playing by Richard's rules, she had compromised her principles. Once she was out of the Drake House, she vowed, she would wash her hands of Richard Winters forever.

Her mind preoccupied, she paid little attention to where she was going, and as she rounded the corner toward Mason's Mercantile, she collided blindly with a man approaching from the opposite direction.

The man grabbed her roughly by the shoulders just as she started to fall. "Stupid bitch! Why don't you watch where you're—"

The man broke off suddenly as he and Samantha recognized each other at the same time.

Arnie Pitts released her. "Mrs. Drury, I'm sorry. I didn't know it was you."

Samantha smoothed her skirts as she struggled to get her bearings. She could not bring herself to look Arnie in the face. Blood and puss had crusted atop a pimple on his cheek that he had been picking at, and the sight sickened her. "It's all right, Arnie. It was my fault for not paying attention to where I was going." She wondered why he was not at work.

Arnie shifted nervously. "Er . . . well . . . good day, Mrs. Drury."

"Good day, Arnie." Samantha could feel his gaze drilling into her back as she walked away.

"Is anything wrong, Mrs. Drury?" the salesclerk at Mason's inquired when she paid for her purchases.

Samantha smiled wanly. "Nothing a cup of willow-bark tea won't cure," she told the young man. "Are the bottled beverages ready for tomorrow's run?"

The clerk nodded vigorously. "Got a new batch in just this morning. I think you'll like the look of the new bottles.

Real good sellers, from what I've been told."

"Good. I'll be by around midmorning to pick them up."

Samantha returned to the restaurant. Sarah was putting another batch of pies into the oven when Samantha went into the kitchen. "It smells good in here," she said, rubbing her throbbing temples. "I don't know what I'd do without you, Sarah."

"Pete Sandoval stopped by while you were out," Sarah said as she closed the oven door. "Said he'll be back around five o'clock. He's interested in driving the wagon for you."

Samantha closed her eyes and expelled her breath in a sigh of relief. She had begun to doubt the wisdom of firing Liam Stern when she was already so shorthanded. Maybe things were finally starting to fall into place after all.

They worked through the afternoon without stopping to rest. It was nearly five when someone knocked at the kitchen door. "I'll get it," Samantha called out, drying her hands on her apron. Sarah was in the dining room, setting up for breakfast.

Instead of Pete Sandoval, whom she had expected, Eulalie Carter stood in the alley. Her eyes were red-rimmed, and her bottom lip was bruised and swollen. Samantha thought of the way Liam Stern had treated Trey's mother and her stomach tensed. She took the other woman by the elbow and drew her into the kitchen. "Eulalie, are you all right?"

Eulalie's chin began to quiver. "I don't know what I'm going to do, Samantha. The rent's due on Friday, and Mr. Sells says if we're late again he's gonna turn us out. Darryl's coming down with the croup again, and I need money for his medicine."

Samantha felt torn. She had barely enough cash on hand to keep the restaurant going for the rest of the week. "I'm sorry, Eulalie. I just don't have the money right now. Maybe if you went to Mr. Sells and explained—"

Eulalie began to cry. "I wouldn't have come here if I had anyone else to turn to."

Samantha chewed on her bottom lip. Her stomach was a mass of knots. She felt terrible sending Eulalie away, and yet she could not help feeling resentful. She took a deep breath. "I need someone to help me with the cooking from five in the morning until two in the afternoon. I can pay you two dollars a day, and you can take home any leftover—"

"I can't come here!" Eulalie blurted out, horrified. "I got a family to take care of!"

"I understand that. That's why I'm offering you the job."

"Jerry would raise the roof if I took a job. I got little ones, and that's where I belong, is home with them. I don't got time to be doing cooking for strangers."

Samantha felt as if she were trapped in the middle of some bizarre nightmare that wasn't making any sense. Eulalie wanted money, but she wasn't willing to work for it, nor had she made any effort to repay what she had already borrowed. Samantha's heart was beating unnaturally fast and her hands were shaking, but she stood her ground. "If you want to work for me, I'll hire you. I'll even pay you on a daily basis, if that's what you want. But I can't afford to keep giving you money. I'll help you, but you must be willing to help yourself first."

Anger flashed in the other woman's eyes. "I always thought you were a good woman, but I was wrong. You don't care about no one else because all you got is yourself to look out for. You don't know what it's like to have to keep a roof over the little ones' heads and food in their bellies.

"Eulalie, listen to me—"

"You just wait, Samantha. Your turn's coming. When the men go on strike next week, there won't be no one eating here. This whole place will go belly up. Then *you* can find out what it's like to not be able to afford a place to live."

Eulalie whirled around and stormed away, leaving Samantha to stare after her in open-mouthed shock. She felt as if the ground had been yanked from beneath her feet. She had been shaken by Eulalie's unexpected reaction to her offer of a job, but even more so by the news of an impending strike. Perspiration beaded across her forehead, and she felt cold. The walls of the room seemed to be closing in on her.

The last time the miners went on strike, Michael was killed.

Samantha turned to find Sarah standing in the doorway, observing her with a troubled frown. "If that don't beat all," Sarah said. "I have children to tend, and I manage to hold down a paying job. That woman's plain lazy, just like her husband."

Samantha folded her arms across her chest and tucked her hands beneath her arms to keep them from shaking. It was not her place to judge Eulalie Carter. If anything, she pitied the woman, but she was quickly learning what a dangerous and exploitative emotion pity could be. "What she said about the strike, Sarah, is it true?"

Sarah shrugged. "I haven't heard anything about a strike. But then, Connor doesn't go to the union meetings."

Later that night, after Sarah had gone home, Samantha confessed her misgivings to Trey over a light supper. "I don't like the sound of it, Trey. Is there no way to stop the men from calling a strike?"

A shadow passed behind Trey's eyes. "We don't know for certain that there will be a strike," he said tonelessly.

The strain in his voice brought Samantha up short. While her own dread of a strike was due more to the unwelcome dredging up of painful memories, Trey was going to have to deal with it firsthand. She regretted adding to his burden. There was a false brightness in her smile. "I'll keep an open ear to the customers' conversations tomorrow morning. Maybe I'll overhear something."

As if he hadn't even heard her, Trey braced his elbows on the edge of the table and lowered his face into his hands. He was tired. Between worrying about Joe, wondering how he was going to come up with the money to fund the Concha's share of the railroad, and now this, there seemed to be no end in sight to the demands on his perseverance. He was beginning to wonder if the battles he was waging against Consolidated Silver and against the miners were even worth fighting. He pressed his fingertips against the ache behind his eyelids, then ran his palms down the length of his face and along his jaw. "You know, Sam," he said wearily, more to himself than to her, "maybe I'm wrong to keep holding out like this. Maybe it would be better to concede defeat and sell the Concha to Consolidated."

Dismayed by the resignation in his voice, Samantha pushed her chair away from the table and stood up. She began to clear away the dishes. "You do that," she threatened, half in jest, "and I'll tell Richard Winters I'll marry him."

Trey's fist crashed down on the table with enough force to make the dishes jump. "Do you think I *want* to sell out?"

Samantha's hand froze in midair, and the color siphoned from her face. Her taunt had been intended to strengthen his resolve, not to anger him. "I—I was only joking," she stammered.

"It was an exceedingly bad joke," Trey ground out. His blue-gray eyes were like shards of ice in his tanned face.

The last thing Samantha wanted was to have his anger directed at her. She knew he was as frustrated by the situation as she was, if not more so. "I'm sorry."

Trey glared at her. "Next time, *think* before you open your mouth."

He might as well have slapped her. Samantha stared at him, dumbstruck. Then anger pierced her pose of stunned immobility and flashed like sunbursts in her gold-flecked eyes. Her nostrils flared. "I said I was sorry," she bit out. "I don't know what more you want from me. It's not my fault all of this is happening."

"I never said it was. I just don't like having Richard Winters thrown into my face." Trey shoved away from the table and stood up. "I have work to do."

The kitchen door slammed loudly after him.

For a long, agonizing moment Samantha just stood there listening to the fading crunch of buggy wheels on the unpaved road, helpless to fight the terrible ache that swelled in her chest and spread outward through her limbs until her whole body seemed to throb with pain.

Her shoulders hunched forward with suppressed sobs and a strangled cry burst in her throat as she flung her arms across the table, sending the dishes flying.

Chapter
Thirteen

"MR. MASON, I can't take these. The miners aren't allowed to drink beer while they're on shift."

The storekeeper's ample belly shook with laughter. "It's not beer," he told Samantha. "Charlie Hires changed the name of his herb tea to root beer, hoping it'll boost sales. This is my first shipment with the new name. You'll be testing the waters, so to speak, with your lunch wagon."

Samantha gave him a weak smile. She wasn't certain she wanted to be a part of anyone's test, but she wasn't in any position to argue.

She had slept fitfully, and her head still throbbed. The argument she'd had with Trey the night before had left a foul taste in her mouth. She still did not quite understand what had brought it about. It troubled her greatly that a wedge had been driven between them just when they were growing so close. Perhaps the disagreement was meant as a warning. Perhaps they were moving too quickly. Perhaps it would be best, she thought dismally, to put a little distance between them, at least while she was trying to sort out her tangled thoughts. She only wished the separation didn't hurt so much.

Once the bottles were packed in ice in the bed of the wagon, Samantha thanked Mr. Mason and climbed up on the seat. Pete Sandoval would be at the restaurant soon, and she wanted to be there when he arrived.

"Good luck to you," Mr. Mason called out as she drove away.

Samantha gripped the reins. I'll need all the luck I can get, she thought. This morning she was not at all confident that the lunch wagon was a good idea.

The breakfast rush had been slower than usual; no doubt word had not gotten around that the Drake House had reopened. None of the customers had made any mention of a strike, and she'd had to bite her tongue to keep from asking outright. Because it was well known around town she had been keeping company with Trey lately, she seriously doubted anyone would confide in her.

Unaware of what she was doing, Samantha drove the wagon right past the restaurant, not stopping until she reached the cemetery.

For several weeks she had neglected coming here, and now the cemetery seemed overgrown and unkempt. She knelt beside Michael's grave and pulled out several clumps of weeds growing around his headstone. Finally her hand stilled, and she just sat there, staring at the dusty gray stone, seeing and feeling nothing. She tried to think of something to say, but words failed her. Michael was gone. She couldn't even talk to his memory anymore, because that, too, had become a blur in her mind.

Yet so many questions remained unanswered. She had almost succeeded in burying the most painful of those questions in the far recesses of her mind, but the rumor of a strike had revived her old fears and uncertainties. While she no longer believed that Trey had had anything to do with the accident that had resulted in her husband's death, Samantha could not help wondering just what Michael had been doing in the mine that day.

With a sigh, she turned her head to look out across the town. It was an ugly town, she thought, as if seeing it for the first time. Only a few years ago the miners' houses, built row upon row when both the town and the mine were prospering, had seemed so clean and new. Now they sagged on their footings. Weeds choked the yards. Windows had been broken out. A fine ash from the smoke that poured from the mill's furnace stacks day and night had settled over everything, dulling colors that had once been bright and turning everything the same dismal shade of gray. The excitement that had driven the town when it was young was gone. Now the miners lived from day to day, not knowing when silver's reign would end and they would find themselves without jobs. Myterra was dying, and it would take nothing less than a miracle to revive it.

A gust of wind whipped a strand of hair across Samantha's eyes. She brushed it away from her face and stood up. As long as there was a breath of life left in the town, she knew she had no choice but to do as the rest of the town's inhabitants did and keep on going about her business as if nothing were amiss. For the time, denial was the only thing keeping Myterra alive.

Squaring her shoulders, she returned to the wagon. Soon the noon whistle would sound. She did not want her first day with the lunch wagon to fail because she was late.

From the window of his office, Trey watched the gathering near the mill. He had given Samantha permission to bring the lunch wagon inside the compound. About fifteen men from the mine and the mill had assembled around Samantha and the wagon to see what she was selling. While the response was not as great as he would have wished for her, for the first day it wasn't bad.

With some relief, Trey noticed that the driver of the wagon appeared to be Pete Sandoval. Of all the men he had recommended to Samantha, Pete was probably the most reliable. If there was potential trouble brewing among the miners, at least Samantha would not be alone.

Suddenly, as if sensing his observation, Samantha turned and looked straight toward him.

His body went rigid. Although he doubted she could see him at that distance, his heart began to pound with slow, heavy beats that made his chest ache. He had not meant to hurt her last night. He did not know why he had suddenly lost patience with her. He felt almost as if he had deliberately driven her away. But why? He loved her and he wanted to marry her. So why did the closeness between them suddenly seem so overwhelming?

A voice behind him jolted him out of his reverie. "Your bookkeeper was not at his desk, so we took the liberty of inviting ourselves in," Ian Hunter said. "Can you spare a few minutes?"

Trey turned away from the window. It took every ounce of willpower he had to keep his voice from trembling. "Hello, Ian. Whittaker. Please, take a seat."

Down by the mill, struggling to keep her disappointment from showing on her face, Samantha slowly turned back toward the wagon. She thought she saw a movement at the window of Trey's office, then decided she was mistaken. She had hoped Trey would be present the first time she brought the lunch wagon into the compound. That he had not appeared hurt her more than any angry words he could have uttered. She tried to tell herself it was because he was busy, but a nagging voice in the back of her mind hinted otherwise. After last night, she thought, it was quite possible that he never wanted to see her again.

After they left the mine compound, at Pete Sandoval's suggestion, they drove the wagon into town. Their first stop was Chandler's Livery.

"Root beer, eh?" Jimmy Chandler asked, scratching his

head as he studied the bottle in his hand. "You sure it won't make me drunk?"

Pete Sandoval laughed. "If it does, it's all in your head, Chandler. It's just sarsaparilla with a fancy name."

By the time they'd been to every livery in town, except the one on Main Street next to the Aurora Saloon, the hardware store, the feed store, and a dozen other places she could not remember, Samantha was of the opinion that Pete Sandoval was more than a driver; he was a born salesman. Another day or two, and she would feel confident staying at the restaurant and just turning the wagon over to him.

"You're good with the customers," she told him as they were heading back toward the Drake House. "They like talking with you."

"Not near as much as I like talking with them," he returned easily. "When I hurt my back down in the stopes and went on disability, I thought I'd go crazy having no one to talk to. I think I'm going to enjoy this job, Mrs. Drury. Thanks for thinking of me."

Samantha hid the ache in her heart behind a smile. "Actually, it was Mr. Stern who recommended you for the job. You should thank him."

They made one final stop, at the jail, before returning to the restaurant, and Samantha went inside alone to see Joe Tochino.

Joe surged up off his bunk when he saw her. The wind had loosened several russet curls from the coil at the nape of Samantha's neck and had also heightened her color. Joe thought she had never looked so pretty, and he told her so. "Love agrees with you," he teased.

Samantha's smile faded. She almost wished she had not told Joe about Trey's offer of marriage. "I brought you fried chicken and biscuits today," she said, changing the subject. "And you have a choice, pumpkin pie or apple?"

Joe had not missed the flash of despair in her eyes. "Samantha, what happened?"

Although she had vowed to keep her troubles to herself, the gentle urging in Joe's voice broke her resistance.

Joe listened intently as Samantha told him an abbreviated version of what had happened. His brows dipped in bewilderment. "Why would the miners want to strike now?" he asked dryly. "They've gotten rid of me, which is what they wanted all along."

"It goes deeper than that this time," Samantha said. She told Joe about the deal Consolidated Silver wanted to strike with the Southern Pacific Railroad and about the pressure they were putting on Trey to sell out. "The men have been led to believe they have a great deal to gain in wages and privileges if the Concha comes under Consolidated's management, so they want Trey to sell the mine. They can't see that in the long run they'll be worse off.

"I'd better go," Samantha said, realizing the lateness of the hour. Pete Sandoval is waiting for me out in the wagon."

"Samantha, wait."

Joe came to the barrier that separated them and closed his hands around the iron bars. His dark eyes were soft with understanding. "When I first realized I loved Maria, it scared the hell out of me. No matter how much I cared for her, I was always saying things to upset her. I think it was my way of protecting myself from getting too close to her too quickly. Be patient with Trey, Samantha. I'm sure he never meant to hurt you. He loves you too much."

Samantha's gaze dropped to the tiny silver crucifix that peeked out between the undone top buttons on Joe's shirt. Her throat tightened. "You miss her, don't you?"

Joe nodded. "More than you'll ever know. That's why it's so important that you don't let Trey's bullheadedness drive you away. Don't make the same mistake I did with Maria. Don't let him get away. He might not admit it, but he needs you. He needs to know that you'll be there for him and not condemn him for what he must do."

Distressed that Joe blamed himself for Maria's exile, Samantha placed her hands over his. "Joe, Maria's leaving was not your fault. You could not have stopped it."

"I could have stopped it," Joe said solemnly. "I waited too long."

All the way home, Samantha thought about what Joe had said. Perhaps Trey did need her. She knew she was miserable without him, and that frightened her. After Michael's death, she had vowed never again to become dependent upon anyone.

Still, was it right for her to deny herself and Trey the happiness that being together brought them simply because she was afraid of loving—and losing—someone again?

When they reached the restaurant, Sarah had finished the baking for the next day's run. She came out of the kitchen, wiping her hands on her apron. "Well? How did it go?"

"Not bad," Pete called out. "Not bad at all."

Although Samantha was not as impressed with the first day's run as Pete Sandoval had been, she said nothing. She doubted they had even turned a profit, but she hoped that by tomorrow word would have gotten out and business would improve. "Do we have room in the icebox for some of this ice?" she asked Sarah. "I hate to see it go to waste."

"I'll look. Oh, before I forget, Maria's brother was here earlier, asking for you."

Samantha's heart stuck in her throat. She hoped nothing had happened to Maria. "Did he say what he wanted?"

"No. Just that he'd stop by this evening on his way home from the mine."

It was late when Roberto Velásquez finally arrived at the

restaurant. Samantha had already sent Sarah and Pete home with enough leftovers to feed their families for several days, and was in the kitchen shaping bread dough into loaves when the knock came at the door.

Wiping her hands on her apron, Samantha flew to the door to let him in. "Roberto, what happened? Is Maria all right?"

Roberto's skin and clothes wore the grime of a day spent below in the stopes. His face was drawn and his cheeks hollow. "Maria is fine, señora. She ask me to tell you do not worry."

Assured that Maria was safe, Samantha remembered the part Roberto had played in removing his sister to a convent in Sonora. She had a difficult time being civil to the young man. "Did you have a safe trip?" she asked. Her voice was strained.

"*Sí*, señora." Roberto shifted uneasily and fidgeted with his hat. "Señora Drury, please understand why we must protect our Maria—"

"Protect her from what?" Samantha interrupted without thinking. "Marauding Apaches?"

"We do not want to see Maria hurt," Roberto said stubbornly.

"What do you think *you've* done to her? Maria and Joe love each other. Joe would never hurt her."

"It is not good for Maria to marry Joe. Maria must be with her own kind. The Mexicanos and the *shkit-ne* are enemies."

Roberto's use of the term *shkit-ne* as well as the bitterness in his voice set Samantha's teeth on edge. "Joe is a human being, Roberto. Or have you forgotten that?"

"He is Apache," Roberto said firmly.

Realizing the futility of trying to reason with someone so set in his opinion, Samantha stopped trying. "Thank you for bringing me news of Maria," she said stiffly. "Now, if you will excuse me, I have work to do."

"Señora, wait. There is more." Roberto nervously moistened his lips. "Maria, she beg me to help Joe Tochino. She say he is falsely accused."

Samantha's heart leaped in her chest, but she cautiously refused to get her hopes up until she'd heard what Roberto had to say. Any concern Roberto Velásquez might show for Joe was shadowed by his dislike of Apaches.

"Joe did not cut the cable, señora. It was Joe's cousin, Eskelta."

Samantha felt as if someone had punched her. Disbelief flickered behind her eyes. "Eskelta? Why?"

"Eskelta was angry when Joe become crew foreman. He think Señor Stern promote Joe because they are friends. He cut the cable and tell everyone that it was Joe, so Joe will be fired."

Samantha could not believe her ears. The harassment Joe had endured from miners who could not accept having an Apache in a position of authority was bad enough; that one of his own people would set out to discredit him was beyond her comprehension. "Have you told Trey about this?" she asked.

Roberto shook his head. "It is not safe for me to go to Señor Stern. The other miners, the ones who talk of a strike, do not want Joe to come back to the Concha. They do not want resistance to the strike. Anyone who is"—Roberto frowned as he searched for the right word—"*simpático* to Señor Stern is not safe."

Samantha was having a difficult time absorbing it all. So there *was* going to be a strike, she thought. And Trey's opponents seemed determined to eliminate those individuals who might stand in their way. Had framing Joe been a part of their plans, or was that, too, an act of revenge by a jealous co-worker? "Roberto, do you know who shot Trey? Or who killed Taza Parks?"

"I do not know, señora. I know Taza Parks spend much money at Mike's Tavern the night before his body is found. Perhaps he steal the money and someone shoot him."

Or someone paid Taza to implicate Joe, then permanently silenced him, Samantha thought. Excitement pulsed through her veins. It was not much, but it might lead to something more substantial, and right now Joe needed all the help he could get. "Thank you for telling me, Roberto. I'm sure Joe will appreciate your help."

Roberto looked down at the hat in his hands. "My family, we do not want our Maria to marry an Apache," he said in a barely audible voice, "but we are not bad people, señora. We do not want to see an innocent man hang."

After Roberto had gone, Samantha hurriedly washed the flour off her hands. She had to see Trey and tell him what she had learned. If she hurried, she could be back by the time the bread dough had risen to the tops of the pans.

Seeing Trey, however, was more difficult than she had anticipated. "I'm sorry, ma'am," the gate guard at the mine told her. "I can't let you in. Mr. Stern does not want to be disturbed."

Samantha had never seen the man before. She wondered if he was a new employee. "Sir, this is very important. Is Paddy Sweeny here? He can vouch for me."

The man eyed her with antagonistic reserve. He knew who Samantha was, even if she didn't appear to recognize him. The woman had a reputation around town for being too damned independent for her own good—just the type of woman he didn't want his own wife turning into. "Mr. Sweeny changed to day shift. I'm the night guard now."

Frustration mixed with alarm surged through Samantha. If Paddy Sweeny now worked the day shift, had Arnie Pitts quit? Or had he been fired? She remembered when they had collided in town, and an uneasy feeling churned in the pit of her stomach. She rubbed her fingertips across her brow in a gesture of distress. "I need to get back to the restaurant," she said. "Do you have a piece of paper? I'd like to leave a message for Mr. Stern."

The man went inside the guard shack. After what seemed an unusually long time, he emerged with a scrap of brown sandwich paper and a pencil. "Will this do?"

Samantha thanked him and hastily scribbled a note to Trey that she needed to speak with him as soon as possible. She gave the paper and the pencil back to the gate guard. "Please see that Mr. Stern gets this before he leaves the compound."

The gate guard watched Samantha's departure with annoyance. If his own wife ever talked to him in that superior tone, he'd give her the back of his hand and remind her just who was boss. Crumpling Samantha's note in his big hand, he tossed it in the waste can. There was more than one way to put an uppity woman in her place.

On the way back to the restaurant, Samantha stopped at the jail. Joe could use a bit of good news.

The door was locked. Samantha went to the window and peered inside, but the building was dark. Neither Sheriff Calder nor any of his deputies appeared to be around. Where was everyone? It wasn't like the sheriff to leave the jail unguarded.

Samantha circled to the back of the building where the jail cells were located. She wondered if Joe was still awake.

No light from the surrounding buildings reached the narrow alley, and it took a moment for Samantha's eyes to adjust to the darkness. As soon as she was able to make out the six iron-barred windows in the thick adobe walls at the rear of the jail, she carefully felt her way through the darkness. The third window should open into Joe's cell, she remembered.

The top of her head barely reached the window sill. Even standing on tiptoe would not allow her to see inside the cell. "Joe, are you awake?" she called softly.

No answer.

She took a deep breath and tried again, a little louder this time. "Joe, it's me, Samantha. Can you hear me?"

"Good thing you identified yourself." A man's voice came from behind her. "Saves me the trouble of having to shoot you."

Samantha gasped and whirled around just as a hand closed around her upper arm in an imprisoning grip. She nearly stumbled over her own feet as he hauled her out of the alley. As they emerged from the alley, a light from the building across the street illuminated the man's face. "Sheriff Calder!"

Instead of releasing her as Samantha had expected him to do, he tightened his grip on her arm and gave her a fierce shake that caused her head to snap back. "What in the hell were you doing back there?" he demanded.

Appalled at being treated like a naughty child who had just been caught at some act of mischief, Samantha tried to jerk her arm free. "If you will stop shaking me, I'll tell you."

Sheriff Calder stopped shaking her, but he did not release her arm. "I'm waiting," he said impatiently.

Samantha had to bite her tongue to keep from blurting out something she might later regret. Antagonizing Sheriff Calder would do nothing to help Joe and might even hurt his case. She took a deep breath. "I needed to speak with Joe, but the building was locked. So I went around back to talk to him through the window."

The sheriff stared at her so long and so hard that Samantha

quailed inwardly. She had the uncomfortable suspicion that he did not believe her. "Mrs. Drury, whatever your reasons for sneaking around behind the jail at this late hour, it was a foolish thing to do. Go home. You can see Tochino tomorrow."

Samantha bristled at his insinuating tone. "Sheriff, I told you why I'm here. I need to see Joe."

"Go home, Mrs. Drury."

"Sheriff, you don't understand. I just found out something that might help his defense."

"In that case, come back in the morning when his attorney is here."

"But I can't come back in the morning. I have a restaurant to run."

Sheriff Calder took Samantha firmly by the shoulders and turned her in the direction of the Drake House. "Good night, Mrs. Drury."

The instant he released her, Samantha turned around. She clenched her teeth and knotted her hands into angry fists as she glared at the sheriff's departing back. First she had been prevented from seeing Trey, and now Joe. If she hadn't been in such a hurry to return to the restaurant in time to rescue her rising bread dough, she would have waited until the sheriff left and then returned to the rear of the jail to talk to Joe. She almost wished she hadn't told Sheriff Calder about having information that might help in Joe's defense. She did not trust the man.

With a sigh of resignation, she turned and started back toward the restaurant. Right now she had no choice but to do as the sheriff ordered.

In the shadows, Silas Jenkins leaned against an adobe wall and lighted a cheroot. The tip of the cigar glowed red in the darkness as he took a long draw. So Samantha Drury had information that might get the Indian cleared of the charges against him, he thought, his mind toying with the scene he had just witnessed between her and the sheriff.

He could not allow that to happen. He was being paid good money to keep the Indian away from the mine during the strike. He was going to have to either get rid of the Indian or make sure Samantha Drury didn't talk.

Jenkins knew that Arnie Pitts would like a chance at shutting up the woman. That was all Pitts had talked about for the last few days, ever since Richard Winters had started paying him to follow her and keep an eye on her. Jenkins had no taste for roughing up women, but Arnie did. He would probably enjoy it.

The problem with Arnie, though, was that he talked too much. No, this was one job he was going to have to take care of himself.

The breakfast rush was the busiest Samantha had ever witnessed. In addition to the usual assortment of miners and townsmen, blue-uniformed soldiers filled the dining room and waited in line outside the front door to get in. "Where did they all come from?" she asked Sarah. Her face was flushed, and her hair had slipped out of its pins to curl wildly about her face. She was out of breath from carrying a heavy stack of dirty plates back to the kitchen.

Sarah Morrissey shook her head. "I can't rightly say. They sure do eat like there's no tomorrow. I swear, if another one orders bacon, my stomach is going to go on strike."

A look of dismay flashed across Samantha's face as she remembered Sarah's condition. "Oh, Sarah, I'm sorry. Sit down and rest for a few minutes. It's not good to be on your feet so much."

Sarah dragged a sleeve across her forehead and gave

Samantha a tired smile. "Don't worry about me. If I wasn't on my feet here, I'd be on them at home."

"Still, I don't want you working so hard you make yourself ill. Do it for me, if not for yourself. I can't afford to lose you." Samantha picked up the plates Sarah had prepared. "When I come back into this kitchen, you had better be sitting down."

She returned to the dining room.

"Can we get more coffee over here?" an impatient voice demanded.

Samantha forced a smile. "Coming right up," she called out. She placed the two plates on a table. "Here you are. Two steak specials. Would you like something else?"

One of the soldiers shook his head, but the other one, a rather unkempt fellow sporting a drooping mustache and sergeant's stripes, grinned at her and placed one hand squarely on her backside. "Some sugar for my coffee?" he drawled suggestively.

Samantha smacked his hand away and stepped out of his reach. "It's on the table, right in front of you," she snapped. Pivoting, she stormed back to the kitchen.

"Men," she mumbled ungraciously as she retrieved the coffee pot from the stove. "Rotten bastards seem to think women were put on this earth solely for their pleasure." She turned to find Pete Sandoval staring at her in open-mouthed affront. When had he arrived? "Thank God you're here," she said by way of apology. "Do you think you can handle the run by yourself this morning? Sarah and I are up to our ears in customers. I won't be able to get away."

Pete nodded. "Sure enough. I know the route like the back of my hand. Don't worry. I'll take care of everything."

Although under ordinary circumstances Samantha would have been pleased, she still felt a little uneasy about letting

Pete go out alone. He knew the route well enough and
had no problems dealing with the customers, but he was
a little slow when it came to handling money. She hoped
he wouldn't allow himself to be cheated. "You'll need to
stop at Jack Petrie's first and get more ice," she reminded
him on his way out the door.

She returned to the dining room with the coffee pot. She
cut a wide path around the mustached soldier who had fondled her. She didn't dare get too close to him; the temptation
to dump the coffee over his head was too great.

Trying hard not to let the incident continue to upset
her, she forced herself to be extra polite as she worked
her way around the dining room, refilling one coffee cup
after another. She stopped by one table and stared down
at the soldier who looked up at her. He was a mere boy,
sixteen or seventeen at the most. Judging from the sad-eyed,
whipped-dog look he was giving her, this was probably
his first time away from home. Her expression softened.
"I haven't seen you gentlemen around here before," she
said. "Where are you from?"

"We're from Fort McCrae, ma'am. We're camped on the
edge of town."

She refilled his cup. "Are you on maneuvers?"

"Well, not really, ma'am. We're going to be protecting
the—"

A sharp yelp sounded in his throat as the soldier across
from him delivered a swift kick to his shins. "Shut your big
mouth, Newman. You know we're not supposed to discuss
our plans."

The younger man turned an uncomfortable shade of red.
He turned his attention to his plate.

Samantha glanced from one man to the other. Icy prickles
touched her skin, and the tiny hairs on her face felt as if they
were standing on end. Aside from the lure of the saloons

and dance halls, the army had only two reasons for being in Myterra. Either the Apaches had gone on the warpath, something they had not done in Pinal County during the seven years since Geronimo's surrender to General Miles, or there was trouble at the mine. She took a deep breath. "Let me know if you need anything else," she managed to get out.

She returned to the kitchen. "Sarah, have you heard anything else about a miners' strike?"

Sarah was sitting at the table with her feet propped up on another chair. She had untied her shoes, and Samantha noticed that her ankles were swollen. She shook her head. "The only thing Connor's told me is that Arnie Pitts got fired. He didn't show up for work two days in a row, and Mr. Stern found out he'd been drinking."

That explained why Arnie had not been manning the guard shack, Samantha thought, but it didn't account for the army's presence in Myterra. Of course, she could be wrong, but why else would the troops be here? And why could Trey not be here when she needed him? He had not stopped by last night, even though she had waited up for him. Now, with the restaurant as busy as it was, she didn't know when she'd get a chance to see either him or Joe.

The breakfast crowd had begun to wane when Pete returned to the restaurant, clearly agitated. His clothes were streaked with dirt, and he had the beginnings of a whopping purple bruise beneath his left eye. "It's the miners," he told Samantha. "They're blocking the entrance to Concha, and they won't let anyone in or out. They got picket signs, and some of them are carrying shovels and pieces of iron pipe. Marty Dennison threatened to overturn the wagon if I didn't get it out of there but quick."

Samantha felt as if events were spinning out of control. Her heart was beating so hard she could feel the blood pulsing in her ears. "Let me wrap a piece of ice in a washcloth for that eye," she said. "Then we can sit down and figure out what to do. Later perhaps I'll take the wagon back up to the mine. If the strikers won't let me into the compound, then maybe *they'll* buy lunch. I can't afford to let all that food go to waste."

"You won't be going anywhere except with me," came an all-too-familiar voice from behind her.

Samantha and Sarah and Pete all turned as Sheriff Calder came into the kitchen from the dining room. Samantha's heart stuck in her throat.

Sheriff Calder eyed Samantha coldly. "Mrs. Drury, I'm placing you under arrest for assisting in the escape of a suspected felon."

Chapter
Fourteen

JOE'S hands were tied behind him, and he was lying face down across the back of a horse. He did not know how long they had been traveling. Although a good hour had passed since he had regained his wits, he continued to feign unconsciousness. He needed time to assess the situation and plan his escape.

He had been awakened before dawn by a sound in his jail cell. He had surged up off his bunk, but before he could see who was there, someone had struck him from behind, knocking him out cold. Now, as he pretended to be unconscious, he felt a painful throbbing behind his eyes and figured he was probably wearing a good-sized lump on the back of his head.

He knew there were two men traveling with him. He recognized Arnie Pitts's voice, but he did not know who the other man was. Judging from the changing heat of the sun on his back, he guessed they were traveling south. The terrain was steeper here. There were fewer trees. They seemed to be climbing higher into the mountains. More than once they crossed deep gullies that had been shaped by flash floods.

Finally they stopped. The men dismounted. Arnie Pitts walked up to the horse that was carrying Joe. He seized Joe's belt and the back of his shirt. "All right, Tochino, time to wake up." He hauled Joe off the horse's back and dropped him onto the ground.

Joe groaned and stirred. Arnie grabbed the neck of Joe's shirt and hauled him to his feet. The ground moved and swayed beneath Joe as he tried to get his bearings. He gritted his teeth against the pounding in his head. The two men blurred before his eyes. He blinked several times, and the images cleared.

The wiry, hard-eyed man pulled his gun and leveled it on Joe. "Untie his hands."

Arnie stared at him in surprise. "What d'ya want to do that for, Jenkins? I thought you wasn't supposed to let him get away."

"Just do as you're told, you fool."

Shaking his head in bewilderment, Arnie took the bowie knife Jenkins handed him and began sawing at the ropes binding Joe's wrists.

As Arnie worked on the ropes, Joe simmered with barely concealed disgust. In his entire life he had met only two or three people for whom he felt outright hatred, and Arnie was one of them. He had disliked the man, for no specific reason, from the first moment he'd seen him. Time and again, when Joe had been forced to stand with him in the confines of the guard shack while signing in, he had nurtured a secret longing to drag Arnie into some back alley and beat his pimply face to a pulp.

The ropes gave way, and a sharp pain knifed through Joe's fingers as the feeling abruptly returned to his hands. He rubbed his chafed wrists while studying the man Arnie had called Jenkins. He'd heard a rumor that Silas Jenkins was in Myterra. Could this be the same man? Joe wasn't certain what role Pitts played in all this, except perhaps to serve as extra muscle.

Suddenly Jenkins chuckled. "I'll bet you're wondering why we brought you here."

Joe said nothing.

"That lawyer of yours," Jenkins said. "He's been asking too many questions. Mr. Winters doesn't like that."

So Richard Winters was involved in this, Joe thought. He was not surprised. Being behind bars had given him a lot of time to think, and he had figured out what had struck him as so odd when Samantha was telling him about the deal Consolidated was trying to work out with the Southern Pacific Railroad. The only logical route for the railroad to take into Myterra was along the Aravaipa Creek basin and through Capitan Pass. If he remembered correctly, Richard Winters's First Territorial Bank held title to that land and was currently leasing the water and grazing rights to ranchers. Even if Trey did have the money to put up for the Concha's share of the railroad, it would still be built on land that Winters, in effect, controlled.

"Just so you don't take it personally," Jenkins continued, "Winters didn't really want you dead. You were more useful to him alive, because he could use you to create a diversion. Unfortunately, that lawyer fellow was gettin' a little too close to the mark with his questions. And that redheaded lady friend of yours didn't do much to help your case, either, with her braggin' to the sheriff that she had information that could get you cleared. So we just had to dirty up your good name. No one will believe you're innocent now that you've gone and busted out of jail."

As Jenkins talked, Joe was scouting out the area. He was careful to keep his gaze averted so that Jenkins and Pitts wouldn't catch on to what he was doing. To the west of the rocks, the land rose sharply, limiting his choices for escape. The only feasible way out was down the mountain, where a rocky outcropping partially blocking the narrow trail gave way to a steep drop down the side of the mountain. If he didn't get battered to death on the rocks, he might be able to make it. He lifted his gaze slightly and studied Jenkins through veiled eyes. "Did you kill Taza Parks?" he asked.

Jenkins shrugged. "It was a payin' job."

"Who paid you? Winters?"

"Who else?"

"But why? What did you have to gain by killing him?"

"Why are you so all-fired concerned? The man was willin' to sell you downriver without battin' an eye. For a couple of bucks, that no-account Apache would have turned his own mother over to the law."

Although Trey had told him that Taza Parks was the one who had implicated him, Joe had clung to an unrealistic thread of hope that Trey was wrong or, at the very least, that Taza had had a good reason for naming him. That Taza had traded both their lives for a bribe made him feel physically ill.

"Did Winters pay you to shoot Treyman Stern?"

"Yup. Unfortunately my aim was a little off that night. I wanted to go back to finish the job, but Winters had other plans for him by then. I think he means to kill Stern himself." Jenkins shook his head. "The man's loco. All he's gonna do is bungle the job."

Joe's heart was pounding with the fierce, steady beat of a war drum. He had no doubt that Jenkins intended to kill him, too. He took a deep breath. "Why are you telling me all this? Wouldn't it have been easier just to shoot me and be done with it?"

"I got my principles. I'll shoot a man in the back, if I have to. But before he dies, I think he's got a right to know who wants him dead."

Joe broke into a run.

The revolver exploded behind him.

A fiery pain stabbed through his right side, the force of

the impact nearly driving him to his knees. Gathering every ounce of strength he possessed, he hurled himself over the rocky ledge, drawing his knees up to his chest and curling into a ball. He hit the ground rolling.

"He's getting away!" Arnie Pitts ran for his horse.

Jenkins lunged, grabbed the reins, and yanked them out of Arnie's hands. "Let him go."

"But Winters wants him dead!"

"I said, let him go."

In frustration, Arnie shoved his hands into his coat pockets. Shifting from one foot to the other, he stared, first at Jenkins, then at the spot where, only seconds ago, Joe had stood. In his pocket, his fingers tightened around the crucifix he had taken off the unconscious Indian, intending to sell it for a couple of dollars. Bewilderment clouded his face. "What d'ya go and do that for, after all the trouble we went to makin' it look like he busted out of jail, then bringin' him up here? By the time we get back to town, it'll be all over the territory who we're workin' for."

"That's what I'm counting on. I figure it's the least we can do for our friend Winters." Jenkins went to his own horse and swung up into the saddle. By the time the Indian got back to Myterra, he intended to be as far out of the territory as he could get. He turned his horse down the trail.

Confused, Arnie ran after him. "Hey, wait a minute! Where's my share of the money?"

"You let the Indian get away," Jenkins called out over his shoulder. "Winters won't like that. Don't guess you'll be getting paid after all, Pitts."

Judge Gates slammed his palm down on his desk and half rose out of his chair. The bald spot on top of his head was as livid as his face. "Young lady, any more out of you, and you're going straight back to jail!" He stared at Samantha long enough to be sure that his threat had sunk in, then lowered his stout frame onto the chair.

Trey's hand tightened warningly on Samantha's shoulder.

Samantha chafed with suppressed resentment. The "evidence" Sheriff Calder had presented against her was so paltry as to be nonexistent, and she was incredulous that Judge Gates would even consider it. It required a supreme effort to keep her voice even. "Your Honor, I don't mean to be disrespectful, but I'm telling you the truth. I did not help Joe break out of jail. All I did was stop by the jail to tell him I'd learned something that would help his case. The front door was locked, so I went around back to talk to him through the window. That's when Sheriff Calder arrived."

"Mrs. Drury, you keep talking about information that will help his case," Sheriff Calder interrupted. "But you haven't given us any idea what that information might be."

Samantha fidgeted. She wasn't sure just how much she should reveal. If what Roberto Velásquez had told her about Eskelta wasn't true, she risked getting him unjustly fired. "Joe wasn't the one who cut the cable at the mine a few weeks ago," she ventured cautiously. "It was someone else."

Trey turned to stare at her. "Who?"

It hurt Samantha to breathe. "Eskelta," she whispered.

Trey frowned. "Joe's cousin?"

"Why in the hell would he do that?" the sheriff demanded.

In halting sentences, Samantha told them what she'd heard about Eskelta being envious of Joe's promotion. "But it's only hearsay," she clarified when she had finished. "I could be wrong."

Judge Gates leaned forward. "Young lady, who told you

Eskelta was the one who cut the cable?"

Samantha bit back the retort that sprang to the tip of her tongue. If Judge Gates called her "young lady" one more time, she was likely to scream. "I can't tell you that."

"Can't or won't?" Judge Gates asked.

Samantha pressed her lips together and returned the judge's glower with one of her own. Puffed-up bureaucrat, she thought derisively.

Sheriff Calder shook his head in disgust. "Mrs. Drury, you're not giving us much to go on."

Judge Gates's eyes narrowed as he studied Samantha. "Did you or did you not return to the jail after your encounter with Sheriff Calder?" he asked.

"I did not." Samantha made no attempt to soften the irritation in her voice. "Even if I'd wanted to, the restaurant kept me so busy I wouldn't have had the time to go back. Besides, why would I want to help Joe escape when I'd just found out something that might *help* him?"

Perry Kendall had been standing to one side, listening to the exchange. He finally stepped forward. "Mrs. Drury has a point, Your Honor. Furthermore, I spoke with Joe Tochino myself earlier yesterday afternoon about a witness I'd located who was willing to testify that Joe did, in fact, take Charlie Cousins home the night Treyman Stern was shot. Mr. Tochino was feeling rather optimistic about winning his case. I believe Mrs. Drury is innocent of the charges against her, Your Honor, and I have a few questions of my own about Mr. Tochino's disappearance."

"Are you trying to say Tochino didn't break out of the Pinal County jail?" Judge Gates asked.

"Your Honor, I'm not saying a word about that until I have more proof. But I can tell you one thing: I firmly believe this entire situation has come about not by happenstance but by design; it was cleverly worked out. By whom I don't know. But I intend to find out."

Judge Gates looked at Samantha. In spite of his warnings, she was clenching and unclenching her hands and glaring at him as if she intended to lunge across his desk to do battle with him. Beside her, Treyman Stern was grim-faced and silent. Gates had not missed the controlling hand Stern had placed on her shoulder. If anyone could keep the woman in line, Stern could. He wondered if the rumors he'd heard were true. They made a handsome couple, Stern with his serious, dark good looks, and Mrs. Drury, who made him think of a wildfire that had been confined by accident to a woman's body. While he had about as much sympathy for independent, outspoken women as he did for Indians, he could not help being intrigued by Samantha Drury. He almost liked her.

He also respected Perry Kendall's opinion.

"Mrs. Drury, I'm going to let you go," Judge Gates told Samantha, "on several conditions. First, under no circumstances are you to leave town. Second, if Mr. Tochino should attempt to contact you, you are to notify Sheriff Calder immediately. Last, but not least, I expect your full cooperation with any investigation into this matter by either Sheriff Calder or Mr. Kendall, preferably without the display of hotheaded belligerence you exhibited in here earlier. Do you understand me?"

Trey felt Samantha bristle at the judge's patronizing tone, and again his hand tightened on her shoulder in a silent warning.

Samantha took a deep breath. She intended to have a word or two with Trey as soon as they left the building. He was beginning to annoy her nearly as much as Judge Gates and Sheriff Calder did. "Yes, sir," she said peevishly.

One shaggy gray eyebrow angled upward.

Samantha remained stubbornly silent. She refused to thank him for his leniency or to apologize for her antagonism.

Despairing of getting even a pretense of gratitude from Samantha, Judge Gates sighed and turned his attention to Trey. "Mr. Stern, since you have agreed to accept responsibility for the young lady, I am going to release her into your custody. You may post the twenty-five-dollar bond with the court clerk downstairs. That will be all. You are dismissed. Sheriff Calder, Mr. Kendall, please remain behind. There is something I wish to discuss with you."

By the time Samantha and Trey left the building twenty minutes later, a crowd had gathered in front of the courthouse. Samantha tried to ignore the stares that followed her down the steps. Some of the onlookers regarded Samantha with open hostility; most were merely curious. The last time a woman had been arrested in Myterra was six months ago, when two prostitutes had engaged in a fistfight in the middle of Main Street.

"Whore!"

The familiarity of the woman's voice caused Samantha to turn.

Eulalie Carter stepped forward and fixed Samantha with an angry glare. "You think you're too good for us, don't you? You can't be bothered with helpin' out your own kind, 'cause you're too busy taking up with murdering Indians!"

Samantha stared at her in open-mouthed shock, too stunned to react. Before she could gather her wits about her, a man she did not know shouted, "Indian-lover!"

Someone else took up the cry, and within seconds the entire crowd was chanting, "Indian-lover! Indian-lover!" A boy of about ten picked up a clod of dirt and hurled it at

Samantha. It struck her shoulder and disintegrated.

The faces in the crowd blurred and swam before her eyes. She thought she saw Maddie Ruskin and Jerry Carter and several others whom she had always considered decent, hardworking people. She did not understand why they would turn against her now.

Trey gripped her elbow. "Come on. Let's get out of here," he whispered.

Eulalie Carter spat on the ground. "You're just a no-good whore, Samantha Drury! Everyone in town knows you're sleeping with Treyman Stern! It wouldn't surprise me if you're sleeping with that Apache scum, too!"

Suddenly Trey released Samantha's elbow. His expression murderous, he pivoted and headed straight for Eulalie.

Samantha grabbed his arm. "Trey, no!"

Eulalie took a step backward, surprise replacing the contempt in her eyes.

Samantha pulled on Trey's arm. "Trey, please, I want to leave."

Trey fought for control. He had come dangerously close to losing his temper. The last thing he needed right now was to be arrested on assault charges. His jaw set in an angry line, he turned and followed Samantha to the buggy.

They wasted no time putting the mob behind them. Trey snapped the reins with such force that the buggy surged forward and Samantha had to grip the edge of the seat to keep from being thrown.

When they were well away from the courthouse, Trey glanced at Samantha. She was sitting stiffly, her jaw thrust forward, staring straight ahead. Her eyes blazed with barely contained anger. As if feeling his gaze on her, she looked away, but not before he had seen the glimmer of tears on her lashes, and he knew the incident had unsettled her more than she was likely to admit. "Are you all right?" he asked, struggling to keep his own anger in check.

A lock of hair had escaped her pins and fallen forward over her face. She brushed it back. "I'm fine," she said curtly.

A muscle in Trey's jaw knotted. He turned his attention back to the road. "You're lucky Judge Gates didn't send you back to jail, Sam. Calling him 'incompetent' wasn't the smartest thing you could have done."

"I'm well aware of that," Samantha shot back. "I couldn't help it. He and Sheriff Calder made me so damned angry I wanted to spit. I have never in my life known anyone to be so condescending. I could swear those two are in cahoots with each other."

"That's ridiculous."

Samantha turned her head to glare at him. "Oh, really? First Joe gets arrested on false charges, and then the same thing happens to me. If you ask me, Calder is just trying to cover up the fact that he can't find the person who shot you."

"If you'd stayed away from that jail in the first place, none of this would have happened. Why didn't you come to me?"

"I tried to come to you, Trey," she said sarcastically. "But *you* didn't want to be disturbed. I even left a message for you with the new gate guard, and you didn't bother to respond to that, either. What else was I supposed to do? Wait outside the gate all night for you?"

Trey cast her a sharp glance. Cobb hadn't given him any message last night when he left the mine compound.

Samantha sighed and rubbed her fingertips wearily across her brow. "I'm sorry. I don't mean to take my frustration out on you. This whole situation has me so tied up in knots that I can't think clearly. I guess I'm just upset over Eulalie Carter behaving the way she did back there. I don't know what I expected from her, but I never thought she'd turn against me that way."

"She was definitely angry," Trey agreed. "What did you do to get her so riled up?"

The accusatory note in Trey's voice was so subtle that Samantha wondered if she had imagined it. "I'll tell you what I did," she said defensively. "I gave her food. I gave her money. Every time that shiftless husband of hers got drunk and gambled away his wages, she came running to me for help. Half the time I gave her more than I was paying Sarah and Maria."

So that's where her money's been going, Trey thought. "How long has this been going on?"

"I don't know. A year, maybe." She tried to brush the dirt off of her shirtwaist. "Eulalie has a lot of nerve, calling me a whore," she continued angrily. "What does she think *she* is, staying with a man who mistreats her and her children the way Jerry Carter does? If that's not prostituting yourself, then what is?"

Samantha's words hit Trey like a slap. He thought of his mother, trapped in a nightmarish marriage to Liam, and suddenly felt as if steel bands were tightening around his chest. It hurt to breathe. "Sam, some women don't have a choice," he said slowly. "They stay with the men who abuse them because they don't have the means to leave, and they'd have nowhere to go if they did."

"Trey, I offered Eulalie a job! And do you know what she did? She got angry! She told me—" Samantha broke off suddenly as she realized too late that what she'd said about Eulalie must have sounded like an indictment of Trey's mother. She looked at him and saw his brittle expression. Guilt streaked through her. Never in her life had she felt as undeserving of anyone's sympathy as she did now. She swallowed hard against the lump that had lodged in her throat. "Trey, I'm sorry."

"Forget it."

She placed a hand on his arm. "I didn't mean to—"

He shrugged off her hand. "I said forget it."

Samantha crossed her arms and retreated as far as the buggy seat would allow. Tears grated behind her eyelids, and she blinked them back. Because she had opened her mouth without thinking, she had unwittingly hurt the one person who meant more to her than anything or anyone else in the world. When was she ever going to learn?

Neither of them spoke during the rest of the ride to the restaurant. Trey did not drive around back this time, but stopped the buggy in front of the Drake House. "I need to get back to the mine," he said tonelessly. "Are you going to be all right here?"

Samantha took a deep breath. She did not want to leave with this tension crackling between them. "I'll be fine. Thanks for coming to the courthouse with me." Her voice quavered.

Trey pressed his fingertips against his burning eyelids. "I'm not angry with you. I just don't like to see you caught in the middle of all this."

"It's a little late for regrets, don't you think?"

"Sam, look at me."

She did, and was shaken to see the lines of fatigue that seemed permanently etched in his face. She wondered if he'd rested at all recently.

Trey knew she wouldn't like what he was about to tell her, and he was already bracing himself for her reaction. "Sam, I want you to stay away from the Concha while the miners are on strike."

Samantha's eyes widened and she opened her mouth to

protest, but Trey continued before she could speak. "I sent a telegram to Colonel Moser down at Fort McCrae, asking him for assistance in keeping order. Unfortunately, the troops he sent up here are nearly as rowdy and undisciplined as the strikers. We'll be lucky if we can get through this strike with a minimum of disruption."

Trey didn't mention the tragedy that had happened at the Concha the last time the miners went on strike, but that was in the forefront of their minds. Samantha moistened her lips. "Trey, I understand your concern. But most of my business comes from the mine and the mill. If I eliminate those two stops from my route, I might as well shut down completely."

"I'm sorry, Sam, but that's the way it has to be."

"Trey, you're going to put me out of business!"

"Samantha, don't start. I'm not in the mood right now for your histrionics."

Histrionics! Samantha stared at him in stunned disbelief. So that was how matters stood between them. At least Richard had been honest about refusing to recognize her needs. Trey, on the other hand, diminished them. Mutiny flashed in her eyes. "You've already said I could bring the lunch wagon into the compound. Does this mean you're withdrawing permission?"

"Until the strike is over, yes."

Samantha's chin shot up defiantly. "A fine one you are to talk about women not having choices, when you are the one interfering with mine. You have no business telling me how to run the restaurant, Trey. If you won't let me into the compound, then I'll stand outside the gate and sell lunches to the strikers."

She gathered her skirts around her and started to climb down from the buggy, but Trey caught her arm, stopping her. "In case you've forgotten, Sam, I'm the one who posted your bond. If having that bond revoked and you back behind bars is the only way I can keep you safe, I won't hesitate to do so."

Angry sparks flashed in Samantha's eyes. "Are you threatening me?"

"I love you, Sam. I don't want to see anything happen to you."

Samantha yanked her arm free of his grasp. "If you love me, Mr. Stern, you certainly have a peculiar way of showing it." Before he could stop her, she jumped down from the buggy and went inside the restaurant, slamming the door behind her.

Sarah hurried out of the kitchen, drying her hands on her apron. Relief flashed across her face, then faded when she saw Samantha's furious expression. "Samantha, are you all right? We were so worried about you!"

Samantha fought to rein in her temper. "Yes, I'm fine. It was all a silly misunderstanding."

Sarah shifted uneasily. She didn't know if Samantha wanted to talk or be left alone. "Mr. Sandoval went home already. He said to tell you he'll be back in the morning to see if you want him to drive the wagon."

"That's fine. Thank you for watching over the place while I was gone. I appreciate your help, Sarah."

"The cleaning up is done. I put the sandwiches from the lunch wagon in the icebox. They should still be good tomorrow."

Samantha nodded. "Why don't you go on home, too, Sarah. This day is already wasted."

"Are we going to reopen in the morning?"

Samantha hesitated. While the practical side of her was not inclined to take lightly any indication of trouble at the mine, Trey's patronizing infuriated her. The restaurant and the lunch wagon were her livelihood. She would be damned if she'd run them into the ground just because Trey asked her to. "Yes, Sarah," she said firmly. "Tomorrow we will open as usual."

Trey slowed the buggy as he neared the mine.

"You there! Get back! You're blocking the entrance!" a cavalry sergeant shouted as he turned his mount, forcing the strikers off the road. About fifty men surged through the opening and headed toward the gate. The soldier's horse reared up, causing some of the men to panic and try to claw their way out of the crowd.

Captain Renfret rode out to meet Trey. "Good afternoon, Mr. Stern. We've been letting the recruits through in groups of twenty. I have several men posted at your headquarters to maintain order."

Trey had to bite his tongue to keep from correcting the officer: they were job applicants, not recruits. And it was the administration building, not his headquarters. "Has there been any trouble?"

"Nothing serious. A fight involving six men broke out about an hour ago, but it was quickly subdued and the men disbursed. Shall I escort you through the gate?"

"Thank you." Trey kept his gaze focused on the road and deliberately blocked out the jeers of the striking miners as he drove through the gate. He was tempted to turn the buggy around and go back to the restaurant and try to reason with Samantha. He understood why she was angry, and he couldn't blame her. Perhaps when she had calmed down she would let him explain why he didn't want her near the mine.

Just this morning he had heard a rumor that Arnie Pitts was now working for Richard Winters. Doing what, he didn't know, but he did not like the idea of Pitts being on Winters's payroll. He didn't trust either of them, and he wouldn't have put it past Pitts to return to the Concha and try to exact revenge for being fired from his job.

About twenty applicants were lined up outside the administration building. A florid-faced sergeant stood on the front steps, issuing orders: "When you go inside, you are to be *quiet*. When you have completed your application and have talked with Mr. Flaherty, you are to come back outside immediately. You, mister, put out that cigar."

When he went inside the building, Trey saw that a long table had been placed against the front wall. Four men sat at the table filling out employment forms. Three others stood in line at the counter. Behind the counter, Amos Flaherty was reviewing the application of the first man in line. Amos, Carl Lemner, and Barney Reese were the only supervisors who had not walked off the job. Amos passed the form to Miles Gilbert, who began taking down the necessary information for an identification tag.

"Next," Amos called out.

Halfway across the room, Trey abruptly stopped. The next man in line looked up suddenly, and their gazes locked. The light in Trey's eyes turned cold. It took every ounce of self-control he had to turn and calmly walk away. He went into his office and closed the door.

"Mister, I asked you a question," Amos said. "What's your name?"

The man turned back to Amos. "Smith. Liam Smith."

Trey sat down behind his desk and dropped his face into his hands. He felt sick to his stomach. He did not want Liam working here.

Still, if Liam had changed over the years, he deserved as fair a shake of the dice as the next man. If he hadn't changed, it would not be long before his old habits resurfaced, and he would be fired. The only thing he was certain of was that he could no longer be objective where his uncle was concerned. The decision to hire or not to hire Liam was best left to Amos.

He was going through the week's mail when he was interrupted by a knock at his door.

Amos opened the door slightly and poked his head into the room. "Have you got a moment, sir?"

Trey motioned to a chair. "Come in, Amos. What's on your mind?"

Amos sat where Trey indicated. "We've hired enough men to replace those on strike, Mr. Stern," he said. "Should I turn the rest away?"

It was all Trey could do not to ask Amos if he had hired Liam. "Don't turn anyone away. Make it clear that we've already hired our limit, but we will still review the qualifications of anyone willing to go on a waiting list. I want you to look over all the applications and make a note of which men you want to hire should there be more openings. I'll trust your judgment."

"Thank you, sir. I'll do that." Amos started to rise.

"Please sit down, Amos. There is something else I wish to discuss with you."

His expression wary, Amos did as he was told. "Is something wrong, Mr. Stern?"

Trey folded the bill of lading he had been reviewing and put it aside. "I'm curious about one of the men on the day shift. Tell me, Amos, what do you know about Eskelta?"

"Someone's coming," Ian Hunter said nervously. "We need to get out of here."

Gaylord Whittaker wrapped the gold shavings in a handkerchief and tucked them in his pocket with the others. "I have what I need. Do you remember the way out?"

Ian placed a finger against his lips in a silent warning. Motioning to the older man to follow, he led Whittaker through a break in the tunnel wall. He moved the boards back into place over the narrow opening and extinguished the lantern, throwing them into absolute darkness.

They waited.

The men's voices grew closer. "How long d'ya suppose the strike's gonna last?"

"From what I hear, a long time. Someone's putting a lot of money behind the strikers."

"Think it'll go through Christmas?"

"Hope so. I need the work."

Through the gaps between the boards, a light flickered, briefly illuminating the tunnel.

"I hear Consolidated Silver wants to take over the mine and put in a new smelter and bring in the railroad and everything," another man said.

Someone snickered. "Unless they quit dragging their feet, they'll never pull it off. You know that man, Winters, the one who owns the bank? He also owns most of the land around here. I heard a rumor that he intends to work a deal with the railroad to allow them free access to the land in return for control over the tracks leading into town."

The voices faded as the miners turned down another tunnel, then were drowned out completely by the muted rumble of the cars on the narrow-gauge track that ran a few hundred feet over their heads.

When it was safe to speak again, Whittaker muttered an oath under his breath. "That bastard is bargaining with Southern Pacific behind our backs. If we don't get control of the mine before Winters cuts a deal with the railroad, we won't have any negotiating leverage at all."

"Stern has already made it clear he won't yield on his terms," Ian reminded him.

"The trick, Hunter, is not to make Stern give in, but to make him *want* to sell."

"The only way Stern will sell is if we guarantee him in writing that the miners will be better off under new management."

"That's not the only way," Whittaker said.

Ian lit the safety lantern. The flame swelled, then flickered precariously before steadying. "Do you have a better idea?"

"Stern will sell," Whittaker said confidently, "if he knows it's the only way the miners will be able to hold on to their jobs."

Chapter
Fifteen

HER face flushed, Samantha set the dirty dishes down on the kitchen table with nearly enough force to break them. After wrapping a dish towel around her hand to protect it, she retrieved the hot coffee pot from the stove. "Put on two more steak specials," she told Sarah. "I'm going to hang out the Closed sign. If we keep serving breakfast, we're not going to have time to take out the lunch wagon." She turned and went back into the dining room.

Outside, in front of the restaurant, horses' hooves pounded the unpaved street accompanied by shouts and cheering. Samantha pressed her lips together in annoyance. All night long, the soldiers from Fort McCrae had been drinking and racing their horses down Main Street. She had not gotten more than a few minutes of sleep.

She was hanging the Closed sign in the front window when a half dozen soldiers arrived at the door.

"Closed!" one of them blurted out in disbelief. "We just got here."

Samantha tried to smile. "I've run out of food," she lied. "You'll have to come back tomorrow."

"But I'm hungry now, and everyone says this place turns out the best breakfasts in town."

Samantha shrugged. "I'm sorry."

Disgruntled, the soldiers went away.

One customer who was already seated shouted, "Hey, lady! What does it take to get some service around here? I asked for some more coffee an hour ago!"

Samantha had to bite her tongue to keep from asking the man where he'd learned to tell time. Deliberately avoiding his gaze, she refilled his cup and moved on to the next table.

The dining room was packed with soldiers. Samantha was beginning to wonder if they were all here instead of at the mine. The miners who usually took their breakfast at the Drake House were conspicuously absent.

She had just finished refilling one soldier's coffee cup when someone gave her backside a fierce pinch. She gasped and whirled around.

The corporal who had pinched her flashed a grin at his companions and leaned back in his chair, tilting it up on its back legs. "Think I could get some honey for my biscuit?" he drawled suggestively.

Anger smoldering in her eyes, Samantha held the coffee pot in a strategic location over the man's head. "Would you care to try that again?"

The soldier's gaze shifted to the coffee pot Samantha carried, then back to her face. The light in his eyes turned cold. "Now, is that any way to treat a United States cavalryman who's here on official military orders?" he chided her.

One of his companions snickered. From the corner of her eye, Samantha saw one man nudge another at the next table. She knew they were all waiting to see what she was going to do next. "I don't care why you're in town," she said icily. "But you've already worn out your welcome here. I want you and your friends to leave."

"Listen, lady, I don't take orders from you. Now, why don't you be a good girl and bring me some honey for my biscuit?" The soldier's gaze lingered impudently on Samantha's bosom, and he slowly ran his tongue between his lips in a lewd gesture. His voice dropped seductively. "On second thought, sugar, bring me another biscuit, too. The one I got here is cold."

Hot color flooded Samantha's face. "I have a better idea," she shot back. "Why don't I warm that one up for you?" Before anyone realized what she was going to do, Samantha dumped the contents of the coffee pot over the biscuit on his plate.

The soldier yelped and brought the front legs of his chair back down to the floor with a thud as the scalding liquid splashed onto his lap. He surged up out of his chair.

Samantha swung the coffee pot at him as he came toward her, but he threw up his arm, deflecting the blow, and knocked the pot from her hand. It clattered loudly on the tile floor. Another soldier caught her from behind, pinning her arms at her sides as he yanked her hard against him. Chairs scraped the floor as men scrambled to clear a space around them.

The corporal she had drenched bent down to pick up the coffee pot. He cursed and jerked his hand away from the hot metal. Snatching his napkin up off the floor where it had fallen, he doubled it over and used it to shield his hand from the heat as he reached for the pot again.

Straightening, he came toward Samantha with the hot coffee pot, a nasty gleam burning in his eyes. "You're a right unfriendly one, aren't you?" he said slowly.

Samantha said nothing. She tried to twist away from the soldier who held her, but his grip on her arms tightened painfully.

The corporal's mouth twisted into a calculating smile. "I think it's time someone taught you a lesson, sugar. Hold her still, Jack."

Fear surged through Samantha's veins as he came toward her with the coffee pot. An eerie silence had fallen over the room. While some of the men fidgeted uneasily, no one came to her defense. The eagerness in their eyes made her feel ill. It was the same look she had witnessed on people's faces when a hanging was about to take place, a kind of sick anticipation that made one wonder just how twisted and perverted people could be.

The soldier raised the coffee pot toward her face. Samantha drew her head back as far as she could, but it was not far enough to escape the scorching waves of heat that emanated from the heavy metal.

"Corporal Lewis! What in the hell do you think you're doing? Sutter! Release that woman!"

Samantha's knees nearly buckled beneath her in horrified relief as the soldier holding her arms suddenly let go. The corporal with the coffee pot took a step back and pivoted.

A tall, thin man with a drooping mustache and master sergeant's stripes on the sleeves of his blue uniform marched into the restaurant. A long, ragged scar along the right side of his face pulled downward on his eyelid. His fearsome glare swept the room. "What in the hell are you men doing here? You're supposed to be up at the mine. I swear, you're the most worthless bunch of cannon fodder I've ever laid eyes on. Get out of here, and get back on duty. *Now!*"

"Aw, c'mon, sarge," one soldier muttered. "We was just having some breakfast. That stuff Mott feeds us down in the mess tent tears up your insides. Can't we finish eating?"

"I said move out!"

"You better listen to what he says," Sarah said from the kitchen doorway. "I got no problem translating for you if you're hard of hearing."

Samantha looked around to find Sarah aiming Maria's sawed-off shotgun into the room. There was a look of blistering determination in Sarah's eyes that she had never seen before. Samantha smoothed her clothes and lifted her chin as the men began trooping out of the restaurant, many of them dragging their feet. A couple of the men left money on the tables, but most didn't. By this time, however, she didn't care if they paid for their food. She simply wanted them to leave.

The tall sergeant cast a derisive gaze over Samantha as if he blamed her for the transgressions of his men, then did an abrupt about-face and marched out of the restaurant.

"Worthless scum," Sarah muttered after everyone had gone. "It would have done my heart good to blast rock salt into every last one of those mangy bastards. What's this thing loaded with, anyway?"

Samantha raked shaking fingers through her hair. "I don't know. Buckshot, I guess. There were two cartridges in it when Maria brought it here."

Sarah turned the gun over in her hands and eyed it critically. "If I were you, I'd go down to Mason's and stock up on cartridges. Things keep up the way they're going in this town, you're liable to need to use this monster."

At midmorning Pete Sandoval arrived. "I don't know if it's a good idea to go near the Concha this morning," he told Samantha. "The strikers are getting bolder. They managed to close the gate for nearly two hours this morning before the soldiers finally decided to show up."

Sarah and Samantha exchanged glances. Samantha was careful to reveal nothing by her expression. She had not told Pete and Sarah that she no longer had permission to take the wagon into the compound. She doubted either of them would be willing to go anywhere near the mine if they knew Trey had told her to stay away. She shrugged nonchalantly. "Let's hope those strikers have worked up an appetite. We can use the money. Pete, if you'll help load all this stuff, we can get started. I'll go with you."

By the time they reached the mine, however, Samantha had begun to question the wisdom of her decision. The road leading to the compound was choked with striking miners, soldiers, and bystanders. Many of the miners carried signs and were chanting, "Full pay for an eight-hour day!"

Pete stopped the wagon. "You still want to do this?" he asked uneasily. His breath fogged in the crisp morning air.

Samantha chewed on her bottom lip as she surveyed the scene before her. "I guess it can't hurt to try. The worst that can happen is that we'll end up going back to the restaurant."

With a sigh, Pete snapped the reins. "That's not the worst," he said ominously.

Samantha searched for a face she recognized. Finally she motioned to Pete and pointed. He directed the wagon toward the crowd.

Seeing her, a miner who sometimes came into the restaurant stepped in front of the wagon, blocking their way. "You can't go in there!" he shouted above the chanting.

Samantha jumped down from the seat. "I don't want to go in," she shouted back. "Most of my regular customers are here, outside the gate."

A uniformed soldier lifted a cover on one of the hampers in the bed of the wagon. "Hey, look! She's got food in here!" He started to reach inside the hamper, but Samantha caught his arm, stopping him.

"Sandwiches," she said firmly, "are fifty cents apiece."

"What the hell's going on here?" Marty Dennison pushed his way through the crowd. He scowled when he saw Samantha. "Are you daft, woman? Get that damned wagon out of here!"

Samantha's chin shot up defiantly. "Pardon me, Mr. Dennison, but I have as much right to be here as you do."

"No one crosses that picket line, Mrs. Drury. Not even you." He paused, then added meaningfully, *"Especially* not you."

The insinuation in his tone served only to make Samantha angrier. Her eyes narrowed as she returned Marty Dennison's glare with one of her own. She was acutely aware of Pete Sandoval behind her, passing out sandwiches and putting money in the cashbox. "I have no intention of crossing the picket line, Mr. Dennison," she said slowly, carefully enunciating each word. "Nor do I have any intention of leaving. Now, if you will please excuse me, I am very busy." She started to turn back to the wagon.

Marty Dennison seized her arm and spun her around. "I told you to leave!"

His grip on her arm made her wince. She tried to pull her arm free, but to no avail. A growing awareness of her vulnerability lent an edge to her voice. "Mr. Dennison, whatever your argument is with Mr. Stern, it doesn't concern me. What does concern me, however, is keeping my restaurant going during this strike. If you want to shut the mine down, that's your right. But don't run me out of business, too."

Dieter Vogel elbowed his way between two men to stand beside Dennison. He eyed Samantha coldly. "The men want you up front," he told Marty.

Marty released Samantha's arm. "Don't say I didn't warn you." The two men disappeared into the crowd.

"Well, well, what have we got here?"

The familiarity of the man's voice caused the fine hair on the back of Samantha's neck to stand up. She whirled around to find herself face to face with the soldier who had tried to burn her with the coffee pot earlier. Her lips thinned.

"May I help you?" she asked icily.

The corporal grazed her with an insolent look. "Is it true what I hear about you sleepin' with the man who owns this mine?"

Hot color flooded Samantha's face. Without answering, she turned back to the wagon.

Just then a stir rumbled through the mob. One man shoved another, who staggered against Samantha, nearly causing her to fall. Pete grabbed her elbow. "You all right?"

She nodded and started to speak, but her words were cut short as several men backed into her, forcing her against the wagon.

"He's coming through!" a man shouted.

In the gap between two men's heads, Samantha saw Trey's buggy slowly inching its way through the crowd. Miners and soldiers pressed against her, smothering her with their closeness. She lost sight of the buggy. Someone elbowed her in the ribs.

"Full pay for an eight-hour day!" a miner yelled. "Get out, Stern! We don't need you!"

Samantha choked back the retort that sprang to her lips. While she was angry with Trey for reasons of her own, she could not help feeling that the miners were being unfair to him. It would serve them right, she thought peevishly, if he were to wash his hands of all of them and sell the Concha.

Suddenly the crowd parted to allow Trey's buggy to pass.

Samantha's breath caught when she saw Trey. His face was pinched and drawn. He had not shaved, and his clothes were rumpled. He must have worked all night, she thought.

Instinctively she started toward him, but stopped when their gazes met. There was no mistaking the smoldering anger in Trey's dark blue-gray eyes as his gaze briefly held hers. The muscles in his jaw tightened. He turned his attention to the road and did not look back.

Hurt swelled in Samantha's chest and choked her throat. Mortification burning in her face, she turned back to the wagon.

The corporal had witnessed the incident with amusement. He snickered. "Looks like you're available after all," he said.

Casting him a derisive glance, Pete Sandoval squeezed between the soldier and Samantha. He leaned close to Samantha and asked in a low voice, "Do you want to leave?"

Samantha shook her head. "We're already here; we might as well make the best of it." Besides, she added to herself, the damage was already done.

Arnie Pitts blew on his hands to warm them. He should have worn his gloves, he thought. He had not expected to have to wait so long for everyone to leave the bank. It had long since grown dark, and what little warmth the sun provided had gone with the daylight. He shoved his hands into his pockets and fidgeted with the crucifix he'd taken from the Indian. He was growing cold and restless.

Still, if he wanted what he was owed, he had to be patient.

It galled him to no end that Jenkins had double-crossed him. Winters was going to be fit to be tied when he found out Tochino had gotten away. Still, Winters had promised him good money to get rid of Tochino, and he was going to pay up. Arnie figured that if he played his cards right, he might be able to talk Winters into paying him to go after Jenkins, too.

Finally the last customer emerged through the heavy wooden doors and descended the steps.

Another hour passed while the two tellers balanced their books and counted their cash and put the money away in the safe. The gaslights in the lobby were dimmed. Only through the windows of Richard Winters's office did the lights continue to burn brightly.

At last the tellers left the building, and Arnie nervously moistened his lips. His hand tightened on the revolver tucked into his belt. He wished he had more bullets, but the drunkard he'd stolen the gun from hadn't been carrying any extras. He hoped he wouldn't need to use the gun, except maybe to scare Winters a little. If necessary, he would just have to make do with the single round that was in the chamber and hope his aim wasn't off. He stepped out of the shadows and started across the street.

The front door of the bank was unlocked. Taking care not to make a sound, he eased it open and stepped inside the dimly lit lobby. Beneath his weight, a floorboard creaked. Arnie froze.

"I'm in my office, Ian," Richard Winters called out.

Arnie's heart pounded in his ears. He hadn't known Winters was expecting a visitor. Damn! If someone showed up before he could get the money from Winters, he was as good as dead.

No longer bothering to be quiet, he pushed the door shut and strode into Richard Winters's office. "Good evening, Mr. Winters."

Richard surged up out of his chair, surprise frozen on his face. He gripped the edge of his desk. "What are you doing here?" he demanded.

Arnie took a deep breath. "I thought you should know, Mr. Winters, Jenkins double-crossed both of us. He let

Tochino get away, then took off without paying me my share of the money."

Richard's blue eyes turned cold, but his expression otherwise remained unchanged. "You disturbed me for *that*?"

"I'll go after Jenkins for you, Mr. Winters. I know where he headed. I know where Tochino is, too. I can get both of them for you."

One corner of Richard's mouth twisted into a smile. "Let me guess," he said caustically. "You'll go after Jenkins and Tochino—for a price."

Arnie shifted nervously and scratched the side of his face. His hand dropped to his waist. Beneath his coat, he fidgeted with the butt of the revolver sticking out above his belt. "I don't need much, Mr. Winters. Just enough to get me to—"

"Get out."

"But, Mr. Winters, if Tochino talks to the law and tells everyone you—"

"I said *get out!*"

Arnie backed away as Richard came around his desk. "Jenkins told him, Mr. Winters. He told Tochino about you wanting to kill Mr. Stern and everything!"

Richard snatched a paper up off the corner of his desk. "Do you see this? Take a good hard look. Look at it!"

Arnie looked at the handbill Winters held out to him. It was a Wanted notice for Joe Tochino. An inappropriate grin spread across his face, and he chuckled. "I guess it don't matter about Tochino getting away after all. Before he gets a chance to talk, someone'll kill him for the reward money." He glanced up to find Winters studying him.

Richard was not smiling. He lifted one fair, well-groomed eyebrow haughtily. "It would be a small matter, Mr. Pitts, to have your name substituted for Mr. Tochino's on this notice."

Arnie's grin faded. "You can't do that."

"You underestimate me, Mr. Pitts. Now, unless it is your desire to have every bounty hunter in the territory looking for you, I suggest you get out of my office immediately. If you have any common sense at all, you'll leave town before daybreak."

First Jenkins had turned on him, and now Winters. Arnie felt his frustration mounting. He had no job; Stern had seen to that. Without any money, he had no place to go. He gripped the revolver. "You'd like that, wouldn't you, having me leave town so I can't tell the sheriff about you?"

Richard expelled his breath in an exaggerated sigh of annoyance. "You are testing my patience, Mr. Pitts. Now, as I am expecting someone shortly, I suggest you do us both a favor and leave before I am tempted to summon the sheriff and have you bodily removed from the premises."

Richard started toward the door, but was brought up short when Pitts pulled his hand from beneath his coat, and he suddenly found himself staring down the barrel of a Colt .45 Single-action Army Model revolver.

"I don't want to shoot you, Mr. Winters, but Tochino knows I was in on this, too. I don't want much. Just what you promised me before and maybe a little extra to get me out of town."

Richard lifted a wary gaze from the revolver to Arnie's face. "All right," he said slowly. "How much money do you need?"

Arnie fidgeted. "Why don't we go see what's in the safe?"

Richard inclined his head toward the door. "The safe is out there." Moving cautiously, he started past Arnie toward the lobby.

Arnie kept the revolver leveled on him as he neared the door of the office. "Get your hands up over your head and don't try nothing stupid, Mr. Winters. I don't want to have to—"

Richard brought his arm down sharply, striking Arnie's forearm and knocking the gun out of his hand. The revolver landed on the carpet.

Momentarily stunned, Arnie stared at his hand, then lifted a startled gaze to Winters's face just as Richard dived for the gun.

Arnie lunged. He grabbed the back of Winters's shirt.

Richard turned and threw his weight against the younger man. Still clutching Winters's shirt, Arnie stumbled backward, knocking over one of the chairs in front of Richard's desk. He went down hard, carrying Richard with him.

Richard rolled to his feet, but Arnie followed right behind him, and before Richard could get his balance, Arnie dived for his legs.

Richard flung his arm out to break his fall, scattering documents across the top of his desk. A poker-hot pain stabbed through his shoulder as he hit the floor. Arnie landed on top of him. Richard shoved him away, and Arnie fell back against the chairs.

Immediately, Richard was on top of him, his hands around Arnie's neck. "You miserable wretch," he ground out between clenched teeth. His face was livid. He pressed his thumbs against Arnie's windpipe. "I'll teach you to come in here and try to blackmail me."

Arnie clawed frantically at the hands fixed around his throat. He could feel the blood pumping behind his eyes. He couldn't breathe.

Over him, Richard Winters's face throbbed in and out of focus. It was an ungodly shade of purple, except for the eyes, which glowed like luminescent blue-white icicles. Winters was banging Arnie's head against the floor and choking him.

Somehow Arnie managed to work his legs up between them, drawing his knees up to his chin and planting his feet squarely against Richard's chest. Then, with every ounce of strength he possessed, he drove his feet into Winters's chest, breaking his hold and shoving him off him. Richard tumbled backward, struck the back of his head on the edge of the desk top, and slumped to the floor.

Gasping for air, Arnie struggled to his knees.

Richard did not move.

Arnie reached over and grasped his shoulder. He gave the other man a firm shake. "Winters?"

Richard's head lolled to one side. Blood was seeping into his hair and the collar of his shirt from a gash on the back of his skull.

Arnie clenched and unclenched his hands. "Damn," he muttered. What was he going to do now? If Winters came to and squealed on him, he was as good as hanged. He had to get out of here. More than that, he had to make sure Winters didn't talk.

He staggered to his feet. There wasn't much time. He had to get Winters out of here before the visitor he was expecting showed up.

Arnie shrugged out of his coat and wrapped it around Winters's head to absorb the flow of blood. Then he grasped the banker's ankles and dragged him away from the desk. Most of the blood on the carpet was hidden in the red-patterned wool, but Arnie did not want to take any chances. He hastily righted the two chairs in front of Winters's desk, strategically placed one of them over the bloodstains, then stacked up the papers that had been scattered in the fight and placed them on top of the desk.

He rubbed the back of his hand across his mouth. He'd done a pretty good job of straightening up, he thought. No one would know there had been a fight in here. When

Winters's visitor arrived, he would think the banker had just stepped out for a moment. By the time anyone thought of looking for a body, Arnie would be well across the county line.

The street was deserted. Arnie dragged Richard's body down the steps and around to the alley, then went back to close the door and to destroy the tracks in the dirt. By the time he returned to the alley, Richard Winters was beginning to regain consciousness. Richard moaned and stirred.

"Not so fast, Winters," Arnie mumbled. With shaking hands, he emptied Richard's pockets of a watch, several coins and a money clip holding several bank notes. He pulled the coat from around Richard's head and wrapped the items inside it. Finally he got to his feet and withdrew the revolver from his belt. He pulled back the hammer. "Sorry you had to go and get yourself robbed and killed, Mr. Winters," he said. His breathing was labored. "But with the company you keep, it was bound to happen sooner or later."

Richard struggled up on one elbow. "Pitts," he gasped. "Help me . . . I'll get you the m-money—"

Arnie pulled the trigger.

"May I come in?"

Trey held open the door of his house and stepped aside to let Ian Hunter pass.

"Nice place you have here," Ian commented as Trey led the way to his study.

"It suits my needs." Trey's tone was guarded. Ian had never visited him at home before. He motioned to a chair. "May I get you some coffee?" he asked.

"No, thank you. I can only stay a few minutes. I have an appointment with Richard Winters." Ian sat down. "Before

I tell you the real reason I came here, I thought you should know that we received a telegram from the home office this morning. Congress repealed the Sherman Silver Purchase Act yesterday."

Trey's stomach suddenly felt as if it had been twisted into a knot. The price of silver was at a record low. Without guaranteed sales to the government, he could not afford to keep the Concha open. Careful to keep his expression schooled, he leaned back in his chair and pensively rubbed his forefinger across his upper lip. His gaze never left Ian's face. "What is Consolidated's next move?"

Ian didn't hesitate. "They're going to force you to sell."

Trey's eyes narrowed. "Would their decision have anything to do with the ore samples you and Whittaker have been taking from the Concha?"

Surprise flickered across Ian's face. "You know about that?"

Until now Trey had only suspected what Ian and Whittaker were up to. Now he knew. He stood up, went to the French doors leading to the courtyard, and stared out into the darkness. Because of political maneuvering by a bunch of bureaucrats in Washington, he was about to lose everything he had spent his adult life working for. And he wasn't alone. Every independent silver mine in the nation was in danger of being shut down because President Cleveland and his old-money friends back east wanted to put the country on a gold standard.

Behind him, Ian said quietly, "Just between you and me—and I'll deny ever saying this—the repeal has hit Consolidated pretty hard. The directors are banking on using the gold the Concha contains to pay off some bad debts and to keep the corporation afloat. If you hold out, you might be able to get the terms you want."

Trey turned to look at him. A frown creased his brow. "If you were in my employ, Ian, I would fire you for revealing information like that to a competitor."

Ian eyed him steadily. "You can't fire someone who has already resigned."

One dark eyebrow shot upward.

"My primary reason for coming here tonight," Hunter said, "and for going to see Winters is to inform you both that Consolidated is sending someone else to negotiate the railroad contract." Ian stood up. "Consolidated has been good to me. I can't deny that. But the company is changing. It's becoming more cutthroat. It's one thing to seize a valuable opportunity; it's another matter to run a man out of business just to get what he has. And that's what Consolidated plans to do to you. They want the gold you're sitting on, and they intend to get it, even if it means breaking you in the process. I won't work for a company that will deliberately set out to ruin a man."

Trey shook his head. "I don't know what to say, Ian. In all honesty, I'm not sorry to see you wash your hands of Consolidated. On the other hand, I hate to see you leave. Will you return to Chicago?"

A twinkle appeared in Ian's eyes. "Actually, I thought I might stay around here. My father left me a little money when he died. Last I heard, there was a mine owner in Myterra who might be interested in obtaining financial backing for his half of a railroad line into town."

Trey was so stunned, it took him a moment to find his voice. "Why are you so eager to invest in the railroad?"

"Because the return is almost guaranteed," Ian replied frankly. "A railroad is impartial. It doesn't care what type of ore is mined in these mountains; it will haul out gold and silver from the Concha as well as copper from the Globe mines. Southern Pacific is considering extending the tracks all the way to Phoenix, linking the territorial capital with the rest of the country. Once that happens, this land is going to open up to all sorts of development. We'd do well to get in on this venture from the beginning, before prices start rising."

Intuitively, Trey knew Ian's offer was sincere, and he knew he and Ian could work well together. Still, he did not want to jump into any arrangement without giving it serious consideration. "That's quite an offer, Ian. I'd like to think it over and get back to you."

"Fair enough. Why don't we discuss it further over breakfast? I can sketch out the general proposal tonight, and we can work out the details tomorrow."

Trey inclined his head. "Is there any place in particular you'd like to meet?" He hesitated to suggest the Drake House. Right now he was still so angry with Samantha for going near the Concha after he'd told her not to that he doubted he could keep a level head if he saw her. The only thing stopping him from having Sheriff Calder revoke her bail was that he did not want to see her back behind bars.

"Have you ever been to Ochoa's Cantina?" Ian asked.

"I've never eaten there, but I know where it is."

"The food is good. Mrs. Ochoa's breakfast specialty is eggs scrambled with chorizos and green chilies."

"Sounds good to me. Meet you there at seven?"

"I'll be there."

On his way back into town, Ian's step was lighter and his shoulders straighter than they had been in months. He was finally beginning to feel good about himself again. He had been growing increasingly disillusioned with Consolidated Silver ever since the home office had placed a gag order on all its employees right after the cave-in that had killed Michael Drury and fifteen others. The enforced silence had hampered the resulting investigations. Hunter's feelings of discontent had increased considerably since Gaylord Whittaker's arrival in Myterra. He didn't know if it was because he suspected that Whittaker had been sent here to keep an eye on him or because of Whittaker's unquestioning acceptance of any underhanded operation the home office wanted done. Either way, he was glad to finally be free of both Whittaker and Consolidated Silver.

Ian was relieved to find the lights still burning in Richard Winters's office when he reached the bank. His visit to Trey had taken longer than he had intended, and he had not expected Winters to wait for him. He went inside. "Winters?"

When he received no response, Ian went to the doorway of Winters's office. The room was empty.

Ian scratched his head. It seemed odd that Winters would leave the bank unlocked and unattended. Finally, not knowing what else to do, he decided to wait. He went into the office and sat in one of the chairs facing Richard's desk.

As the minutes dragged by with agonizing slowness and Richard Winters still did not return, Ian's uneasiness mounted. There was something odd about the office, something he could not quite put a finger on.

Everything was in its place, Ian thought as his gaze roamed the office. It wasn't as if Richard had left in a hurry, leaving a file open or papers scattered about his desk. But then, Richard Winters didn't scatter much of anything, even when he was working. The man was tidy to a fault. The papers on his desk were always stacked with military precision, and his pen holder was kept at a particular angle.

Even his chair was always turned a certain way.

Then realization dawned, and Ian's eyes narrowed critically as he stared at the papers on Richard's desk. They were stacked neatly—neatly, that is, unless one was judging by Richard Winters's standards. Several pages stuck out beyond the rest, and they were lying at a slightly crooked angle on one corner of the desk. Even the chairs in front of the desk were not placed at so precise an angle as usual. A sudden chill touched the base of Ian's spine, causing gooseflesh to erupt on his skin.

Ian stood up and stepped away from the desk. He had a peculiar feeling that Richard Winters had not been the last person in this office. Someone else had been here. Had someone gone through Winters's papers, hoping to find something?

As he stared at the desk, Ian noticed that the chair he had been sitting in was quite a bit farther away from the desk than the other one, making the arrangement look awkward in a way he had not noticed when he'd first entered the office.

Something was wrong, terribly wrong.

With the intention of finding Sheriff Calder, Ian started to leave, but again his attention was involuntarily drawn to the chair in which he had been sitting. He went to the chair and stared down at it, puzzled by the odd attraction it held for him.

If he had been arranging the furniture, even without Winters's fetish for neatness, he thought, he would have placed the chair farther to the left and closer to the desk. As it was, whoever sat in it would be an observer rather than a participant in any conversation. On a whim, he picked up the chair and moved it to the spot he felt was more appropriate.

Then he saw the stain.

The barely noticeable coloration suggested that something had been spilled on the carpet. Ian knelt down and touched the darkened area.

It was wet.

Ian raised his hand. There was blood on his fingertips.

Samantha had finished setting up for the breakfast rush and had checked the locks on the doors when she heard a noise in the alley. She blew out the lantern, then went to the pantry and retrieved Maria's shotgun.

The kitchen doorknob turned and clicked several times. Holding her breath, Samantha slowly made her way across the darkened kitchen with the shotgun, her heart pounding in her ears.

There was a faint knock on the kitchen door, followed by coughing. Then a familiar voice rasped hoarsely, "Samantha?"

Samantha put down the shotgun, threw back the bolt, opened the door, and was nearly knocked down as Joe pitched forward.

She caught his arm to keep him from falling. "Joe! What are you doing here? Are you all right?"

Even as she spoke, she knew he wasn't all right. His breathing was strained, and he was leaning heavily on her. She led him to a chair, then closed and bolted the door. Her hands were shaking so badly she could barely light the lamp.

"Oh, my God!" She pressed a hand over her mouth to keep from being sick.

Joe was sitting slumped over, his right arm pressed close to his side. His clothes were torn, his face bruised and scraped. Blood saturated the right side of his shirt, and the stain appeared to be spreading.

"Joe, look at you! You're bleeding all over the place! What happened? Were you shot?"

"I'll be all right." Joe tried to catch his breath. "The bullet went clear through."

"I'm going to get Dr. Goss."

"No! There are Wanted posters all over town. If anyone finds out I'm here, I'll be hanged without a trial."

"Joe, you need to see a doctor."

"There's no time. Samantha, listen to me. Richard Winters is behind all this. He hired a gunman to shoot Trey and Taza. I'm guessing he paid Taza to tell Sheriff Calder that he saw me shoot Trey. Then Winters had Taza killed so he couldn't talk."

Samantha froze. There was a terrible pressure in the middle of her chest, making her heart feel as if it would explode. "Why?" she whispered.

"I don't know why. Perhaps Winters wants control of the mine." Briefly, Joe told her everything that had happened since he was hit over the head in his jail cell. "You need to warn Trey," he told her when he'd finished his story. "Winters intends to kill him."

Samantha took a deep, unsteady breath to try to calm her reeling emotions. She did not want to believe Richard was responsible for the shootings, and yet instinct told her it was true. "Let me see to your wound first," she said shakily. "Then you need to get out of here. I don't want to take a chance that someone may have seen you. I've already been ordered to inform Sheriff Calder if you try to contact—"

Samantha gasped and whirled around as someone banged loudly on the kitchen door.

"Mrs. Drury, it's Sheriff Calder."

Samantha stared at Joe in wide-eyed disbelief. The color had completely drained from her face, making her red hair seem almost garish against her unnatural pallor.

Joe pushed himself up off the chair. "I need to hide," he whispered. Pain was etched in the lines of his face.

Samantha looked around frantically. There was no place in the house where Sheriff Calder would not be able to find him if he decided to try. She nodded toward the pantry. "Over there."

Sheriff Calder knocked again. "Mrs. Drury, I know you're in there. Open this door."

Samantha felt as if she would be ill. Had Sheriff Calder followed Joe to the restaurant? Even if he hadn't, one peek through the kitchen window would have effectively ended any search. She waited until Joe was safely inside the pantry, then wiped her damp palms on her skirt and went to the door. She slid back the bolt and opened the door.

Sheriff Calder's expression was so grim that Samantha's heart turned over in her chest. She knew he had come after Joe. "What can I do for you, Sheriff?" Her voice sounded as if it belonged to someone else.

The sheriff removed his hat. He looked not at her but past her, his eyes focusing on a point behind her. His brows drew together. "Expecting trouble?"

Samantha turned and followed his gaze. The shotgun was still lying on the kitchen table. She had forgotten to put it away. "I heard noises in the alley earlier. It turned out to be nothing." It was not entirely a lie.

Sheriff Calder turned his attention back to her, and his probing gaze searched her face. For what, Samantha didn't know. The intensity of his stare made her uneasy.

Finally Sheriff Calder drew himself up to his full height and took a deep breath. "Mrs. Drury, Richard Winters was killed tonight," he said firmly. "I found his body in the alley behind the bank. He had been shot once in the chest, and there was a gash on the back of his head, as if he'd been struck with a heavy object."

Samantha's hand flew to her mouth. Richard was dead?

Before she could recover her wits, Sheriff Calder reached into his pocket. "I found this on the ground near the body." He removed his hand from his pocket. A dainty silver chain and crucifix dangled from his fingers.

Samantha's breath caught in her throat. Her startled gaze flew to the sheriff's face.

Calder coiled the chain in the palm of one hand and returned it to his pocket. "I can see you recognize the crucifix. It's the same one Joe Tochino was wearing when he broke out of jail."

Samantha had to bite her tongue to keep from blurting out the truth about Joe's supposed escape from jail, but she knew Sheriff Calder would demand to know how she'd come by such privileged information. She took a deep breath. "Maria gave it to him," she said in a low voice.

"Have you seen him?"

"No." Her voice wavered. This latest turn of events had left her feeling as if someone had jerked the ground from beneath her feet.

Sheriff Calder sighed. "Mrs. Drury, unless you wish to return to jail, you had best answer me truthfully. Has Joe Tochino been here?"

Samantha felt her anger mounting. The fact that Sheriff Calder was questioning her word had less to do with her credibility than with his opinion of her as a person. She thrust out her chin and glared at him. "Would you care to come in and look for him?" she asked sarcastically. She prayed he had not looked through the kitchen window and seen Joe for himself.

For a brief second the anger in Sheriff Calder's eyes hardened into hatred. Then it was gone. "That won't be necessary." He put his hat back on. "I'm sorry to have troubled you. Good night, Mrs. Drury."

After she closed the door, Samantha's knees nearly buck-led beneath her in terrified relief. She had almost expected the sheriff to take her up on her ungraciously rendered invitation. She waited until she heard the sheriff ride away, then closed the kitchen curtains.

Unsteady on his feet, Joe emerged from the pantry. He clutched the back of a chair for support. "I guess we won't need to warn Trey about Winters after all," he said uneven-ly.

Samantha crossed her arms. She was shaking so badly, she could hardly speak. "Who would have had reason to kill him, Joe?"

"Who *didn't* have a reason? What did the sheriff mean about you returning to jail?"

"It's a long story." Samantha went to the stove and poured hot water from the kettle into a shallow bowl, then retrieved several clean dish towels and a linen tablecloth from the pantry. She nodded at the chair. "You'd better sit down before you faint. And take off that shirt so I can see to your wound."

While she cleaned Joe's bullet wound and bound his torso with strips torn from the tablecloth, Samantha told him what had happened since the night he'd disappeared from the Myterra jail.

As she talked about her arrest and about the miners' strike, Joe noticed that Samantha did not mention Trey's name at all. "I don't have a good feeling about you staying here alone, Samantha," he said when she finished.

Samantha gave him a wan smile. She didn't have a good feeling about anything that had happened in this town lately. Gathering up the remaining strips of linen, she draped the torn tablecloth over her arm and picked up the washbasin. "I'm the last person you should be worrying about, Joe. Don't move. I'll go find something for you to wear."

Joe gripped her arm. "What happened between you and Trey?"

The memory of Trey's earlier reaction caused Samantha's chest to constrict abruptly. When she tried to swallow, her throat hurt. For as long as she lived, she would never forget the look of contempt on Trey's face when he saw her outside the mine compound. She avoided Joe's gaze. "Nothing happened."

"Samantha, something is wrong. I can see it in your eyes."

She sighed. "Right now Trey is angry with me, and I can't say that I blame him. I'd rather not talk about it, Joe. Please?"

They'd probably quarreled, Joe thought. With two people as headstrong as Trey and Samantha were, he was surprised they weren't at each other's throats more often. He released her arm. "I'll respect your wishes," he said quietly. "On one condition."

She cast Joe a disgruntled glance. "What condition?"

"That you iron out your differences and not let this discord between you turn into something that can't be mended. If this is some petty disagreement that you're not even likely to remember a few months down the road, don't let it drive a permanent wedge between you. He's a good man, Samantha. Don't let him slip away."

"The way you let Maria slip away?" There was no mistaking the sarcasm in Samantha's voice.

Pain flickered behind Joe's eyes. "That's not fair."

"When is life ever fair, Joe? Tell me that."

Before Joe could answer, Samantha left the room.

Little was said between them over the next half hour. Finally, dressed in Michael Drury's clothes, Joe prepared to leave. Samantha handed him a parcel. "Here is some food to get you through the next few days. Promise me you'll be careful?" Samantha's voice was strained.

Joe took the bundle and thanked her. "I appreciate your going out on a limb for me."

"That's what friends are for." Samantha's attempt at nonchalance fell short. Her throat tightened. *That's what friends are for.* Trey had said the same thing to her. She took a shaky breath. "I'm sorry for the remark I made about Maria. Forgive me?"

Sliding one arm around her shoulders, Joe drew her near and kissed her forehead. "There's nothing to forgive," he said softly. "Take care, *querida.* If Trey doesn't come to his senses soon and marry you, I might just come back here when all the commotion has died down and court you myself."

Tears stung Samantha's eyes. Remembering something, she ran back to the table and picked up the shotgun. "Take this with you. You might need it."

Joe started to object, but Samantha silenced his protest with a shake of her head. "Consider it one final gift from Maria," she said thickly.

After Joe had gone, Samantha leaned against the kitchen door as numb shock began to set in. Although she had never loved Richard Winters, she had come close to marrying him. Now he was dead, and Joe was being blamed for the murder. When was this nightmare ever going to end?

She had to reach Trey. Regardless of how he felt about her right now, he would want to help Joe. Until the real killer was found, none of them would be safe.

Joe had told her that Silas Jenkins was the man Richard had hired to kill Trey. He was still out there somewhere, as was Arnie Pitts. Whoever had taken Maria's crucifix from Joe while he was unconscious had killed Richard.

Whatever the man had to gain from killing Richard Winters, he no longer had a reason to kill Trey.

Unless perhaps he wanted to finish the job he'd started.

Fully aware that she was probably allowing her imagination to get the best of her, Samantha fetched her coat and blew out the lanterns. She had to warn Trey, no matter how ridiculous her theory sounded. If she did nothing, and something happened to him, she would never forgive herself.

The night was still when she slipped out into the darkness and pulled the kitchen door shut behind her. Even the sounds of revelry coming from the saloons and dance halls seemed unusually subdued. She shivered and turned up her collar. She wished she had thought to give Joe a blanket to take with him.

She decided to go to Trey's house first. As tired as he had looked this morning, she would not have been surprised if he had driven home and gone straight to bed. Although, knowing Trey, as long as there was a job to be done, he would keep working, regardless of how exhausted he might be. If he wasn't at home, she would look for him at the mine. She would not give up until she had found him, even if she had to lie to get past the gate guard.

As she neared the part of town where Trey lived, a vague uneasiness began gnawing at her insides. The buildings were closer together here, and the streets narrower. She thought of the night Trey was shot in front of his own house, and her uneasiness grew. Drawing her coat tighter around her and clenching her teeth to keep them from chattering, she quickened her step. The sooner she reached Trey, the better.

Suddenly she froze. Was it only her imagination or had she heard the crunch of gravel? She listened, but her heart was pounding so loud in her ears she could not have heard anything, and when she looked around, she saw nothing. She resumed walking.

She heard the sound again, closer this time. She whirled around. Someone grabbed her from behind, and a hand closed over her mouth, smothering her scream.

Samantha clawed frantically at the hand covering her mouth, but to no avail. The man tightened his arm around her middle, cutting off her air and lifting her feet off the ground. She kicked at his shins with her heels.

He yanked her hard against him. "Pipe down, Mrs. Drury, or you won't leave me any choice but to *make* you be still!"

Sheriff Calder?

Samantha stopped fighting.

Sheriff Calder took his hand away from Samantha's mouth. Gripping her upper arm, he spun her around to face him. "I had a feeling you'd try to warn Stern about your friend Tochino. Well, it won't work, Mrs. Drury. This time I'm going after Tochino without any interference from you or from Stern." Still gripping her arm, he steered her none too gently down the street in the direction from which she had just come.

Samantha had to run to keep up with the sheriff's long-legged stride. There was a hard, cold knot in the pit of her stomach just like one she'd gotten as a child when she accidentally swallowed a chunk of ice. Only this time the coldness was not from ice but from fear. "Where are you taking me?" she demanded.

"Where I should have kept you the first time you gave me trouble," Sheriff Calder retorted. "In jail!"

Samantha's fear ballooned into panic, overriding her sense of reason. She rammed her elbow into the sheriff's ribs. He grunted, and his grip on her slackened. Yanking her arm free, Samantha broke into a run.

"Get back here!" Sheriff Calder shouted. He sprinted after her. His arms closed around her from behind.

Samantha began to scream.

Sheriff Calder covered her mouth with his hand and gave her head a stern shake. "Be quiet!" he hissed in her ear.

Samantha sank her teeth into his thumb.

The sheriff yelped and yanked his hand away from her face. "Damn you!"

Samantha wrenched herself out of his grasp, but before she could get away, a fiery pain exploded in the back of her head, and her entire world slipped into darkness.

Chapter
Sixteen

JOE stopped and crouched beside a boulder to catch his breath. Closing his eyes, he rested his forehead against the cold stone and fought back the weakness that rolled over him in nerve-deadening waves. He wanted to lie down somewhere and sleep for a long, long time. He felt feverish.

He thought of Richard Winters, and anger only increased his sense of helplessness. He was being blamed for this murder, too, and there was nothing he could do to clear his name. For whatever reason, Sheriff Calder seemed determined to convict him.

He was not aware of having fallen asleep until the snapping of a twig in the underbrush jolted him awake. Suddenly alert, he strained his ears to listen.

Nothing. It must have been a rabbit, he thought. He relaxed somewhat.

The sleep had done him good. He felt a little stronger now, and more clearheaded. He opened and closed his hands several times to work the stiffness out of his fingers. The night was cold and clear. He thought of building a fire, then decided against it.

The stars were beginning to fade in their clarity. It would be light soon, and he knew he should start traveling again. Yet still he delayed. He did not know what was holding him back, except that running away did not feel right. If he went back, he risked being caught and hanged without a trial. Men would do anything for a reward. But if he did not go back, he might never get a chance to clear himself of the charges against him. He would always be a wanted man.

Finally he arrived at a decision. He would go back, but he would stay hidden until it was safe for him to be seen in the open. If he could find Perry Kendall and explain what had happened to him, perhaps the attorney could convince Sheriff Calder and Judge Gates that he was innocent.

By the time Joe reached Myterra, it was daylight. Avoiding the main streets, he made his way through the narrow alleys until he reached the Drake House.

From the front of the restaurant, he could hear loud banging and cursing. Careful to keep from being seen, he slipped between the buildings and looked around the corner.

Two men Joe had never seen before were standing in front of the restaurant. One of them gave the door a fierce kick and swore loudly, "Damn it all! How's a working man supposed to eat when places don't open up like they're supposed to?"

"Aw, c'mon, Bubba," the man's companion pleaded. "Give it up. She ain't openin' up just 'cause you want her to. Let's go somewheres else."

Joe ducked back into the shadows. He felt uneasy. Samantha didn't usually close down on a weekday. He wished he knew where she was. Returning to the rear of the restaurant, he tried the kitchen door, but it was locked. He cupped his hands around his eyes and peered through the window. He could see no one.

Unable to shake the disturbing feeling that something had happened to Samantha after he left last night, Joe went to the door and pounded on it. "Samantha! Are you in there? Samantha, answer me!"

Behind him, a woman gasped.

Joe's heart leaped into his throat. He pivoted.

Sarah Morrissey pressed one hand against her heart. "Mr. Tochino, you frightened the daylights out of me!" she blurted out. Then, as she seemed to remember the Wanted posters she had seen, Sarah's eyes widened and her voice dropped to a whisper. "What are you doing here?"

Joe figured he hadn't frightened her nearly half so much as she had him, but he didn't say so. "There's no time to explain right now, Mrs. Morrissy. Do you know where Samantha is?"

Sarah shook her head. "The place was locked up when I came to work this morning, and Samantha didn't answer the door. After the trouble we had here yesterday, I thought she might have changed her mind about opening."

Joe's eyes narrowed. "What trouble?"

"It was those soldiers from Fort McCrae. A couple of them got real cheeky with her yesterday during the breakfast rush, and when she told them to leave, they grabbed her. One of them held her, and the other one was going to burn her face with the coffee pot. They might have hurt her really bad if their sergeant hadn't come along when he did and told them to get to work."

Joe muttered an oath under his breath. Samantha hadn't told him about any trouble at the restaurant. "Would you recognize the two men?"

Sarah nodded. "The sergeant called one of them Corporal Lewis. I can't remember the other one's name. But I could pick them both out if I had to."

Joe rubbed a hand over his jaw as he worried over what to do next. His earlier strength had left him, and he was beginning to feel ill. Still, if Samantha was in trouble, he had to help her. "I'm going inside," he said.

Dredging up every ounce of strength he possessed, Joe stepped back and gave the door a fierce kick with the sole of his boot. The lock split, and the door opened with a splintering crash.

No one was in the kitchen. Joe immediately went through the dining room to Samantha's small bedroom off the rear hall.

The open trunk containing Michael Drury's old clothes was still sitting in the middle of the floor, and Samantha's bed looked as if it had not been slept in.

On the bureau, next to the washbasin, Joe saw the torn tablecloth and the linen strips she had used last night to clean his wound. In the washbasin, more pieces of linen floated in a pool of bloodied water. Alarm surged through Joe's veins. It was not like Samantha to let a mess like that sit overnight. He went back to the kitchen.

"Mrs. Morrissey, I want you to go get Sheriff Calder. Tell him Samantha is missing. Don't tell him you saw me, or he'll waste his time coming after me instead of looking for Samantha. I'm going up to the mine to see what I can find out."

"Do you think those soldiers might have come back for Samantha?" Sarah asked.

Although Joe suspected Samantha's disappearance was due to something far more threatening than a couple of hot-headed soldiers amusing themselves at a woman's expense, he kept his speculations to himself. He started toward the door. "I don't know, ma'am," he said, "but I intend to find out."

The cantina owner's daughter, a tall, slender girl of eighteen or nineteen with soft, dark brown hair braided and wrapped around her head in a coronet, brought Trey a cup of coffee and in halting English asked for his order.

In Spanish, Trey explained that he was waiting for someone. An attractive blush fused into the girl's cheeks and she hurried back to the kitchen. Trey suppressed a chuckle. He had a pretty good idea why Ian had wanted to come here.

The situation at the mine worried him. As soon as word got out that the Sherman Silver Purchase Act had been repealed, panic would likely follow. The strikers were going to push even harder for Consolidated to assume ownership of the Concha. Anyone with any common sense at all would be able to figure out that he did not have the funds necessary to keep the mine open on his own unless major changes were made, changes that could entail substantial reductions in manpower.

He had lain awake much of the night, trying to reach a decision. He could not, in good conscience, ask the miners to make sacrifices on his behalf. They had nothing to gain by his retaining ownership of the mine. If anything, they risked a cut in pay and the possibility of losing their jobs. At this point it no longer even mattered whether the men were paid in cash or scrip. What mattered now was being paid at all.

It was a quarter past seven when Ian arrived at the cantina. There were shadows beneath his eyes, and he looked as if he had not rested well. He pulled out a chair, sat down, and apologized for being late. "Have you heard about Richard Winters?" he asked.

Something in Ian's voice touched a warning chord in the back of Trey's mind. He slowly put down his coffee cup. "What about him?"

"He wasn't at the bank last night when I got there. There were bloodstains on the carpet. The sheriff found his body in the alley behind the bank. He'd been shot."

Trey felt as if someone had punched him in the gut. He had never liked Richard Winters, but he had never wished for the man's death. "Winters is dead?"

Ian nodded. "His money and valuables were gone. It appeared as if he had been robbed, but Sheriff Calder seemed to think otherwise. From the questions he was asking me, I got the impression he believed the murder was premeditated."

Until Ian had offered to finance Trey's half of the railroad, Trey mused, Richard Winters had been Consolidated Silver's only potential competition for railroad shares. "Do you think Consolidated could be behind the shooting?" he asked.

A troubled expression clouded Ian's eyes. "Why would they want him dead? Because Winters went behind Consolidated's back and was negotiating with Southern Pacific on his own?"

Although that bit of information was news to Trey, he was careful to keep his surprise from showing. "Winters was also funding the strikers," he said evenly.

Ian let his breath out slowly. "I didn't know that. I wondered how the miners could afford to go without work for any length of time. The union treasury has been broke since the last strike. I heard that from one of the mill workers."

The girl who had waited on Trey returned to their table with a cup for Ian and a fresh pot of coffee. Trey noticed that she had changed into a clean dress and apron and that she cast shy glances at Ian from beneath her lashes as she filled their cups and took their orders.

After the girl returned to the kitchen, Trey told Ian of his decision. "I'm going to sell the Concha to Consolidated."

Ian stared at him in astonishment. "Just like that? I thought you were going to hold out until Consolidated met your terms."

"If they want use of the railroad, they'll meet my terms."

The dismay in Ian's eyes slowly turned to amusement, then to admiration. "Are you considering using your profits from the sale of the mine to buy Consolidated's share of the railroad?"

"If Consolidated is as strapped for cash as you implied, they're not going to be in a good financial position to buy both the mine and the railroad shares."

"They're not going to want to let go of those railroad shares," Ian cautioned.

"True. But if I retain ownership of the mine and am forced to close it down, they're going to have a railroad running right through the middle of a ghost town. I'm betting they won't want to take that chance."

Before Ian could respond, the girl who had waited on them came into the room with Amos Flaherty. She pointed toward the table where they were sitting, and Amos came toward them. His face was red, as if he'd been running, and his expression was distraught.

Trey pushed back his chair and stood up. Something was wrong. Amos would not have followed him here otherwise.

Amos fidgeted with his hat. "I asked around, sir, and some of the boys said they saw you come here." He cast Ian Hunter a wary glance.

"It's all right, Amos. Ian is a friend. What happened?"

Although Amos still looked doubtful, he turned his attention back to Trey. "There's trouble up at the Concha, sir. The strikers took control of the mine. They're ordering everyone out of the stopes. Carl Lemner tried to stop them, and they jumped him. He's hurt bad, sir."

Trey snatched his hat off the seat of the chair beside him and tossed a coin on the table. "Where's Carl now?"

"Down at the doc's. A couple of us managed to get him out and into a wagon."

If the strikers destroyed the mine, Trey thought, there would be nothing left to sell, and his efforts would have been for naught. But what angered him above all was that men who had remained loyal to him during the strike were getting hurt. "Ian, we'll have to schedule this meeting for another time. I need to get back to the mine." He started toward the door with Amos close on his heels.

Ian bolted out of his chair. "I'm coming with you."

Outside the cantina, the air was tinged with a sharp, acrid smell that stung the back of Trey's nose and caused his eyes to water. He instinctively turned his gaze up the hill toward the mine. Even from here, he could see the thick black smoke that engulfed the mill. He swore inwardly. There was enough dynamite stored in Michael Drury's old office to blow up the entire compound. The fire had to be contained before it spread to the administration building.

All the way to the Concha, Trey prayed he was not too late.

More than two thousand men choked the road leading to the mine entrance. Mounted soldiers were trying in vain to drive back a swarm of rioters who were attempting to rush the gate. Railcars used to haul the ore out of the tunnels had been rolled across the gate, blocking the entrance. A volley of shots exploded in the crowd. Someone screamed. Strikers and onlookers shoved in panic to escape the chaos.

Leaving the horse and buggy at the bottom of the hill, Trey waded through the rioters until he located Captain Renfret. "What in the hell is going on here? You're supposed to be keeping order."

The officer looked frustrated. "I'm sorry, sir. I couldn't stop them."

Trey had to bite his tongue to keep from castigating the officer with accusations of incompetence. He turned to Amos. "Go up to the hoisting station and sound the alarm," he shouted over the din. "We have to get everyone out of the mine before that dynamite catches." He started toward the gate.

Two men caught him by the arms and held him back. "Hey, mister, you can't go in there!"

Barely controlled rage boiling in his veins, Trey shrugged them off. He glared at the men. "Who is in charge here?"

Recognition flickered in one man's eyes, and for a second he appeared unsure of what to do next. "Uh . . . Marty Dennison is, sir," the man stammered. "Him and Mr. Vogel."

"Where are they?"

The man jerked his head toward the compound. "Up at the mine office, Mr. Stern."

Curbing the almost overwhelming urge to knock a few heads together, Trey pushed his way through the crowd. Anyone with the inclination to stop him backed off after seeing the determined set of his jaw and the raw fury blazing in his eyes.

At the gate he catapulted up onto one of the railcars and jumped down on the other side. Flames from the burning mill had spread and licked at the dry brush that grew along the fence. Ahead of him, the entire hill was shrouded in smoke.

Many of the men inside the compound were armed. Through the smoke, Trey saw John Ruskin, carrying a rifle, pass only a few feet away from him as he marched several men toward the gate. They were not regular miners, but replacements who had been hired to work during the strike.

The miners called them scabs, non-union workers who crossed picket lines during a strike. Trey had never been completely comfortable with the term; it seemed to place the blame for the miners' woes on the wrong shoulders.

Closing the distance between them in three long strides, Trey seized John Ruskin's collar and swung the big man around. "How many men are still below?" he demanded.

Recovering his balance before his wits, the miner shook his head. "I—I don't know, sir," he sputtered.

"Then find out!" Trey ground out. "Get everyone out of that mine. Then get your tail up to the pumping station and get this fire under control before we all get blown to pieces."

Remembering himself, John Ruskin pulled himself up to his full height and waved his rifle in Trey's face. "I don't take orders from anyone except—"

"You'll do as you're told, Ruskin, or I'll see to it that you never work in another mine in this territory!"

Any objection the miner might have made was snuffed out by the grating of metal on metal. Trey turned just in time to see a hundred-foot section of steel fencing come crashing down. There was no time to get out of the way. Mentally and physically, he braced himself for the stampede of rioters.

Samantha opened her eyes and swallowed hard against the bile that rose in her throat as the ceiling spun precariously above her. She had to resist the urge to close her eyes again to shut out the sharp pain pulsing in her head.

Morning was just breaking. The light that filtered in through the barred window was gray and unwelcoming. Gradually the room came into focus, and Samantha realized that she was in a jail cell.

The last thing she remembered was Sheriff Calder grabbing her from behind as she tried to run away from him. After that, her memories were a blur of pain and darkness.

Sheriff Calder must have struck her on the head. Why else would it hurt so much?

Her skirt was tangled around her legs, and her coat was twisted, making movement difficult. Somehow she managed to push herself upright and swing her feet over the side of the narrow cot. Her hair hung askew, prevented from falling down completely by the pins that jabbed her scalp. She tugged out the remaining pins and shoved them into her coat pocket. Fighting against the dizziness that threatened to overwhelm her, she slowly stood up and made her way across the cell toward the iron bars.

"Hello!" she shouted. "Is anyone out there? Sheriff Calder!"

There was no answer. The door separating the corridor of mean little cells from the sheriff's office was closed. She shouted again, louder this time.

Nothing.

Samantha swore silently. This was insane. She did not belong here. Why Sheriff Calder was so determined to have her locked up was beyond her. Last night he'd said something about going after Joe. She wondered if that was what he was doing now. If so, it might be hours, or even days, before he returned.

The jail cell was cold. Bars blocked the small, high openings, but there was no glass in the windows to protect the prisoners from the elements. She crossed her arms, as much from nervousness as from the cold, and began pacing. She had to find a way to get out of here.

Her head was throbbing so hard that she began to feel sick to her stomach. She stopped pacing and rubbed her temples with her fingertips. Disjointed thoughts pounded through her head.

Richard was dead.

Joe was on the run.

She had missed the breakfast rush.

She bit down on her bottom lip to stifle the terrified laughter that welled in her throat. Here she was, in jail, with no imminent chance of being released, and all she could think about was missing the breakfast rush. She had to get herself under control before she succumbed to hysteria.

Taking a deep breath, she forced herself to think calmly and rationally.

It was a good thing she had missed the breakfast rush, she told herself. As soon as Sarah realized she was missing, she would go for help. At least, Samantha hoped she would. But then, Sarah might not realize she was missing. Sarah might think she'd overslept or simply decided to close for the day.

Then she remembered the hairpins, and her hopes escalated. She delved into her coat pocket. It might work. It was worth a try, and it would give her something to concentrate on besides going crazy with worry.

Kneeling beside the cell door, she reached around the bars and inserted the pin into the keyhole from the outside.

She did not know how long she worked. At one point she had nearly succeeded in triggering the locking mechanism when the end of the hairpin broke off inside the keyhole. Muttering a curse, she took another hairpin from her pocket.

That was when she heard the noise. It was very faint and sounded as if it was coming from outside the jail.

She listened. The sound came again. Someone was knocking on the front door. Then she heard a woman's voice calling out to Sheriff Calder.

Sarah!

Samantha scrambled to her feet. "Sarah!" she shouted as loud as she could. "Sarah! Do you hear me?"

Panic pulsed through her veins as she realized that Sarah might not be able to hear her.

Then she remembered the window.

Without wasting another second, she dragged the cot away from the wall and positioned it beneath the window. She climbed up on the cot. "Sarah! *Sarah!*"

She shouted until she was hoarse.

"Samantha? Is that you?"

Samantha's legs nearly buckled in relief. Gripping the iron window bars, she rose up on tiptoe. She could barely see the top of Sarah's head through the window. "Sarah, thank goodness you found me. You have to get me out of here!"

"But the sheriff's not here, and the door is locked."

Samantha thought a moment. "Break the window, and open the door from the inside," she said. "The keys should be on the peg just inside the door."

"All r-right," Sarah stammered. "Just hold on a minute."

Samantha sank down on the thin mattress and covered her face with her hands. She was shaking so badly she could hardly think. As soon as Sarah got her out of here, she had to find Trey. Joe needed him. *She* needed him. She needed to feel the warm security of his arms around her. She needed him to hold her and assure her that everything was going to be all right.

The tinkling of broken glass jolted her back to the present. She bolted off the cot.

After what seemed an eternity, the door separating the cells from the sheriff's office inched open, and Sarah stuck her head around the corner. "Samantha?"

"I'm down here."

Glancing guiltily over her shoulder, Sarah tiptoed to the cell. She held up the heavy metal ring with its multiple keys. "I found them."

"Why are you whispering?"

"Because we're going to get caught!"

The absurdity of the situation struck both women simultaneously. Sarah's shoulders began to shake with suppressed mirth. Samantha clamped her hand over her mouth as a fit of laughter seized her. "What are you going to tell Connor?" she asked when she finally caught her breath.

"That you threatened to fire me if I didn't break you out of jail," Sarah managed to get out between giggles. She selected a key and inserted it into the lock. "If I get arrested, Samantha, I'm never going to forgive you."

Realizing how much Sarah was risking for her, Samantha sobered. She reached between the bars and covered the other woman's hand with her own. "Sarah, I don't know how I'll ever repay you for doing this, but I will. I promise."

Understanding reflected in Sarah's eyes. "Don't fret about it. You don't owe me anything."

Oh, but I do, Samantha thought. *More than you know*.

As Sarah tested each key in the lock, Samantha explained the events of the previous night and how she had come to be back in jail.

Sarah snapped her head up to stare at her. "Mr. Winters is dead?"

Samantha nodded. "Sheriff Calder thinks Joe killed him. He's out looking for Joe now."

"He won't have far to look, that's for sure. Mr. Tochino is here in town."

"You saw him?"

"He was at the restaurant this morning, asking for you. I told him about those soldiers trying to have their way with you yesterday, and he asked me to come here and tell the sheriff that you were missing."

Samantha shook her head in disbelief. "He's going to get himself caught. Do you know where he is now?"

"He went to the mine. I think he means to go after those men." Sarah drew her brows together in consternation. "I can't get any of the keys to work. I think something is stuck down inside the lock."

Samantha groaned. "My hairpin," she said apologetically. "I was trying to pick the lock."

Sarah got down on her knees so she could peer into the keyhole. "Hold on a bit. I think I may have it."

After a minute, the lock gave way. Sarah stood up and pulled the cell door open.

"You did it! Sarah, you're wonderful!"

"I'm a criminal, that's what I am."

"You're an angel," Samantha corrected.

Suddenly the wail of the warning whistle from the Concha pierced the air with its terrifying high-low warble.

For several long, agonizing seconds, Samantha's heart seemed to stop beating entirely.

Sarah's eyes widened, and she pressed one hand against her heart. "Good Lord, what now?" she whispered.

"Sarah, is Connor working today?" Samantha shouted over the whistle.

Sarah shook her head. "No . . . his back . . ."

Thank goodness, Samantha thought. The last thing Sarah needed was to have her husband injured, or worse.

An intense, gut-twisting fear gripped Samantha's stomach, making her feel ill. *Trey.* Every fiber of her being told her he was at the mine and that he was in terrible danger. Dear God, let him be safe, she prayed.

She took Sarah's arm. "Come on, Sarah. Let's get out of here."

Outside, they could see the smoke billowing up from the mine compound.

"It's the mill!" Sarah cried. "It's on fire!"

"It's more than just the mill. Oh, my God, Sarah! If the fire takes out the pumping station, the mine will flood!" Samantha turned and took the other woman by both hands.

"Sarah, please, go home and ask Connor to round up every-one he can find. We need to put that fire out!"

"What about you? Where are you going?"

"I'm going to the mine."

Sarah seized Samantha's arm, preventing her escape. "You can't go up there! It's too dangerous."

"I have to, Sarah. Trey needs all the help he can get."

"You'll just be in the way."

"Sarah, you don't understand!" Samantha's voice echoed the desperation in her eyes. "I lost one man I loved to that blasted mine; I'm not going to lose another."

"Samantha!"

Samantha didn't hear her. She was already halfway down the street.

Samantha stopped first at the restaurant and dragged every spare blanket she owned out of the closet. Please don't let me be too late, she silently begged. More than once she nearly stumbled beneath the heavy load as she made her way up the hill toward the mine.

She was not prepared for the destruction that greeted her when she reached the compound. Long sections of the new fence that Trey and Michael had erected shortly before Michael's death were lying on the ground. Over-turned railcars blocked the road, and the guard shack lay on its side about fifty feet away from its foundation.

Of what had once been the stamp mill, all that remained were the huge crushing stones and a skeleton of charred framing timbers. The assay office and the pumping sta-tion were completely gone. The roof of the administra-tion building was engulfed in flame. Men were passing buckets of water to one another to try to extinguish the blaze, but as fast as they worked, cinders from the burn-ing roof fell on the surrounding ground, igniting the dried grass.

Samantha pushed her way through the chaos toward one of the men in the bucket line. "Pour water on these," she ordered. "We can use them to beat out the flames."

A few minutes later, armed with a dripping blanket, Samantha took up a position near the burning building and began beating out the flames spreading along the ground toward the foundation of the building. Smoke stung her eyes and choked her throat, and it was not long before her arms began to throb with pain, but she forced herself to keep moving. She couldn't let the flames get near the walls, she thought frantically. Trey could replace the roof, but once the walls caught, the dry wood would ignite as quickly as if someone had doused the building with lamp oil.

Suddenly Trey burst through the wall of smoke. He grabbed the first man in the bucket line by the front of his shirt. "There's dynamite in that building!" he shouted above the din. "Leave it! Get away from here!" He released the miner, and the man nearly stumbled over himself as he scrambled to put a safe distance between himself and the burning building.

"Get back!" Trey shouted. His voice cracked with hoarseness. "All of you! Get away from the building."

Just then there was a loud splintering crash as the roof of the building caved in.

Overcome with exhaustion, Samantha let the blanket drop, and wiped her forehead with an aching arm as she took deep gulping breaths so thick with smoke they made her lungs ache. She wanted so badly to lie down and rest that it took a concentrated effort to remain standing. Hardly aware of what she was doing, she lifted the blanket and brought it down hard, smothering the flames that nipped at the hem of her skirt.

"*Sam!*"

Trey's voice pierced her weariness, and Samantha looked

up in time to see him bearing down on her. He was covered with soot and dirt, and his clothes were torn. There was a wild, desperate look on his face that she had never seen before.

Tears of futility and exhaustion filled Samantha's eyes. She did not need to hear Trey tell her it was too late to save the building. She already knew that. Everything he had worked so hard for was gone, and there was nothing she could do to bring it back. Never in her life had she felt as helpless as she did now.

In the next few seconds everything seemed to happen at once. Trey's hand clamped around her arm, wrenching a startled cry from her throat. With a force that felt as if it would yank her arm from its socket, he jerked her around and hauled her away from the burning building.

Gripped with confusion and terror, Samantha lost her hold on the blanket and half ran, half stumbled after him, barely able to see through the blur of tears and smoke as she struggled to keep up with his long-legged stride.

Without warning, Trey hurled her ahead of him and threw his entire weight against her, slamming into her with enough impact to drive the air from her lungs as she hit the rocky ground. Gasping for air, Samantha tried to lift her head, but Trey shoved her head back down to the ground and shifted his weight over her, shielding her with his body.

Behind them, with volcanic violence, the administration building exploded.

Chapter
Seventeen

BLAST followed blast as the cases of dynamite ignited in the inferno. All around them, men were screaming and running to escape the explosion. Samantha stifled a cry as they were showered with dirt and splinters and live cinders. Trey swung his arm over her head and pressed her face to the ground. Beneath them, the earth seemed to move of its own accord. Through it all, the warning whistle never stopped blaring. Samantha felt as if she were in the middle of some horrible nightmare from which she could not awaken.

After what seemed an eternity, Trey moved. He grasped Samantha's shoulder and pulled her with him as he sat up. "Are you all right?" he shouted above the deafening noise.

There was a persistent ringing in Samantha's ears that would not go away, but as far as she could tell, she was not injured. She nodded numbly.

Still holding on to her, Trey struggled to his feet. Samantha gripped the front of his shirt as the world reeled precariously around her. Her body ached in a thousand places, and she felt ill. She had completely forgotten about the dynamite that was stored in Michael's old office. Her stomach moved up toward her throat, and she had to swallow hard to keep from retching.

Trey tilted her head back and smoothed her hair away from her dirt- and soot-smudged face. Holding her face between his hands, Trey stared down into the liquid amber-flecked eyes he had grown to love, and a painful lump lodged in his throat as he was filled with the realization of how close he had come to losing her. Fighting for composure, he brushed a streak of dirt from her cheekbone with his thumb. He had to shout to be heard. "I need your help, Sam. Go into town and get Dr. Goss. Tell him we need him here. Can you do that for me?"

Tears of terrified relief filled Samantha's eyes, and she had to quell the urge to throw herself into Trey's arms. Afraid she might crumble if she tried to speak, she nodded.

Trey released her, and a numbing ache settled in his chest as he watched her departing back.

Over the next several hours, strikers and scabs, their differences temporarily forgotten, worked side by side to put out the blaze and carry the injured to safety. Marty Dennison, Dieter Vogel, and Gaylord Whittaker had been killed in the explosion, and thirty other men were injured, some seriously. That there had not been greater loss of life and limb was no small miracle; when the cases of dynamite ignited, the resulting blast had driven debris more than two hundred feet into the air.

Inside the hoisting station, its walls blackened with smoke, the cables screeched, indicating that the cage was coming to the surface. Trey hauled himself to his feet and waited for the cage to emerge from the darkness of the shaft. His clothes were scorched and torn, and every muscle in his body felt as if it had been trampled.

There was a loud clang of metal against metal as the cage reached the platform and the door was opened.

The dismal faces on the search crew as the men trooped sullenly into the hoisting station relayed the bad news.

Amos Flaherty shook his head. "I'm sorry, sir." His voice trembled with exhaustion. "The shaft has collapsed. We can't get below the first pair of crosscuts."

Trey swore under his breath and pressed his fingertips against his burning eyelids. "How many men are still missing?" he asked wearily.

Connor Morrissey hung the last available identification tag on its peg. "Four at last count, Mr. Stern. Sam Hawkins, Jonathan Weiss, Emery Taylor, and Liam Smith."

The muscle in Trey's jaw knotted, and he stared at Connor so long and so hard that the other man visibly quailed. "I'll check again, Mr. Stern," he muttered.

Ignoring him, Trey turned toward the door. "We'll try going in through the old entrance."

Amos followed Trey to the door. "Sir, those tunnels are unstable. The blast dislodged the bracing timbers. Jiggle the wrong one and a million tons of dirt will come crashing down on our heads."

Trey did an abrupt about-face. The lines in his face were taut with fatigue, and his blue-gray eyes were like unyielding slivers of slate in his tanned face. "I'm well aware of the dangers, Amos. For that reason, this search is strictly voluntary. Those of you who wish to remain behind may do so. I will not hold it against you."

The men shifted uneasily and exchanged glances. Amos sighed wearily. "I'll go with you."

Another man signaled with a raised forefinger. "Me, too."

"Count me in," another said.

In one form or another, every man in the hoisting station agreed to participate in the search. "We'll go the long way, down through Hayden Creek Canyon and up the mine road to the old entrance. I don't want to take a chance that our trooping across the hill will cause a cave-in below. Does everyone have a safety lantern?"

His earlier hesitancy gone, Amos inclined his head. "Lanterns, ropes, picks. You name it, Mr. Stern; we got it."

Trey's gaze touched upon each man in the hoisting station in unspoken gratitude. "Keep your eyes open when we go in," he instructed. "If any one of you should see anything unusual, you're to tell the rest of us immediately. Likewise, at the first sign of poison gases, we're getting out. Is that understood?"

Mumbled assent rippled through the group. Trey took a deep breath. "Let's go."

By midday Joe knew he was on the right trail. He hunkered down and studied the tracks in the dirt. The freshly made hoofprints were not as deep as earlier ones, indicating that the rider was not driving his horse as hard. By his reckoning, the man he was hunting was no more than a few hours ahead of him.

He knew he was following only one horse, but who its rider was, he could not yet determine. He was willing to bet it was either Arnie Pitts or Silas Jenkins. Maria's crucifix had given that much away.

Joe had been wearing the crucifix the night Pitts and Jenkins had taken him out of the Myterra jail, and one of them had stolen it from around his neck while he was unconscious. He didn't know if the killer had dropped the necklace or intentionally left it by Richard Winters's body. The only thing he knew was that he was being framed for a murder he did not commit.

It troubled him that Samantha had disappeared shortly after tending to his wound. Had Arnie or Jenkins seen him go into the restaurant? If so, either man could safely assume that he had told Samantha about being abducted from the jail and about the part they had played in carrying out

Richard Winters's instructions. If Joe had been seen going to the restaurant, Samantha was in serious danger.

After resting awhile and eating one of the sausage biscuits that Samantha had packed for him the night before, Joe continued on his way. Although he was traveling on foot and was hampered by his injuries, his skill at tracking and his familiarity with the terrain provided him with shortcuts that a man on a horse would not have been able to take. By stopping every few miles to rest, he had managed steadily to close the distance between him and his quarry.

It was nearly dusk when, from a high ridge, he spotted a horse watering at a stream that trickled through the narrow canyon below. The horse was saddled. Its rider, Joe reasoned, could not be far away.

Careful to keep to high ground, Joe slowly made his way along the ridge until he was directly above the horse. He settled down behind a stand of jojoba shrubs thick with tiny gray-green oval leaves and rested Maria's sawed-off shotgun across his knees.

He did not have long to wait. After a few minutes a man appeared in the clearing below with an armload of wood. After dropping the wood with a clatter, the man straightened and absently scratched his arms. Then he pushed back his hat and knelt to arrange the wood for a campfire.

Arnie Pitts. Joe was not surprised. It would be like Arnie to kill Richard Winters and then run.

Samantha was nowhere to be seen. If Arnie had not brought her along when he fled town, then where was she? What had he done with her? Joe intended to get some answers, even if he had to drag them out of Arnie Pitts.

Joe waited while Arnie built a fire and rummaged through his saddlebags. Finally Arnie returned to the fire and sat down on the ground with his knees drawn up to his chest. Darkness had quickly settled on the canyon, and the firelight flickered eerily off Arnie's face as he gnawed on a strip of dried beef. He did not appear to be armed, but Joe wanted to be certain before he moved in.

He picked up a small rock and balanced it in his hand. His gaze traveled to the horse grazing idly by the stream. He drew back his arm, took aim, and let the rock fly.

The rock struck the horse on the hindquarters. The horse surged forward and took off downstream.

Arnie scrambled to his feet. "Hey! Come back here!" he yelled. He ran after the horse, but went only a few yards before he gave up the chase. Swearing loudly, he returned to the campfire. In a fit of temper, he yanked his hat off and threw it on the ground. "Damned stupid animal!" he cursed.

It was all the proof Joe needed. If Arnie had been armed, he would have drawn his weapon the instant the horse spooked.

Soundlessly Joe inched his way down the rocky slope.

Arnie had once again hunkered down by the fire when Joe emerged into the clearing. His back was to Joe, and he had wrapped his arms around himself. His teeth chattered with cold as he uttered every damning statement he could think of about his runaway horse.

Only a few feet away from him, Joe trained the shotgun on Arnie's back and waited.

After a few minutes, Arnie shifted his weight onto his knees and held his hands out to the fire to warm them. "Damned stupid horse," he muttered. "How in the hell am I supposed to get to Tucson now?"

"You could try walking," Joe suggested.

Arnie leaped to his feet and spun around. His eyes grew wide with fear as he stared wordlessly at Joe. Finally his breathing quickened, and he sputtered, "Y-you!"

Joe's eyes were hard and dark in his rigid face. "You thought I was dead, didn't you?"

Arnie swallowed hard, then shook his head vehemently. "You d-don't understand," he stammered. "It wasn't my fault that J-Jenkins—" His gaze darted to the shotgun in Joe's hands and he nervously ran his tongue across his lips. Panic flickered behind his eyes. "Just g-give me a chance. I-I can explain everything."

Joe pulled back the hammer of the shotgun with a distinct click that resonated off the canyon walls. "Good," he said tonelessly. "Start talking."

Near the mouth of the old mine entrance, Samantha stood with Ian Hunter and a score of others awaiting news of those still not accounted for. As the sun went down, an eerie silence had settled over the compound. The acrid smell of smoke and gunpowder hovered over the valley. Lanterns bobbed in the darkness, illuminating the faces of those who waited. "Why do you think they're taking so long?" Samantha asked in a low voice. As she spoke, her breath fogged in the chill night air.

Ian shook his head. "I don't know. But I wish like hell they'd get out of there before this entire hill caves in on them."

Samantha crossed her arms and shuddered. She was acutely aware of the risks that Trey and the others in the search crew were taking, and the thought that she could lose Trey the same way she'd lost Michael was never far from the forefront of her mind. "Trey won't stop searching until he has found everyone," she said in a strained voice. "He feels responsible for those men."

"Maybe I should have gone below with them."

Samantha turned her head to study Ian. Even though he had done a fair job of helping extinguish the fire, Samantha knew from his uncallused hands and his slender build that Ian Hunter was unaccustomed to physical labor. "You'd only have gotten in the way," she said quietly.

At first Ian did not respond, and Samantha thought she might have offended him. When he finally spoke, there was a note of pained regret in his voice. "I keep thinking about the last explosion here," he said. "I wasn't much help then, either."

"There wasn't a thing any of us could have done to save those men," Samantha said woodenly.

"Not all of them, perhaps. But I could have stopped your husband from going below. At least he'd be alive today."

Samantha's heart slowed to a standstill, and she felt a terrible pressure in her chest. She moistened her lips. "What do you know about that day?" she asked in a small voice.

Ian shrugged. "Not much. I was with Drury at the mill. The men were having trouble assembling one of the furnaces. One of the miners came running in. He said he had an important message for your husband. Drury took him aside. They talked for a few minutes; then both of them took off running out the door. They were halfway to the hoisting station before I caught up with them. I asked Drury what was wrong, and he said there was no time to explain, that he had to get the rest of the men out of the mine."

Samantha closed her eyes and groaned inwardly as waves of frustration and impotent rage washed over her. All the months she had spent suspecting Trey of causing Michael's death, then questioning Michael's presence in the mine that day, while the truth had remained just beyond their grasp. Her throat constricted, and it took all the self-control she could summon to maintain her composure. All day long she had been on the verge of tears, but never more so than at this moment. "Why didn't you tell anyone about this before now?" she asked. Her voice quavered.

Ian cast her an apologetic glance. "I had my reasons. Unfortunately, they no longer seem valid. I'm sorry. I didn't mean to stir up painful memories for you."

Samantha took a deep, unsteady breath. "I suppose I should be grateful to finally know the truth about that day."

The sharp edge on Samantha's voice pricked Ian like a thorn. He turned to look at her, and the retort that had sprung to the tip of his tongue died when he saw the pain in her tear-brightened eyes. Her arms were folded defensively in front of her and her mouth was compressed into a thin white line. He saw her throat work convulsively several times as she struggled for control. "To be honest, I don't know who planted the dynamite in the Kingman stope," he said quietly. "I'm not even sure your husband knew it was there. All I know is that he gave up his life to save the others. Your husband was a brave man, Mrs. Drury."

Samantha's bottom lip quivered, and she caught it between her teeth to still it. With her fingertips, she wiped away a tear that ran down her cheek. "Thank you," she said in a choked voice.

At the mine entrance, someone shouted, "They're coming out!"

After what seemed an eternity, two men emerged from the mouth of the tunnel, their knees bent beneath the weight of the body they carried.

Samantha choked back a gasp.

The men placed the body on the ground.

A minute later two more men came out of the mine. They, too, carried between them the twisted, broken body of a man.

A raw, primitive grief overwhelmed Samantha, and she pressed her fist against her mouth to stifle the cry of anguish that swelled in her throat. Bitterness and a sense of helpless defeat assailed her. Didn't anyone ever die of natural causes in a mining town? Did every death carry with it the horror and violence of catastrophe?

Ian placed a steadying hand on Samantha's shoulder.

Not until the third body had been taken from the mine did Trey appear. When he stepped outside, his legs nearly buckled beneath him, and he threw out his hand to steady himself.

Samantha tore free of Ian's grasp and hurried to him.

Trey caught her in his arms and pulled her close. He buried his face in her hair, and his large frame shook convulsively. "I couldn't . . . save them."

"You did what you could," Samantha murmured against his shirtfront. "No one could ask for more."

"Liam . . ." Trey said in a low voice. "He's still . . . down there."

Liam? Was he one of the missing men? As the implication behind the revelation began to sink in, Samantha felt her insides knot. She pulled back and tilted her head to look up at Trey. His face was gray and pinched, and death haunted his eyes. Samantha placed her hand flat on his chest where his coat hung open. Through his shirt she could feel his heart beating unnaturally fast. "You're not thinking of going back down there, are you?"

Trey slowly shook his head in a bizarre gesture of denial and resignation. "I have no choice, Sam. Liam is still down there somewhere. I have to find him."

Suddenly Samantha felt so angry she longed to lash out at someone. That Trey would risk his life for a man who, in her estimation, had done little to deserve it, made her blood hot. She struggled to keep her voice calm. "You've already done everything you can, Trey. If the others didn't survive, Liam probably didn't either. There's no point in risking your life just to pull one more body out of that tunnel."

"She's right, Stern," Ian said behind her. "It's unlikely that anyone could have survived the cave-in. It would be foolhardy to go back down there now."

In the end, Trey conceded.

He sent one of the men into town for a wagon and arranged to have the bodies taken to the funeral parlor. Two of the dead were bachelors, but the third had left a wife and two children back in St. Louis. In the morning he would make arrangements to contact the widow and have the man's belongings shipped home.

Only a few hours of darkness remained when Trey and Samantha trudged down the hill toward town.

Neither of them spoke. Trey's thoughts churned with misgivings. While a part of him said he'd done everything he could, another part of him said he should have kept looking until he found his uncle.

Why? a voice in the back of his mind whispered vengefully. What did Liam ever do to deserve your concern? Why should you risk your life looking for him after the way he treated you and your mother?

In his mind he tried changing the identities of the men whose bodies they'd found. Suppose Liam had been among them. Would he have continued the search for the fourth man?

Probably not. After finding the first three bodies, they had dug through an extra hundred feet of dirt and rubble with no success. Liam had been nowhere near the others.

Still, Trey could not shake the uneasy feeling that his decision to stop searching was going to haunt him for a long, long time.

They had just reached the edge of town when Trey stumbled, nearly bringing both of them to their knees. Samantha caught his arm to steady him. "Are you all right?"

Trey placed a reassuring hand over hers. "I'm fine, Sam. I just wasn't paying attention to where I was going."

Samantha wasn't fooled. Trey was nearly dead with exhaustion. "Do you want to go to your house or to the restaurant?" she asked.

Trey rubbed one hand over the side of his face. "That's fine," he said wearily, not answering her question. He didn't care where they went as long as he could lie down and sleep.

Samantha decided to take him to his house, since it was closer. She slid her arm around his waist. "As soon as we get home, I'll fix you a hot bath, and you can get out of those dirty clothes. I'll fix you something to eat. You must be famished."

Trey did not answer, and Samantha fell silent as they slowly made their way through the narrow packed-dirt streets. She tried not to dwell on how they were going to get through the coming months, but the disquieting thoughts would not go away. She knew she would have to close the Drake House. The mine and the mill were gone and, with them, ninety-five percent of Myterra's jobs. Most of the townspeople would probably pull up stakes and move on to other mining towns.

She still had Trey, she reminded herself. Somehow they would find a way to start over and build a new life together. At least now, any suspicions she might have had about Trey's culpability for Michael's death were buried for good. Even starting over with nothing seemed less formidable than trying to build a future on a foundation haunted by shadows of the past.

As they neared his house, Trey's instincts suddenly awakened, and his body tensed. Samantha glanced up at his taut face. "What is it?"

He did not answer.

Samantha followed his gaze.

In the shadow of the adobe walls, a man lay slumped on the ground in front of Trey's house with his face pressed against the heavy wooden door. He lifted his arm and pounded halfheartedly on the door. His words were slurred. "C'mon, Tyler, lemme in. You can't turn me away. I'm kin. I brou' you up like you was my own."

Liam!

Every nerve in Trey's body felt stretched to the point of breaking. He told himself he should have known. As soon as it became apparent that Liam was not with the others in the mine, he should have known where his uncle would be. He thought of the men who had endangered their lives searching for him when all along Liam was in some saloon in Myterra nursing a bottle of whiskey, and every ounce of hatred and disgust he had ever felt for his uncle rose to the surface like a wound that had never healed. If Liam had died with the others, he might have felt some shred of compassion for him. Now all he felt was an intense, slow-burning rage.

Samantha's hand tightened on his arm. "Trey?"

He removed Samantha's hand from his arm. "Excuse me, Sam. I have some unfinished business to take care of."

With an unwavering sense of purpose, Trey closed the distance between himself and Liam in less than half a dozen determined strides. Seizing his uncle by the shirtfront, he hauled him to his feet.

A sour smell hung over Liam like a cloud as he sagged drunkenly against Trey. "Tyler, is 'at you?"

Trey pushed him away. Liam's identification tag still hung from a chain around his neck; he had neglected to turn it in at the hoisting station as required when he left the mine. Trey grasped the tag and gave it a jerk that broke the chain. He dangled the tag before Liam's face.

"Do you see this, Liam?" he ground out between clenched teeth. "Because of this, nine men just spent sixteen hours digging through a cave-in to try to find you! And where were you, Liam? Tell me that. Tell me what *you* were doing while good, decent men were risking their lives searching for your mangy carcass!"

With one hand Liam gripped the front of Trey's shirt for support. He jabbed a forefinger into Trey's chest. "You don' talk to me 'at way, Tyler. I'll take a belt to your backside and pu' the fear of the Almighty in you, so help me."

Trey pried Liam's hand off his shirt and flung it away from him. He took a step backward and flexed the muscles in his right hand. "You go right ahead, Liam," he said with deadly calm. "Do whatever you want. I'm ready for you."

Filled with horror at the realization of what was happening, Samantha flew to Trey's side and grabbed his arm. "Trey, don't!"

Trey shook off Samantha's hand. "Stay out of this, Sam. It doesn't concern you."

Samantha pushed her way between the two men. "Trey, he's not worth it. Leave him alone!"

His face rigid with barely leashed anger, Trey placed his hands beneath Samantha's arms, lifted her off the ground, and set her out of the way. Grasping her shoulders, he gave her a stern shake. "This is between Liam and me, Samantha. Stay out of it! Do you understand me?"

"Trey, I'm begging you! I don't want you fighting!"

Without warning, Liam seized the back of Trey's coat and swung him around with surprising strength. Before Trey could regain his balance, Liam smashed his fist into Trey's face, sending him sprawling.

Choking back a scream, Samantha hurried to Trey and knelt beside him as he struggled to rise on one elbow. Fear echoed in her voice. "My God, you're bleeding! Are you all right?"

Trey sat up and wiped the back of his hand across his mouth. His hand came away smeared with blood. "I'm fine, Sam. Now please get out of the way and let me handle this."

Above them, Liam swayed unsteadily on his feet. "C'mon, Tyler. Stand up and take your whuppin' like a man."

Samantha grabbed Trey's arm. "Trey, don't. He's drunk. It wouldn't be a fair fight."

Cynicism hardened Trey's eyes. "Tell my mother that," he said bitterly. He staggered to his feet.

Liam snickered. "You ne'er was much of a man, Tyler, always hidin' behind your ma's skirts. I tried to make a man outta you. I done my best by you, and you still growed up to be a yellow-livered coward."

Liam's face blurred and distorted before Trey's eyes as his uncle's taunts awakened memories he had long since buried in the far recesses of his mind. He was ten years old, and Liam was hitting him across the back with a length of framing lumber. He saw his mother crying and trying to stop him, and Liam backhanding her across the mouth. Something in Trey's mind snapped.

He swung.

Liam ducked the blow and plowed his head into Trey's belly, knocking him off his feet.

Samantha scrambled out of the way as the two men crashed to the ground and rolled over and over in the dirt. With her back pressed against the adobe wall, she watched in mute horror as Trey fastened his hands around Liam's neck and slammed the back of his head into the ground over and over again. There was a crazed look in Trey's eyes that made her feel physically ill. She swallowed hard to keep from being sick.

Liam wedged a knee between them and shoved, breaking the hold Trey had on him. Trey rolled to his feet just as Liam came up swinging. Trey threw up his arm, deflecting the blow intended for his head. He drove his fist into Liam's stomach, causing him to grunt and double over. Before Liam could recover, Trey brought both his fists up under Liam's chin. Dazed, Liam staggered backward.

Trey caught him by the shirtfront, keeping him from falling. For a moment he just stood there with one hand on his uncle's shoulder, holding him steady. Both men were breathing heavily. Finally Liam glanced up at his nephew through a glaze of pain and drunkenness. An inappropriate grin touched one corner of his mouth, and a noise that was a cross between a chuckle and a groan sounded in his throat. "I guess . . . I had you pegged wrong," he mumbled.

Trey's eyes missed nothing as they took in every feature of his uncle's aging, unshaven face. He dropped his hand from Liam's shoulder, and both men just stood there, each assessing the other. Trey picked up Liam's hat, which had landed in the dirt, and handed it to him.

Liam clutched the hat against his chest.

"One more thing," Trey said slowly, deliberately. "This one's for Ma." Drawing back his arm, he smashed his fist into Liam's jaw, sending him reeling. Liam landed on his back. He groaned and tried to sit up, then collapsed in the dirt.

Trey turned and walked away.

Samantha was leaning against the building, head bowed, one hand pressed over her eyes. Trey couldn't tell if she was crying or not. He gently took her arm. "It's over."

Samantha dropped her hand away from her face. Her face was strained, but her eyes were dry. Her gaze rested on Liam, passed out in the middle of the street.

"He'll sleep it off," Trey said. "In the morning he probably won't even remember what happened."

Samantha gritted her teeth. No, but I will, she thought unhappily.

Once they were inside the house, Trey lit the lamps while Samantha started the stove and put on a kettle of water to boil. Neither of them spoke. As Samantha busied herself in the kitchen, Trey noticed that she seemed to go out of her way to avoid looking at him.

"Shall I take your coat?" he asked when she finished washing her hands.

Samantha shrugged out of her coat and handed it to him, then turned back to the sink. "The water will be hot in a few minutes. Do you want to bathe first or eat first?" Her voice was clipped and businesslike.

"Sam, look at me."

Samantha squared her shoulders, as if bracing herself, and turned to face him. Dismay flickered in her eyes as she got her first glimpse of his grime-blackened face in the light. Her gaze darted away from his face without ever quite meeting his. "You're a mess. Let me get you something to wash your face with." Turning back to the sink, she wet a dish towel beneath the pump and had started to wring it out when she felt him close behind her.

Trey took the towel from her and dropped it into the sink, then wrapped his arms around her from behind and pulled her against him.

Samantha stiffened.

Trey's breath was warm against her ear. "Sam, I'm sorry you had to witness what happened out there with Liam. Maybe I was wrong. Maybe you were right, and I should have just left him alone. I don't know. In the morning I'll probably feel like a jackass for picking a fight with a drunk old man. But for tonight it was something I had to do. I hope you'll try to understand."

Samantha leaned her head back against Trey's shoulder. "I do understand," she said in a choked voice. "And I'm not angry about Liam."

"Then what is it, sweetheart?"

Samantha took a deep breath. "When you were down in that mine today, I was so . . . scared . . ." Her voice faltered. "I was terrified that something would happen to you and that we'd never get a chance to build a life together. I kept thinking that if only I had married you when you first asked me, instead of waiting . . ."

Taking her by the shoulders, Trey turned her around to face him. Her eyes, bright with unshed tears, shone like giant topaz stars in her soot-streaked face. "Sam, I hope you know I have no intention of dying any time soon."

Samantha started to shake her head. "That's not what I meant."

"I know what you meant," Trey said quietly. His expression turned somber. "I no longer have anything to offer you. The mine has caved in. The mill's gone. Sam, you're going to be marrying a man who probably went bankrupt today."

"Trey, I don't care if we never have another dime between us. You are what matters to me. Not money. Not the mine. Not the restaurant. *You*."

Trey drew her into his arms and brushed his lips against the top of her head. "I love you," he murmured. He paused, then added regretfully, "If I wasn't so damned tired, I'd take you into the bedroom and show you how much."

Samantha wrapped her arms around Trey's waist and hugged him with all the strength she had left. "I love you too," she said shakily. "I'm just sorry it took me so long to realize it."

After Trey had gone into the bedroom to get out of his soiled clothes, Samantha leaned over the sink and rested her forehead against the cold iron pump handle. A painful lump had wedged itself in her throat, and she was dangerously close to bursting into tears. She told herself that everything was going to be all right. Trey was safe. Nothing and no one could hurt him now. Not the mine. Not Richard Winters—

She suddenly realized that with all the commotion at the mine she had completely neglected to tell Trey about Richard's murder and about everything else that had happened. Straightening up, she grabbed the wet dish towel out of the sink, wrung it out, and began scrubbing her face and neck. "I almost forgot to tell you," she called out. "I saw Joe last night. He'd been shot, but it was just a flesh wound. I think he's going to be all right. He said Richard Winters had paid Arnie Pitts and Silas Jenkins to get him out of town and kill him, but Joe got away. Richard also paid Taza Parks to tell the sheriff he saw Joe shoot you, then had him killed too, so he couldn't talk."

When she didn't get a response, Samantha put down the towel and went to the door. "Trey, did you hear me?"

Although lamplight shone through the open doorway, no sound or movement came from the room. Samantha made her way across the silent hall to the bedroom. "Trey?"

He was sound asleep.

His clothes were on the floor beside the bed where he'd dropped them after taking them off. Still wearing his drawers, he was sprawled on his back on the bed with his feet sticking out over the edge of the mattress and one arm thrown up over his head. Beneath the coat of grime he was wearing, fatigue was so deeply etched in the lines of his face that Samantha wondered if it would ever go away.

She sighed and shook her head. "You're going to get pneumonia lying there like that," she scolded softly. Going to the bed, she worked the extra blanket out from under his legs, shook it out, and draped it over him. As she finished tucking the blanket around his shoulders, she gently brushed the back of her hand across his cheek. "I love you," she whispered.

Moving quietly, she placed his shoes under the bed so he wouldn't stumble over them in the morning, then bent down to retrieve his shirt and pants. A small heavy object fell out of his pants pocket and clattered to the floor. Puzzled, Samantha knelt and picked it up.

It was a chunk of pure gold the size of a walnut. Samantha turned it over and weighed it in her hand. She had never seen anything like it. Realizing that Trey's pants had seemed unusually heavy when she picked them up, she set the gold nugget on the floor and went through the rest of his pockets.

She found a half dozen such nuggets of varying sizes, the largest being the size and shape of a small hen's egg. Samantha set the gold pieces on the floor and sat back on her heels to stare at them in amazement.

Then the full import of what she had discovered set in and sobered her. Trey must have found the gold when they were digging through the tunnel to search for the trapped miners. If that was the case, he would want to go back down in the mine as soon as possible and start digging.

She tried to feel excited about the discovery, but couldn't. The prospect of spending her days worrying about him, not knowing when he would go down in those tunnels never to return, was painfully daunting. Now for the first time she began to realize why she had put off marrying him. It wasn't because she didn't love him or because she treasured her independence. It was because she was afraid of losing him the same way she'd lost Michael.

With a sigh, Samantha picked up the gold nuggets and placed them on top of the trunk beneath the window, then draped Trey's pants and shirt over her arm and blew out the lamp. For a moment she just stood there in the darkness listening to the sound of Trey's breathing.

It was a comforting sound, and it filled her with an odd sense of peace that she had not felt in a long time. Hugging Trey's clothes close to her heart, she made a silent vow to try to overcome her fears. If Trey wanted to rebuild the mine, she would stand behind him. She would learn to trust in his judgment and have faith that he loved her enough never to take unnecessary risks or make her worry needlessly. Never, she vowed, would she ask him to be less than he was.

Judge Gates set the brief to one side of his desk and leaned back in his chair. His expression was somber. "Mrs. Drury, in light of the evidence Mr. Kendall was able to unearth in his investigations, and the signed confession Arnie Pitts gave Sheriff Calder, all charges against you have been dropped."

Even though Samantha had been almost certain of the outcome, relief surged through her at hearing Judge Gates's decision. "Thank you," she said.

"However," Judge Gates continued. "There is, I believe, the small matter of a broken window. I have spoken with Sheriff Calder, and he is willing to settle out of court. If you will agree to replace the glass in the front door of the sheriff's office, he will consider the case closed."

Although Samantha felt that Sheriff Calder should replace his own window, since he was to blame for erroneously arresting her in the first place, she wisely kept her opinion to herself and agreed to the judge's terms.

"Good," Judge Gates said decisively. He pushed back his chair and stood up. "Now that this disagreeable business has been settled, we can move on to more pleasant matters. Mr. Kendall, you may let the others in now."

Perry Kendall, who had been standing quietly to one side while Judge Gates talked to Samantha, went to the door and opened it. Trey and Joe had been waiting in the corridor. Judge Gates had dismissed the charges against Joe the day before. Both men stood up when the door opened. Trey's gaze immediately sought Samantha's. In the two weeks that had passed since the disaster at the mine, Trey seemed to have aged permanently. Samantha could tell from the small crease between his brows that he too had harbored some concerns over her meeting with the judge, although probably for different reasons.

Trey and Joe entered the judge's chambers, and Perry Kendall closed the door after them. Trey went to Samantha's side. Slipping her hand into his, she pulled him down to her level and whispered into his ear, "You can relax now. I didn't tell him he was incompetent."

Judge Gates cleared his throat and said solemnly, "Samantha Drury and Treyman Stern, I'm not going to go into a lengthy discourse about the responsibilities of marriage. You are both mature adults"—his gaze rested on Samantha as he paused, and one gray brow arched meaningfully—"and I am sure you are cognizant of what you are getting into. Before we begin, however, does anyone present know of any reason why this union should not take place?"

After the brief ceremony had ended and the appropriate documents were signed, Trey escorted Samantha to the waiting buggy. "I'm proud of you," he said as he helped her up onto the seat. "For a moment there, I thought you were going to give Judge Gates a piece of your mind."

Samantha arranged her skirts around her and folded her hands in her lap. "I don't know what gave you that idea," she said with deadpan seriousness. "I promised you I would be nice to him until after we were safely married."

Trey circled around the buggy and climbed up beside her. The small white scar at the corner of his mouth disappeared when he grinned. "Mrs. Stern, I have the distinct feeling that being married to you is going to be anything but safe."

Perry Kendall and Joe had followed them out of the courthouse. Joe braced one hand on the side of the buggy. His dark eyes were unreadable as they rested on Samantha. "You take care of her, Trey. She's a very special woman."

Trey looked at Samantha, and his expression gentled. "I know," he said quietly.

An awkward silence settled over the tiny group. Samantha looked down at her hands and wondered if Joe still thought about Maria. As if sensing her disquiet, Trey took both her hands in one of his and gave them a reassuring squeeze.

Joe took a deep breath. "Before you go," he said with forced lightness, "there's something I want to tell you." He glanced around at Perry Kendall. "Mr. Kendall has agreed to provide me with the necessary references and letters of recommendation for admission to the university and then to law school."

For a moment they just sat there, stunned by Joe's announcement. Trey was the first to speak. "Joe, that's wonderful news. I think you'll make a fine attorney." He extended his hand. "Congratulations!"

Samantha's initial shock gave way to dismay. "Does that mean you'll be leaving Myterra?"

Joe inclined his head. "For a time, yes. After that, I want to return to the reservation at San Carlos to practice law. I want to make sure that what happened to me doesn't happen to others among my people." He looked at Trey. "You once told me that if I was going to give you my resignation I'd better have a damned good reason. I hope this qualifies."

"I can't think of a better reason," Trey said with deep sincerity. "I'm glad you've found what you want to do with your life."

Unlike the last time Trey and Samantha left the court-house together, no angry mob followed them. A peaceful calm had settled over the town. In the distance, the sound of hammering echoed in the crisp autumn air.

Samantha's gaze automatically turned up the hill toward the Concha where work crews were busy rebuilding the mine's offices. The mill's smokestacks still loomed over Myterra, but they were no longer operational. Samantha was secretly glad that Consolidated Silver had decided to rebuild the new stamp mill in another town. She was not going to miss the soot and the smoke one bit.

"Are you sorry I sold the mine?" Trey asked beside her.

Samantha flashed him a smile. "Not especially. Are you?"

Trey's brows drew together as he pondered that one. "I think I was at first. But the more I thought about it, the more I realized that Consolidated can offer this town a better chance for recovery than I can. And I'll get to stay on as a consultant. I can't ask for more than that."

"It won't be the same as running it yourself."

"I know. But the truth is, my priorities have changed. The mine is no longer the most important thing in my life."

In spite of herself, Samantha felt a warm blush creep into her cheeks. Tucking her arm into his, she leaned against him and asked coyly, "May I ask what is?"

Although he intended to make certain that Samantha never had reason to doubt that she was the most important thing in his life, Trey could not resist teasing her. Careful to keep his eyes fixed on the road and his expression dead serious, he replied solemnly, "Dessert."

Samantha drew back in startled affront. That was the last response she had expected him to give. "Dessert? Do I dare ask what we are having for dessert that is so special?"

Laughter welled up inside Trey, warming his deep blue-gray gaze and making his broad shoulders shake with barely contained mirth. "Freckles."